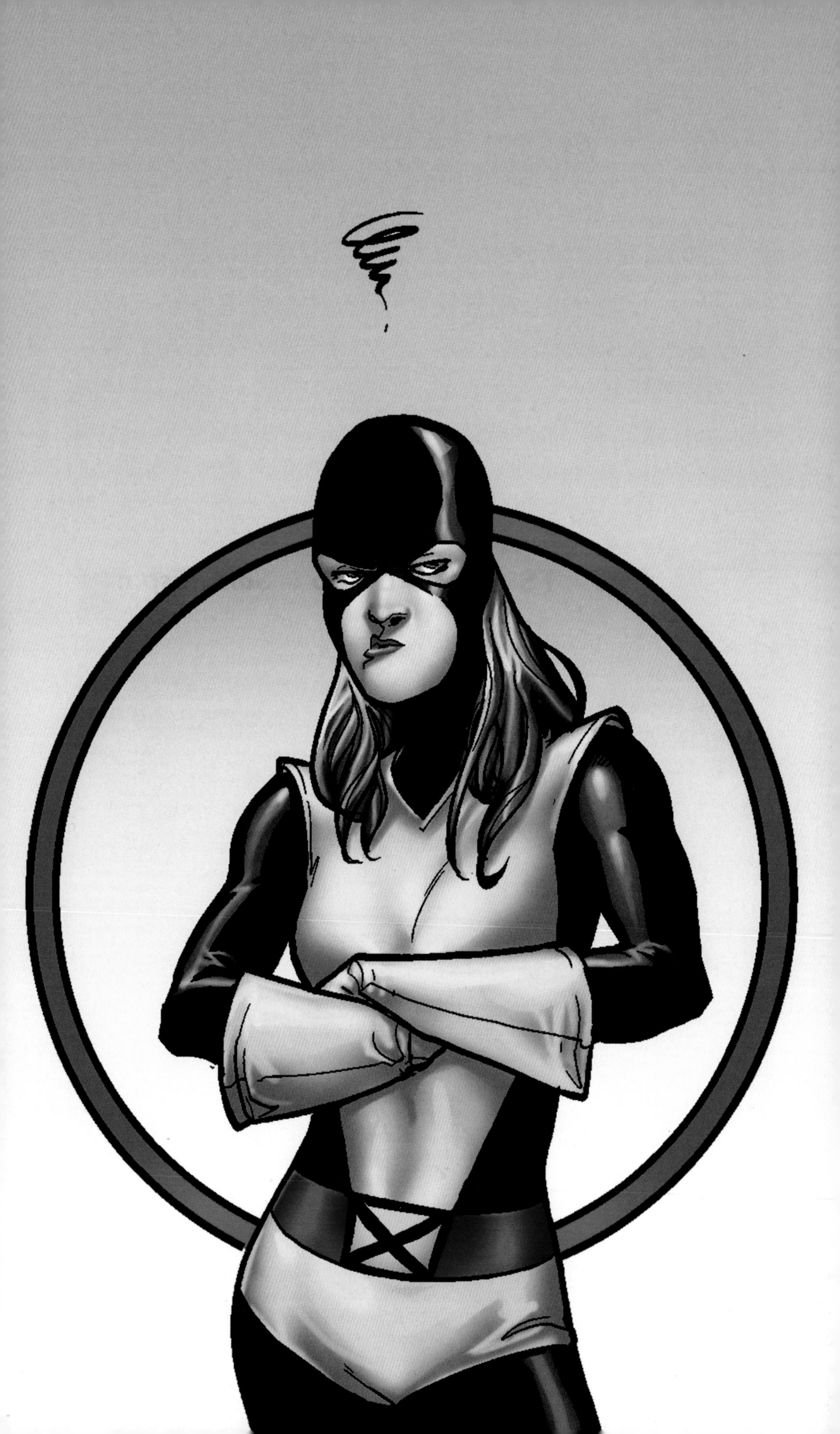

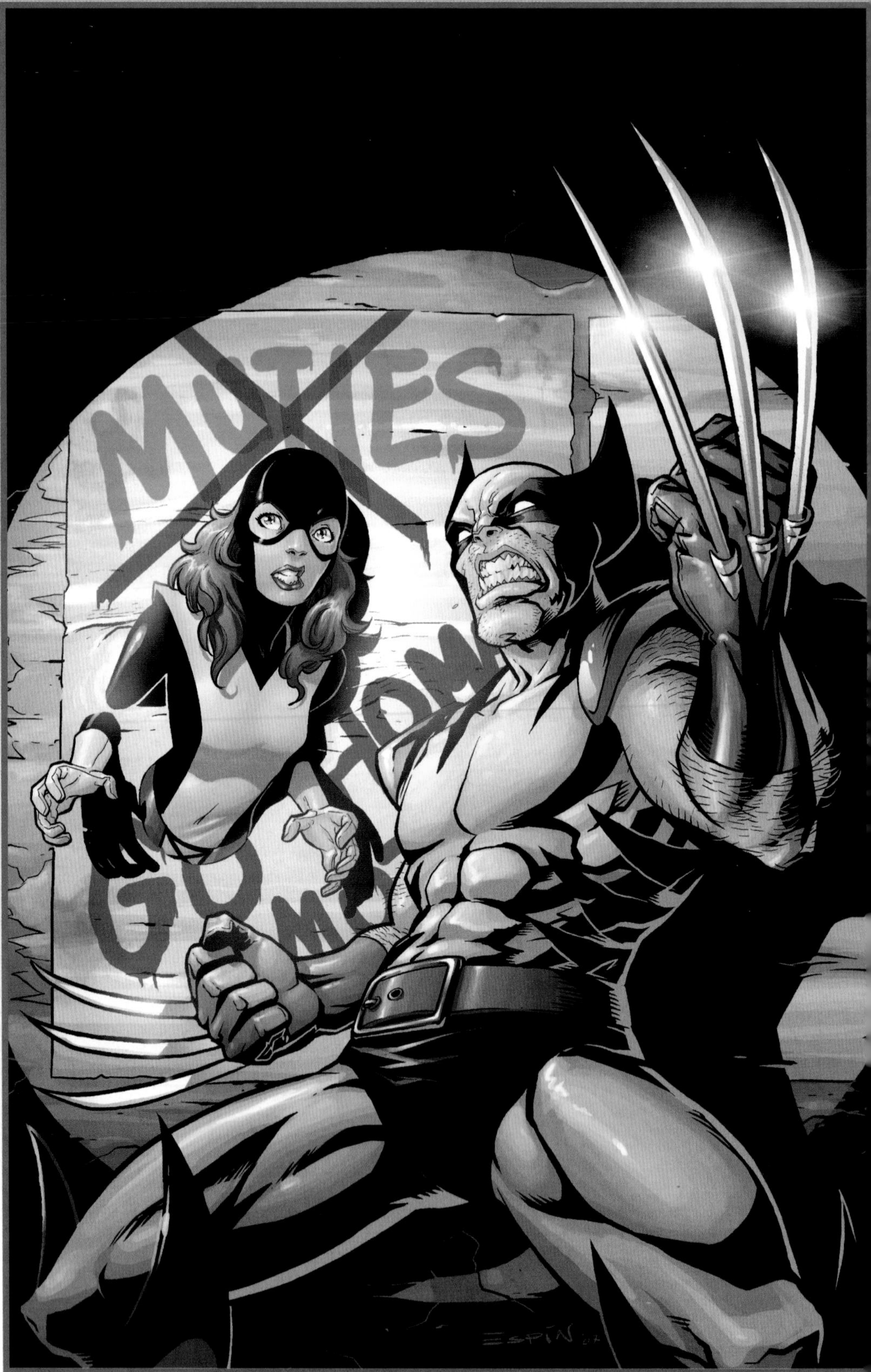

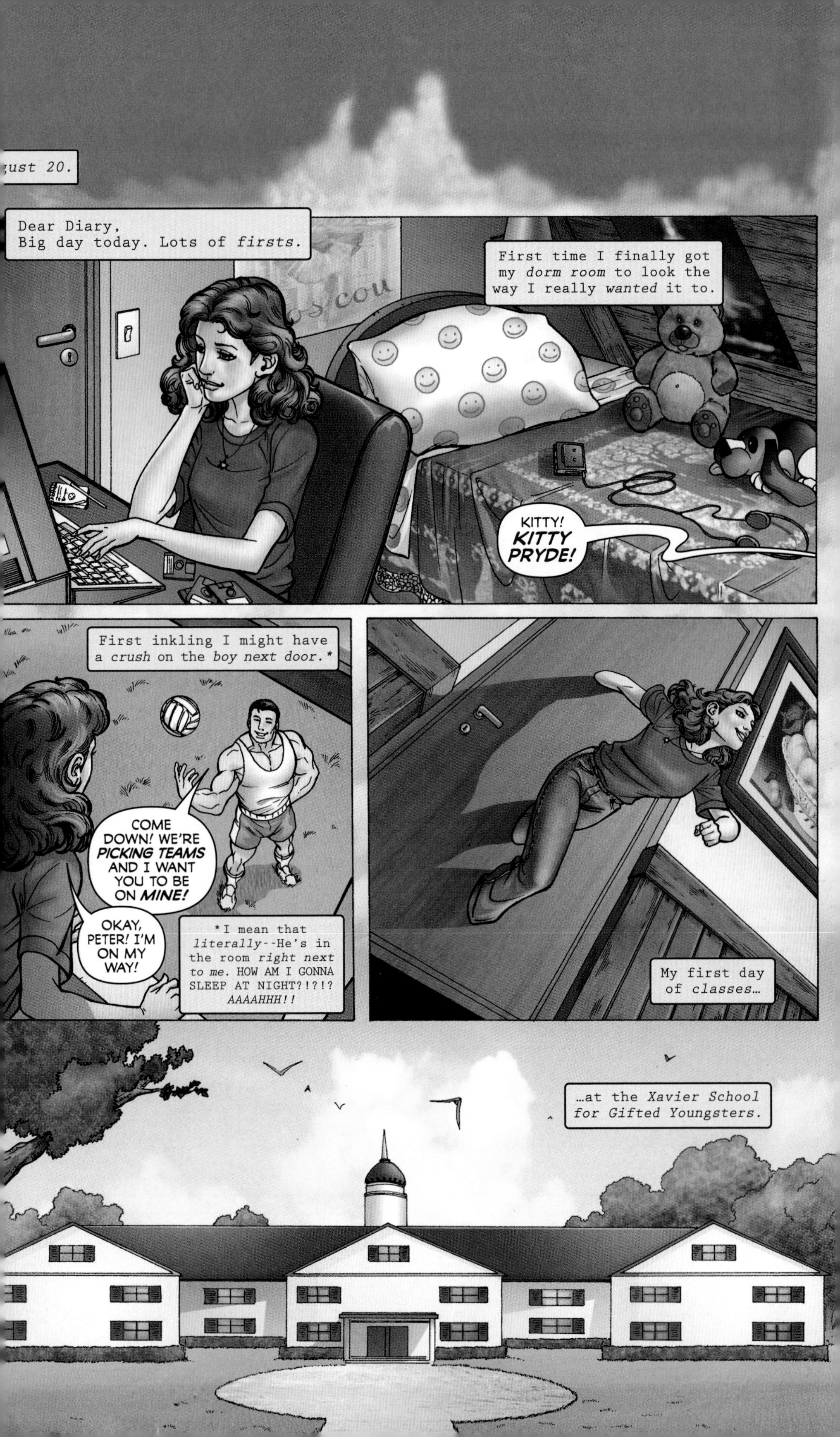

gust 20.
Dear Diary,
Big day today. Lots of *firsts*.
First time I finally got my *dorm room* to look the way I really *wanted* it to.
KITTY! ***KITTY PRYDE!***
First inkling I might have a *crush* on the *boy next door.**
COME DOWN! WE'RE ***PICKING TEAMS*** AND I WANT YOU TO BE ON ***MINE!***
OKAY, PETER! I'M ON MY WAY!
*I mean that *literally*--He's in the room *right next to me.* HOW AM I GONNA SLEEP AT NIGHT?!?!? *AAAAHHH!!*
My first day of *classes*...
...at the *Xavier School for Gifted Youngsters.*

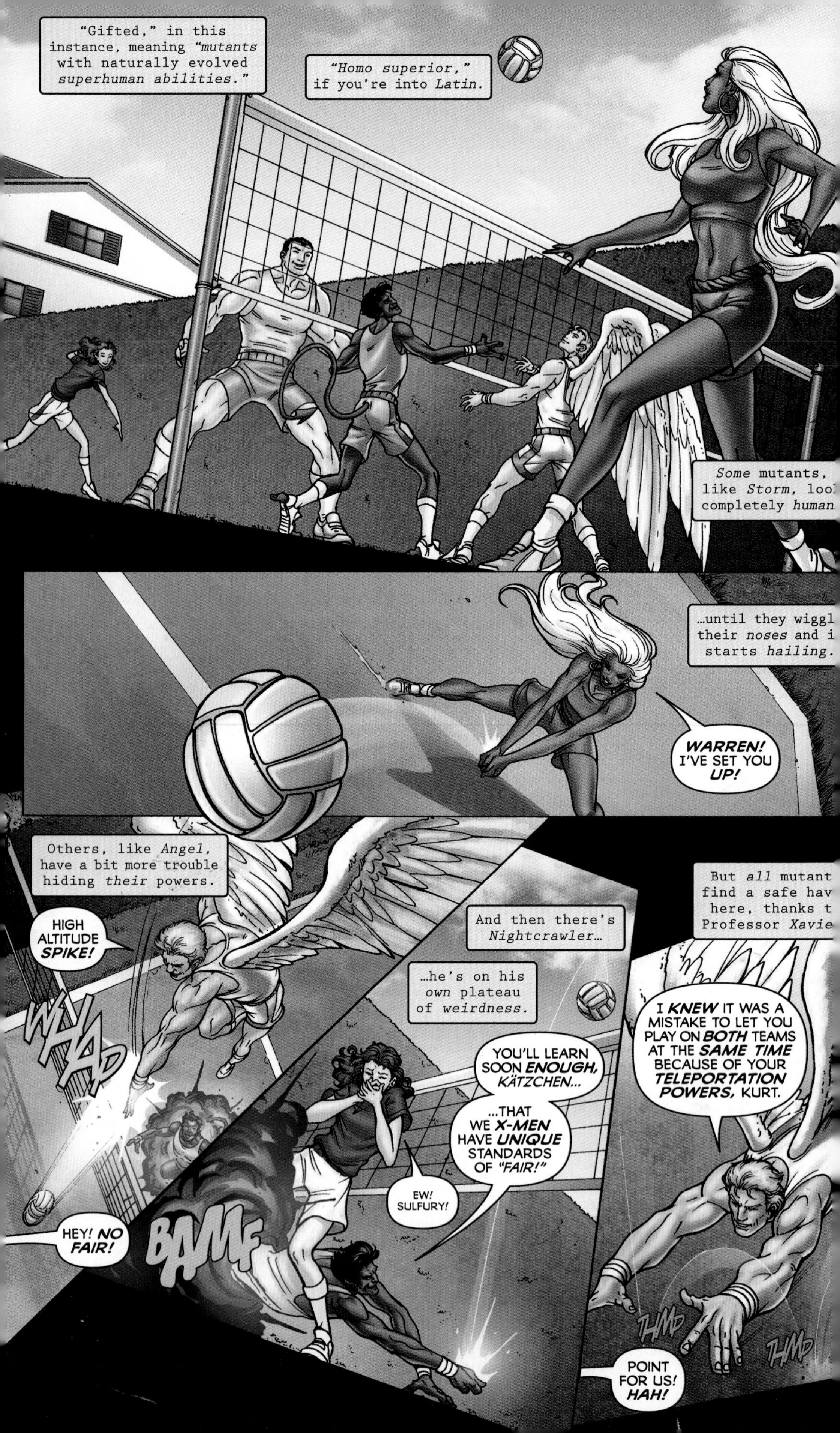
"Gifted," in this instance, meaning "mutants with naturally evolved superhuman abilities."
"Homo superior," if you're into Latin.
Some mutants, like Storm, lool completely human
...until they wiggl their noses and i starts hailing.
WARREN! I'VE SET YOU UP!
Others, like Angel, have a bit more trouble hiding their powers.
HIGH ALTITUDE SPIKE!
WHAP
HEY! NO FAIR!
And then there's Nightcrawler...
...he's on his own plateau of weirdness.
BAMF
YOU'LL LEARN SOON ENOUGH, KÄTZCHEN...
...THAT WE X-MEN HAVE UNIQUE STANDARDS OF "FAIR!"
EW! SULFURY!
But all mutant find a safe hav here, thanks t Professor Xavie
I KNEW IT WAS A MISTAKE TO LET YOU PLAY ON BOTH TEAMS AT THE SAME TIME BECAUSE OF YOUR TELEPORTATION POWERS, KURT.
THMP
THMP
POINT FOR US! HAH!

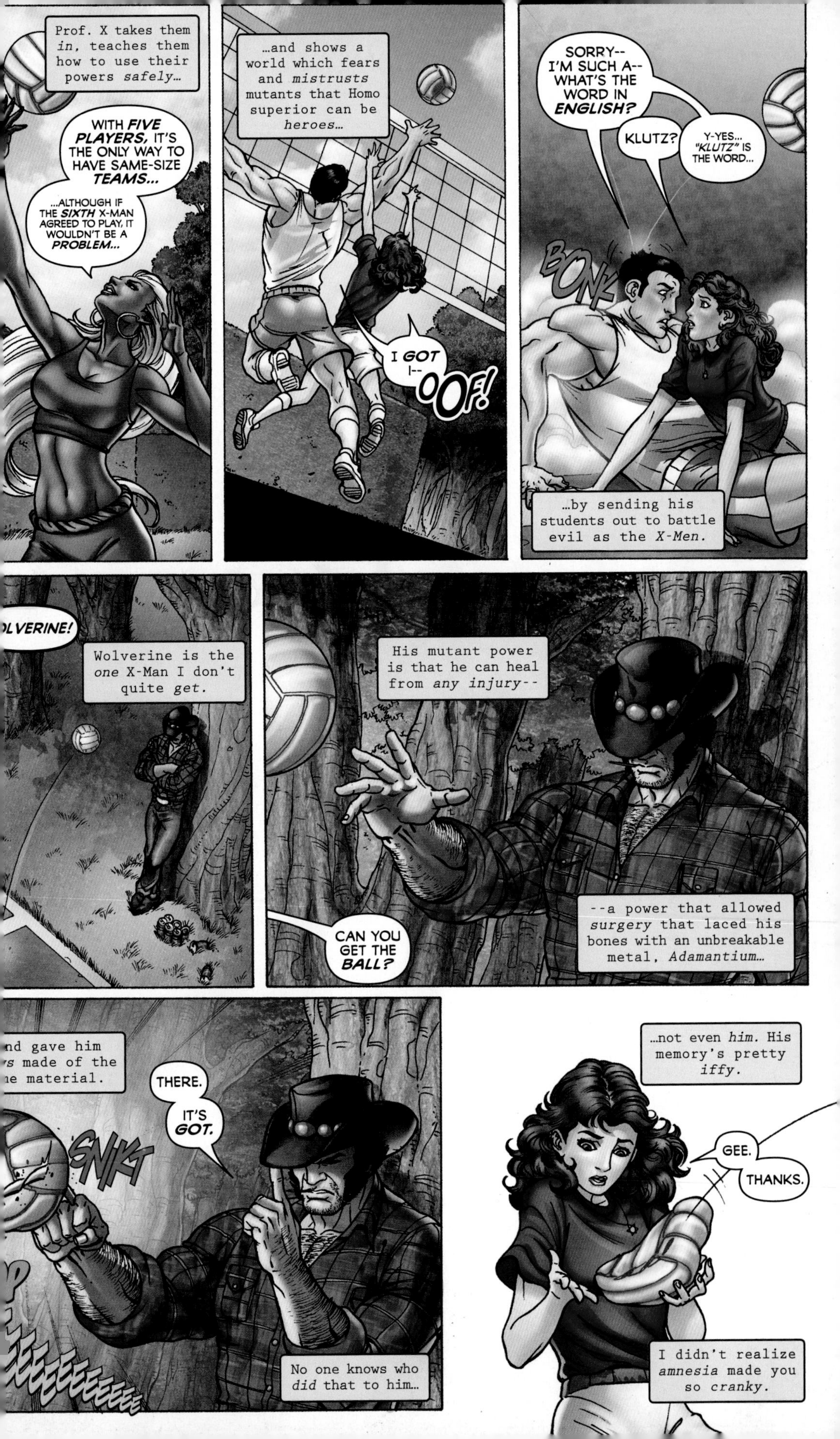

Prof. X takes them *in*, teaches them how to use their powers *safely*...
WITH *FIVE PLAYERS,* IT'S THE ONLY WAY TO HAVE SAME-SIZE *TEAMS...*
...ALTHOUGH IF THE *SIXTH* X-MAN AGREED TO PLAY, IT WOULDN'T BE A *PROBLEM...*
...and shows a world which fears and *mistrusts* mutants that Homo superior can be *heroes*...
I *GOT* I--
OOF!
SORRY-- I'M SUCH A-- WHAT'S THE WORD IN *ENGLISH?*
KLUTZ?
Y-YES... *"KLUTZ"* IS THE WORD...
BONK
...by sending his students out to battle evil as the *X-Men*.
LVERINE!
Wolverine is the *one* X-Man I don't quite *get*.
His mutant power is that he can heal from *any injury*--
CAN YOU GET THE *BALL?*
--a power that allowed *surgery* that laced his bones with an unbreakable metal, *Adamantium*...
nd gave him
s made of the
ne material.
THERE.
IT'S *GOT.*
SNIKT
No one knows who *did* that to him...
...not even *him*. His memory's pretty *iffy*.
GEE.
THANKS.
I didn't realize *amnesia* made you so *cranky*.

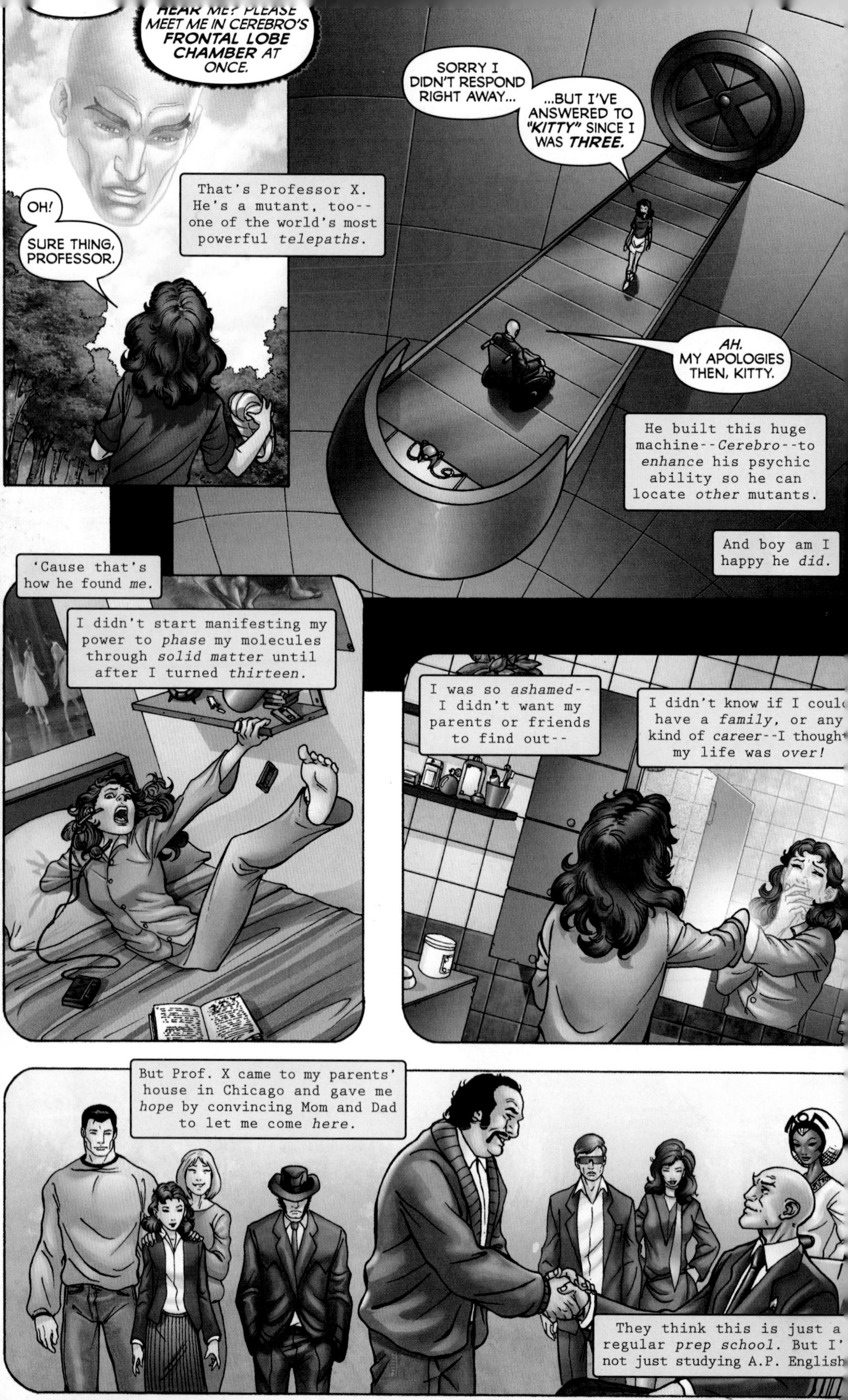
HEAR ME? PLEASE MEET ME IN CEREBRO'S FRONTAL LOBE CHAMBER AT ONCE.
OH!
SURE THING, PROFESSOR.
That's Professor X. He's a mutant, too--one of the world's most powerful telepaths.
SORRY I DIDN'T RESPOND RIGHT AWAY...
...BUT I'VE ANSWERED TO "KITTY" SINCE I WAS THREE.
AH. MY APOLOGIES THEN, KITTY.
He built this huge machine--Cerebro--to enhance his psychic ability so he can locate other mutants.
And boy am I happy he did.
'Cause that's how he found me.
I didn't start manifesting my power to phase my molecules through solid matter until after I turned thirteen.
I was so ashamed--I didn't want my parents or friends to find out--
I didn't know if I coul have a family, or any kind of career--I though my life was over!
But Prof. X came to my parents' house in Chicago and gave me hope by convincing Mom and Dad to let me come here.
They think this is just a regular prep school. But I' not just studying A.P. English

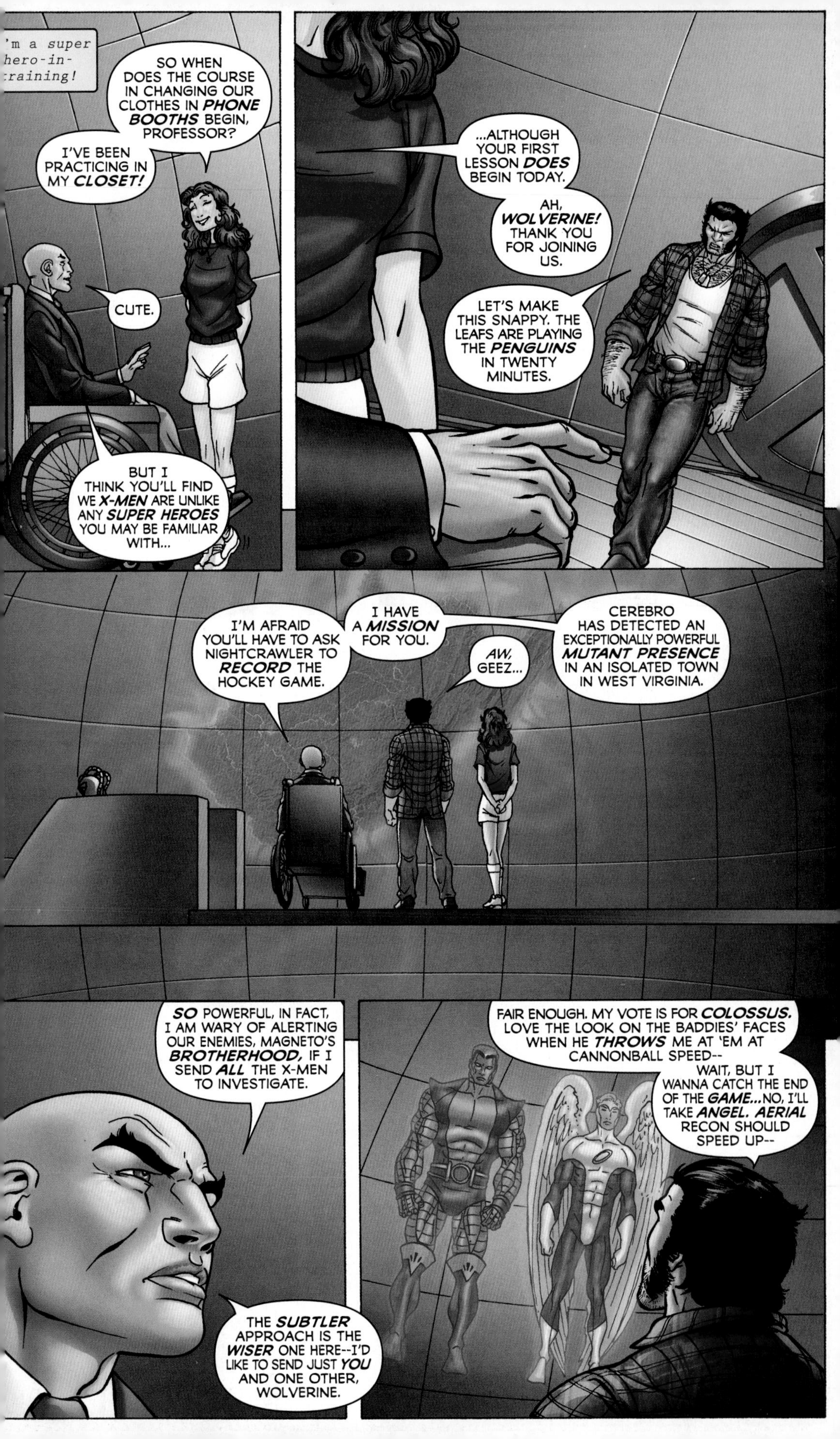
'm a super hero-in-training!
SO WHEN DOES THE COURSE IN CHANGING OUR CLOTHES IN PHONE BOOTHS BEGIN, PROFESSOR?
I'VE BEEN PRACTICING IN MY CLOSET!
CUTE.
BUT I THINK YOU'LL FIND WE X-MEN ARE UNLIKE ANY SUPER HEROES YOU MAY BE FAMILIAR WITH...
...ALTHOUGH YOUR FIRST LESSON DOES BEGIN TODAY.
AH, WOLVERINE! THANK YOU FOR JOINING US.
LET'S MAKE THIS SNAPPY. THE LEAFS ARE PLAYING THE PENGUINS IN TWENTY MINUTES.
I'M AFRAID YOU'LL HAVE TO ASK NIGHTCRAWLER TO RECORD THE HOCKEY GAME.
I HAVE A MISSION FOR YOU.
CEREBRO HAS DETECTED AN EXCEPTIONALLY POWERFUL MUTANT PRESENCE IN AN ISOLATED TOWN IN WEST VIRGINIA.
AW, GEEZ...
SO POWERFUL, IN FACT, I AM WARY OF ALERTING OUR ENEMIES, MAGNETO'S BROTHERHOOD, IF I SEND ALL THE X-MEN TO INVESTIGATE.
THE SUBTLER APPROACH IS THE WISER ONE HERE--I'D LIKE TO SEND JUST YOU AND ONE OTHER, WOLVERINE.
FAIR ENOUGH. MY VOTE IS FOR COLOSSUS. LOVE THE LOOK ON THE BADDIES' FACES WHEN HE THROWS ME AT 'EM AT CANNONBALL SPEED--
WAIT, BUT I WANNA CATCH THE END OF THE GAME...NO, I'LL TAKE ANGEL. AERIAL RECON SHOULD SPEED UP--

NO... ...I'D LIKE YOU TO BRING *KITTY.*

WHAT?!

ME?

HER?

BUT--SHE HASN'T GONE ON A SINGLE *MISSION* YET!

THAT WOULD BE THE *IDEA.* IT HAS BEEN *SOME TIME* SINCE I ACCEPTED MY *FIRST CLASS* OF X-MEN.

BACK THEN, I TAUGHT ALL THEIR CLASSES *MYSELF.* BUT THOSE STUDENTS WERE ALL RELATIVELY *YOUNG.*

YOU *NEW* X-MEN ARE MUCH *OLDER,* MORE *EXPERIENCED.* I THINK OUR *YOUNGER* STUDENTS, LIKE KITTY, SHOULD GAIN THE *BENEFIT* OF THAT.

CALL IT...A INTERNSHI YOU WILL

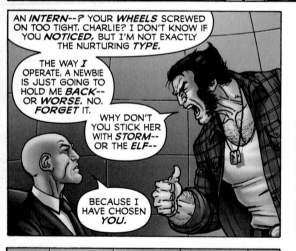

AN *INTERN*--? YOUR *WHEELS* SCREWED ON TOO TIGHT, CHARLIE? I DON'T KNOW IF YOU *NOTICED,* BUT I'M NOT EXACTLY THE NURTURING *TYPE.*

THE WAY *I* OPERATE, A NEWBIE IS JUST GOING TO HOLD ME *BACK*-- OR *WORSE.* NO. *FORGET* IT.

WHY DON'T YOU STICK HER WITH *STORM*-- OR THE *ELF*--

BECAUSE I HAVE CHOSEN *YOU.*

AND IF YOU *DON'T* DO IT, I, IN TURN, WILL FEEL MUCH *LESS* INCLINED...

...TO CONTINUE PROBING YOUR *MIND* FOR YOUR LOST *MEMORIES.*

WE AIN'T HAD OUR *LAST WORDS* ABOUT THIS, CHARLIE.

CHARLES.

WHAT

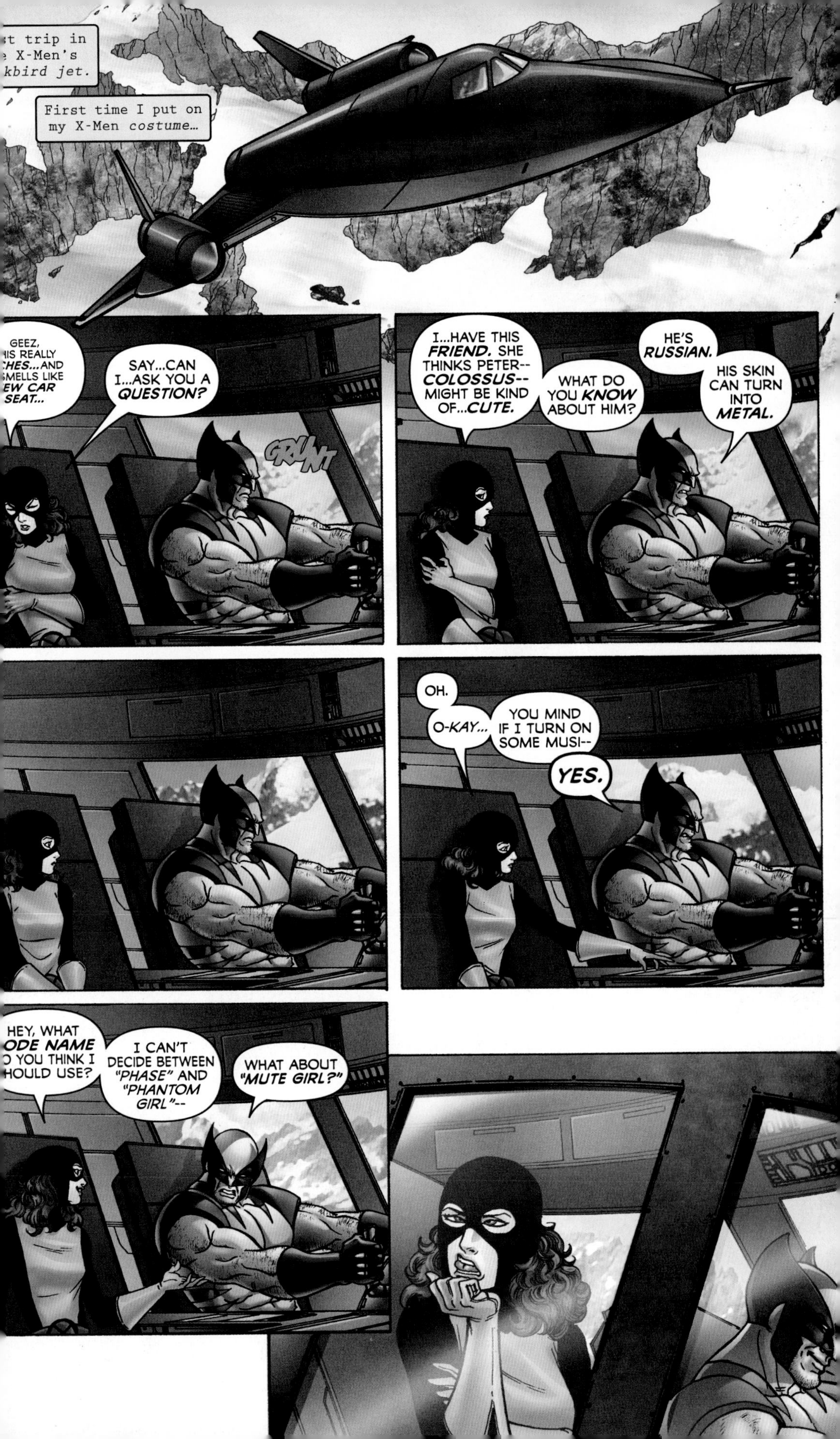

t trip in
X-Men's
kbird jet.
First time I put on my X-Men costume...
GEEZ, HIS REALLY CHES...AND SMELLS LIKE EW CAR SEAT...
SAY...CAN I...ASK YOU A QUESTION?
GRUNT
I...HAVE THIS FRIEND. SHE THINKS PETER-- COLOSSUS-- MIGHT BE KIND OF...CUTE.
WHAT DO YOU KNOW ABOUT HIM?
HE'S RUSSIAN.
HIS SKIN CAN TURN INTO METAL.
OH.
O-KAY...
YOU MIND IF I TURN ON SOME MUSI--
YES.
HEY, WHAT ODE NAME O YOU THINK I HOULD USE?
I CAN'T DECIDE BETWEEN "PHASE" AND "PHANTOM GIRL"--
WHAT ABOUT "MUTE GIRL?"

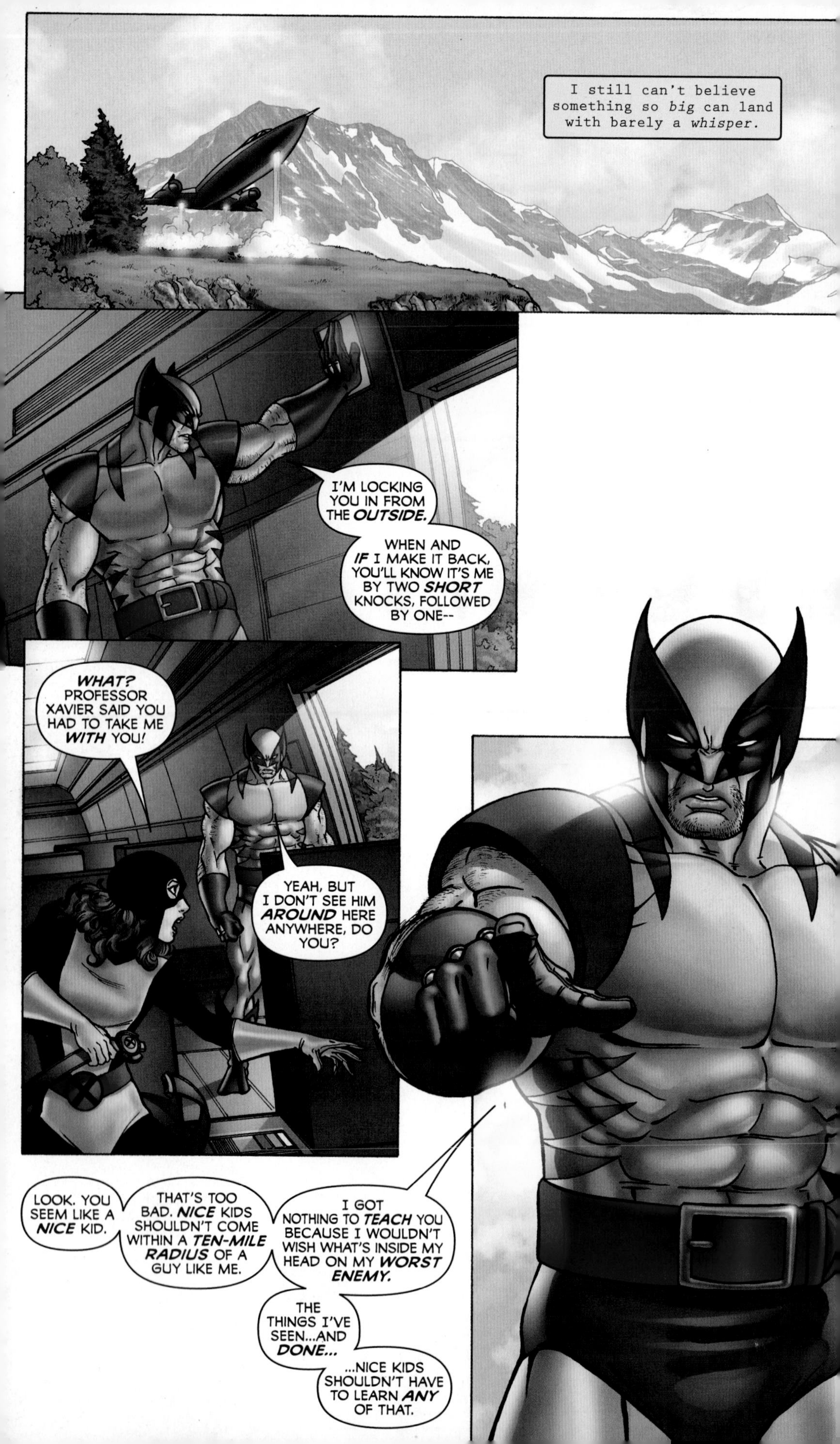

I still can't believe something so *big* can land with barely a *whisper.*
I'M LOCKING YOU IN FROM THE ***OUTSIDE.***
WHEN AND ***IF*** I MAKE IT BACK, YOU'LL KNOW IT'S ME BY TWO ***SHORT*** KNOCKS, FOLLOWED BY ONE--
WHAT? PROFESSOR XAVIER SAID YOU HAD TO TAKE ME ***WITH*** YOU!
YEAH, BUT I DON'T SEE HIM ***AROUND*** HERE ANYWHERE, DO YOU?
LOOK. YOU SEEM LIKE A ***NICE*** KID.
THAT'S TOO BAD. ***NICE*** KIDS SHOULDN'T COME WITHIN A ***TEN-MILE RADIUS*** OF A GUY LIKE ME.
I GOT NOTHING TO ***TEACH*** YOU BECAUSE I WOULDN'T WISH WHAT'S INSIDE MY HEAD ON MY ***WORST ENEMY.***
THE THINGS I'VE SEEN...AND ***DONE...***
...NICE KIDS SHOULDN'T HAVE TO LEARN ***ANY*** OF THAT.

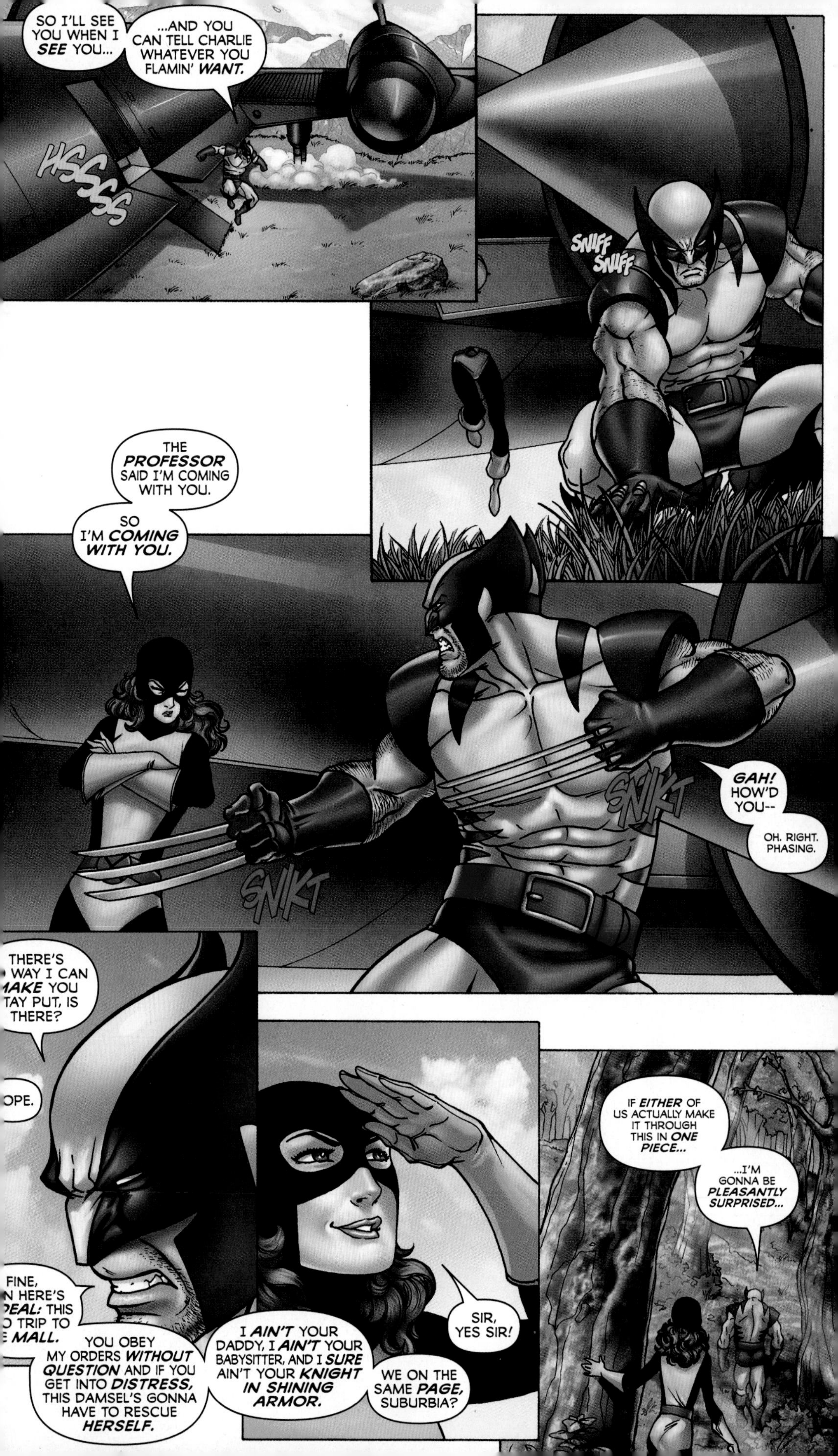

SO I'LL SEE YOU WHEN I *SEE* YOU...
...AND YOU CAN TELL CHARLIE WHATEVER YOU FLAMIN' *WANT.*
HSSSSS
SNIFF SNIFF
THE *PROFESSOR* SAID I'M COMING WITH YOU.
SO I'M *COMING WITH YOU.*
SNIKT
SNIKT
GAH! HOW'D YOU--
OH. RIGHT. PHASING.
THERE'S WAY I CAN *MAKE* YOU TAY PUT, IS THERE?
OPE.
FINE, N HERE'S *DEAL:* THIS TRIP TO *MALL.*
YOU OBEY MY ORDERS *WITHOUT QUESTION* AND IF YOU GET INTO *DISTRESS,* THIS DAMSEL'S GONNA HAVE TO RESCUE *HERSELF.*
I *AIN'T* YOUR DADDY, I *AIN'T* YOUR BABYSITTER, AND I *SURE* AIN'T YOUR *KNIGHT IN SHINING ARMOR.*
WE ON THE SAME *PAGE,* SUBURBIA?
SIR, YES SIR!
IF *EITHER* OF US ACTUALLY MAKE IT THROUGH THIS IN *ONE PIECE...*
...I'M GONNA BE *PLEASANTLY SURPRISED...*

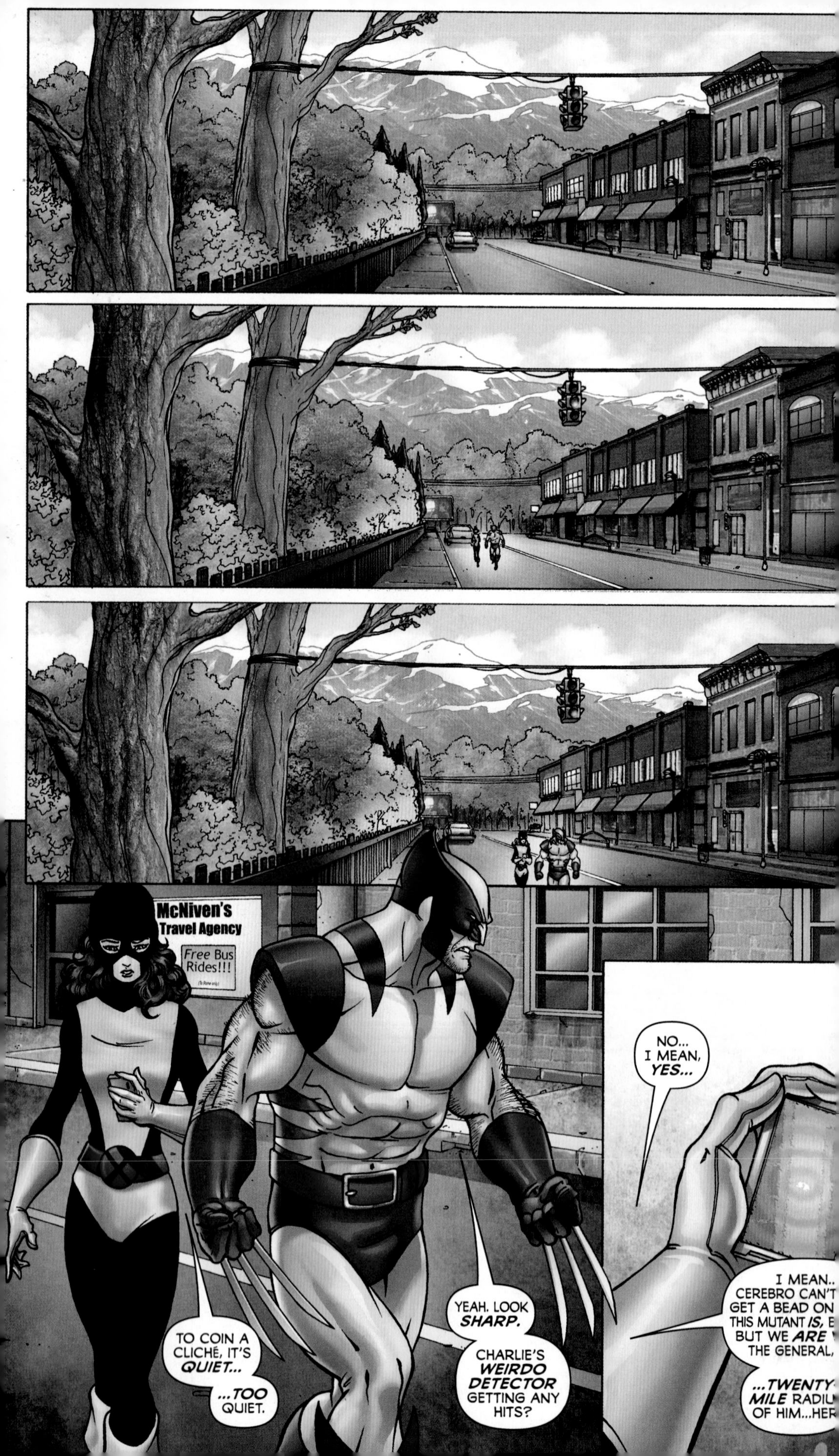
McNiven's
Travel Agency
Free Bus Rides!!!
TO COIN A CLICHÉ, IT'S *QUIET...*
...TOO QUIET.
YEAH. LOOK *SHARP.*
CHARLIE'S *WEIRDO DETECTOR* GETTING ANY HITS?
NO... I MEAN, *YES...*

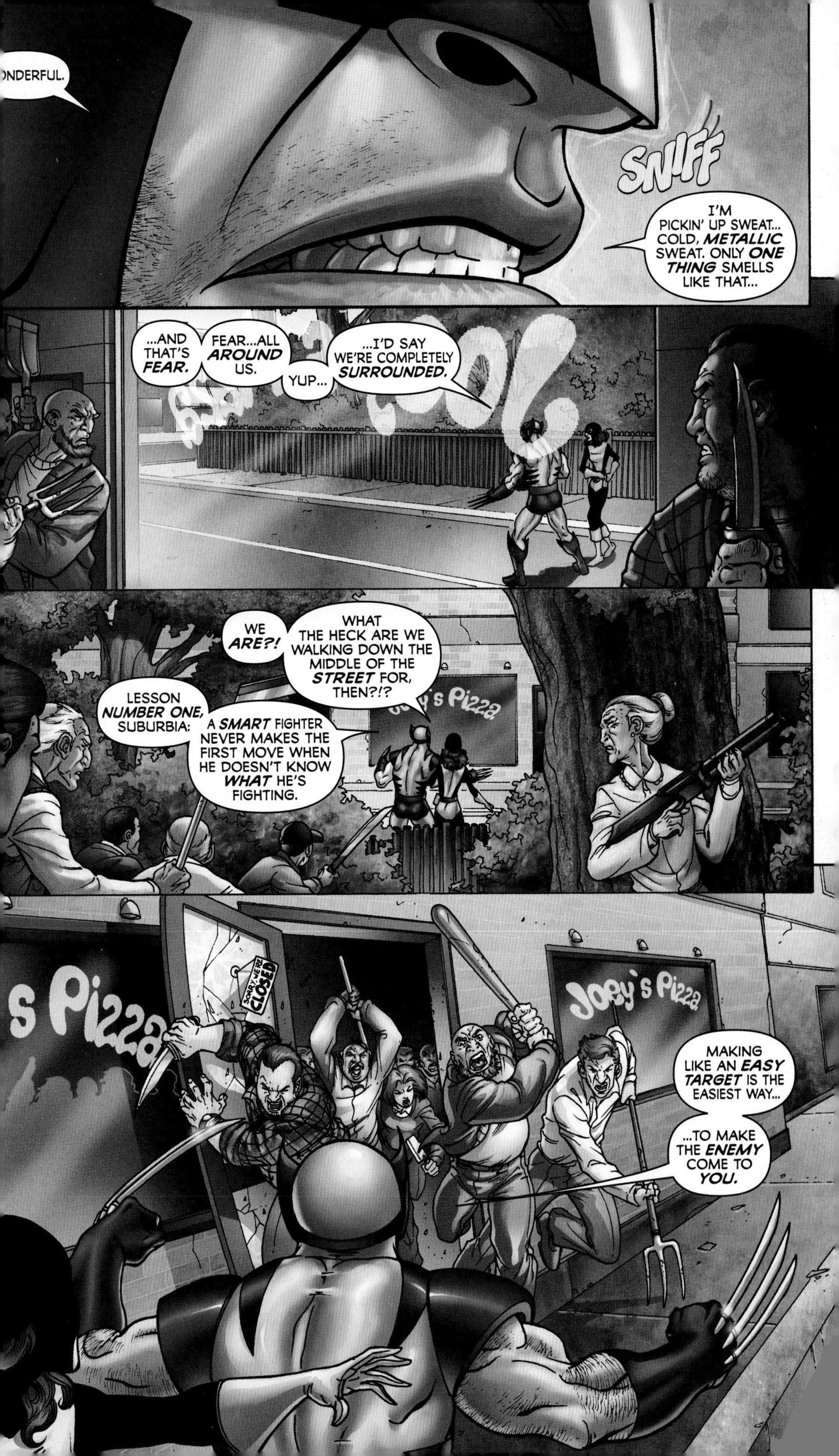

ONDERFUL.
SNIFF
I'M PICKIN' UP SWEAT... COLD, METALLIC SWEAT. ONLY ONE THING SMELLS LIKE THAT...
...AND THAT'S FEAR.
FEAR...ALL AROUND US.
YUP...
...I'D SAY WE'RE COMPLETELY SURROUNDED.
WE ARE?!
WHAT THE HECK ARE WE WALKING DOWN THE MIDDLE OF THE STREET FOR, THEN?!?
Joey's Pizza
LESSON NUMBER ONE, SUBURBIA:
A SMART FIGHTER NEVER MAKES THE FIRST MOVE WHEN HE DOESN'T KNOW WHAT HE'S FIGHTING.
s Pizza
SORRY WE'RE CLOSED
Joey's Pizza
MAKING LIKE AN EASY TARGET IS THE EASIEST WAY...
...TO MAKE THE ENEMY COME TO YOU.

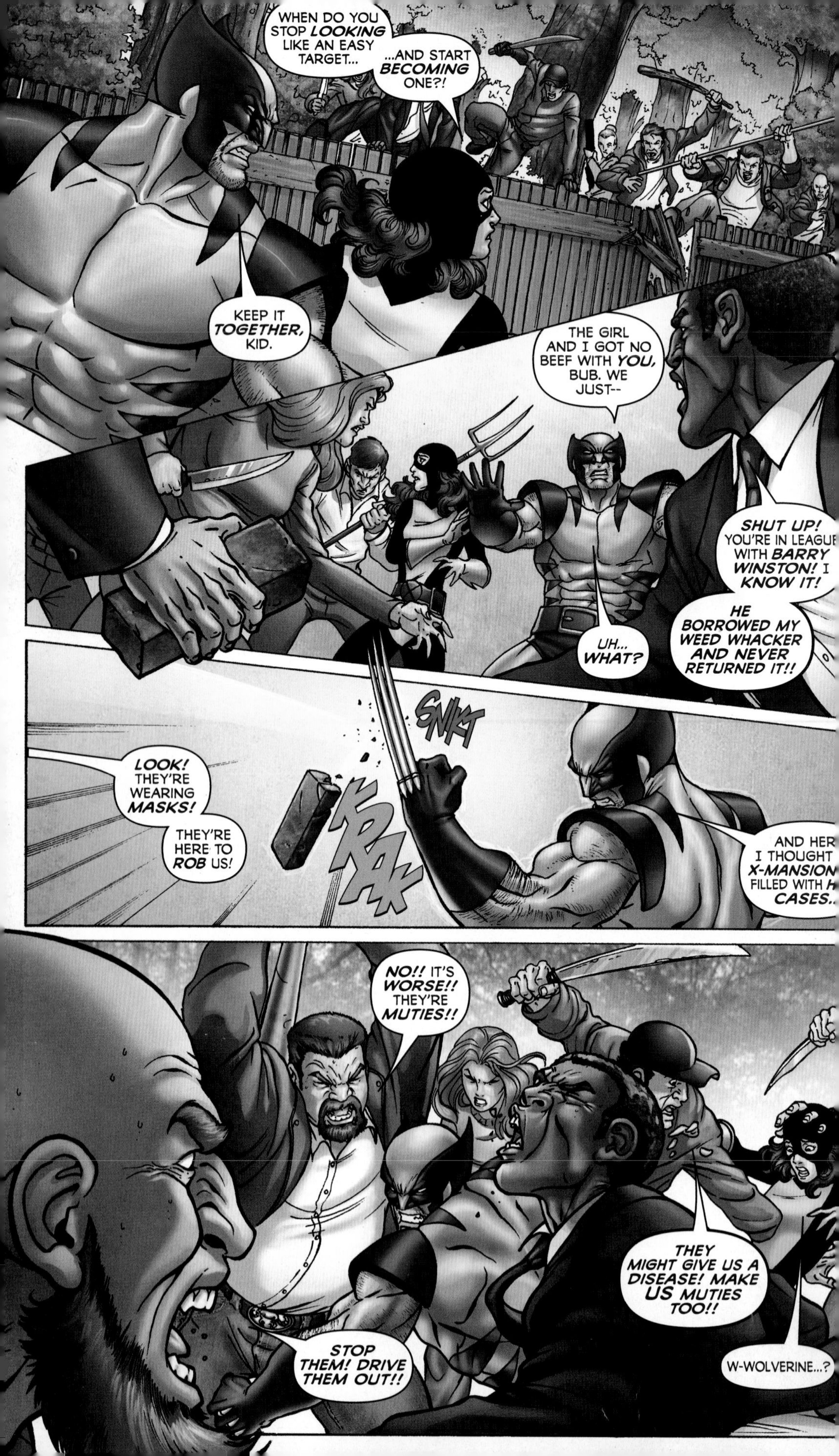
WHEN DO YOU STOP LOOKING LIKE AN EASY TARGET...
...AND START BECOMING ONE?!
KEEP IT TOGETHER, KID.
THE GIRL AND I GOT NO BEEF WITH YOU, BUB. WE JUST--
SHUT UP! YOU'RE IN LEAGUE WITH BARRY WINSTON! I KNOW IT!
HE BORROWED MY WEED WHACKER AND NEVER RETURNED IT!!
UH... WHAT?
SNIKT
LOOK! THEY'RE WEARING MASKS!
THEY'RE HERE TO ROB US!
KRAK
NO!! IT'S WORSE!! THEY'RE MUTIES!!
THEY MIGHT GIVE US A DISEASE! MAKE US MUTIES TOO!!
STOP THEM! DRIVE THEM OUT!!
W-WOLVERINE...?

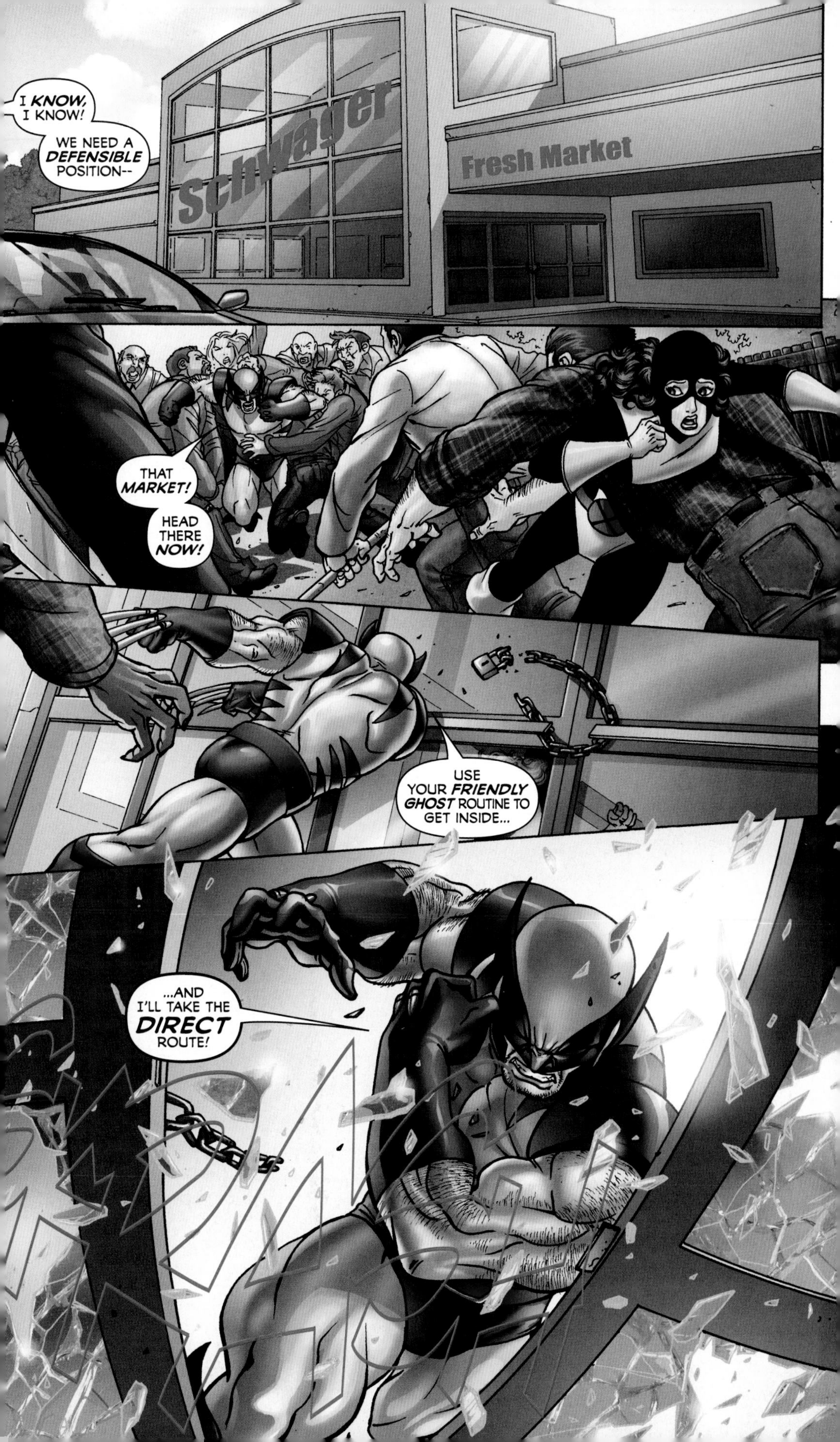

I KNOW, I KNOW!
WE NEED A DEFENSIBLE POSITION--
Schwager
Fresh Market
THAT MARKET!
HEAD THERE NOW!
USE YOUR FRIENDLY GHOST ROUTINE TO GET INSIDE...
...AND I'LL TAKE THE DIRECT ROUTE!

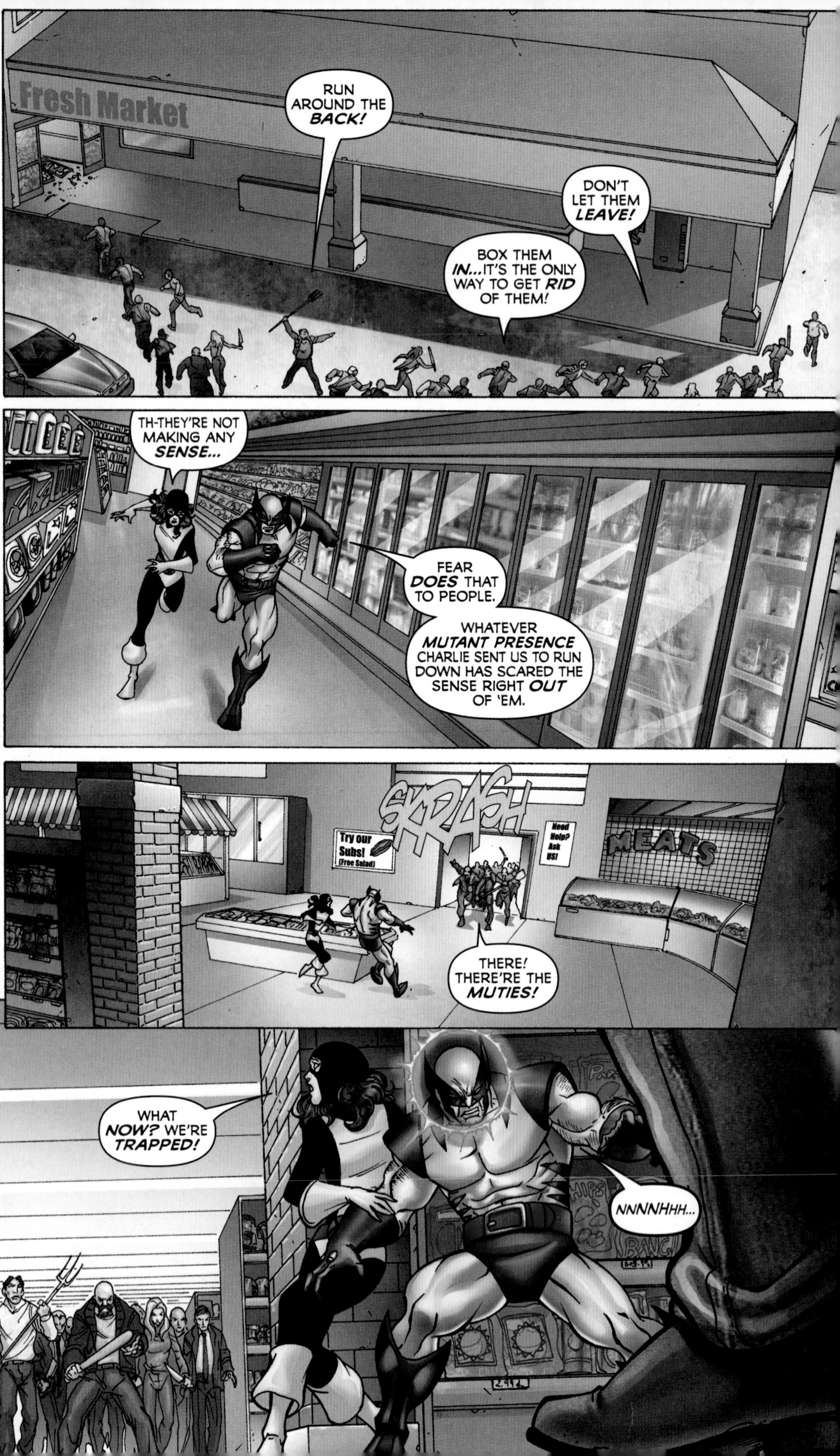
Fresh Market
RUN AROUND THE BACK!
DON'T LET THEM LEAVE!
BOX THEM IN...IT'S THE ONLY WAY TO GET RID OF THEM!
TH-THEY'RE NOT MAKING ANY SENSE...
FEAR DOES THAT TO PEOPLE.
WHATEVER MUTANT PRESENCE CHARLIE SENT US TO RUN DOWN HAS SCARED THE SENSE RIGHT OUT OF 'EM.
SKRASH
Try our Subs! (Free Salad)
Need Help? Ask US!
MEATS
THERE! THERE'RE THE MUTIES!
WHAT NOW? WE'RE TRAPPED!
NNNNHHH...

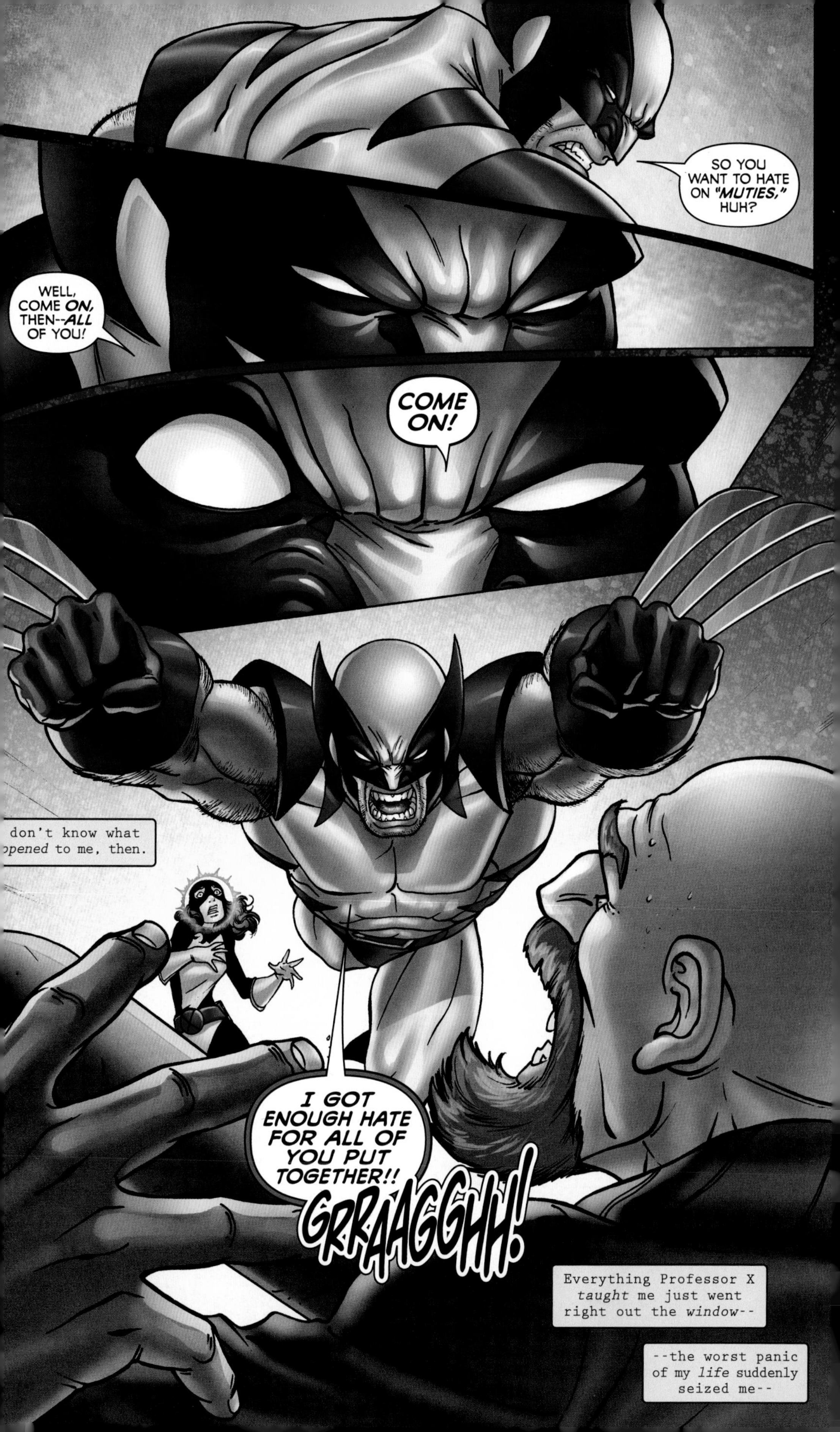
SO YOU WANT TO HATE ON "MUTIES," HUH?
WELL, COME ON, THEN--ALL OF YOU!
COME ON!
don't know what
opened to me, then.
I GOT ENOUGH HATE FOR ALL OF YOU PUT TOGETHER!!
GRRAAGGHH!
Everything Professor X taught me just went right out the window--
--the worst panic of my life suddenly seized me--

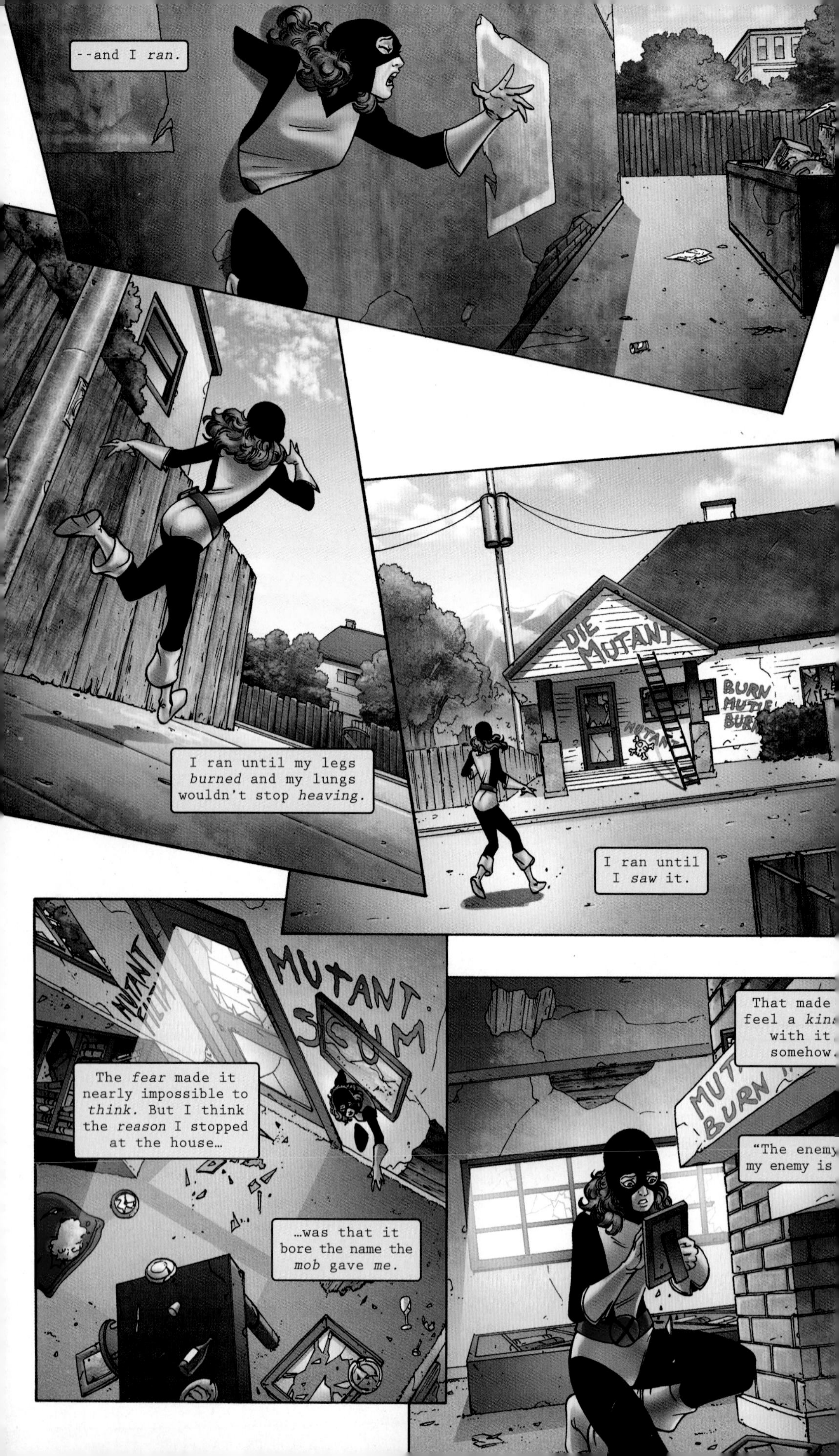
--and I *ran*.
I ran until my legs *burned* and my lungs wouldn't stop *heaving*.
DIE MUTANT
BURN MUTIE
I ran until I *saw* it.
MUTANT FILTH
MUTANT SCUM
The *fear* made it nearly impossible to *think*. But I think the *reason* I stopped at the house…
…was that it bore the name the *mob* gave *me*.
That made
feel a kin
with it
somehow.
“The enemy
my enemy is

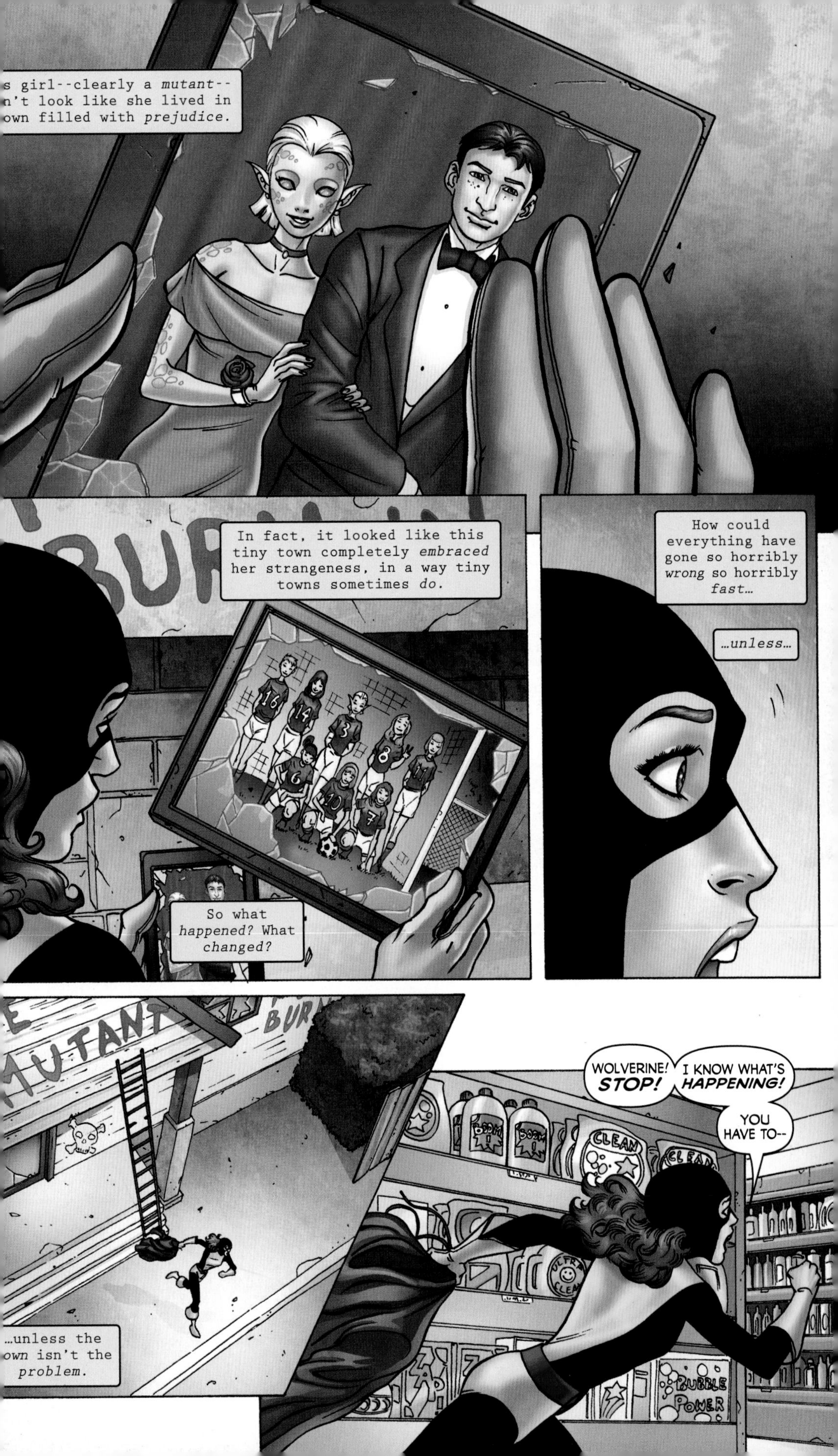
s girl--clearly a mutant--
n't look like she lived in
own filled with prejudice.
In fact, it looked like this tiny town completely embraced her strangeness, in a way tiny towns sometimes do.
So what happened? What changed?
How could everything have gone so horribly wrong so horribly fast...
...unless...
MUTANT
BUR
...unless the
own isn't the
problem.
WOLVERINE! STOP!
I KNOW WHAT'S HAPPENING!
YOU HAVE TO--
CLEAN
BUBBLE POWER

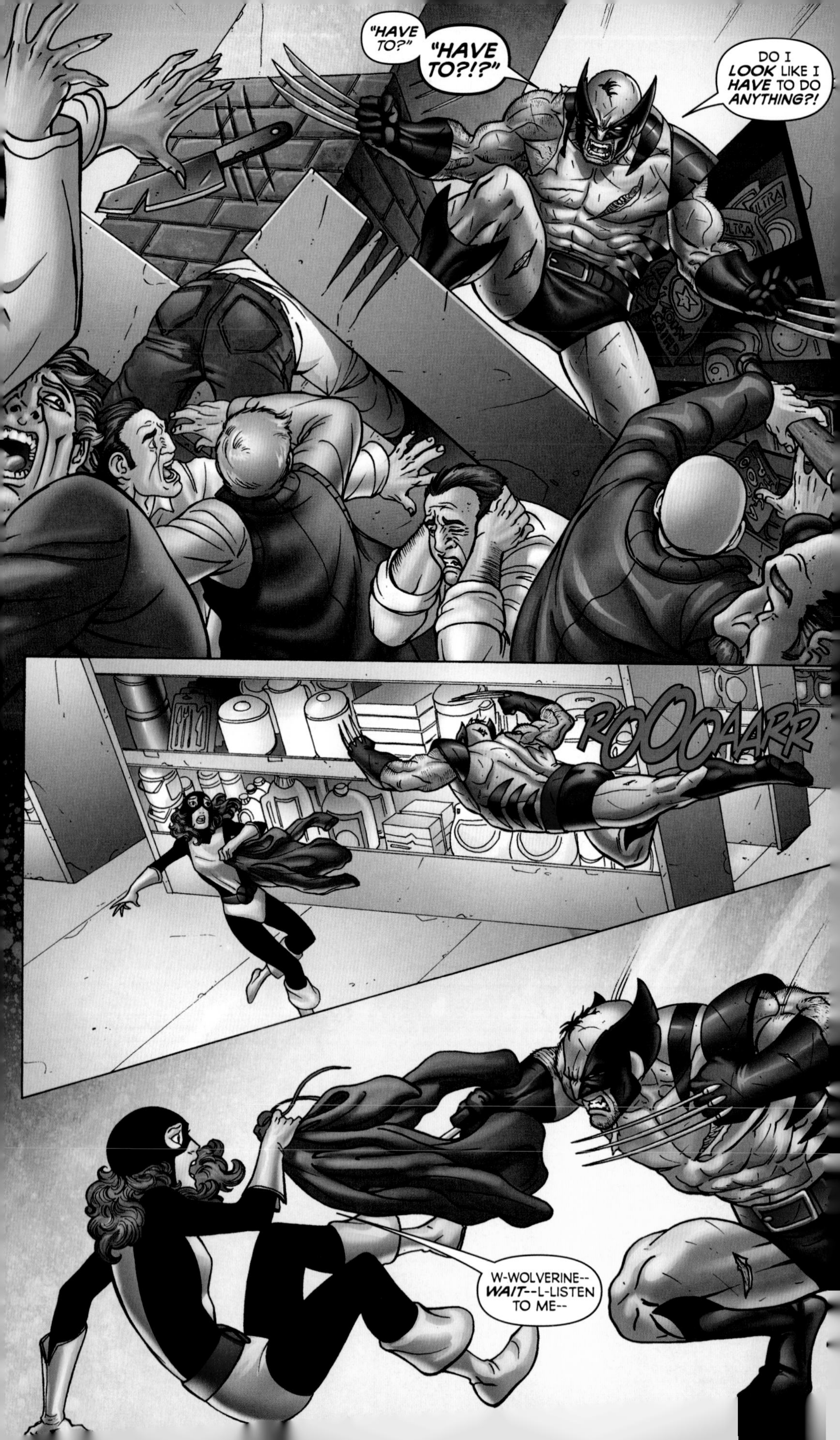
"HAVE TO?"
"HAVE TO?!?"
DO I LOOK LIKE I HAVE TO DO ANYTHING?!
ROOOOAARR
W-WOLVERINE-- WAIT--L-LISTEN TO ME--

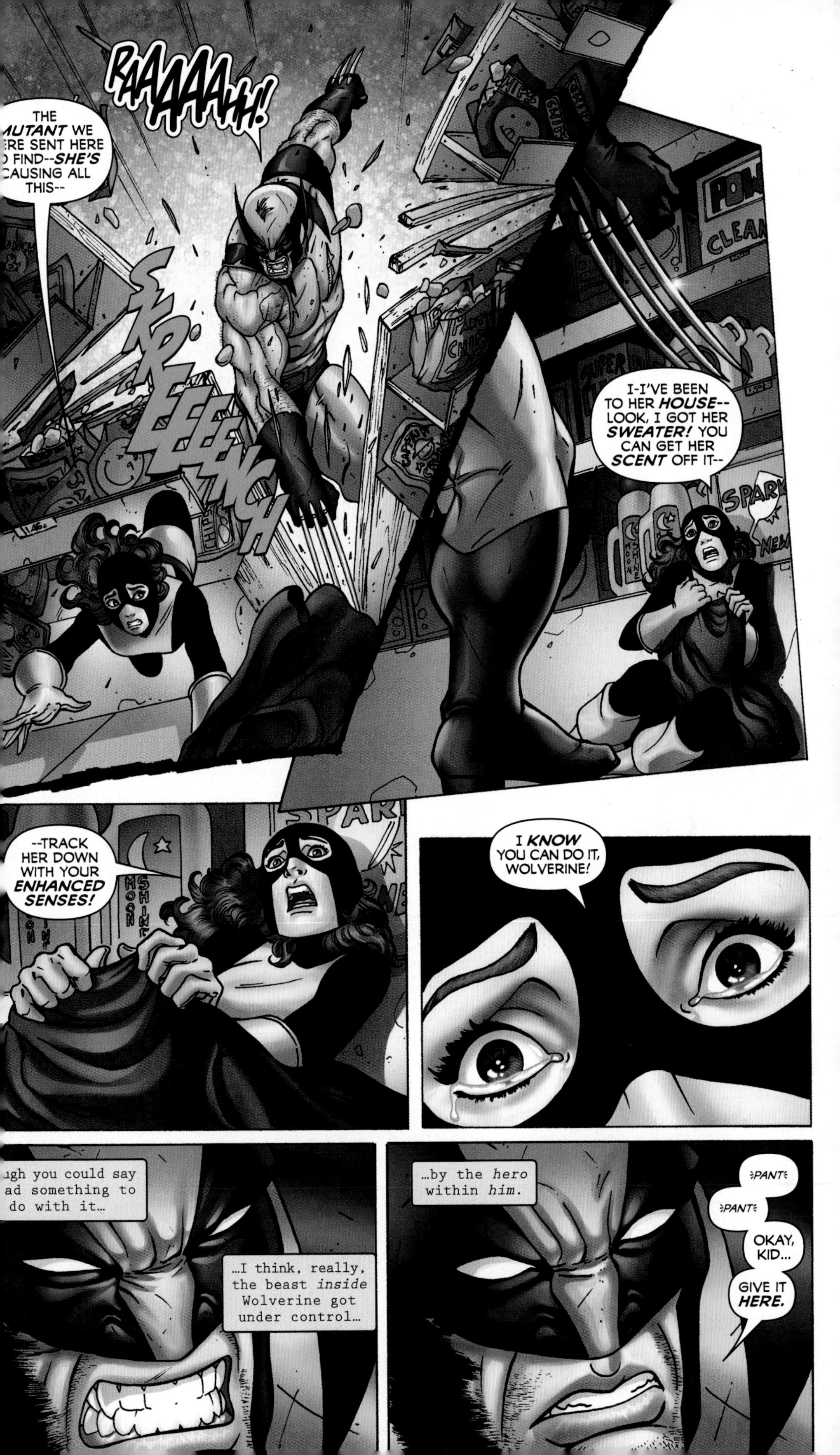
RAAAAAHH!
THE MUTANT WE ERE SENT HERE D FIND--SHE'S CAUSING ALL THIS--
SKREEEEEENCH
I-I'VE BEEN TO HER HOUSE-- LOOK, I GOT HER SWEATER! YOU CAN GET HER SCENT OFF IT--
--TRACK HER DOWN WITH YOUR ENHANCED SENSES!
I KNOW YOU CAN DO IT, WOLVERINE!
ugh you could say ad something to do with it...
...I think, really, the beast inside Wolverine got under control...
...by the hero within him.
PANT
PANT
OKAY, KID...
GIVE IT HERE.

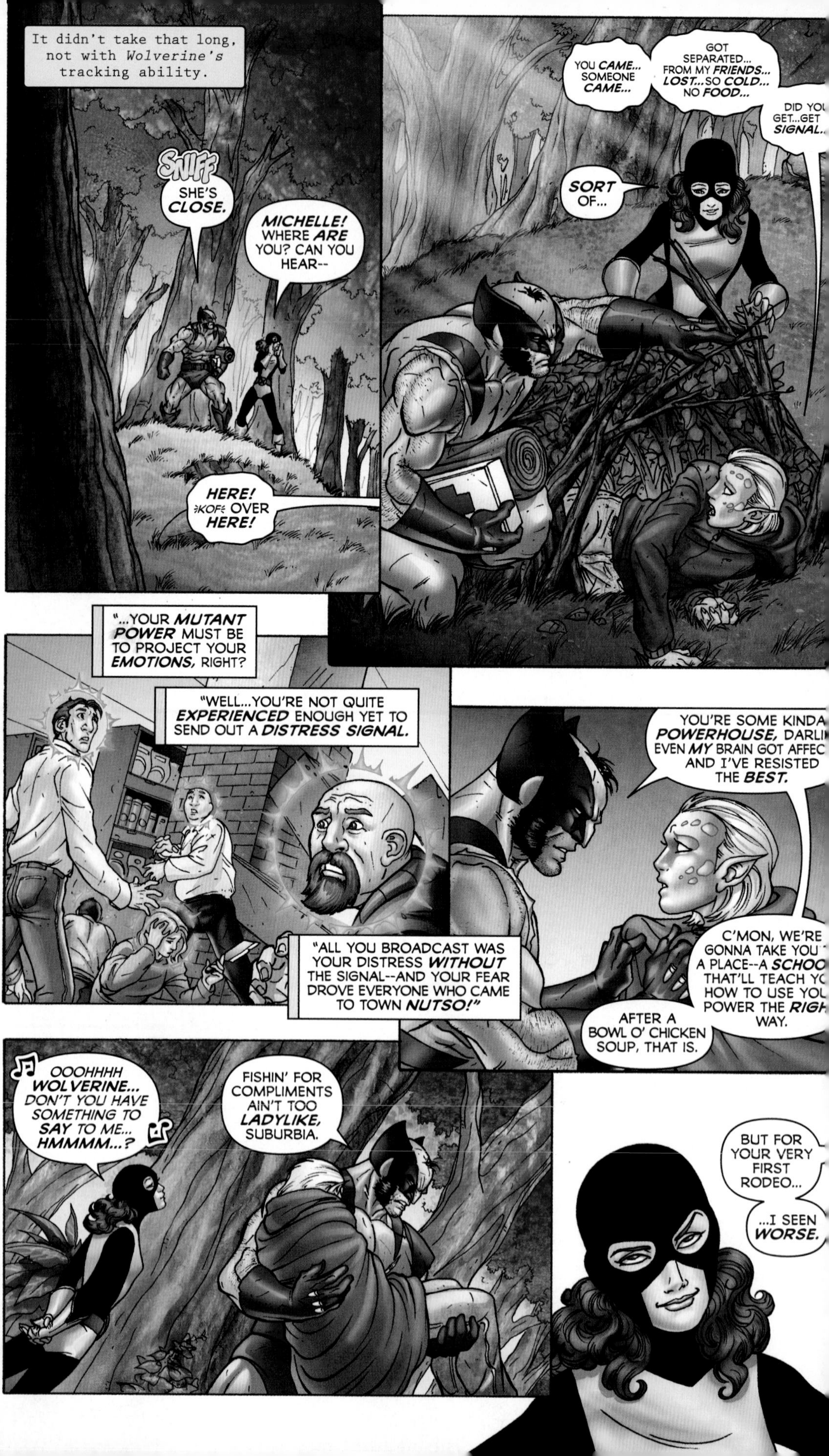

It didn't take that long, not with *Wolverine's* tracking ability.
SNIFF
SHE'S CLOSE.
MICHELLE! WHERE ARE YOU? CAN YOU HEAR--
HERE! KOF OVER HERE!
YOU CAME... SOMEONE CAME...
GOT SEPARATED... FROM MY FRIENDS... LOST...SO COLD... NO FOOD...
DID YOU GET...GET SIGNAL...
SORT OF...
"...YOUR MUTANT POWER MUST BE TO PROJECT YOUR EMOTIONS, RIGHT?
"WELL...YOU'RE NOT QUITE EXPERIENCED ENOUGH YET TO SEND OUT A DISTRESS SIGNAL.
"ALL YOU BROADCAST WAS YOUR DISTRESS WITHOUT THE SIGNAL--AND YOUR FEAR DROVE EVERYONE WHO CAME TO TOWN NUTSO!"
YOU'RE SOME KINDA POWERHOUSE, DARLI EVEN MY BRAIN GOT AFFEC AND I'VE RESISTED THE BEST.
C'MON, WE'RE GONNA TAKE YOU A PLACE--A SCHOO THAT'LL TEACH YO HOW TO USE YOU POWER THE RIGH WAY.
AFTER A BOWL O' CHICKEN SOUP, THAT IS.
OOOHHHH WOLVERINE... DON'T YOU HAVE SOMETHING TO SAY TO ME... HMMMM...?
FISHIN' FOR COMPLIMENTS AIN'T TOO LADYLIKE, SUBURBIA.
BUT FOR YOUR VERY FIRST RODEO...
...I SEEN WORSE.

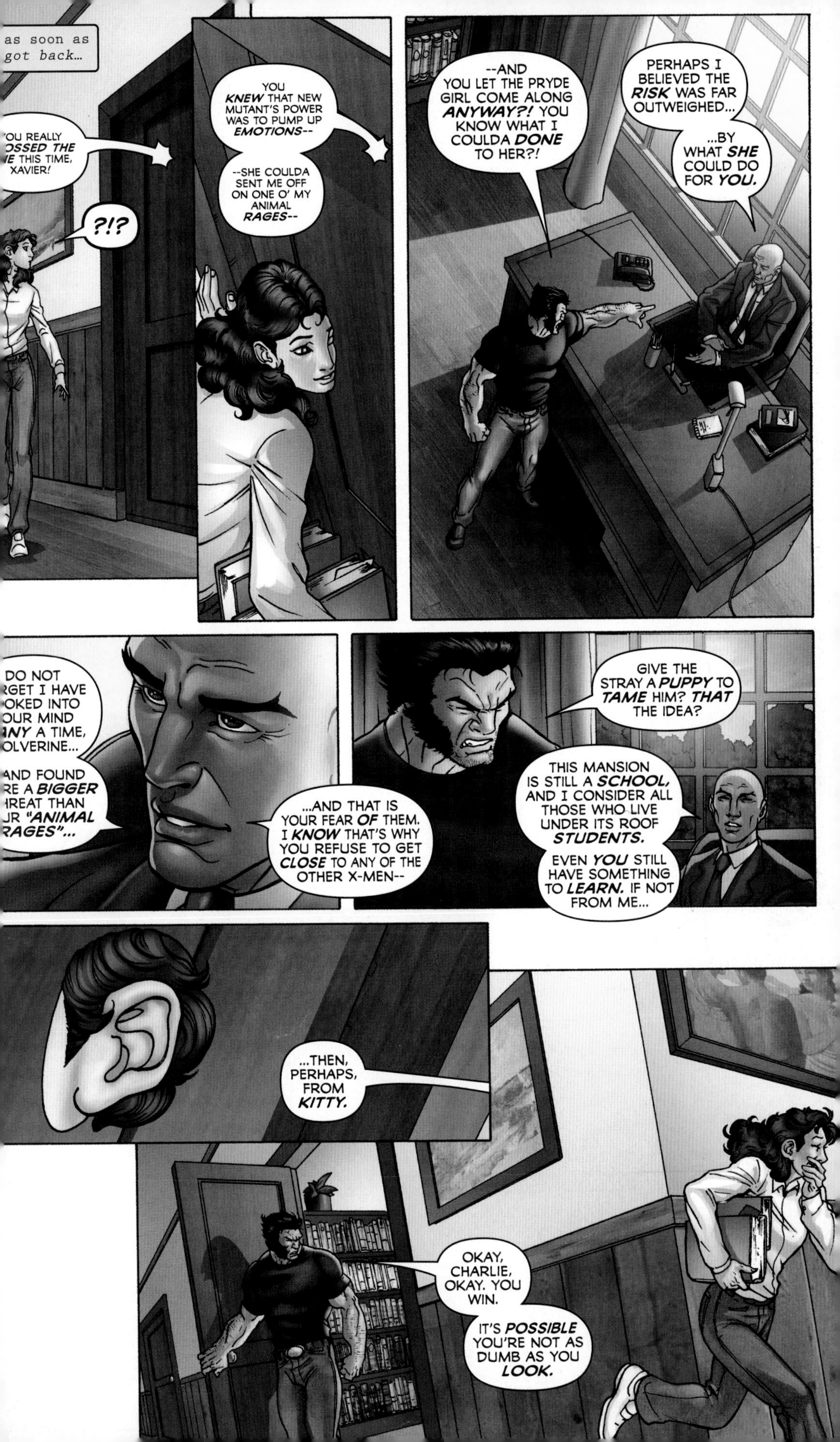

as soon as
got back...
OU REALLY
OSSED THE
E THIS TIME,
XAVIER!
?!?
YOU KNEW THAT NEW MUTANT'S POWER WAS TO PUMP UP EMOTIONS--
--SHE COULDA SENT ME OFF ON ONE O' MY ANIMAL RAGES--
--AND YOU LET THE PRYDE GIRL COME ALONG ANYWAY?! YOU KNOW WHAT I COULDA DONE TO HER?!
PERHAPS I BELIEVED THE RISK WAS FAR OUTWEIGHED...
...BY WHAT SHE COULD DO FOR YOU.
DO NOT
RGET I HAVE
OKED INTO
OUR MIND
NY A TIME,
OLVERINE...
AND FOUND
RE A BIGGER
HREAT THAN
UR "ANIMAL
RAGES"...
...AND THAT IS YOUR FEAR OF THEM. I KNOW THAT'S WHY YOU REFUSE TO GET CLOSE TO ANY OF THE OTHER X-MEN--
GIVE THE STRAY A PUPPY TO TAME HIM? THAT THE IDEA?
THIS MANSION IS STILL A SCHOOL, AND I CONSIDER ALL THOSE WHO LIVE UNDER ITS ROOF STUDENTS.
EVEN YOU STILL HAVE SOMETHING TO LEARN. IF NOT FROM ME...
...THEN, PERHAPS, FROM KITTY.
OKAY, CHARLIE, OKAY. YOU WIN.
IT'S POSSIBLE YOU'RE NOT AS DUMB AS YOU LOOK.

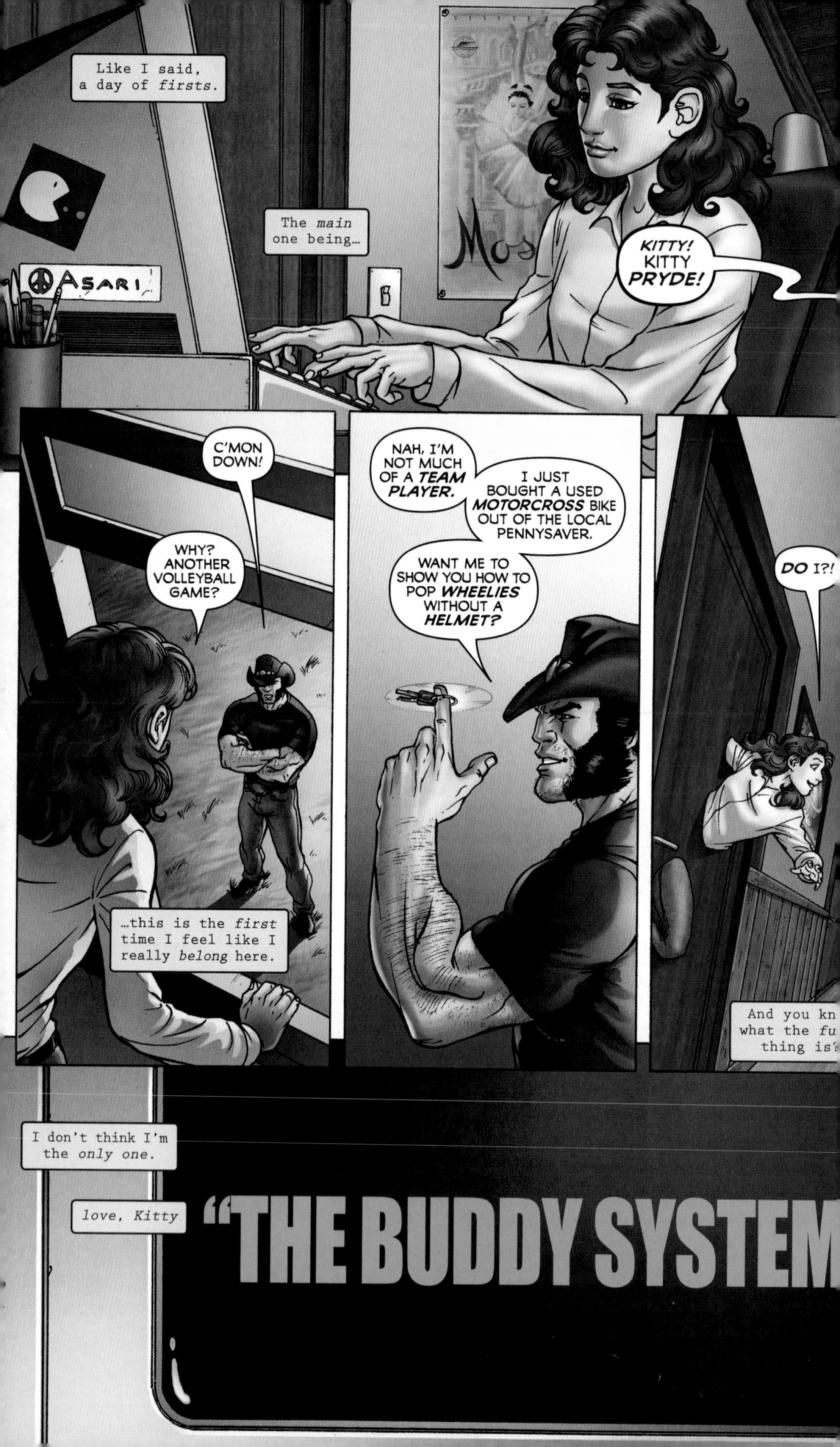
Like I said, a day of *firsts*.
The *main* one being...
ASARI
KITTY! KITTY PRYDE!
C'MON DOWN!
WHY? ANOTHER VOLLEYBALL GAME?
...this is the *first* time I feel like I really *belong* here.
NAH, I'M NOT MUCH OF A *TEAM PLAYER.*
I JUST BOUGHT A USED *MOTORCROSS* BIKE OUT OF THE LOCAL PENNYSAVER.
WANT ME TO SHOW YOU HOW TO POP *WHEELIES* WITHOUT A *HELMET?*
DO I?!
I don't think I'm the *only one.*
love, Kitty
"THE BUDDY SYSTEM

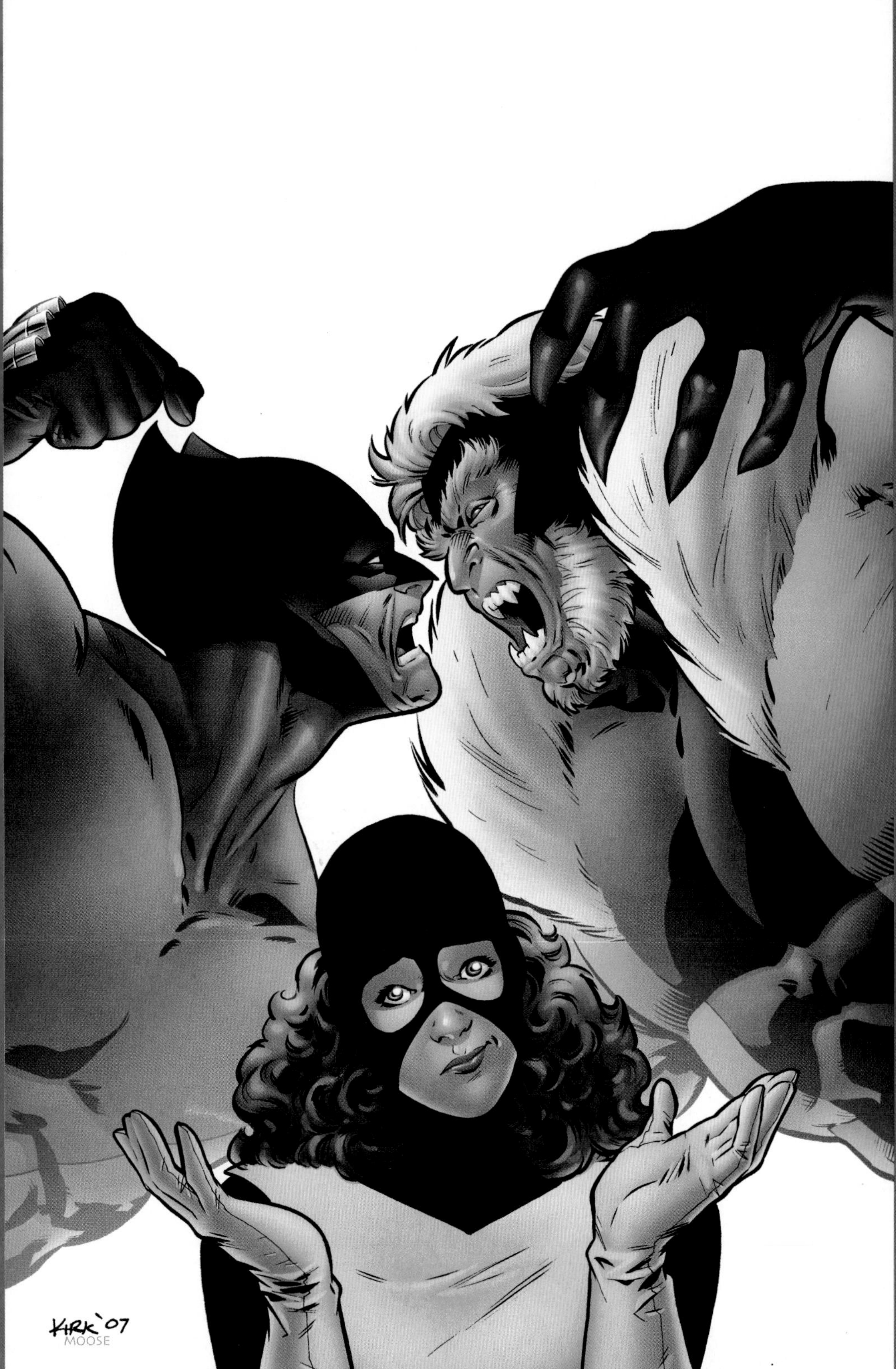
KIRK '07
MOOSE

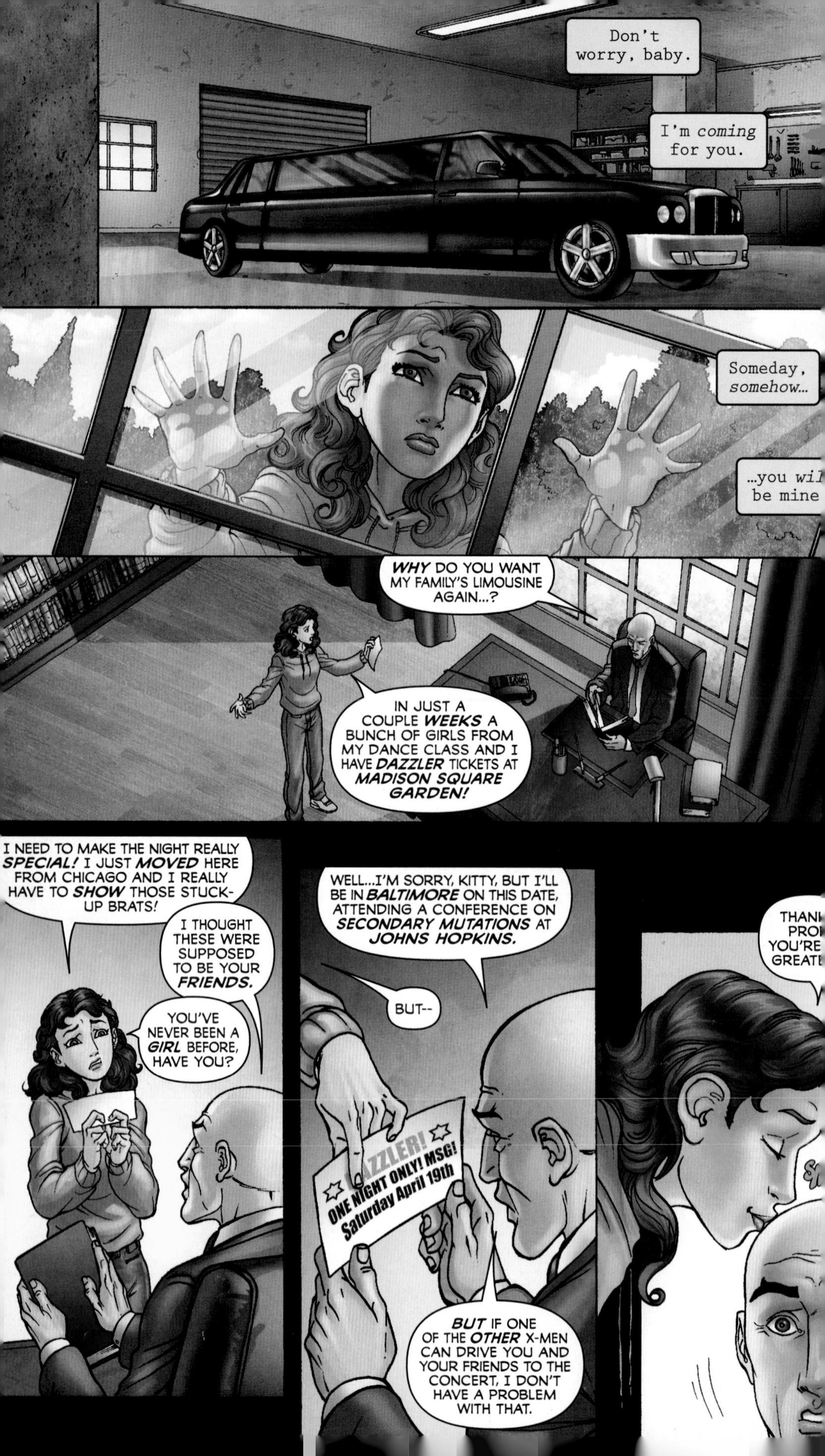
Don't worry, baby.
I'm *coming* for you.
Someday, *somehow*...
...you *wil*
be mine
WHY DO YOU WANT MY FAMILY'S LIMOUSINE AGAIN...?
IN JUST A COUPLE ***WEEKS*** A BUNCH OF GIRLS FROM MY DANCE CLASS AND I HAVE ***DAZZLER*** TICKETS AT ***MADISON SQUARE GARDEN!***
I NEED TO MAKE THE NIGHT REALLY ***SPECIAL!*** I JUST ***MOVED*** HERE FROM CHICAGO AND I REALLY HAVE TO ***SHOW*** THOSE STUCK-UP BRATS!
I THOUGHT THESE WERE SUPPOSED TO BE YOUR ***FRIENDS.***
YOU'VE NEVER BEEN A ***GIRL*** BEFORE, HAVE YOU?
WELL...I'M SORRY, KITTY, BUT I'LL BE IN ***BALTIMORE*** ON THIS DATE, ATTENDING A CONFERENCE ON ***SECONDARY MUTATIONS*** AT ***JOHNS HOPKINS.***
BUT--
ONE NIGHT ONLY! MSG!
Saturday April 19th
BUT IF ONE OF THE ***OTHER*** X-MEN CAN DRIVE YOU AND YOUR FRIENDS TO THE CONCERT, I DON'T HAVE A PROBLEM WITH THAT.

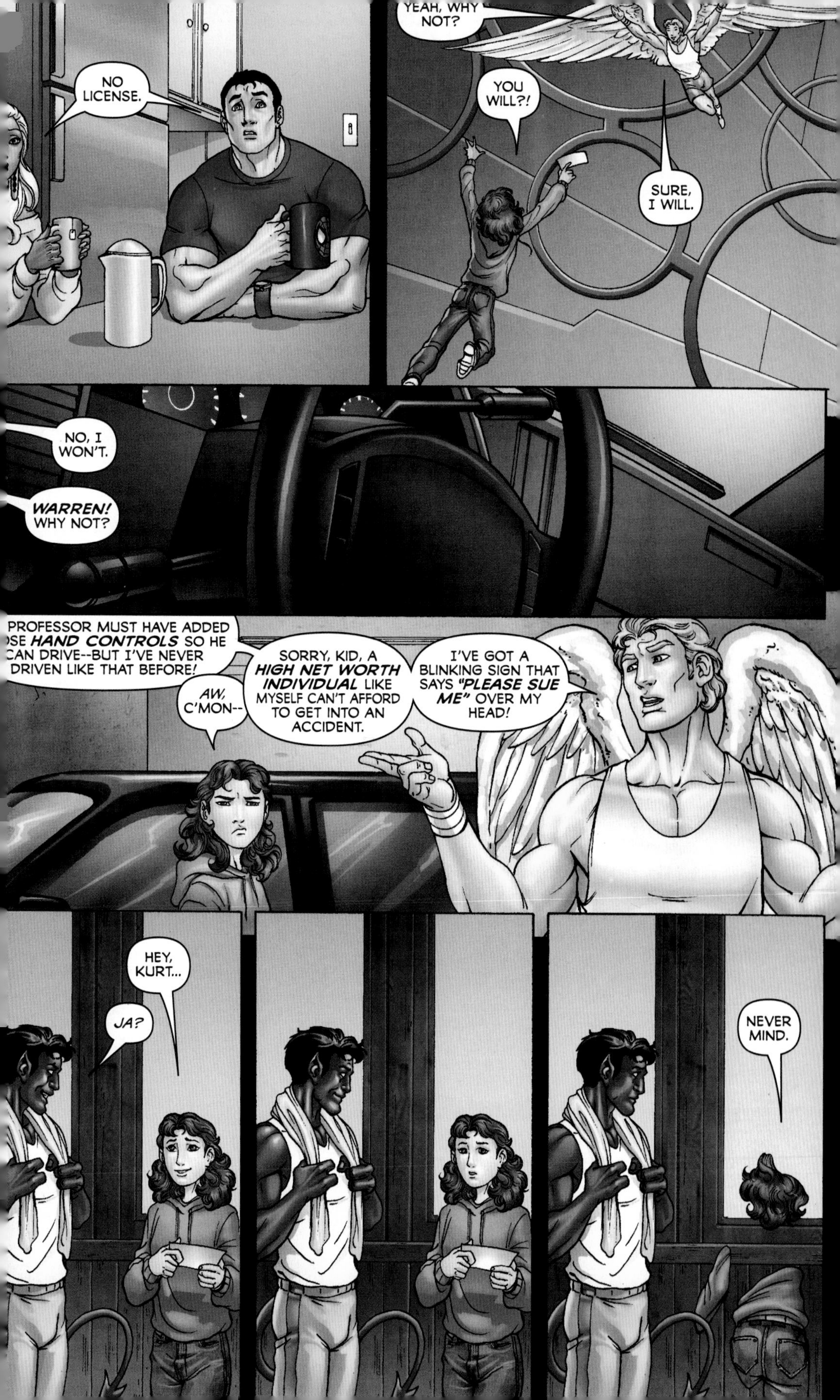

NO LICENSE.
YEAH, WHY NOT?
YOU WILL?!
SURE, I WILL.
NO, I WON'T.
WARREN! WHY NOT?
PROFESSOR MUST HAVE ADDED
OSE HAND CONTROLS SO HE
CAN DRIVE--BUT I'VE NEVER
DRIVEN LIKE THAT BEFORE!
AW, C'MON--
SORRY, KID, A HIGH NET WORTH INDIVIDUAL LIKE MYSELF CAN'T AFFORD TO GET INTO AN ACCIDENT.
I'VE GOT A BLINKING SIGN THAT SAYS "PLEASE SUE ME" OVER MY HEAD!
HEY, KURT...
JA?
NEVER MIND.

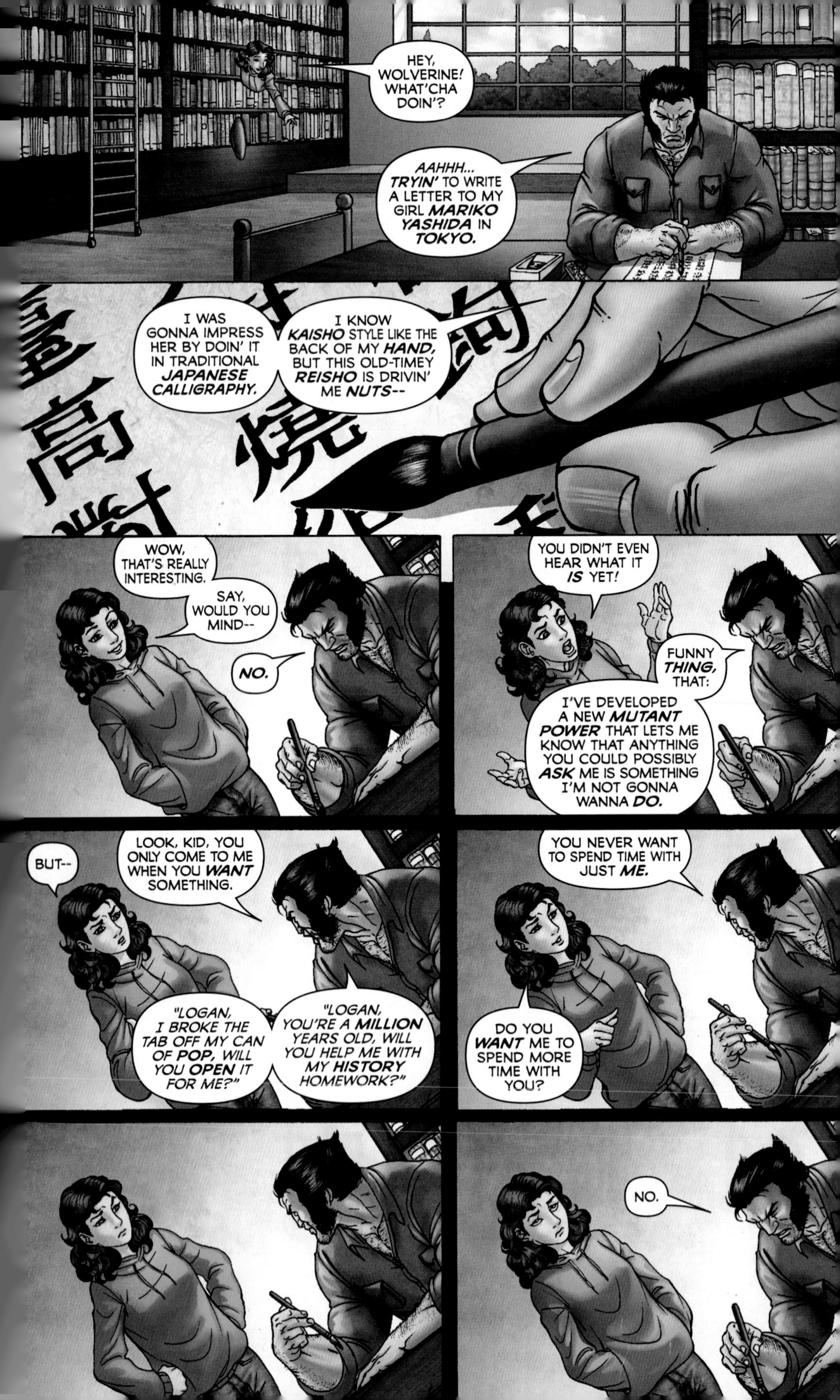
HEY, WOLVERINE! WHAT'CHA DOIN'?
AAHHH... TRYIN' TO WRITE A LETTER TO MY GIRL MARIKO YASHIDA IN TOKYO.
I WAS GONNA IMPRESS HER BY DOIN' IT IN TRADITIONAL JAPANESE CALLIGRAPHY.
I KNOW KAISHO STYLE LIKE THE BACK OF MY HAND, BUT THIS OLD-TIMEY REISHO IS DRIVIN' ME NUTS--
WOW, THAT'S REALLY INTERESTING.
SAY, WOULD YOU MIND--
NO.
YOU DIDN'T EVEN HEAR WHAT IT IS YET!
FUNNY THING, THAT:
I'VE DEVELOPED A NEW MUTANT POWER THAT LETS ME KNOW THAT ANYTHING YOU COULD POSSIBLY ASK ME IS SOMETHING I'M NOT GONNA WANNA DO.
BUT--
LOOK, KID, YOU ONLY COME TO ME WHEN YOU WANT SOMETHING.
"LOGAN, I BROKE THE TAB OFF MY CAN OF POP, WILL YOU OPEN IT FOR ME?"
"LOGAN, YOU'RE A MILLION YEARS OLD, WILL YOU HELP ME WITH MY HISTORY HOMEWORK?"
YOU NEVER WANT TO SPEND TIME WITH JUST ME.
DO YOU WANT ME TO SPEND MORE TIME WITH YOU?
NO.

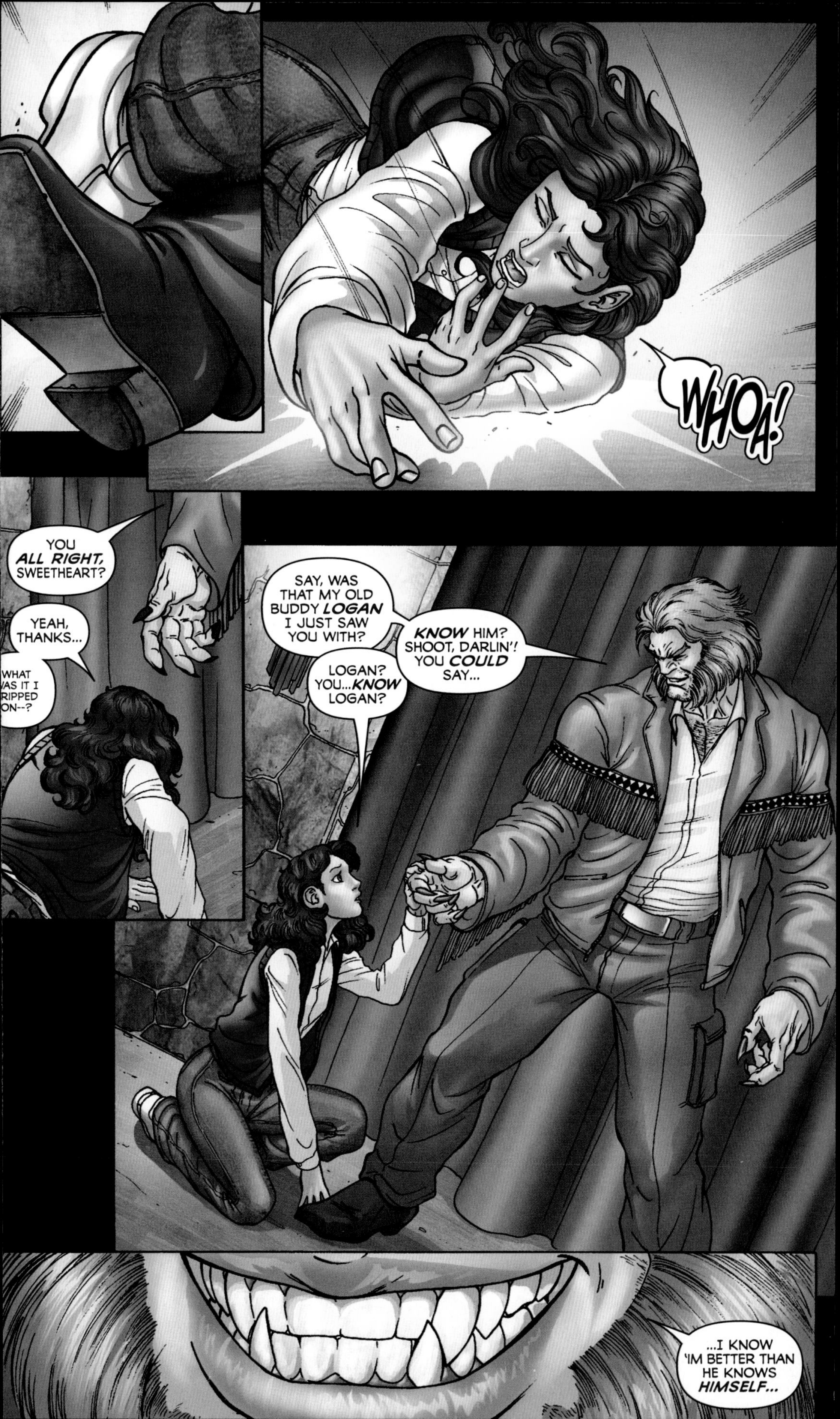
WHOA!
YOU ALL RIGHT, SWEETHEART?
YEAH, THANKS...
WHAT WAS IT I TRIPPED ON--?
SAY, WAS THAT MY OLD BUDDY LOGAN I JUST SAW YOU WITH?
LOGAN? YOU...KNOW LOGAN?
KNOW HIM? SHOOT, DARLIN'! YOU COULD SAY...
...I KNOW 'IM BETTER THAN HE KNOWS HIMSELF...

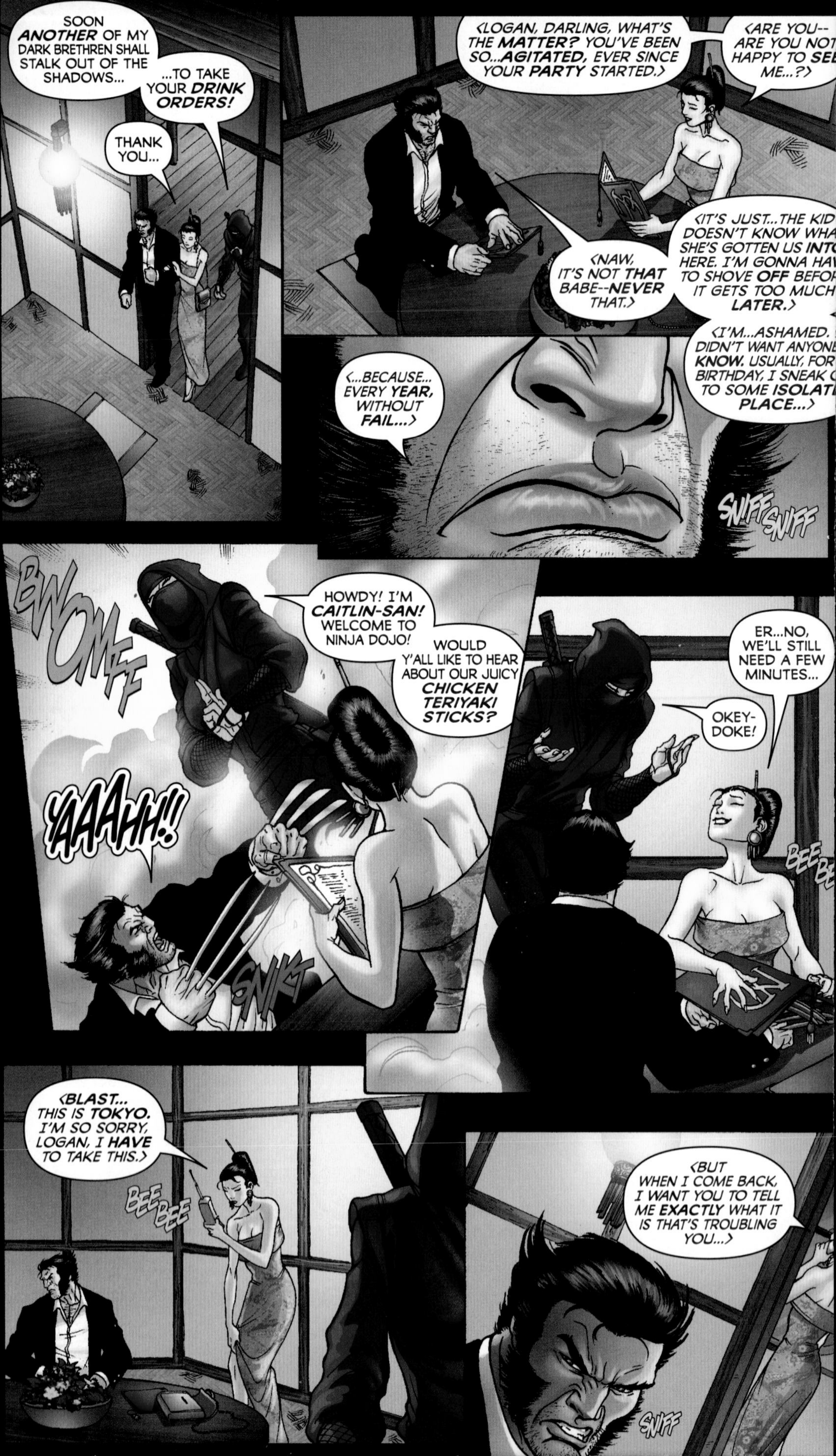
SOON ANOTHER OF MY DARK BRETHREN SHALL STALK OUT OF THE SHADOWS...
...TO TAKE YOUR DRINK ORDERS!
THANK YOU...
<LOGAN, DARLING, WHAT'S THE MATTER? YOU'VE BEEN SO...AGITATED, EVER SINCE YOUR PARTY STARTED.>
<ARE YOU-- ARE YOU NOT HAPPY TO SEE ME...?>
<NAW, IT'S NOT THAT BABE--NEVER THAT.>
<IT'S JUST...THE KID DOESN'T KNOW WHAT SHE'S GOTTEN US INTO HERE. I'M GONNA HAVE TO SHOVE OFF BEFORE IT GETS TOO MUCH LATER.>
<...BECAUSE... EVERY YEAR, WITHOUT FAIL...>
<I'M...ASHAMED. I DIDN'T WANT ANYONE TO KNOW. USUALLY, FOR MY BIRTHDAY, I SNEAK OFF TO SOME ISOLATED PLACE...>
SNIFF SNIFF
BWOMFF
HOWDY! I'M CAITLIN-SAN! WELCOME TO NINJA DOJO!
WOULD Y'ALL LIKE TO HEAR ABOUT OUR JUICY CHICKEN TERIYAKI STICKS?
YAAAHH!!
SNIKT
ER...NO, WE'LL STILL NEED A FEW MINUTES...
OKEY-DOKE!
BEE BEE
<BLAST... THIS IS TOKYO. I'M SO SORRY, LOGAN, I HAVE TO TAKE THIS.>
BEE BEE
<BUT WHEN I COME BACK, I WANT YOU TO TELL ME EXACTLY WHAT IT IS THAT'S TROUBLING YOU...>
SNIFF

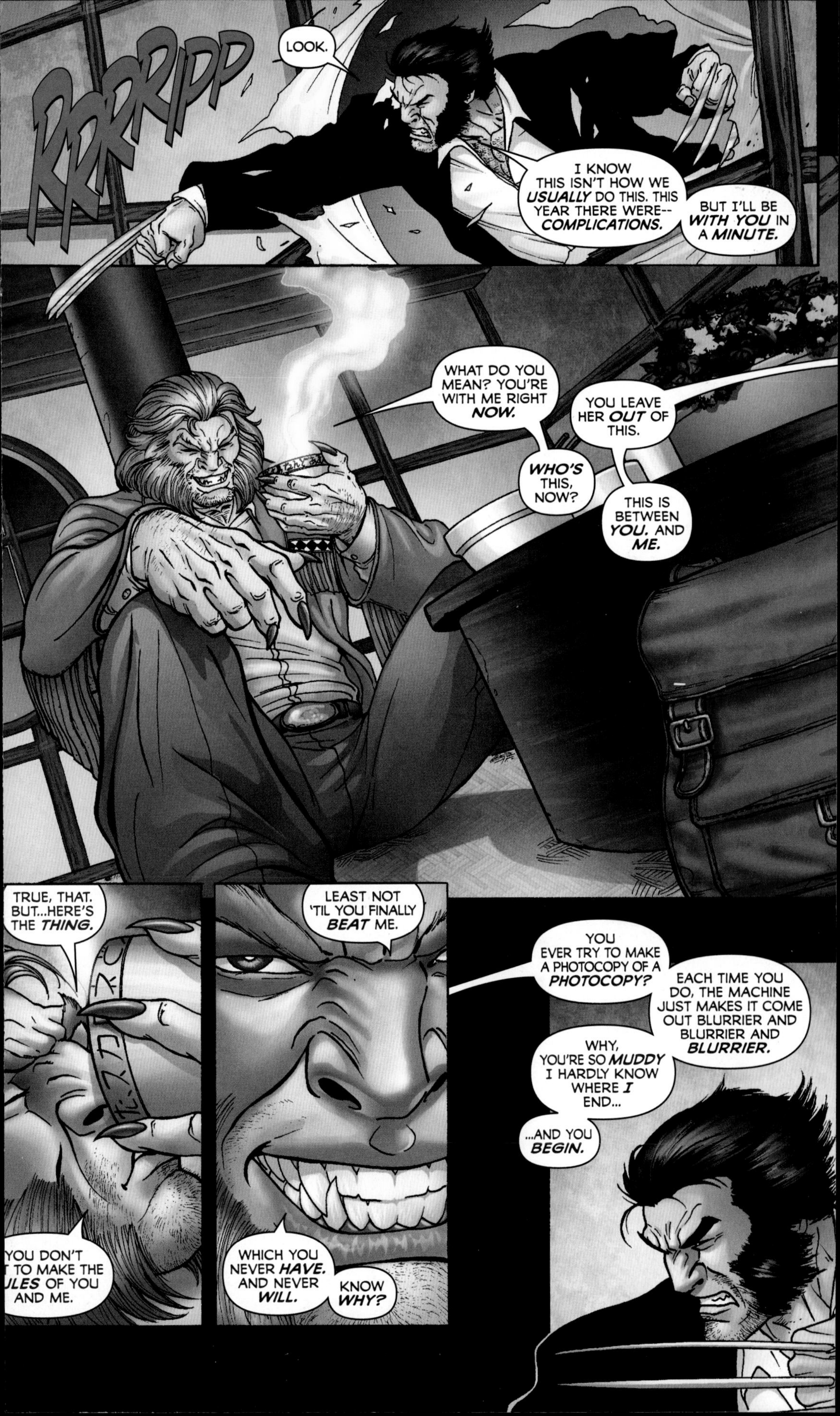
RRRRIPP
LOOK.
I KNOW THIS ISN'T HOW WE USUALLY DO THIS. THIS YEAR THERE WERE-- COMPLICATIONS.
BUT I'LL BE WITH YOU IN A MINUTE.
WHAT DO YOU MEAN? YOU'RE WITH ME RIGHT NOW.
WHO'S THIS, NOW?
YOU LEAVE HER OUT OF THIS.
THIS IS BETWEEN YOU. AND ME.
TRUE, THAT. BUT...HERE'S THE THING.
LEAST NOT 'TIL YOU FINALLY BEAT ME.
WHICH YOU NEVER HAVE. AND NEVER WILL.
KNOW WHY?
YOU EVER TRY TO MAKE A PHOTOCOPY OF A PHOTOCOPY?
EACH TIME YOU DO, THE MACHINE JUST MAKES IT COME OUT BLURRIER AND BLURRIER AND BLURRIER.
WHY, YOU'RE SO MUDDY I HARDLY KNOW WHERE I END...
...AND YOU BEGIN.

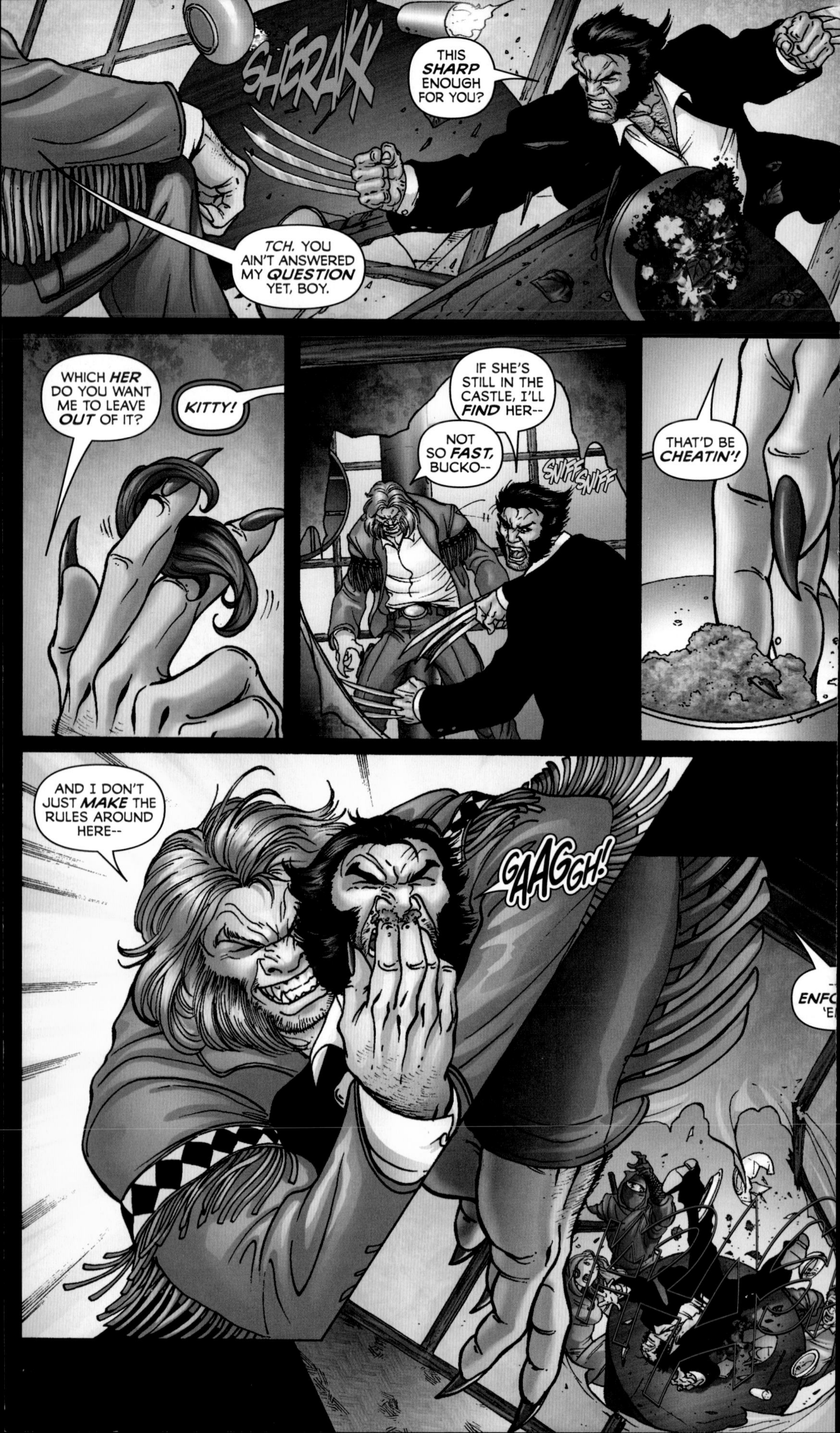
SHERAKK
THIS SHARP ENOUGH FOR YOU?
TCH. YOU AIN'T ANSWERED MY QUESTION YET, BOY.
WHICH HER DO YOU WANT ME TO LEAVE OUT OF IT?
KITTY!
IF SHE'S STILL IN THE CASTLE, I'LL FIND HER--
NOT SO FAST, BUCKO--
SNIFF SNIFF
THAT'D BE CHEATIN'!
AND I DON'T JUST MAKE THE RULES AROUND HERE--
GAAGGH!

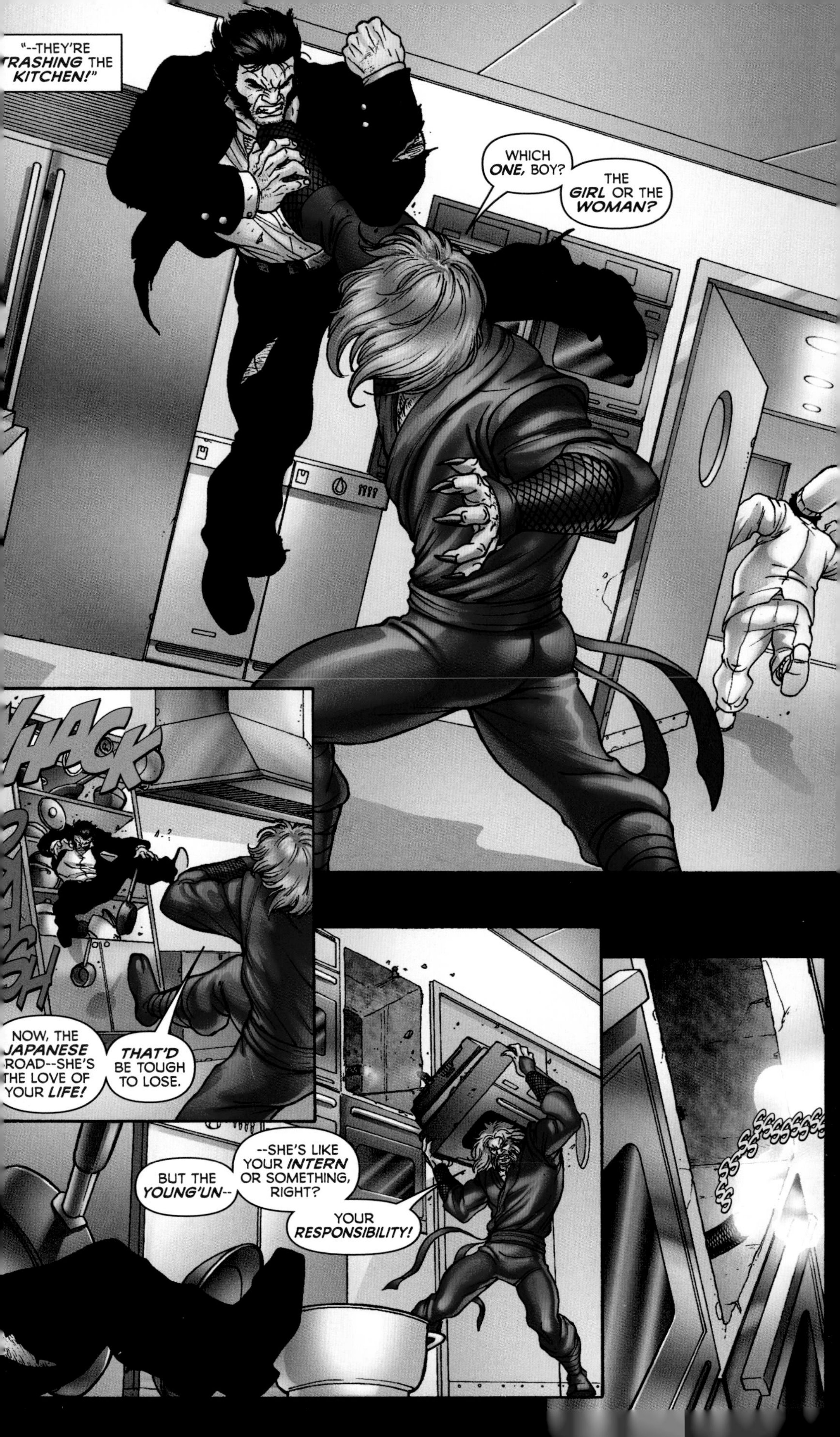
"--THEY'RE TRASHING THE KITCHEN!"
WHICH ONE, BOY?
THE GIRL OR THE WOMAN?
HACK
NOW, THE JAPANESE BROAD--SHE'S THE LOVE OF YOUR LIFE!
THAT'D BE TOUGH TO LOSE.
BUT THE YOUNG'UN--
--SHE'S LIKE YOUR INTERN OR SOMETHING, RIGHT?
YOUR RESPONSIBILITY!

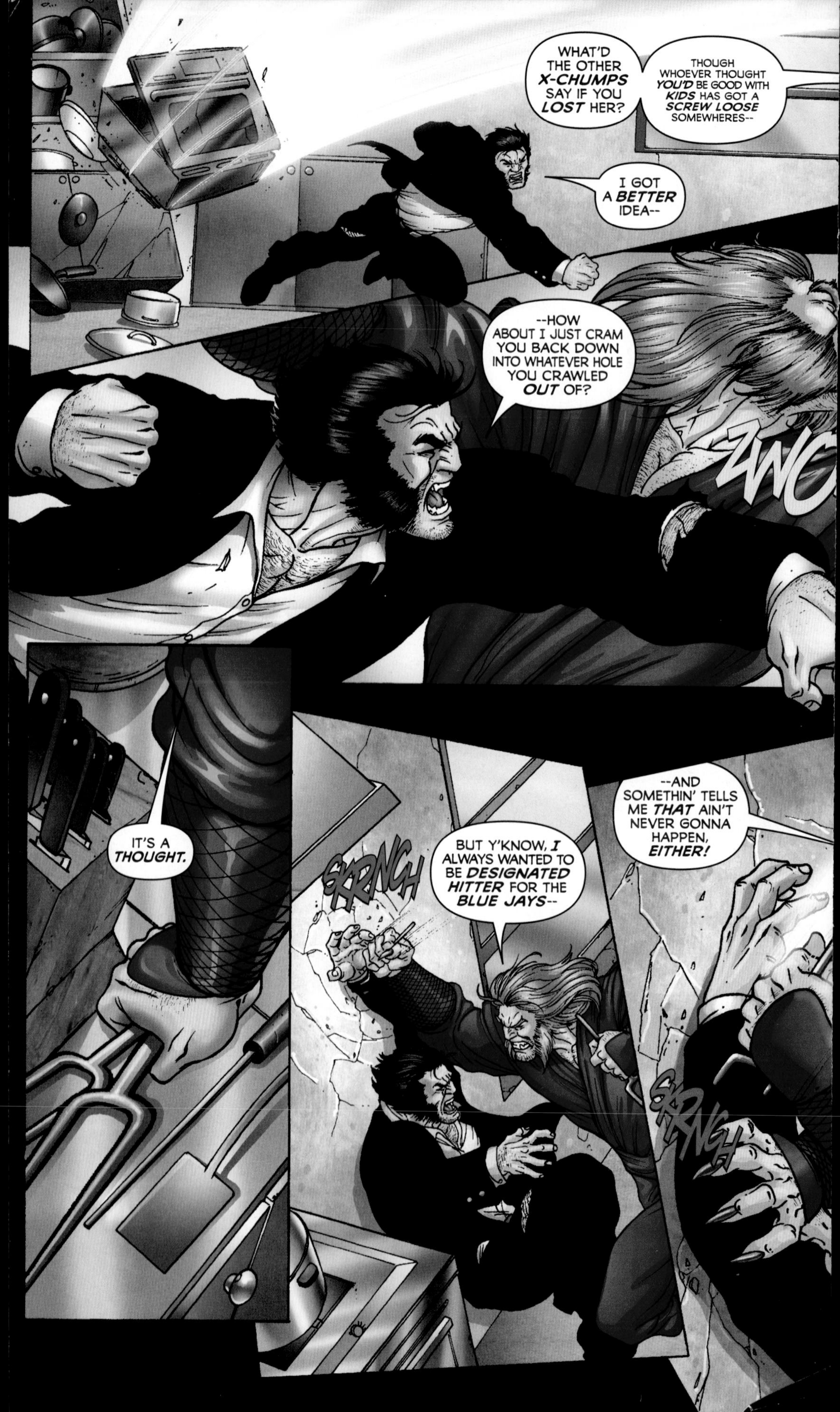

WHAT'D THE OTHER X-CHUMPS SAY IF YOU LOST HER?
THOUGH WHOEVER THOUGHT YOU'D BE GOOD WITH KIDS HAS GOT A SCREW LOOSE SOMEWHERES--
I GOT A BETTER IDEA--
--HOW ABOUT I JUST CRAM YOU BACK DOWN INTO WHATEVER HOLE YOU CRAWLED OUT OF?
IT'S A THOUGHT.
SKRNCH
BUT Y'KNOW, I ALWAYS WANTED TO BE DESIGNATED HITTER FOR THE BLUE JAYS--
--AND SOMETHIN' TELLS ME THAT AIN'T NEVER GONNA HAPPEN, EITHER!
SKRNCH

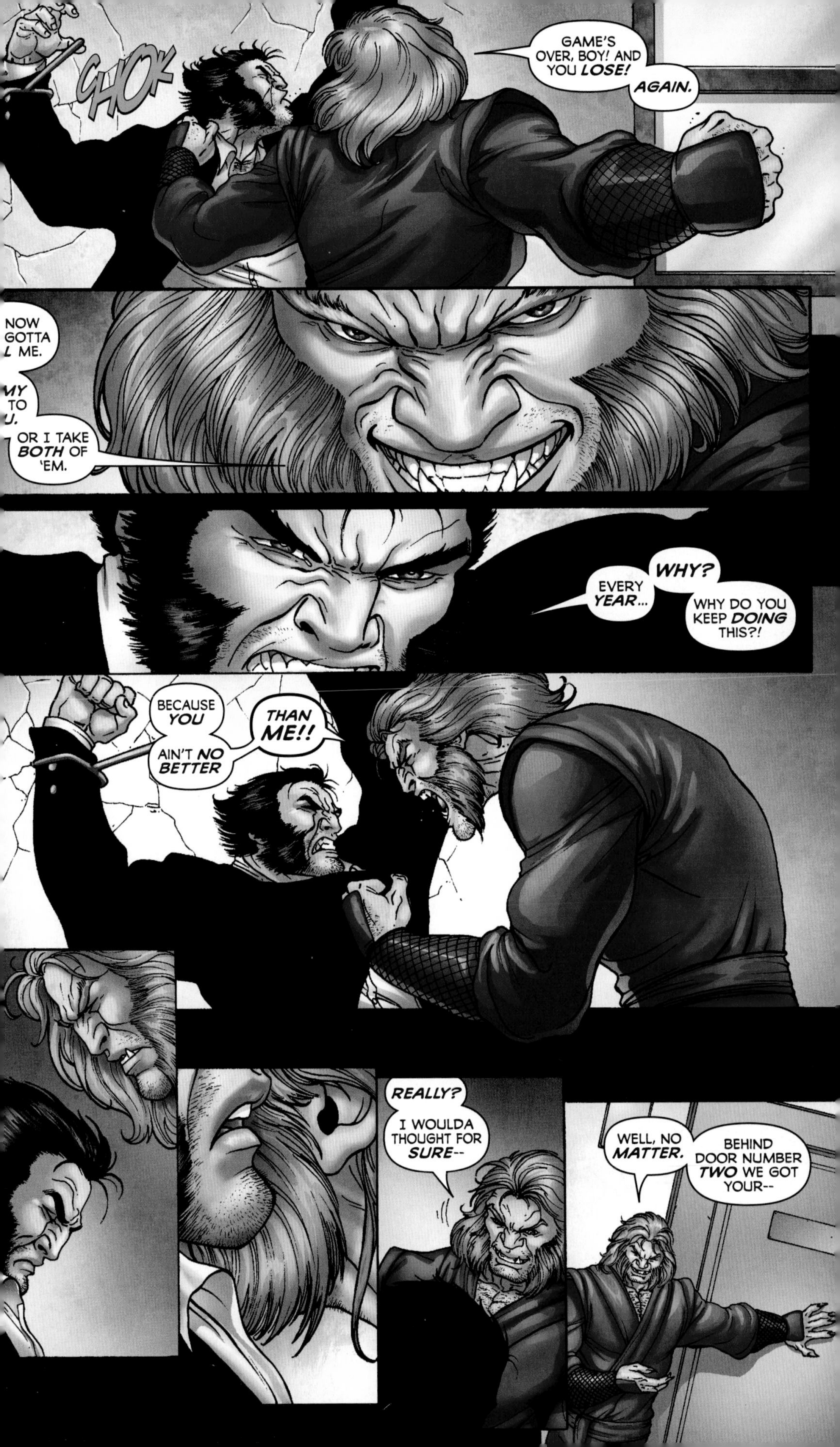

CHOK
GAME'S OVER, BOY! AND YOU LOSE!
AGAIN.
NOW GOTTA ME.
TO
OR I TAKE BOTH OF 'EM.
EVERY YEAR...
WHY?
WHY DO YOU KEEP DOING THIS?!
BECAUSE YOU
AIN'T NO BETTER
THAN ME!!
REALLY?
I WOULDA THOUGHT FOR SURE--
WELL, NO MATTER.
BEHIND DOOR NUMBER TWO WE GOT YOUR--

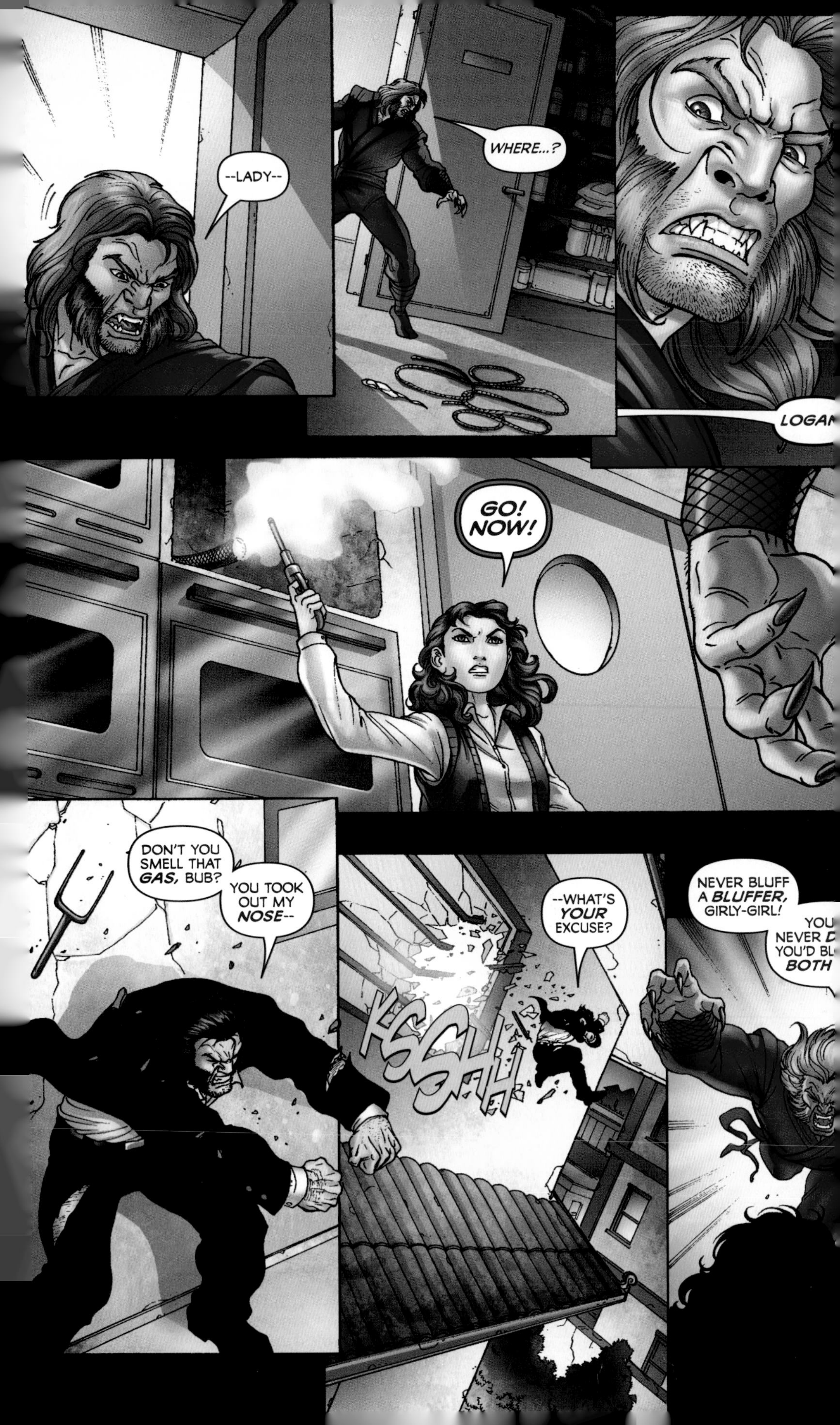
--LADY--
WHERE...?
LOGAN
GO! NOW!
DON'T YOU SMELL THAT GAS, BUB?
YOU TOOK OUT MY NOSE--
--WHAT'S YOUR EXCUSE?
KSSHH
NEVER BLUFF A BLUFFER, GIRLY-GIRL!

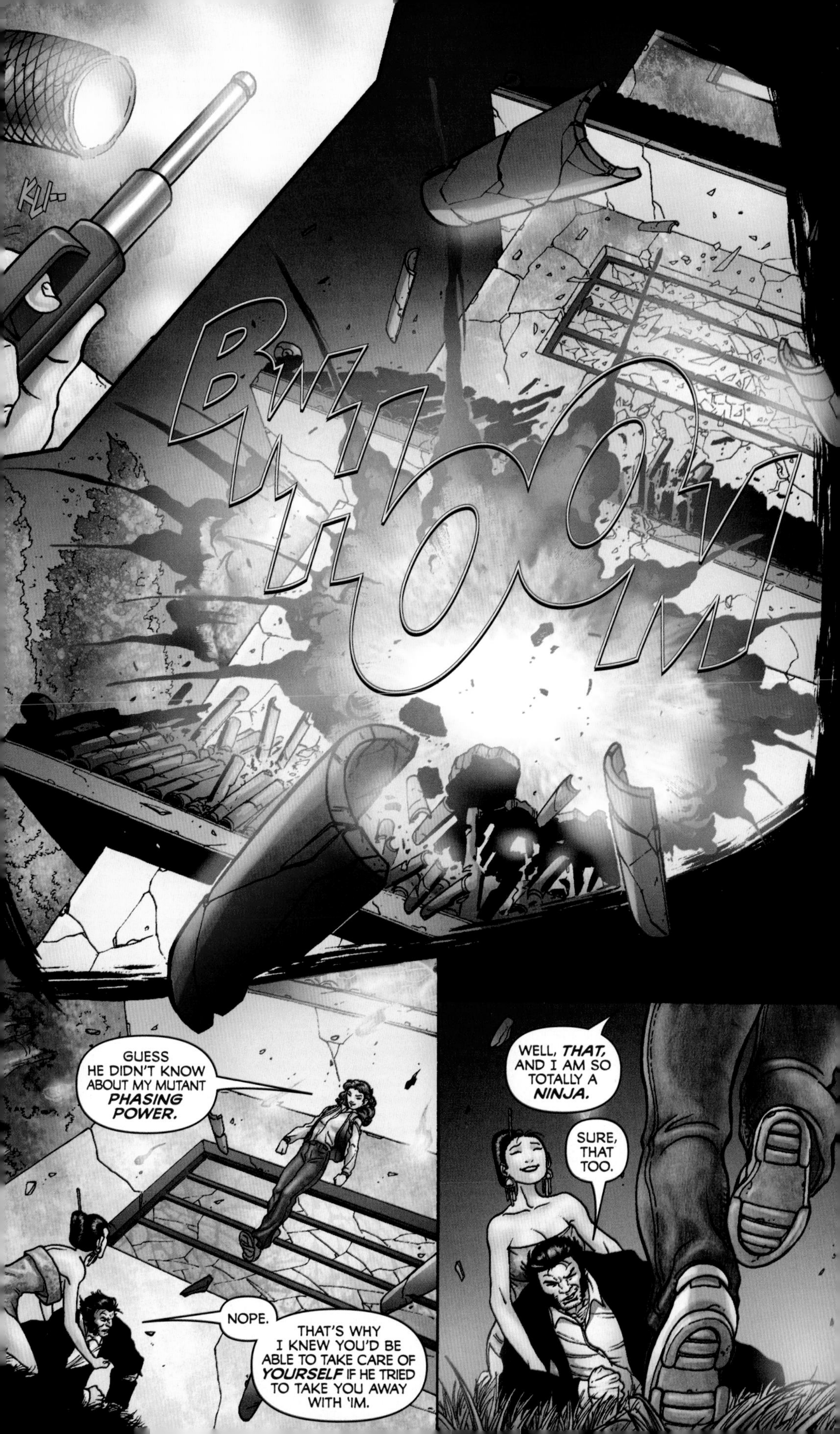
KLI-
BWOOM
GUESS HE DIDN'T KNOW ABOUT MY MUTANT PHASING POWER.
NOPE.
THAT'S WHY I KNEW YOU'D BE ABLE TO TAKE CARE OF YOURSELF IF HE TRIED TO TAKE YOU AWAY WITH 'IM.
WELL, THAT, AND I AM SO TOTALLY A NINJA.
SURE, THAT TOO.

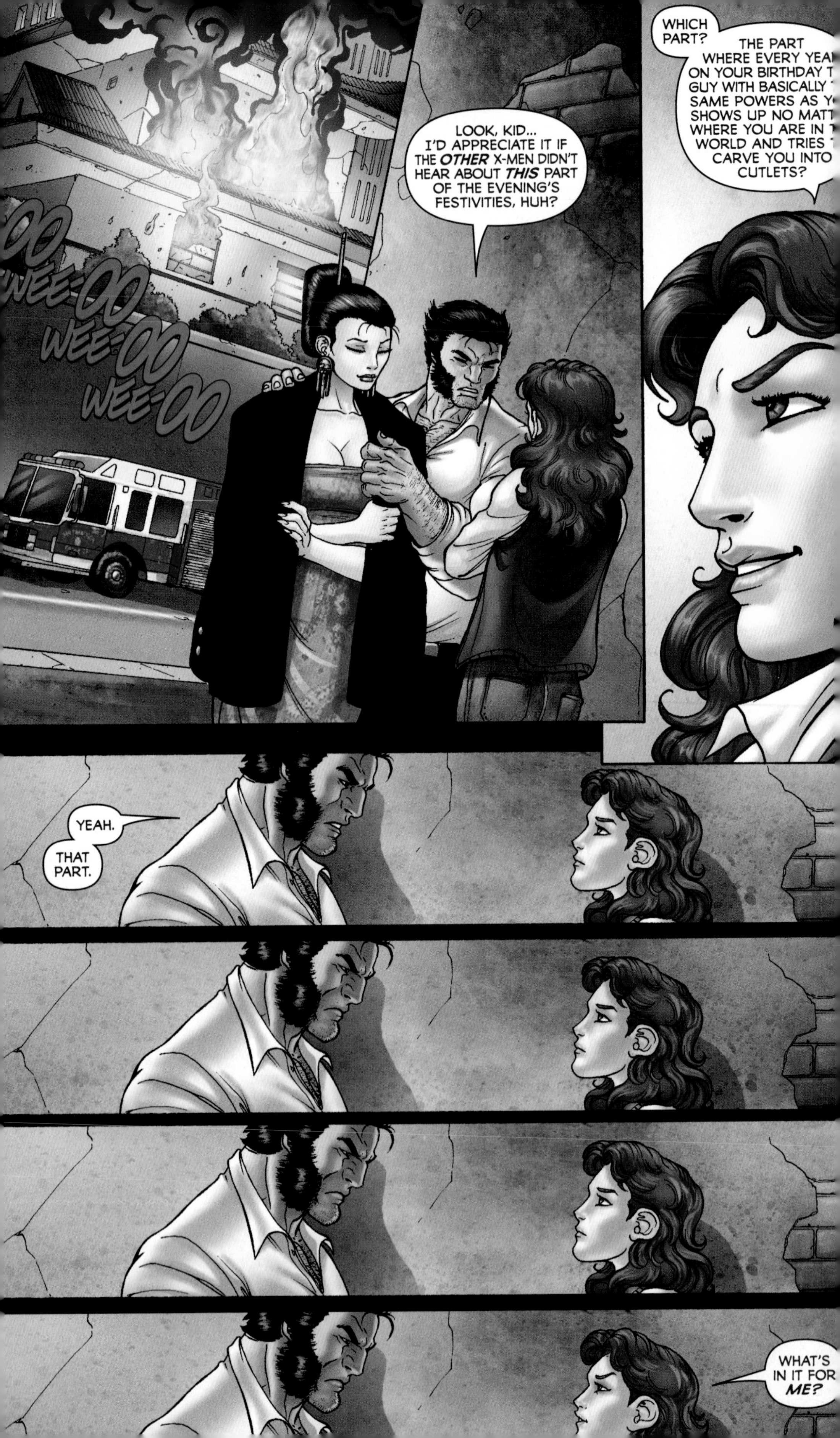
OO
WEE-OO
WEE-OO
WEE-OO
LOOK, KID... I'D APPRECIATE IT IF THE ***OTHER*** X-MEN DIDN'T HEAR ABOUT ***THIS*** PART OF THE EVENING'S FESTIVITIES, HUH?
WHICH PART?
THE PART WHERE EVERY YEA ON YOUR BIRTHDAY T GUY WITH BASICALLY SAME POWERS AS Y SHOWS UP NO MATT WHERE YOU ARE IN WORLD AND TRIES CARVE YOU INTO CUTLETS?
YEAH.
THAT PART.
WHAT'S IN IT FOR ***ME?***

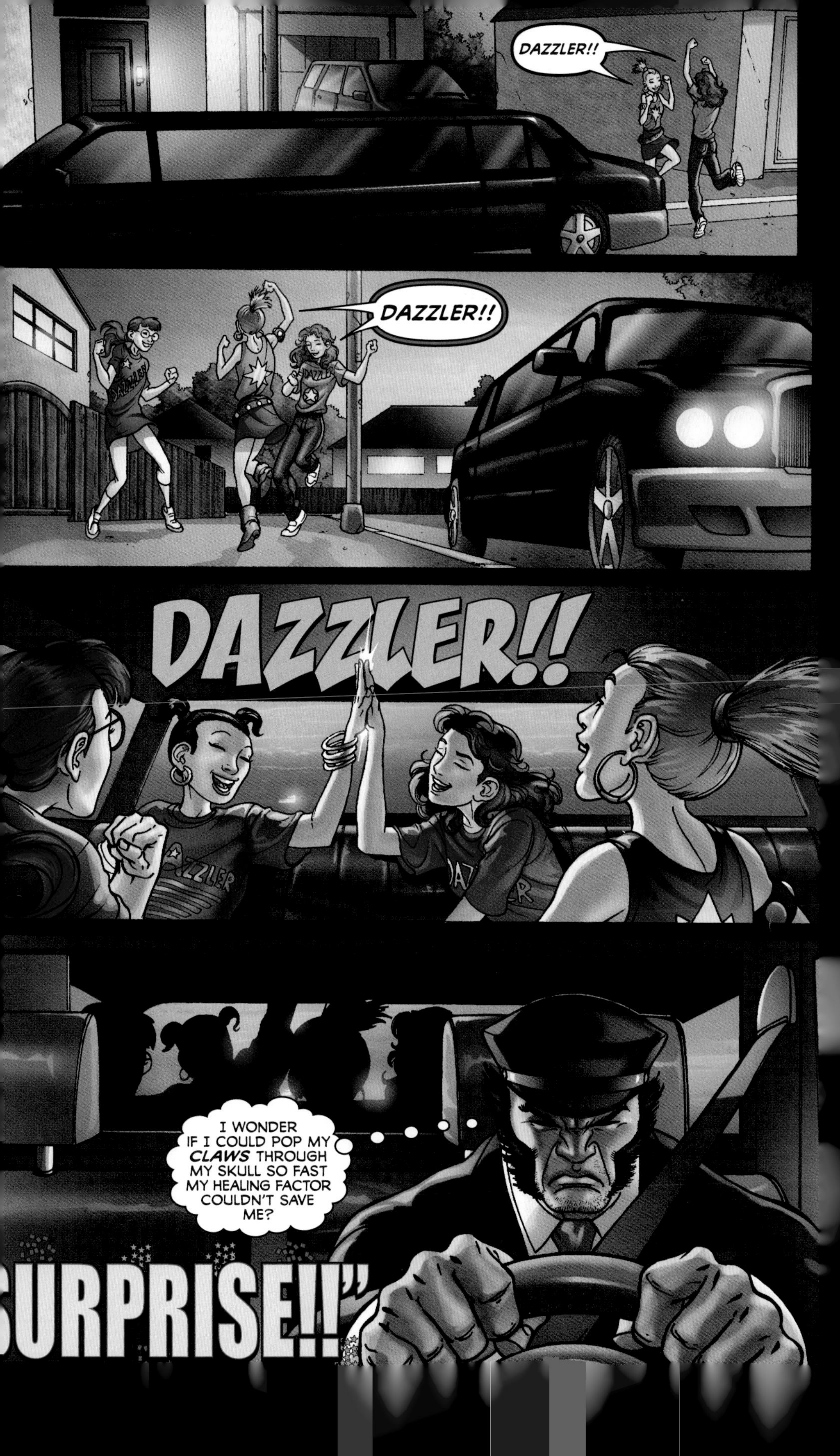
DAZZLER!!
DAZZLER!!
DAZZLER!!
I WONDER IF I COULD POP MY *CLAWS* THROUGH MY SKULL SO FAST MY HEALING FACTOR COULDN'T SAVE ME?
SURPRISE!!"

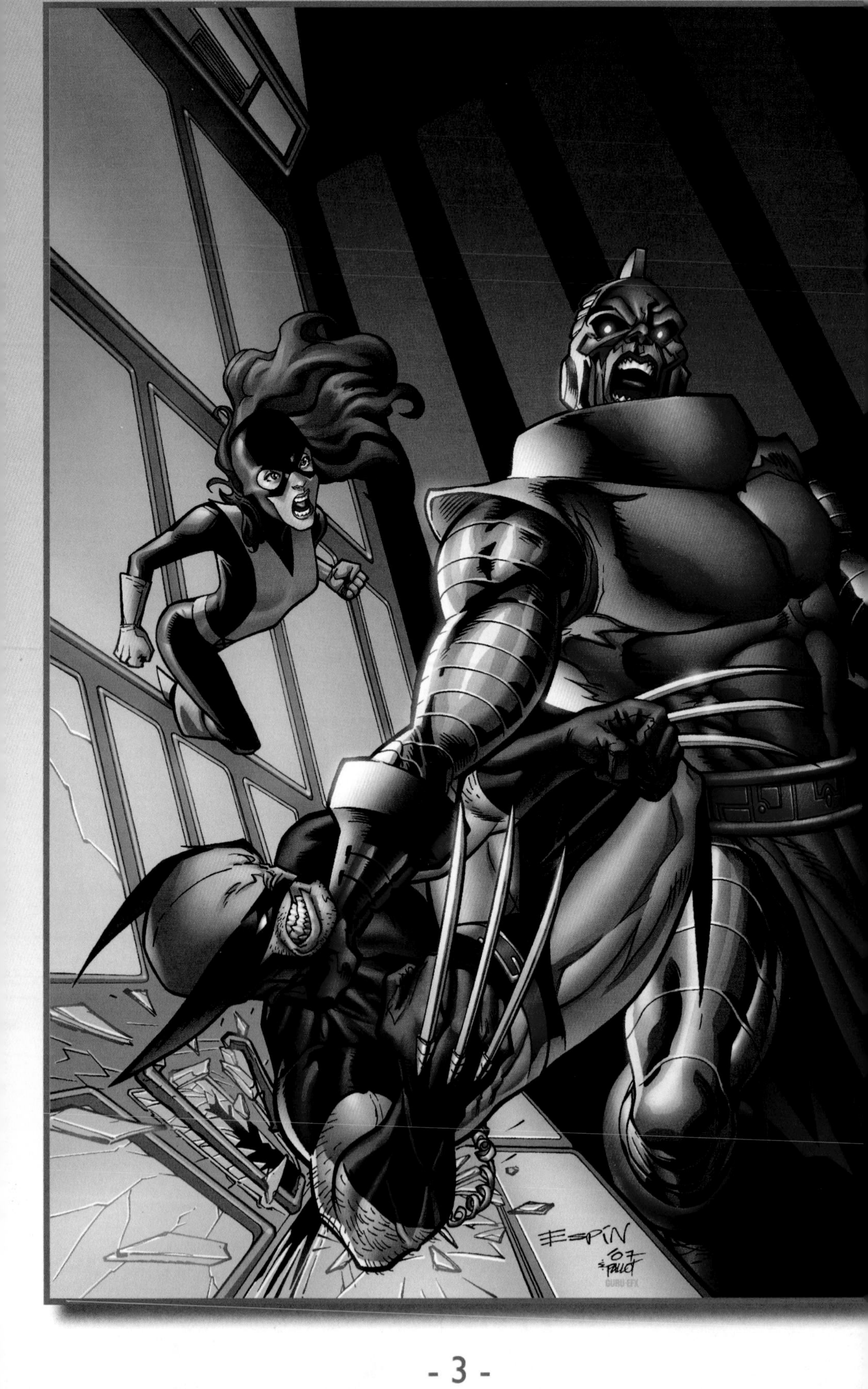

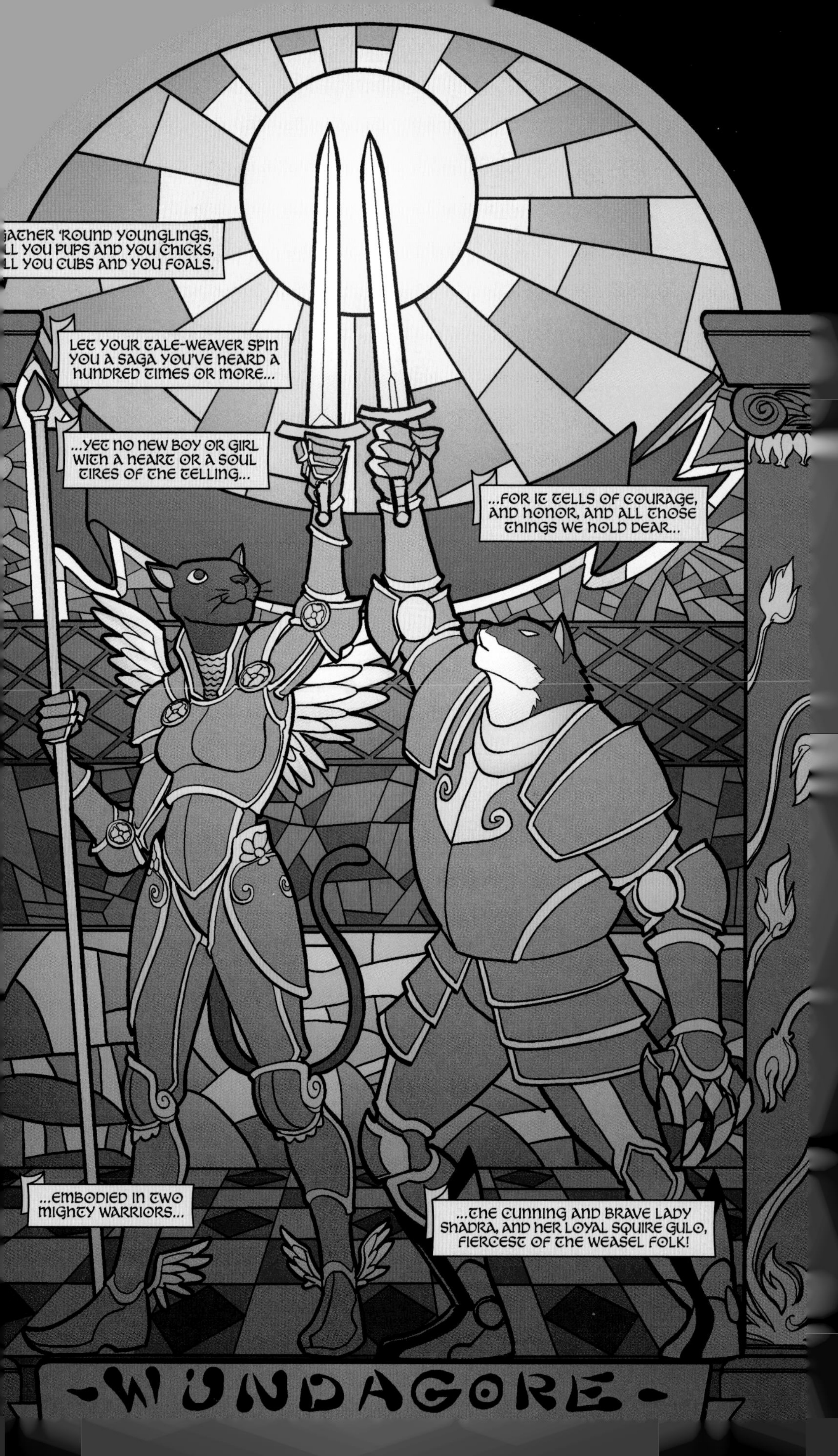
GATHER 'ROUND YOUNGLINGS,
LL YOU PUPS AND YOU CHICKS,
LL YOU CUBS AND YOU FOALS.
LET YOUR TALE-WEAVER SPIN YOU A SAGA YOU'VE HEARD A HUNDRED TIMES OR MORE...
...YET NO NEW BOY OR GIRL WITH A HEART OR A SOUL TIRES OF THE TELLING...
...FOR IT TELLS OF COURAGE, AND HONOR, AND ALL THOSE THINGS WE HOLD DEAR...
...EMBODIED IN TWO MIGHTY WARRIORS...
...THE CUNNING AND BRAVE LADY SHADRA, AND HER LOYAL SQUIRE GULO, FIERCEST OF THE WEASEL FOLK!
-WUNDAGORE-

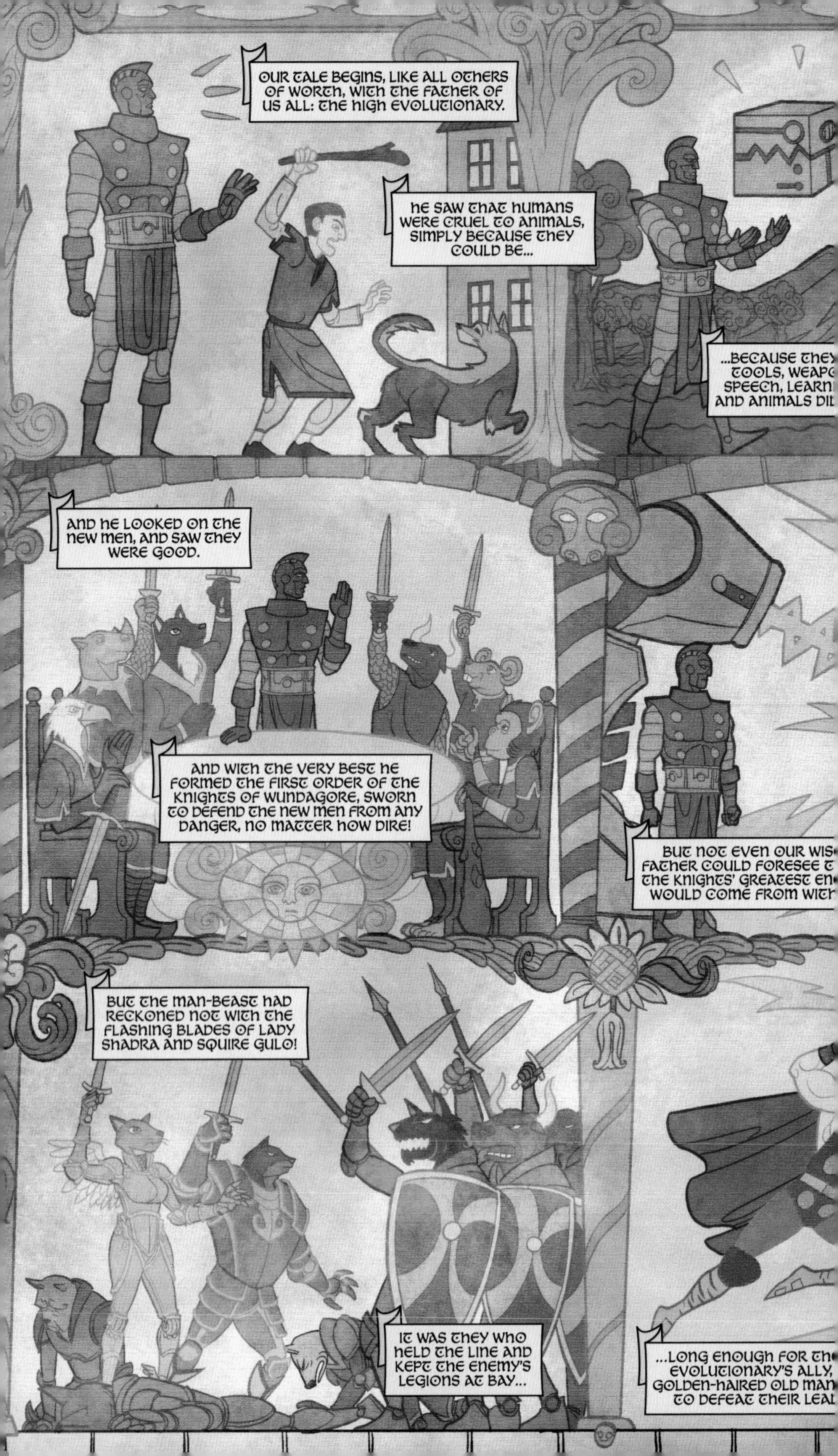
OUR TALE BEGINS, LIKE ALL OTHERS OF WORTH, WITH THE FATHER OF US ALL: THE HIGH EVOLUTIONARY.
HE SAW THAT HUMANS WERE CRUEL TO ANIMALS, SIMPLY BECAUSE THEY COULD BE...
...BECAUSE THEY TOOLS, WEAPO SPEECH, LEARN AND ANIMALS DI
AND HE LOOKED ON THE NEW MEN, AND SAW THEY WERE GOOD.
AND WITH THE VERY BEST HE FORMED THE FIRST ORDER OF THE KNIGHTS OF WUNDAGORE, SWORN TO DEFEND THE NEW MEN FROM ANY DANGER, NO MATTER HOW DIRE!
BUT NOT EVEN OUR WIS FATHER COULD FORESEE T THE KNIGHTS' GREATEST EN WOULD COME FROM WITH
BUT THE MAN-BEAST HAD RECKONED NOT WITH THE FLASHING BLADES OF LADY SHADRA AND SQUIRE GULO!
IT WAS THEY WHO HELD THE LINE AND KEPT THE ENEMY'S LEGIONS AT BAY...
...LONG ENOUGH FOR TH EVOLUTIONARY'S ALLY, GOLDEN-HAIRED OLD MAN TO DEFEAT THEIR LEA

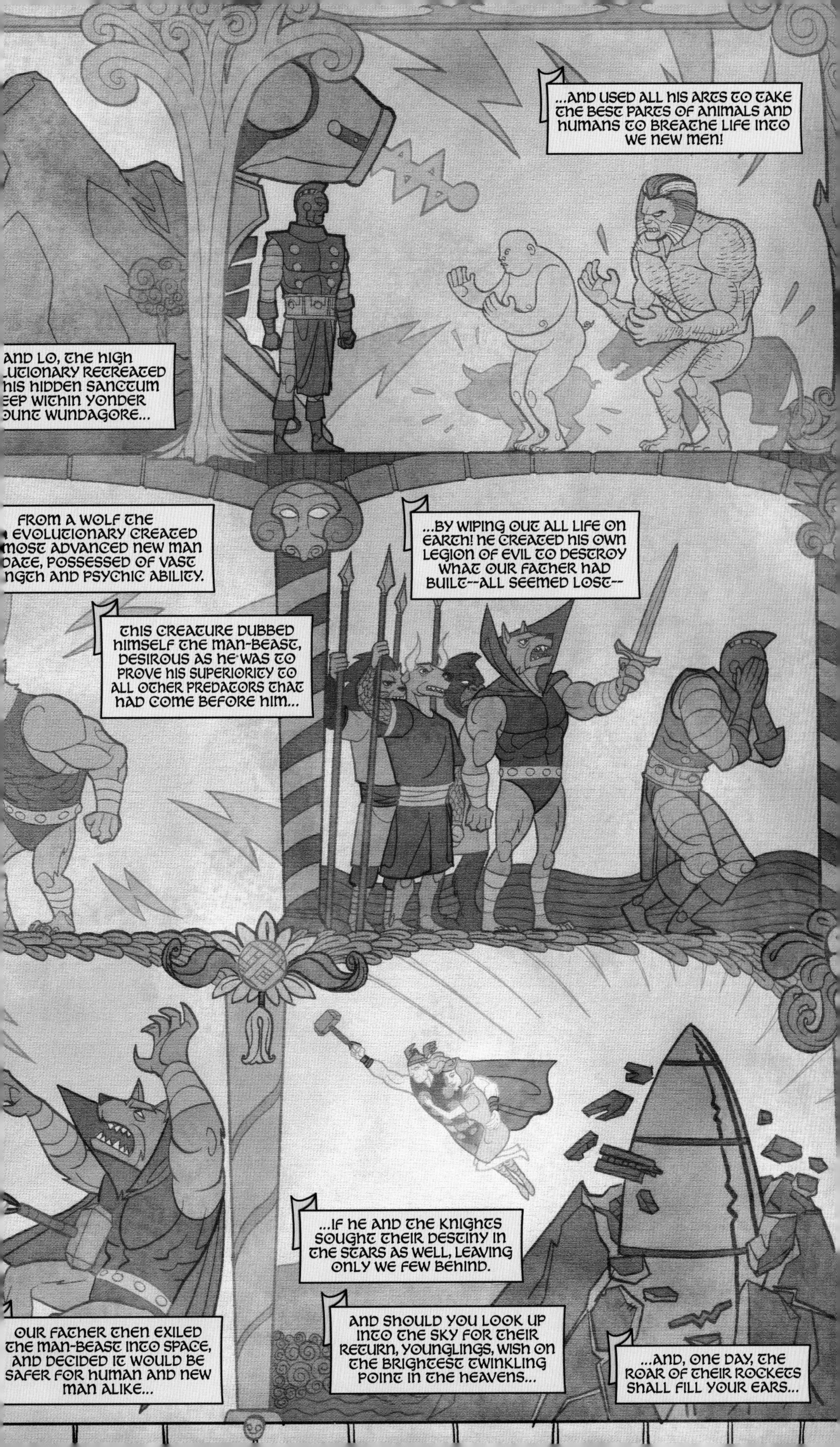

AND LO, THE HIGH
LUTIONARY RETREATED
HIS HIDDEN SANCTUM
EEP WITHIN YONDER
OUNT WUNDAGORE...
...AND USED ALL HIS ARTS TO TAKE THE BEST PARTS OF ANIMALS AND HUMANS TO BREATHE LIFE INTO WE NEW MEN!
FROM A WOLF THE
EVOLUTIONARY CREATED
MOST ADVANCED NEW MAN
DATE, POSSESSED OF VAST
NGTH AND PSYCHIC ABILITY.
THIS CREATURE DUBBED HIMSELF THE MAN-BEAST, DESIROUS AS HE WAS TO PROVE HIS SUPERIORITY TO ALL OTHER PREDATORS THAT HAD COME BEFORE HIM...
...BY WIPING OUT ALL LIFE ON EARTH! HE CREATED HIS OWN LEGION OF EVIL TO DESTROY WHAT OUR FATHER HAD BUILT--ALL SEEMED LOST--
OUR FATHER THEN EXILED THE MAN-BEAST INTO SPACE, AND DECIDED IT WOULD BE SAFER FOR HUMAN AND NEW MAN ALIKE...
...IF HE AND THE KNIGHTS SOUGHT THEIR DESTINY IN THE STARS AS WELL, LEAVING ONLY WE FEW BEHIND.
AND SHOULD YOU LOOK UP INTO THE SKY FOR THEIR RETURN, YOUNGLINGS, WISH ON THE BRIGHTEST TWINKLING POINT IN THE HEAVENS...
...AND, ONE DAY, THE ROAR OF THEIR ROCKETS SHALL FILL YOUR EARS...

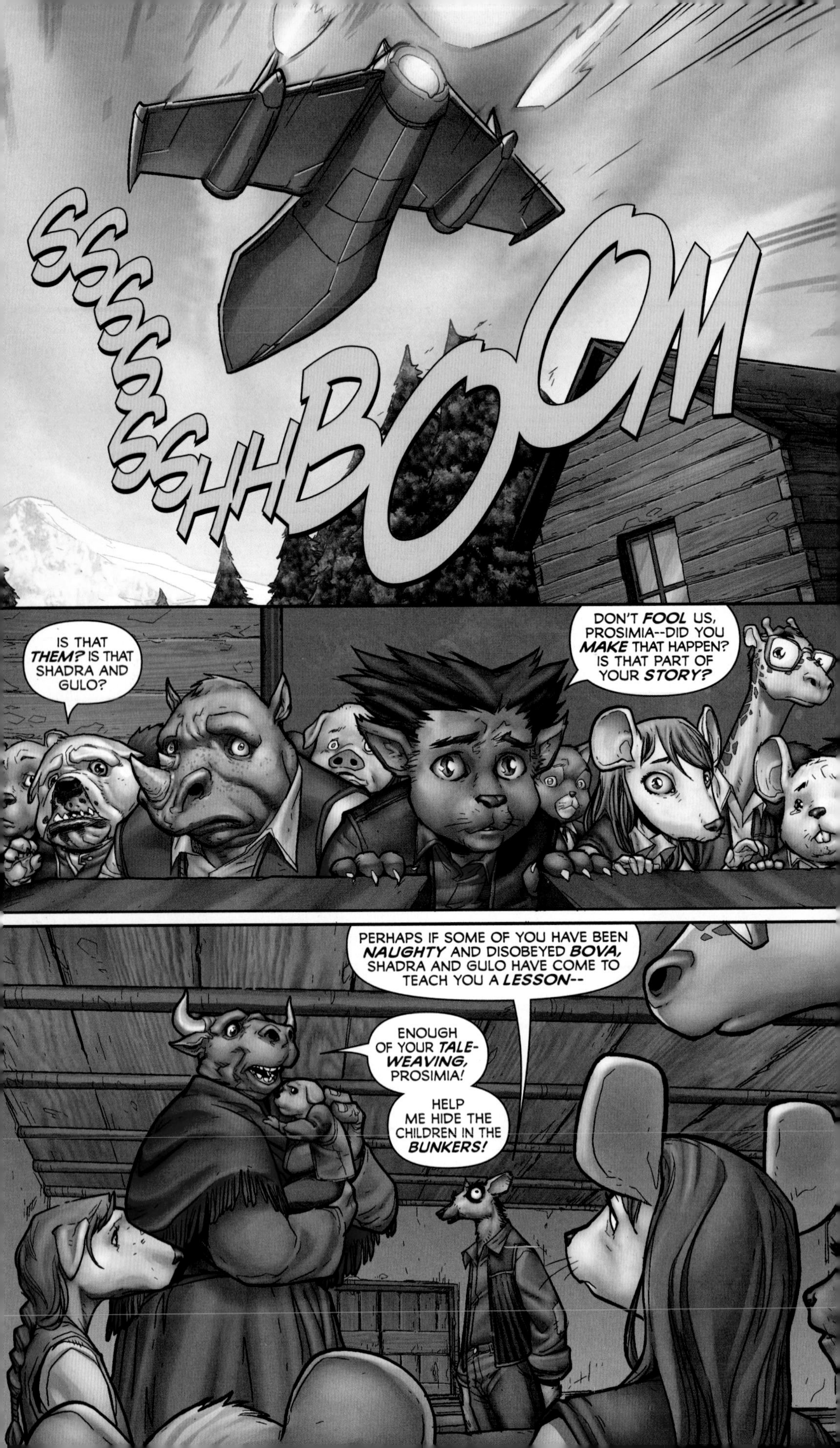
SSSSSSSHHBOOM
IS THAT *THEM?* IS THAT SHADRA AND GULO?
DON'T *FOOL* US, PROSIMIA--DID YOU *MAKE* THAT HAPPEN? IS THAT PART OF YOUR *STORY?*
PERHAPS IF SOME OF YOU HAVE BEEN *NAUGHTY* AND DISOBEYED *BOVA,* SHADRA AND GULO HAVE COME TO TEACH YOU A *LESSON--*
ENOUGH OF YOUR *TALE-WEAVING,* PROSIMIA!
HELP ME HIDE THE CHILDREN IN THE *BUNKERS!*

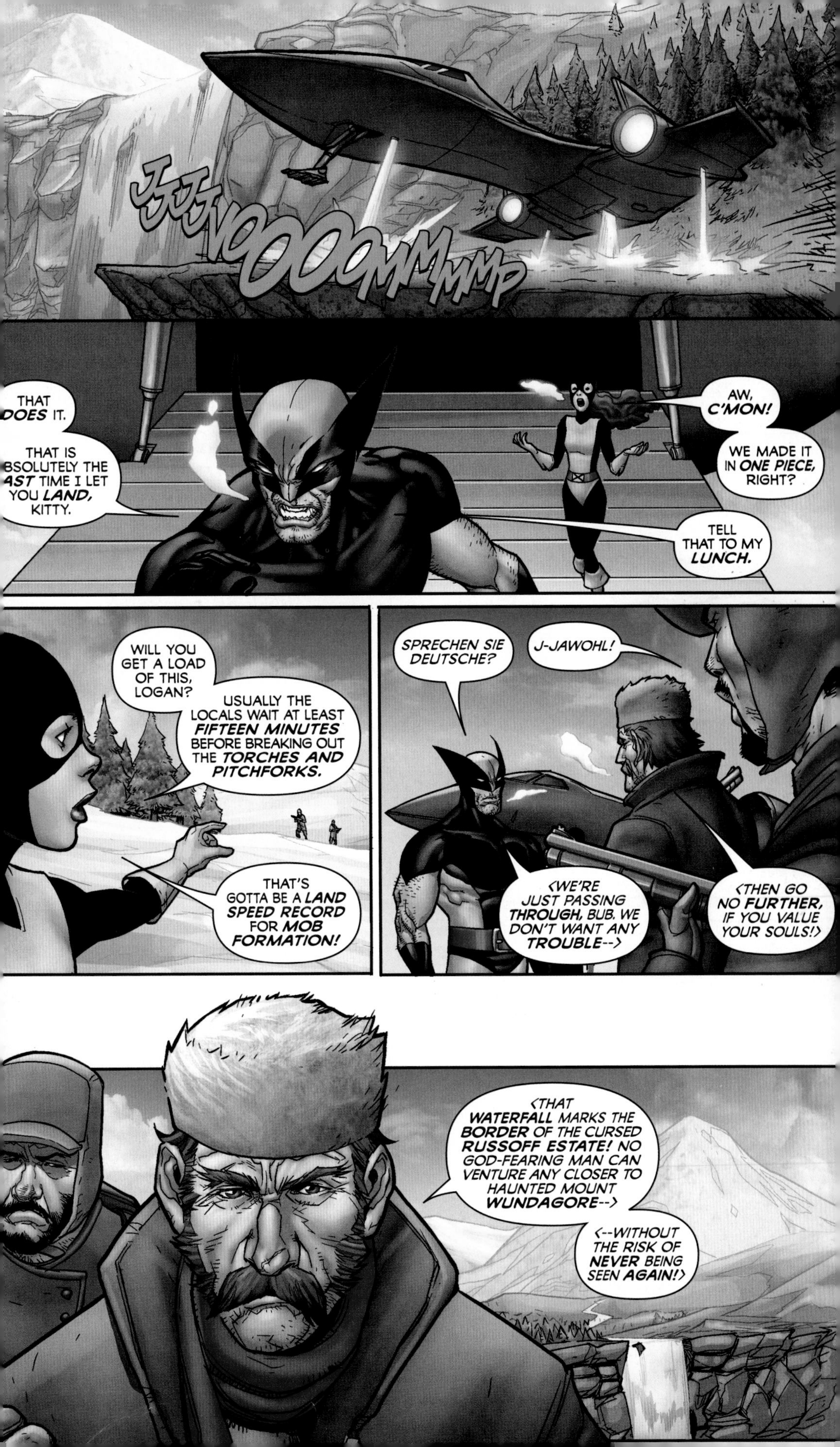

JJJVOOOOMMMMP
THAT DOES IT.
THAT IS BSOLUTELY THE AST TIME I LET YOU LAND, KITTY.
AW, C'MON!
WE MADE IT IN ONE PIECE, RIGHT?
TELL THAT TO MY LUNCH.
WILL YOU GET A LOAD OF THIS, LOGAN?
USUALLY THE LOCALS WAIT AT LEAST FIFTEEN MINUTES BEFORE BREAKING OUT THE TORCHES AND PITCHFORKS.
THAT'S GOTTA BE A LAND SPEED RECORD FOR MOB FORMATION!
SPRECHEN SIE DEUTSCHE?
J-JAWOHL!
<WE'RE JUST PASSING THROUGH, BUB. WE DON'T WANT ANY TROUBLE-->
<THEN GO NO FURTHER, IF YOU VALUE YOUR SOULS!>
<THAT WATERFALL MARKS THE BORDER OF THE CURSED RUSSOFF ESTATE! NO GOD-FEARING MAN CAN VENTURE ANY CLOSER TO HAUNTED MOUNT WUNDAGORE-->
<--WITHOUT THE RISK OF NEVER BEING SEEN AGAIN!>

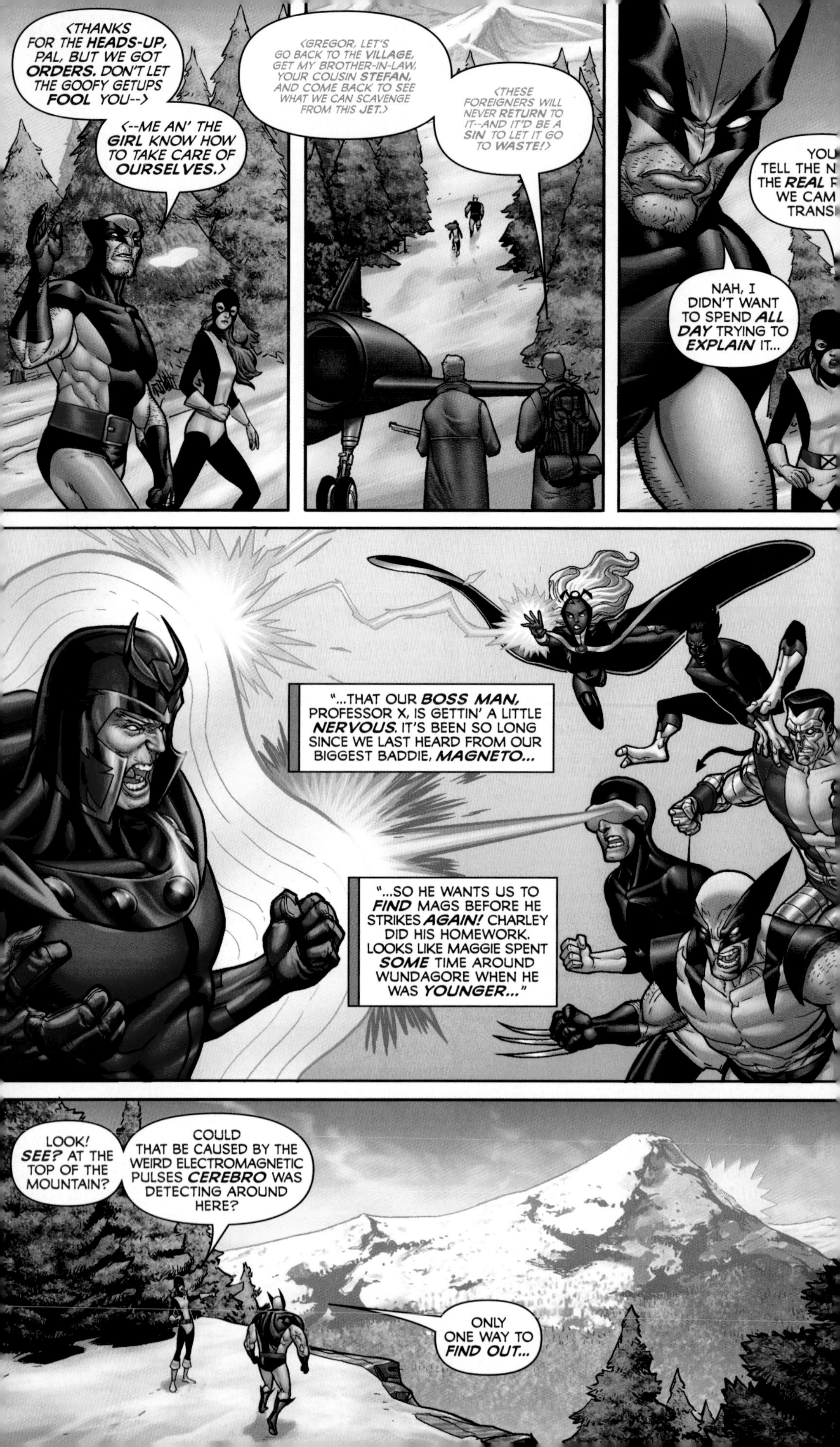

<THANKS FOR THE **HEADS-UP,** PAL, BUT WE GOT **ORDERS.** DON'T LET THE GOOFY GETUPS **FOOL** YOU-->
<--ME AN' THE **GIRL** KNOW HOW TO TAKE CARE OF **OURSELVES.**>
<GREGOR, LET'S GO BACK TO THE **VILLAGE,** GET MY BROTHER-IN-LAW, YOUR COUSIN **STEFAN,** AND COME BACK TO SEE WHAT WE CAN SCAVENGE FROM THIS **JET.**>
<THESE FOREIGNERS WILL NEVER **RETURN** TO IT--AND IT'D BE A **SIN** TO LET IT GO TO **WASTE!**>
YOU TELL THE THE **REAL** WE
NAH, I DIDN'T WANT TO SPEND **ALL DAY** TRYING TO **EXPLAIN** IT...
"...THAT OUR **BOSS MAN,** PROFESSOR X, IS GETTIN' A LITTLE **NERVOUS.** IT'S BEEN SO LONG SINCE WE LAST HEARD FROM OUR BIGGEST BADDIE, **MAGNETO...**
"...SO HE WANTS US TO **FIND** MAGS BEFORE HE STRIKES **AGAIN!** CHARLEY DID HIS HOMEWORK. LOOKS LIKE MAGGIE SPENT **SOME** TIME AROUND WUNDAGORE WHEN HE WAS **YOUNGER...**"
LOOK! **SEE?** AT THE TOP OF THE MOUNTAIN?
COULD THAT BE CAUSED BY THE WEIRD ELECTROMAGNETIC PULSES **CEREBRO** WAS DETECTING AROUND HERE?
ONLY ONE WAY TO **FIND OUT...**

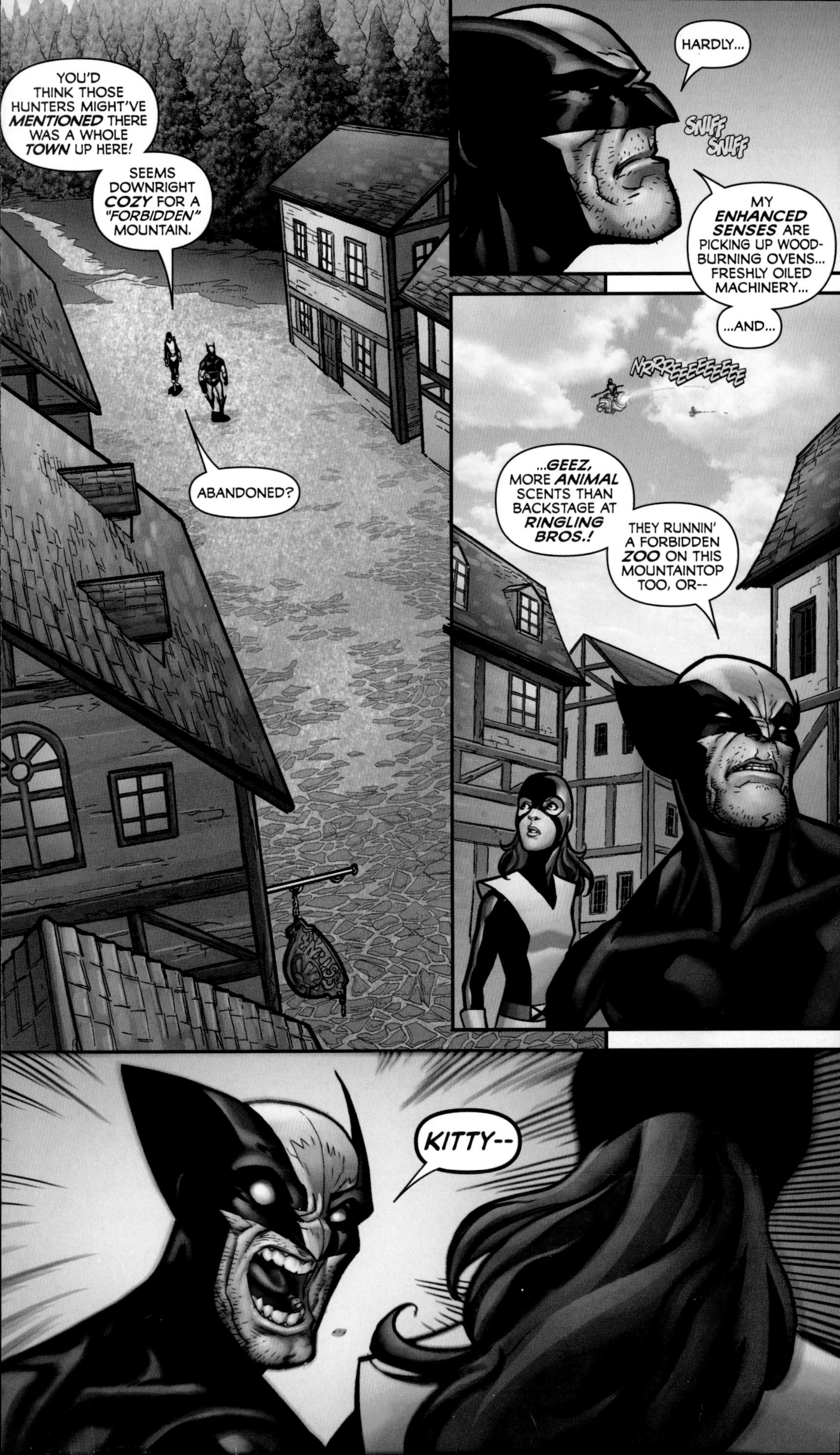

YOU'D THINK THOSE HUNTERS MIGHT'VE *MENTIONED* THERE WAS A WHOLE *TOWN* UP HERE!
SEEMS DOWNRIGHT *COZY* FOR A *"FORBIDDEN"* MOUNTAIN.
ABANDONED?
HARDLY...
SNIFF SNIFF
MY *ENHANCED SENSES* ARE PICKING UP WOOD-BURNING OVENS... FRESHLY OILED MACHINERY...
...AND...
NRRREEEEEEEEE
...*GEEZ,* MORE *ANIMAL* SCENTS THAN BACKSTAGE AT *RINGLING BROS.!*
THEY RUNNIN' A FORBIDDEN *ZOO* ON THIS MOUNTAINTOP TOO, OR--
KITTY--

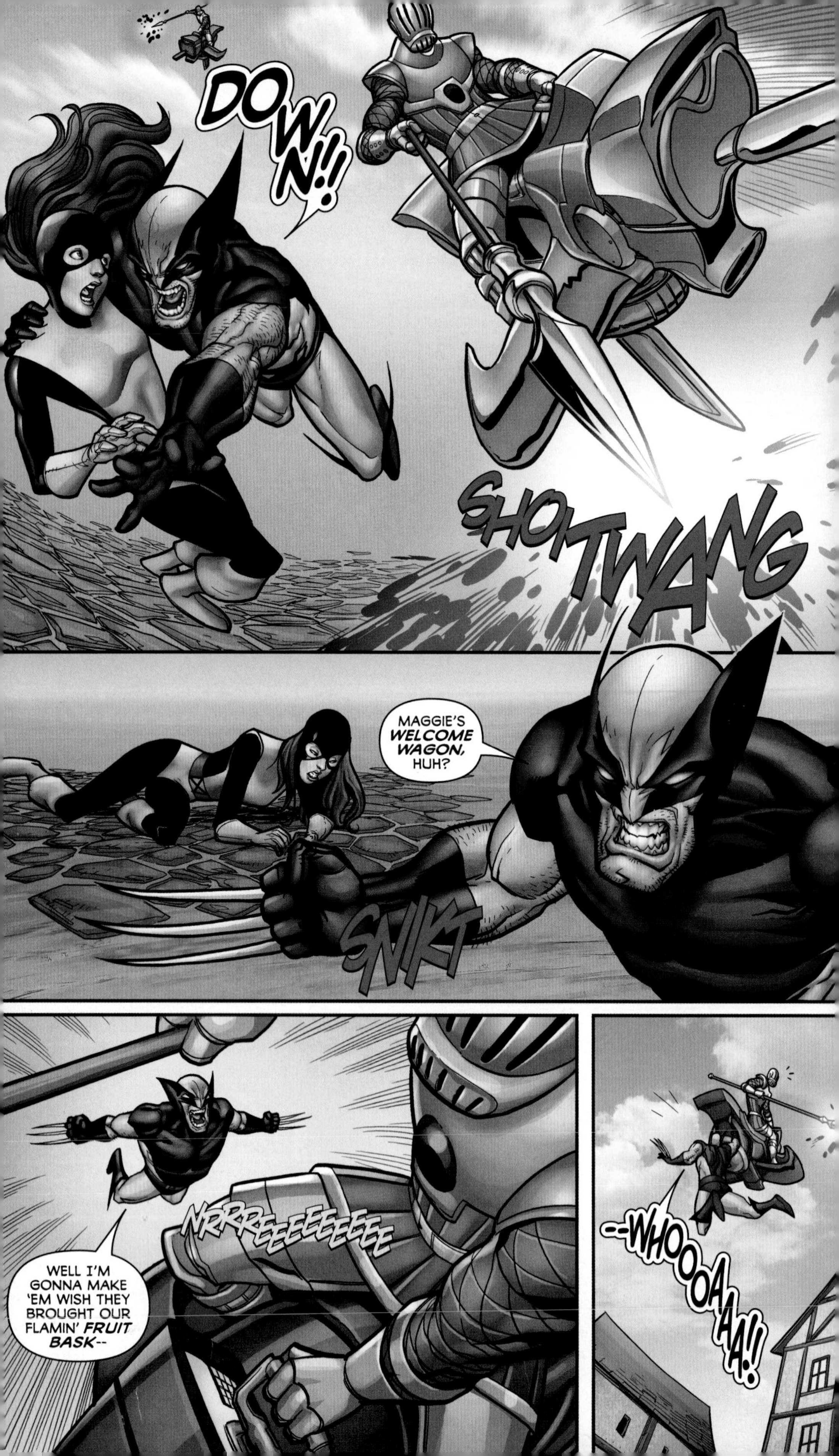
DOWN!!
SHOK
TWANG
MAGGIE'S *WELCOME WAGON,* HUH?
SNIKT
WELL I'M GONNA MAKE 'EM WISH THEY BROUGHT OUR FLAMIN' *FRUIT BASK--*
NRRREEEEEEEEE
--WHOOOAAA!!

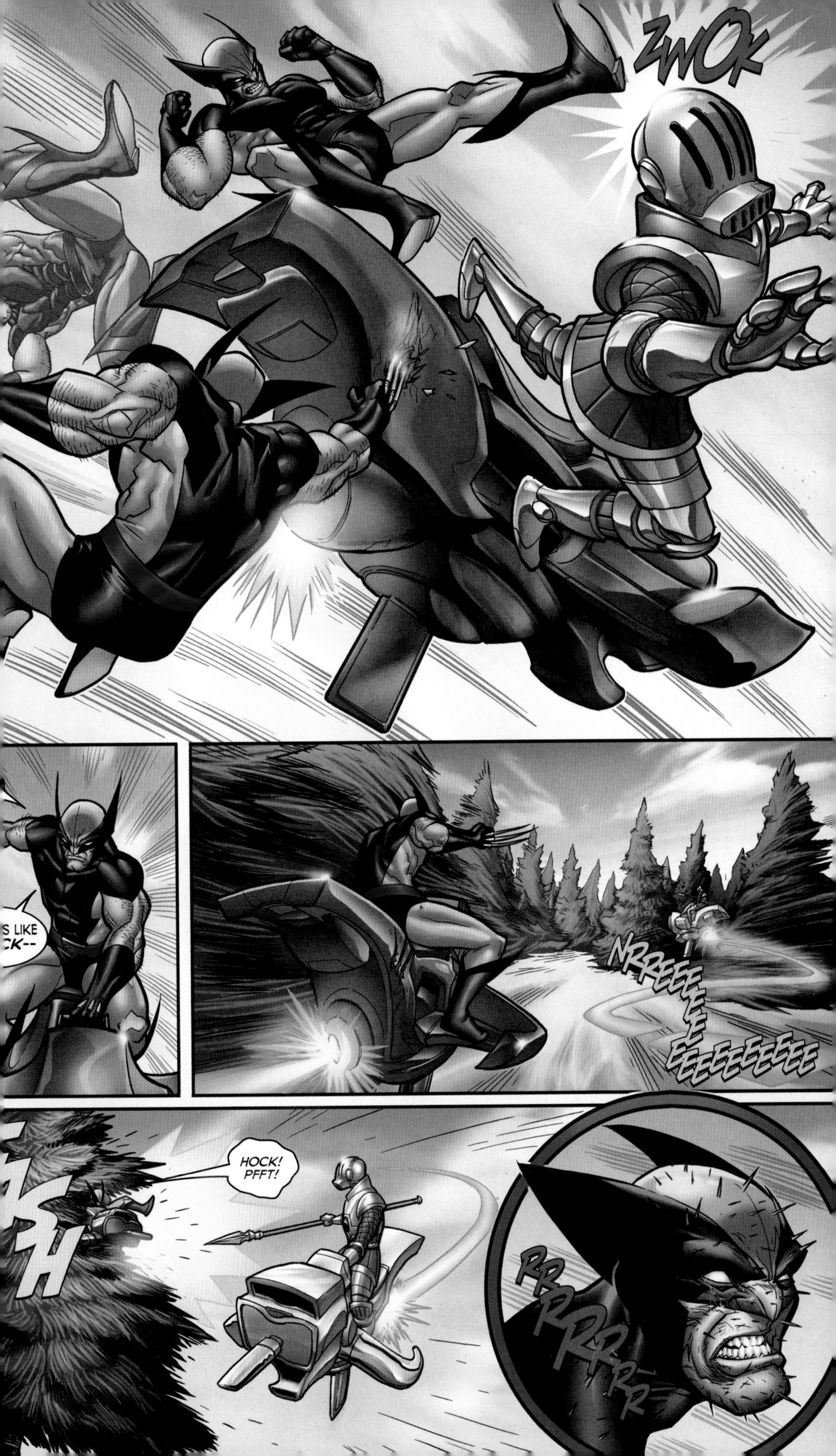
ZWOK
S LIKE
CK--
NRREEEEEEEEEEEEEE
HOCK! PFFT!
RRRRRRRR

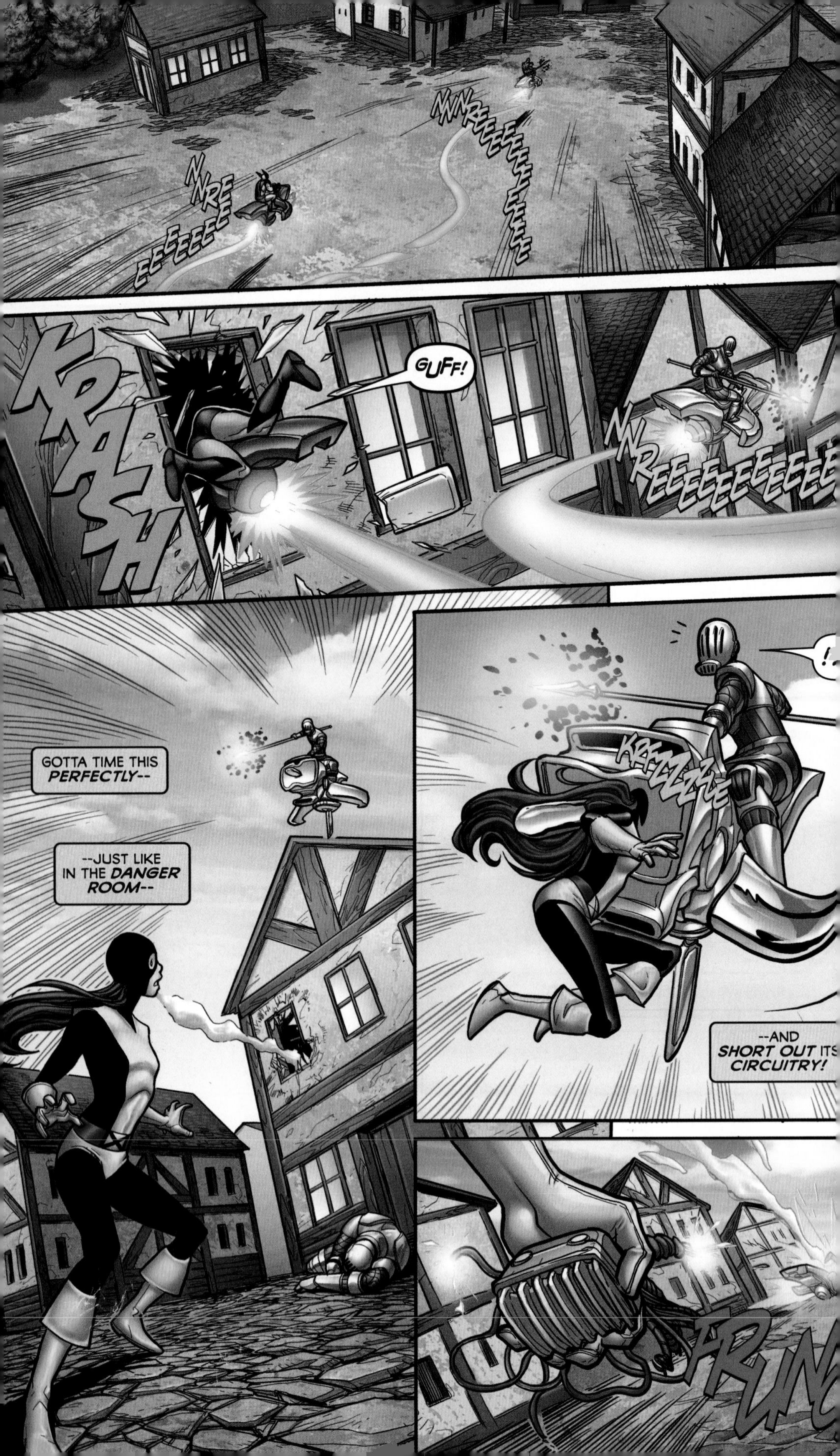

NNRE EEEEEEE
NNNREEEEEEEEEEEE
KRASH
GUFF!
NNREEEEEEEEEEEEE
GOTTA TIME THIS PERFECTLY--
--JUST LIKE IN THE DANGER ROOM--
!
--AND SHORT OUT ITS CIRCUITRY!

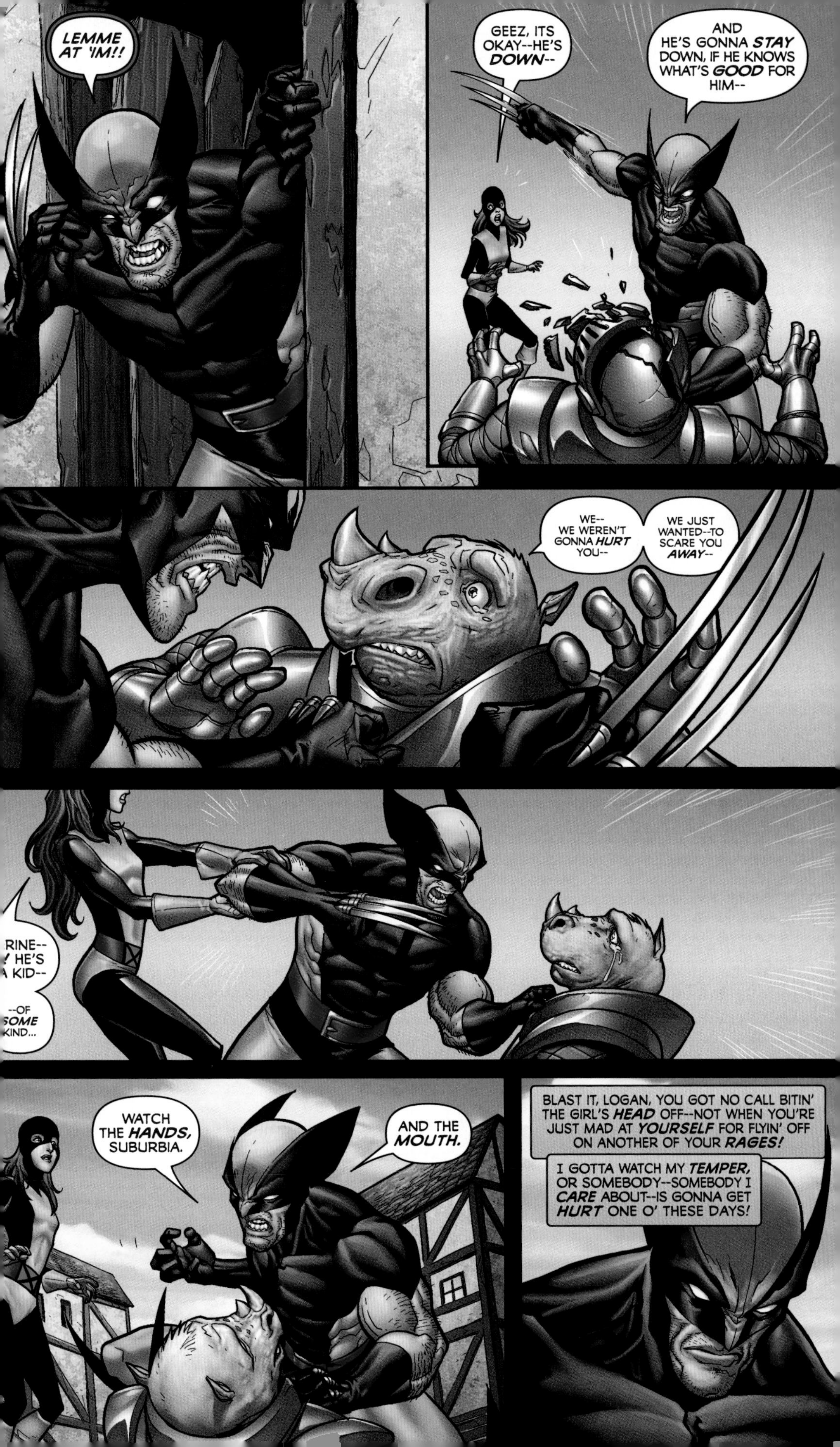
LEMME AT 'IM!!
GEEZ, ITS OKAY--HE'S DOWN--
AND HE'S GONNA STAY DOWN, IF HE KNOWS WHAT'S GOOD FOR HIM--
WE-- WE WEREN'T GONNA HURT YOU--
WE JUST WANTED--TO SCARE YOU AWAY--
RINE-- HE'S KID--
--OF SOME KIND...
WATCH THE HANDS, SUBURBIA.
AND THE MOUTH.
BLAST IT, LOGAN, YOU GOT NO CALL BITIN' THE GIRL'S HEAD OFF--NOT WHEN YOU'RE JUST MAD AT YOURSELF FOR FLYIN' OFF ON ANOTHER OF YOUR RAGES!
I GOTTA WATCH MY TEMPER, OR SOMEBODY--SOMEBODY I CARE ABOUT--IS GONNA GET HURT ONE O' THESE DAYS!

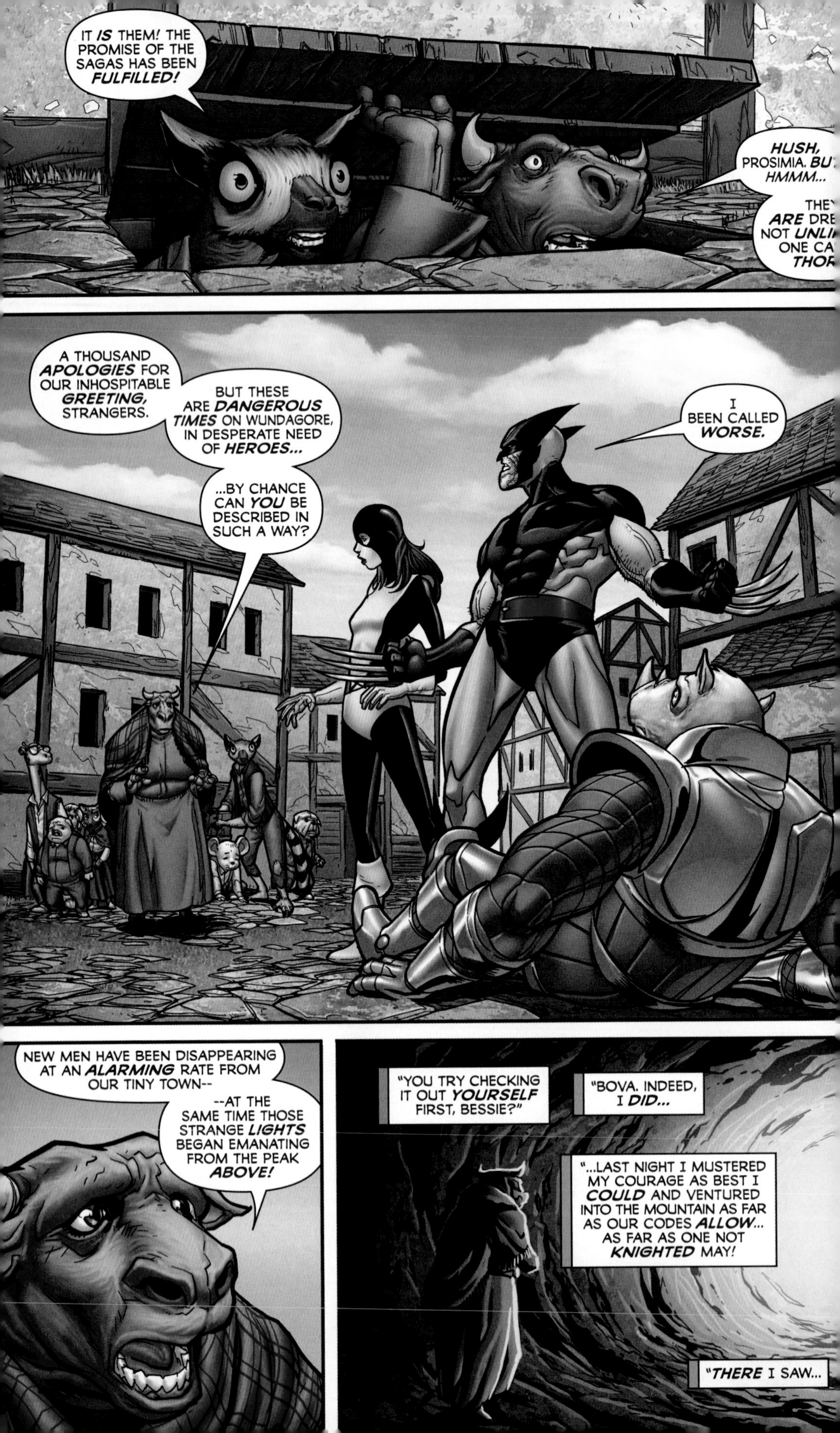
IT IS THEM! THE PROMISE OF THE SAGAS HAS BEEN FULFILLED!
HUSH, PROSIMIA. BU HMMM...
THE ARE DRE NOT UNLI ONE CA THOR
A THOUSAND APOLOGIES FOR OUR INHOSPITABLE GREETING, STRANGERS.
BUT THESE ARE DANGEROUS TIMES ON WUNDAGORE, IN DESPERATE NEED OF HEROES...
...BY CHANCE CAN YOU BE DESCRIBED IN SUCH A WAY?
I BEEN CALLED WORSE.
NEW MEN HAVE BEEN DISAPPEARING AT AN ALARMING RATE FROM OUR TINY TOWN--
--AT THE SAME TIME THOSE STRANGE LIGHTS BEGAN EMANATING FROM THE PEAK ABOVE!
"YOU TRY CHECKING IT OUT YOURSELF FIRST, BESSIE?"
"BOVA. INDEED, I DID...
"...LAST NIGHT I MUSTERED MY COURAGE AS BEST I COULD AND VENTURED INTO THE MOUNTAIN AS FAR AS OUR CODES ALLOW... AS FAR AS ONE NOT KNIGHTED MAY!
"THERE I SAW...

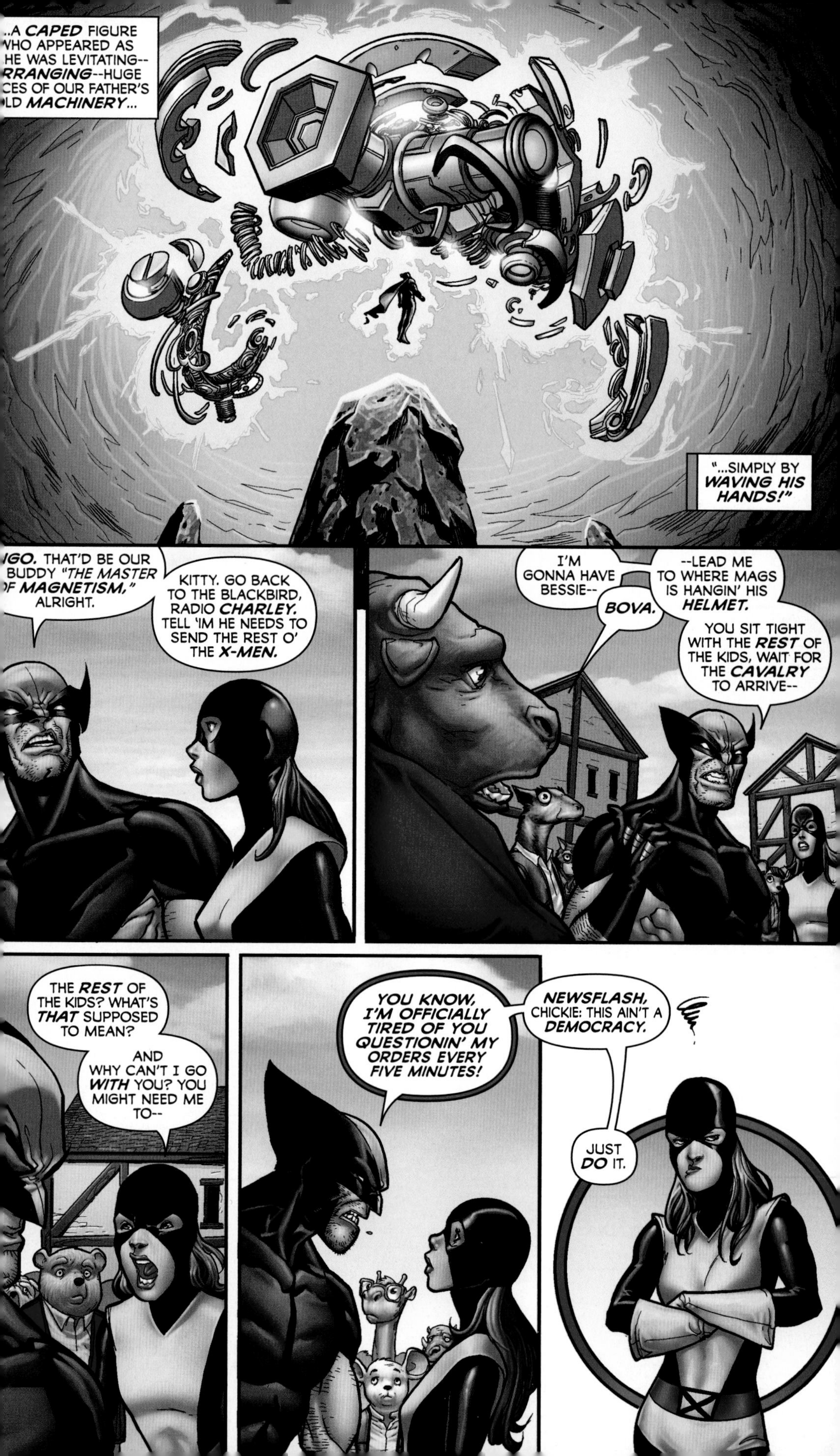

..A CAPED FIGURE WHO APPEARED AS HE WAS LEVITATING-- RRANGING--HUGE CES OF OUR FATHER'S LD MACHINERY...
"...SIMPLY BY WAVING HIS HANDS!"
IGO. THAT'D BE OUR BUDDY "THE MASTER F MAGNETISM," ALRIGHT.
KITTY. GO BACK TO THE BLACKBIRD, RADIO CHARLEY. TELL 'IM HE NEEDS TO SEND THE REST O' THE X-MEN.
I'M GONNA HAVE BESSIE--
BOVA.
--LEAD ME TO WHERE MAGS IS HANGIN' HIS HELMET.
YOU SIT TIGHT WITH THE REST OF THE KIDS, WAIT FOR THE CAVALRY TO ARRIVE--
THE REST OF THE KIDS? WHAT'S THAT SUPPOSED TO MEAN?
AND WHY CAN'T I GO WITH YOU? YOU MIGHT NEED ME TO--
YOU KNOW, I'M OFFICIALLY TIRED OF YOU QUESTIONIN' MY ORDERS EVERY FIVE MINUTES!
NEWSFLASH, CHICKIE: THIS AIN'T A DEMOCRACY.
JUST DO IT.

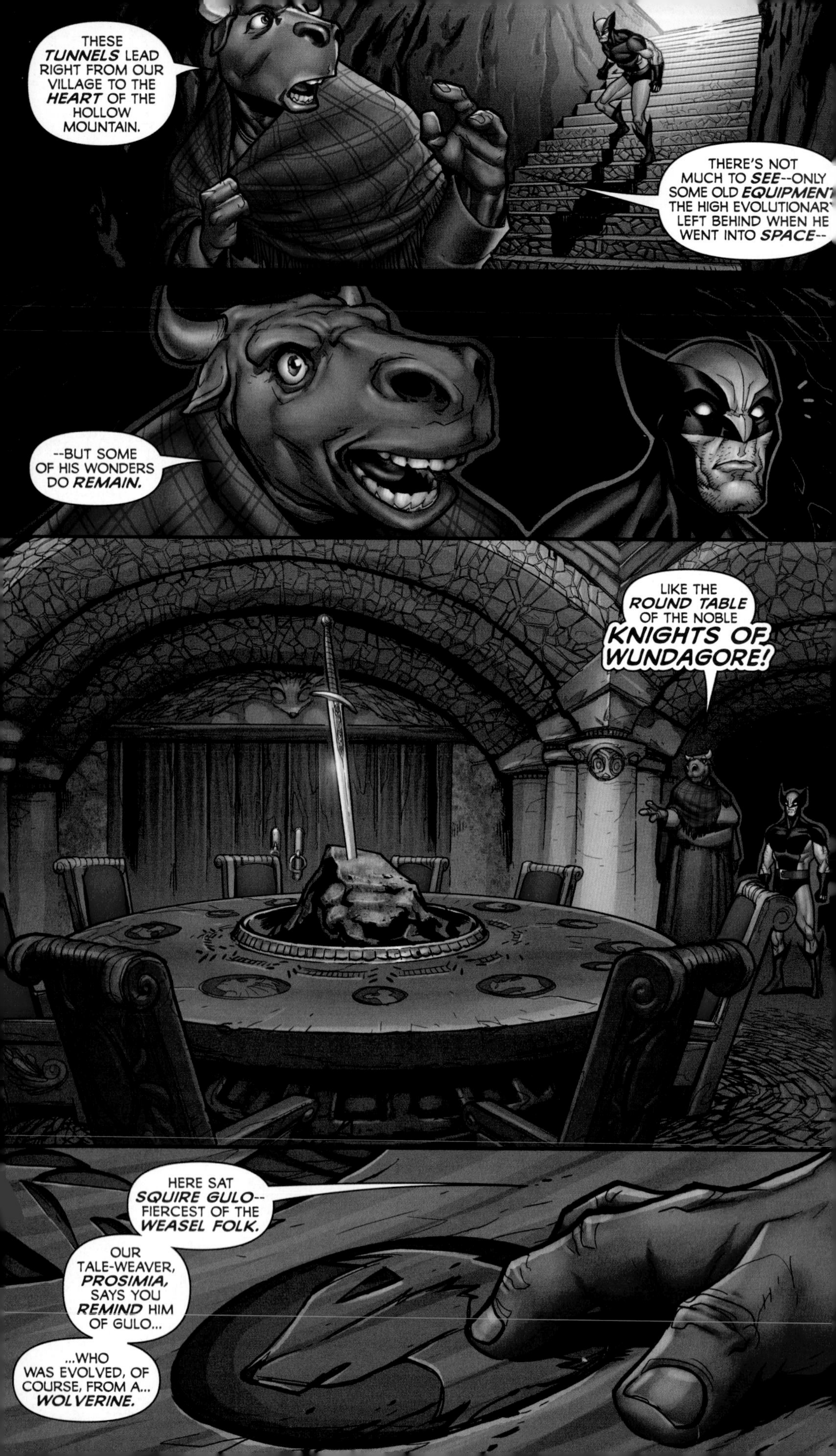
THESE TUNNELS LEAD RIGHT FROM OUR VILLAGE TO THE HEART OF THE HOLLOW MOUNTAIN.
THERE'S NOT MUCH TO SEE--ONLY SOME OLD EQUIPMENT THE HIGH EVOLUTIONARY LEFT BEHIND WHEN HE WENT INTO SPACE--
--BUT SOME OF HIS WONDERS DO REMAIN.
LIKE THE ROUND TABLE OF THE NOBLE KNIGHTS OF WUNDAGORE!
HERE SAT SQUIRE GULO-- FIERCEST OF THE WEASEL FOLK.
OUR TALE-WEAVER, PROSIMIA, SAYS YOU REMIND HIM OF GULO...
...WHO WAS EVOLVED, OF COURSE, FROM A... WOLVERINE.

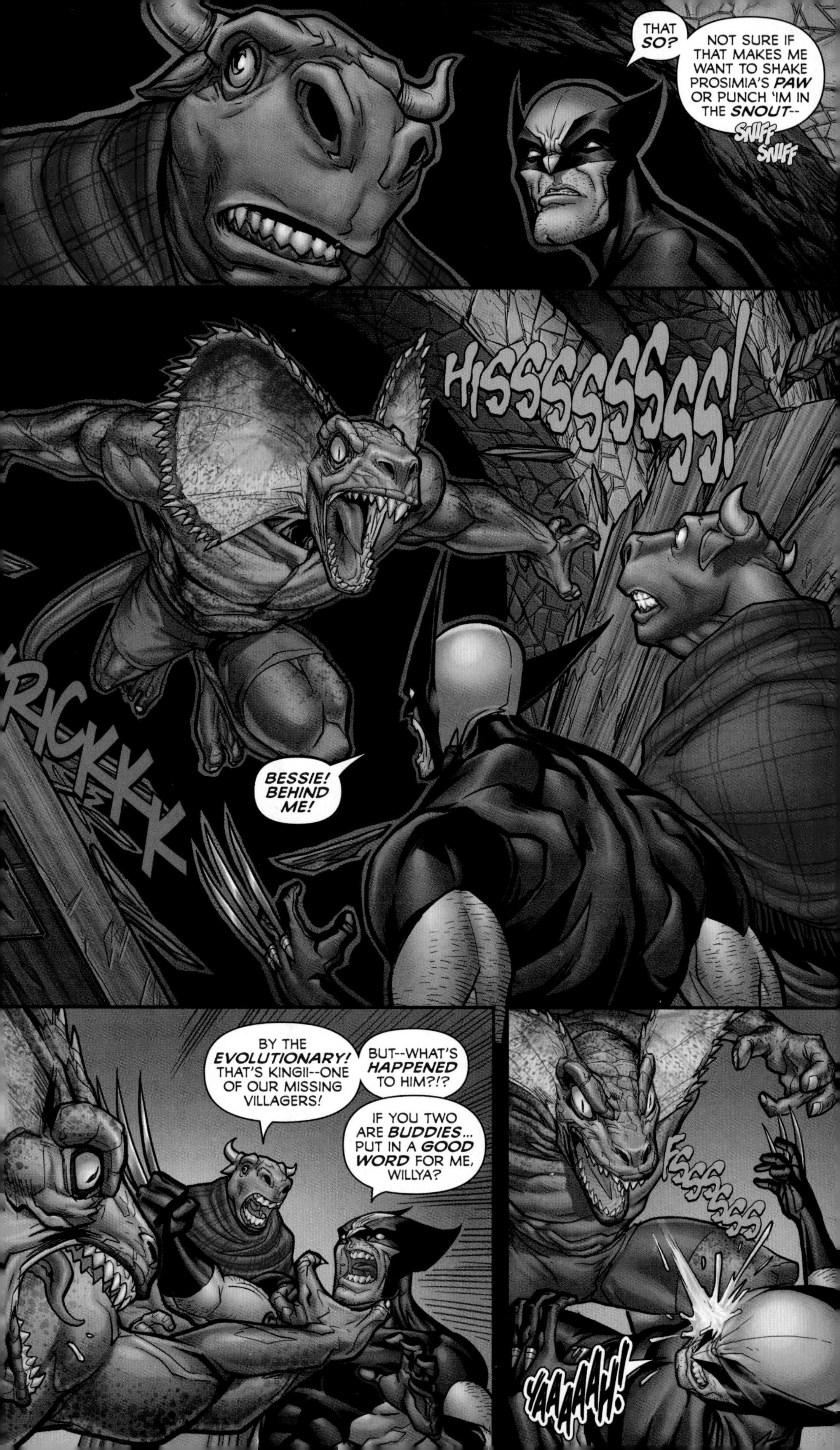
THAT SO?
NOT SURE IF THAT MAKES ME WANT TO SHAKE PROSIMIA'S PAW OR PUNCH 'IM IN THE SNOUT--
SNIFF SNIFF
HISSSSSSSSS!
KRICKKKK
BESSIE! BEHIND ME!
BY THE EVOLUTIONARY! THAT'S KINGII--ONE OF OUR MISSING VILLAGERS!
BUT--WHAT'S HAPPENED TO HIM?!?
IF YOU TWO ARE BUDDIES... PUT IN A GOOD WORD FOR ME, WILLYA?
FSSSSSSS
YAAAAAH!

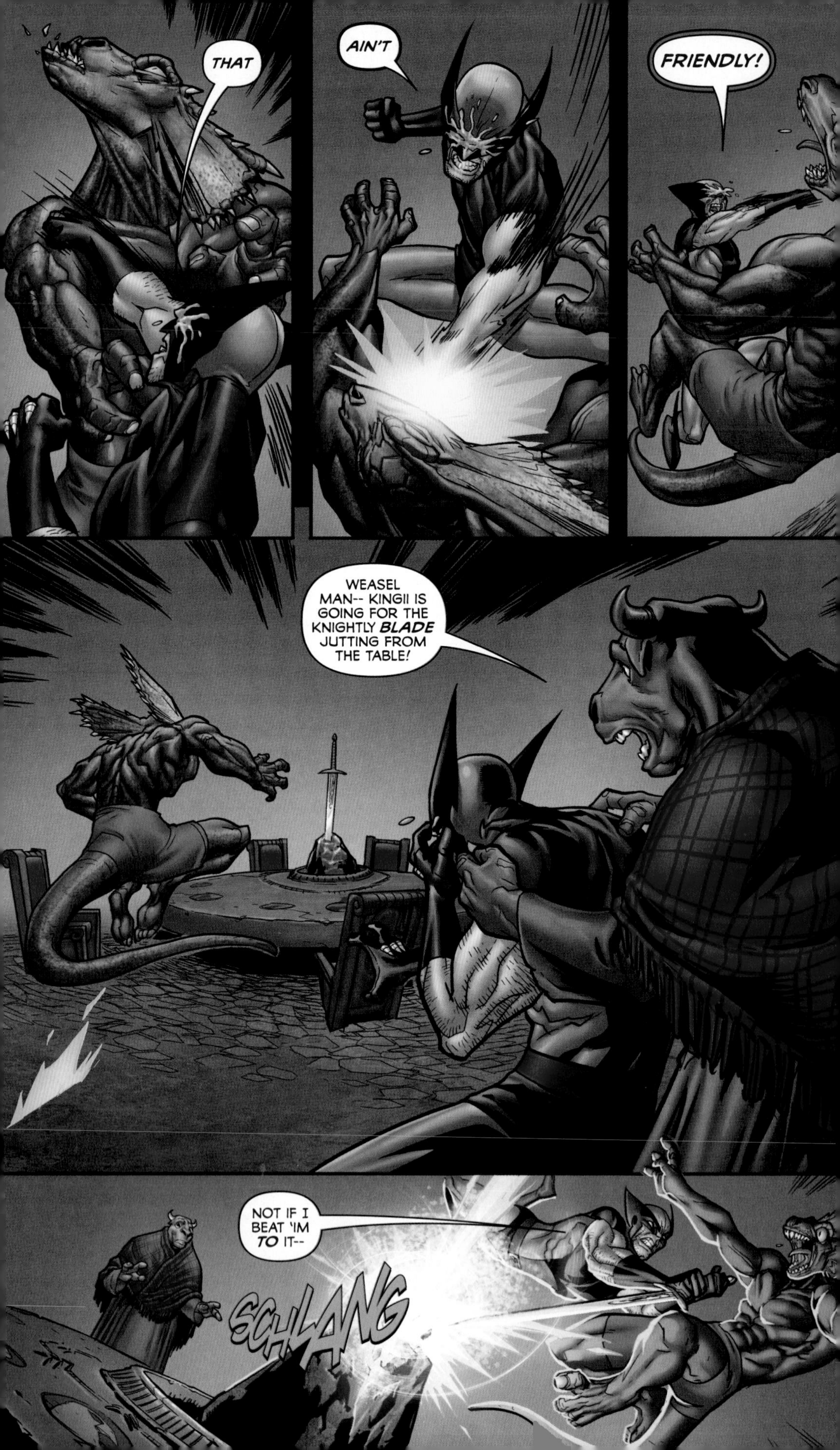
THAT
AIN'T
FRIENDLY!
WEASEL MAN-- KINGII IS GOING FOR THE KNIGHTLY *BLADE* JUTTING FROM THE TABLE!
NOT IF I BEAT 'IM *TO* IT--
SCHLANG

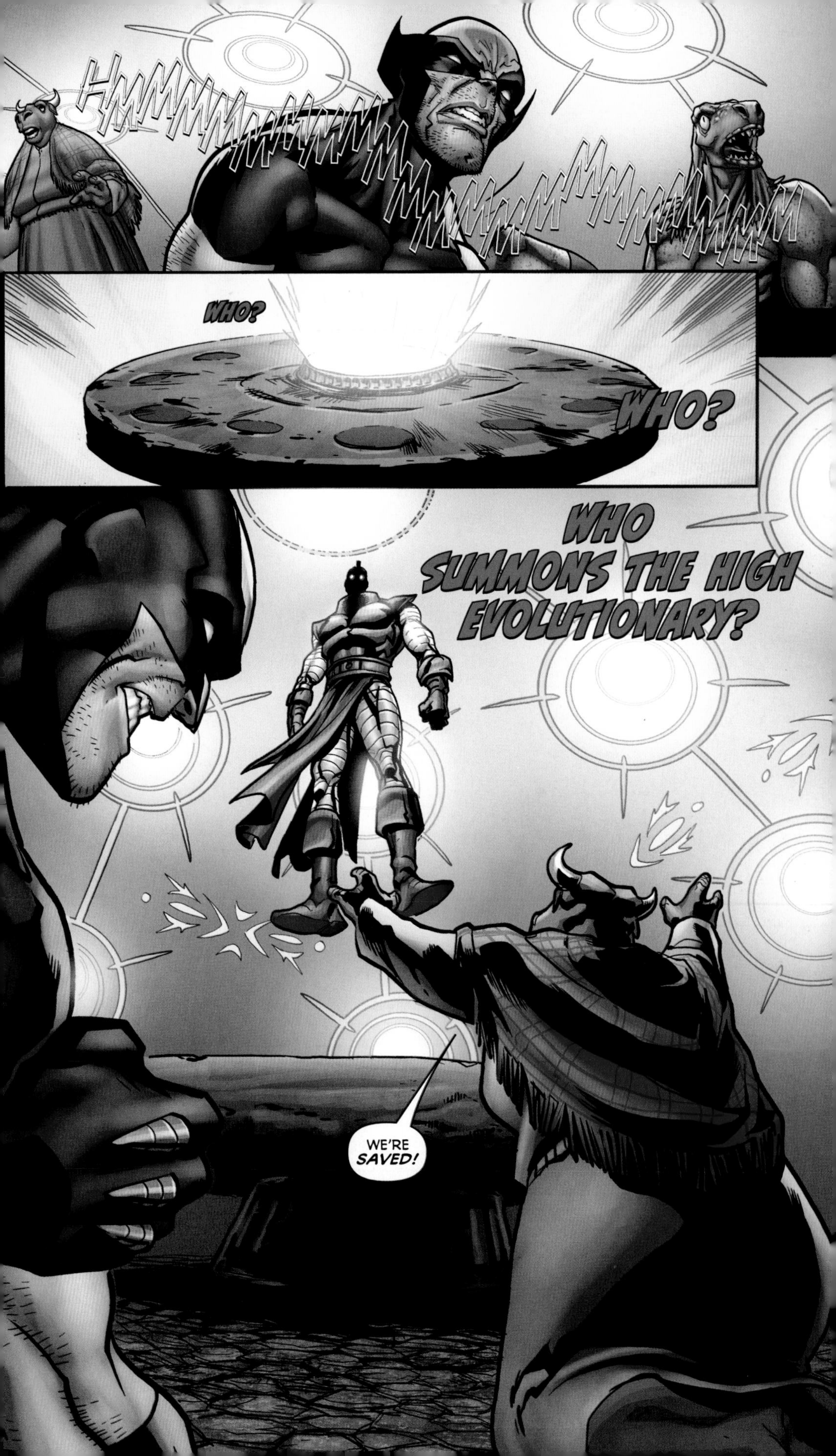
HMMMMMMMMMMMMMMMMMMMMMMMMMMM
WHO?
WHO?
WHO SUMMONS THE HIGH EVOLUTIONARY?
WE'RE SAVED!

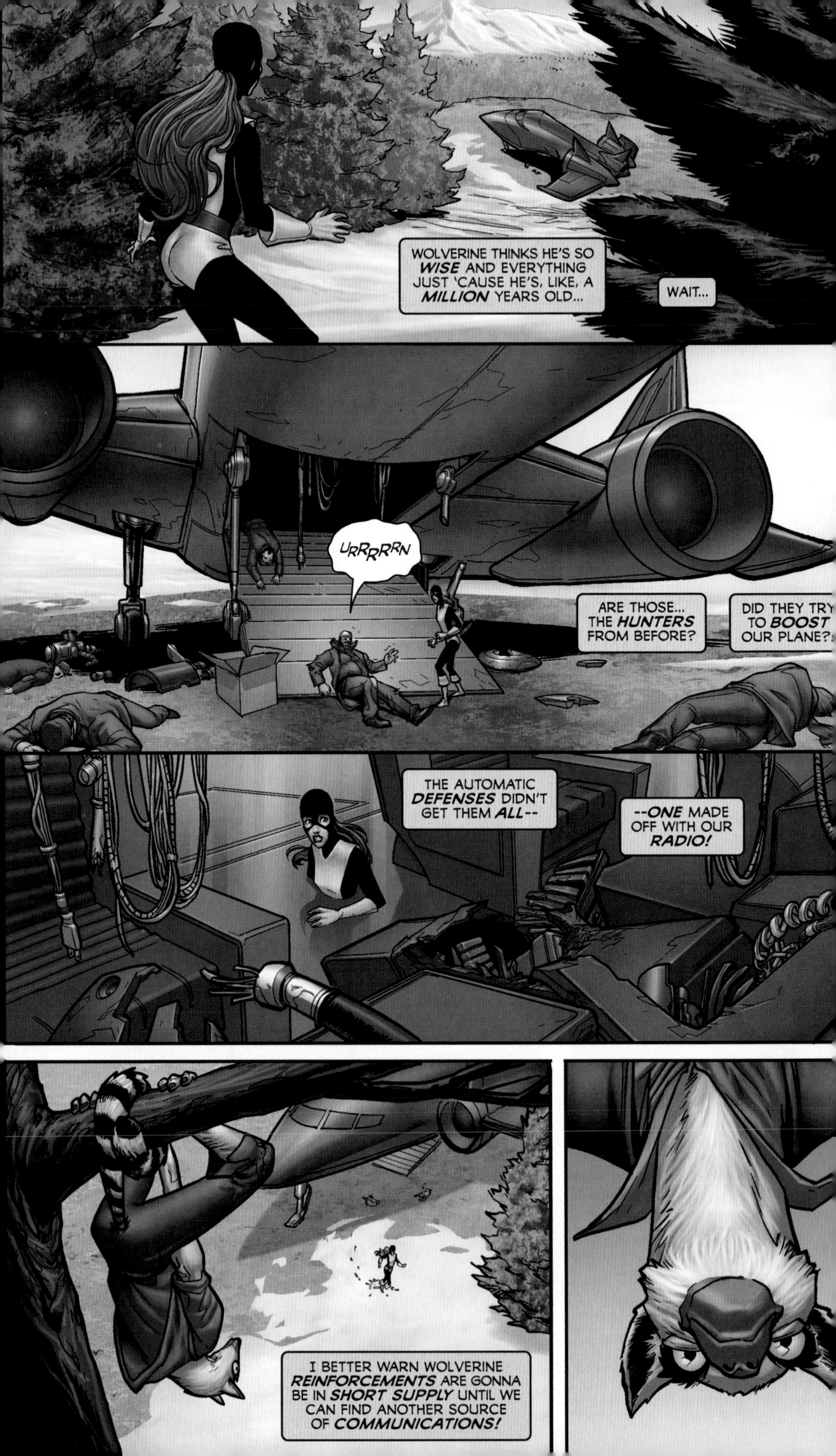

WOLVERINE THINKS HE'S SO WISE AND EVERYTHING JUST 'CAUSE HE'S, LIKE, A MILLION YEARS OLD...
WAIT...
URRRRRN
ARE THOSE... THE HUNTERS FROM BEFORE?
DID THEY TRY TO BOOST OUR PLANE?
THE AUTOMATIC DEFENSES DIDN'T GET THEM ALL--
--ONE MADE OFF WITH OUR RADIO!
I BETTER WARN WOLVERINE REINFORCEMENTS ARE GONNA BE IN SHORT SUPPLY UNTIL WE CAN FIND ANOTHER SOURCE OF COMMUNICATIONS!

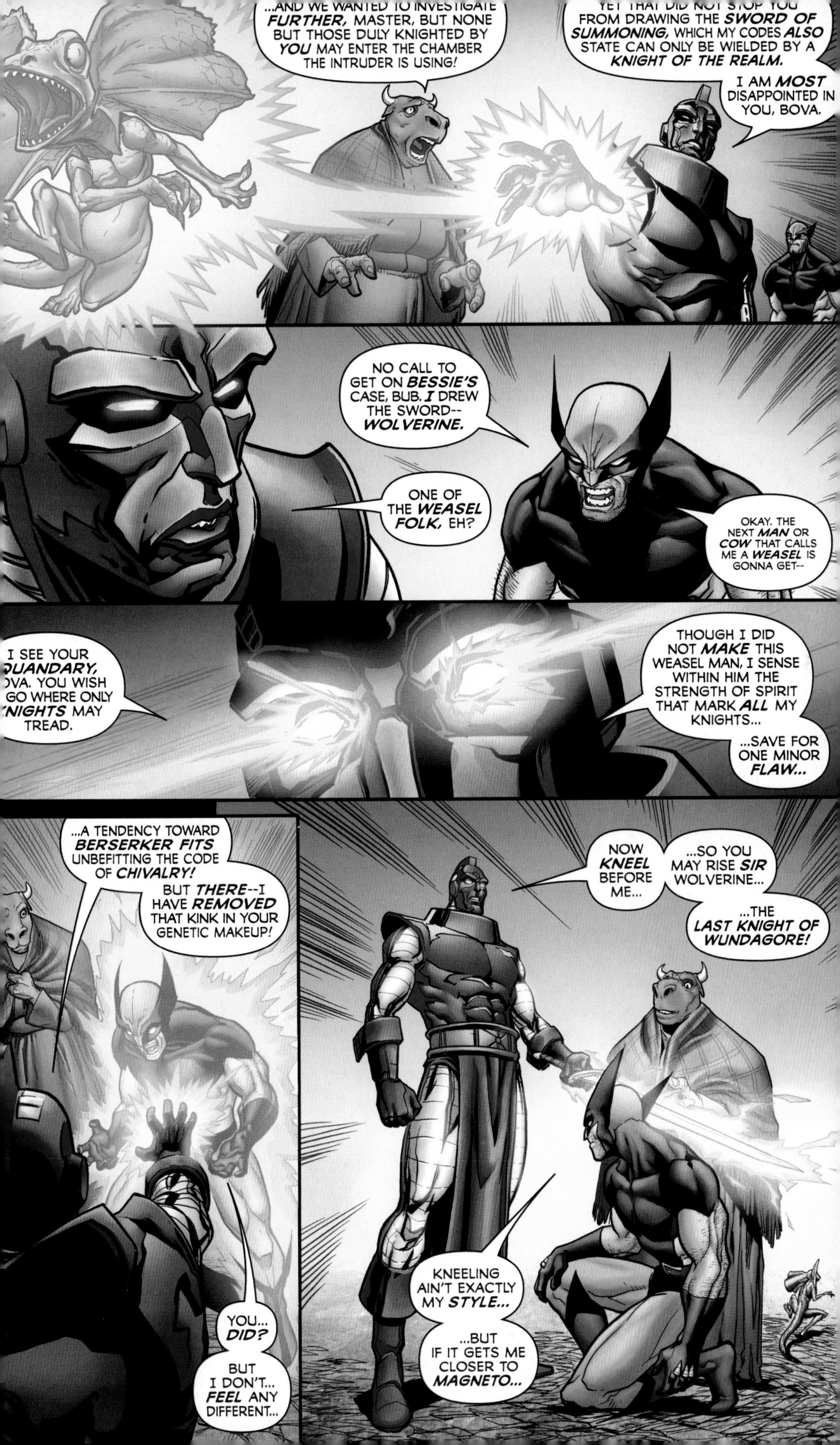
...AND WE WANTED TO INVESTIGATE FURTHER, MASTER, BUT NONE BUT THOSE DULY KNIGHTED BY YOU MAY ENTER THE CHAMBER THE INTRUDER IS USING!
YET THAT DID NOT STOP YOU FROM DRAWING THE SWORD OF SUMMONING, WHICH MY CODES ALSO STATE CAN ONLY BE WIELDED BY A KNIGHT OF THE REALM.
I AM MOST DISAPPOINTED IN YOU, BOVA.
NO CALL TO GET ON BESSIE'S CASE, BUB. I DREW THE SWORD-- WOLVERINE.
ONE OF THE WEASEL FOLK, EH?
OKAY. THE NEXT MAN OR COW THAT CALLS ME A WEASEL IS GONNA GET--
I SEE YOUR QUANDARY, BOVA. YOU WISH TO GO WHERE ONLY KNIGHTS MAY TREAD.
THOUGH I DID NOT MAKE THIS WEASEL MAN, I SENSE WITHIN HIM THE STRENGTH OF SPIRIT THAT MARK ALL MY KNIGHTS...
...SAVE FOR ONE MINOR FLAW...
...A TENDENCY TOWARD BERSERKER FITS UNBEFITTING THE CODE OF CHIVALRY!
BUT THERE--I HAVE REMOVED THAT KINK IN YOUR GENETIC MAKEUP!
YOU... DID?
BUT I DON'T... FEEL ANY DIFFERENT...
NOW KNEEL BEFORE ME...
...SO YOU MAY RISE SIR WOLVERINE...
...THE LAST KNIGHT OF WUNDAGORE!
KNEELING AIN'T EXACTLY MY STYLE...
...BUT IF IT GETS ME CLOSER TO MAGNETO...

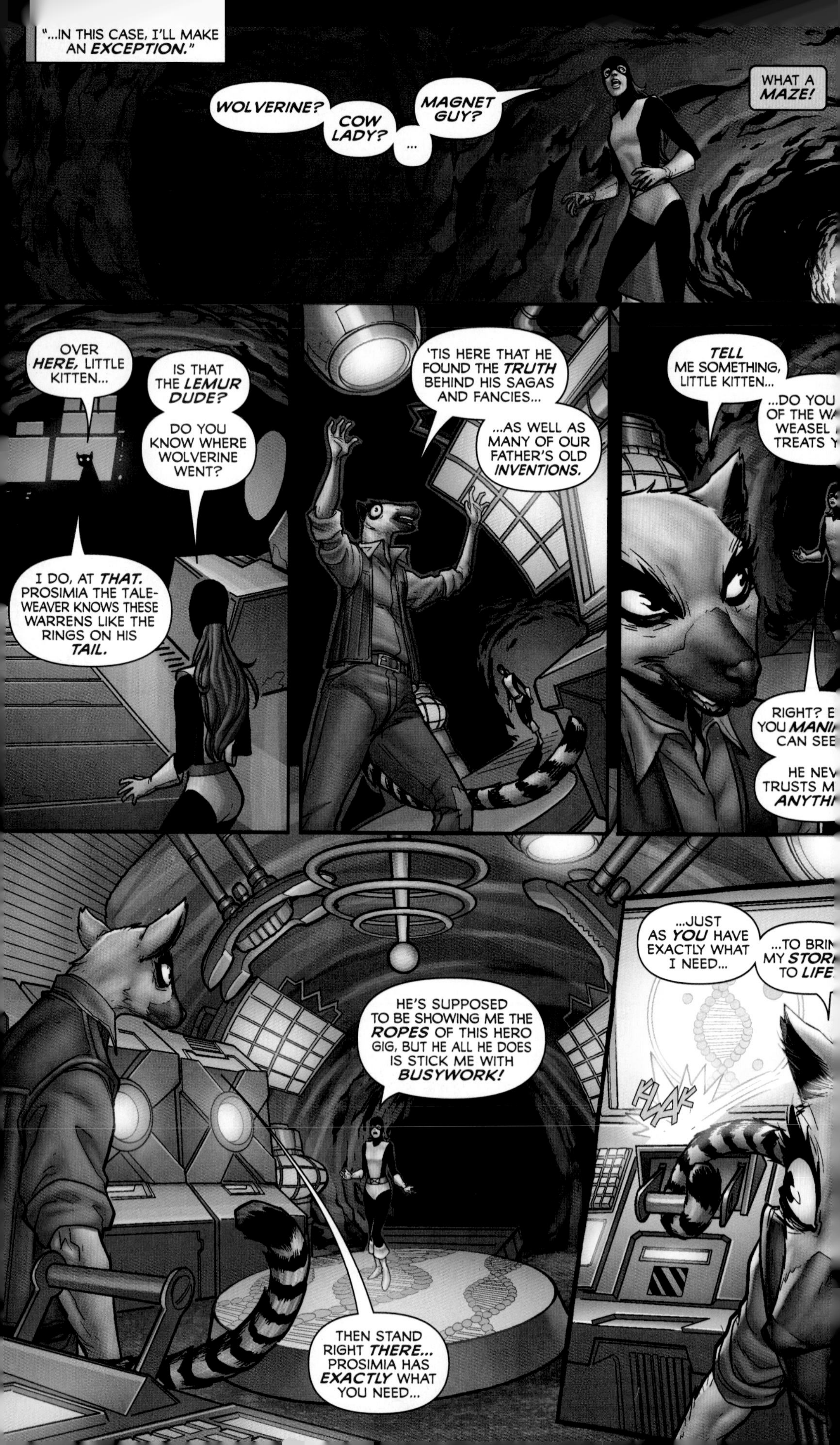
"...IN THIS CASE, I'LL MAKE AN EXCEPTION."
WOLVERINE?
COW LADY?
...
MAGNET GUY?
WHAT A MAZE!
OVER HERE, LITTLE KITTEN...
IS THAT THE LEMUR DUDE?
DO YOU KNOW WHERE WOLVERINE WENT?
I DO, AT THAT. PROSIMIA THE TALE-WEAVER KNOWS THESE WARRENS LIKE THE RINGS ON HIS TAIL.
'TIS HERE THAT HE FOUND THE TRUTH BEHIND HIS SAGAS AND FANCIES...
...AS WELL AS MANY OF OUR FATHER'S OLD INVENTIONS.
TELL ME SOMETHING, LITTLE KITTEN...
HE'S SUPPOSED TO BE SHOWING ME THE ROPES OF THIS HERO GIG, BUT HE ALL HE DOES IS STICK ME WITH BUSYWORK!
THEN STAND RIGHT THERE... PROSIMIA HAS EXACTLY WHAT YOU NEED...
...JUST AS YOU HAVE EXACTLY WHAT I NEED...
KLAK

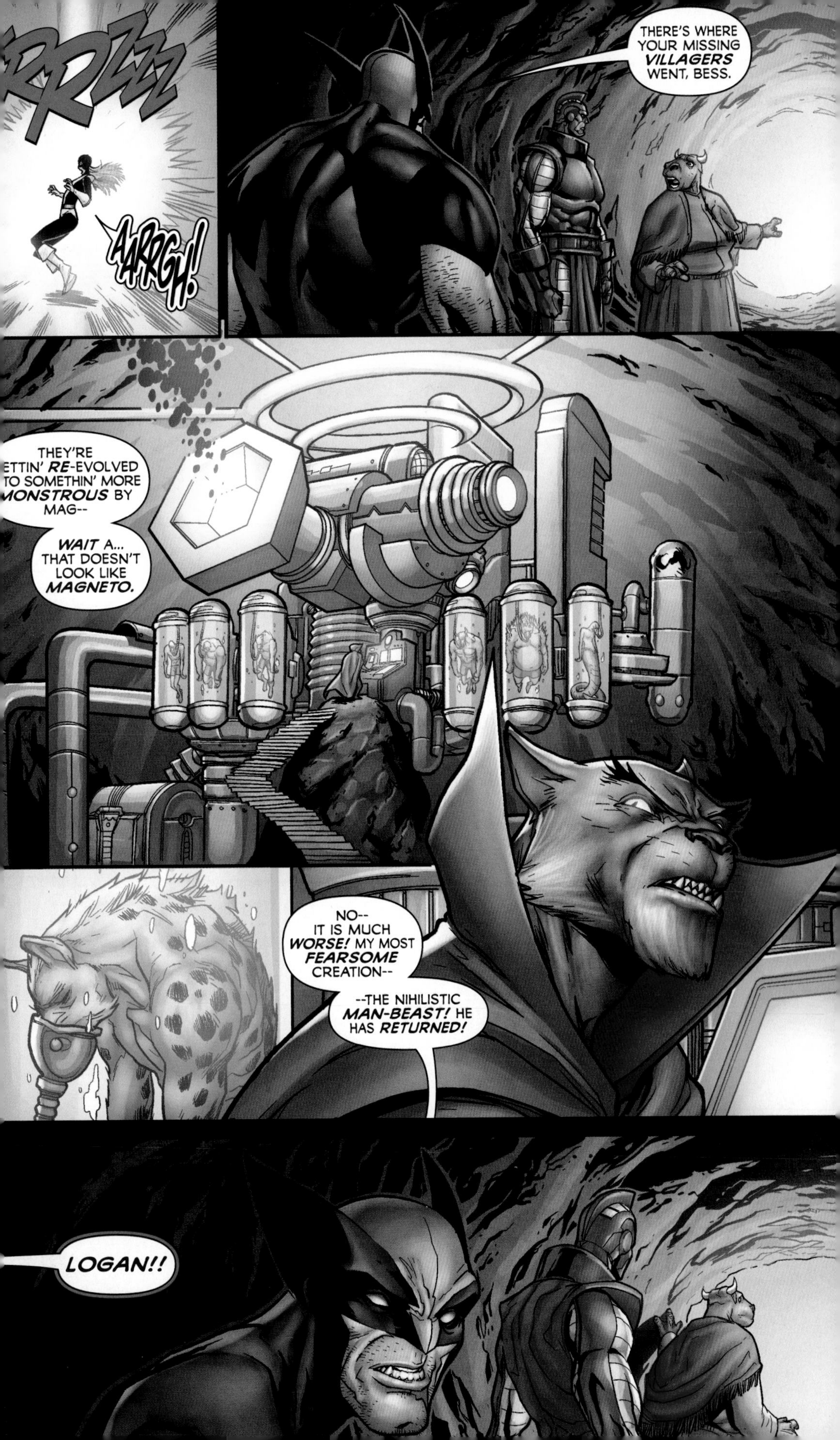
RRZZZZ
AARRGH!
THERE'S WHERE YOUR MISSING VILLAGERS WENT, BESS.
THEY'RE ETTIN' RE-EVOLVED TO SOMETHIN' MORE MONSTROUS BY MAG--
WAIT A... THAT DOESN'T LOOK LIKE MAGNETO.
NO-- IT IS MUCH WORSE! MY MOST FEARSOME CREATION--
--THE NIHILISTIC MAN-BEAST! HE HAS RETURNED!
LOGAN!!

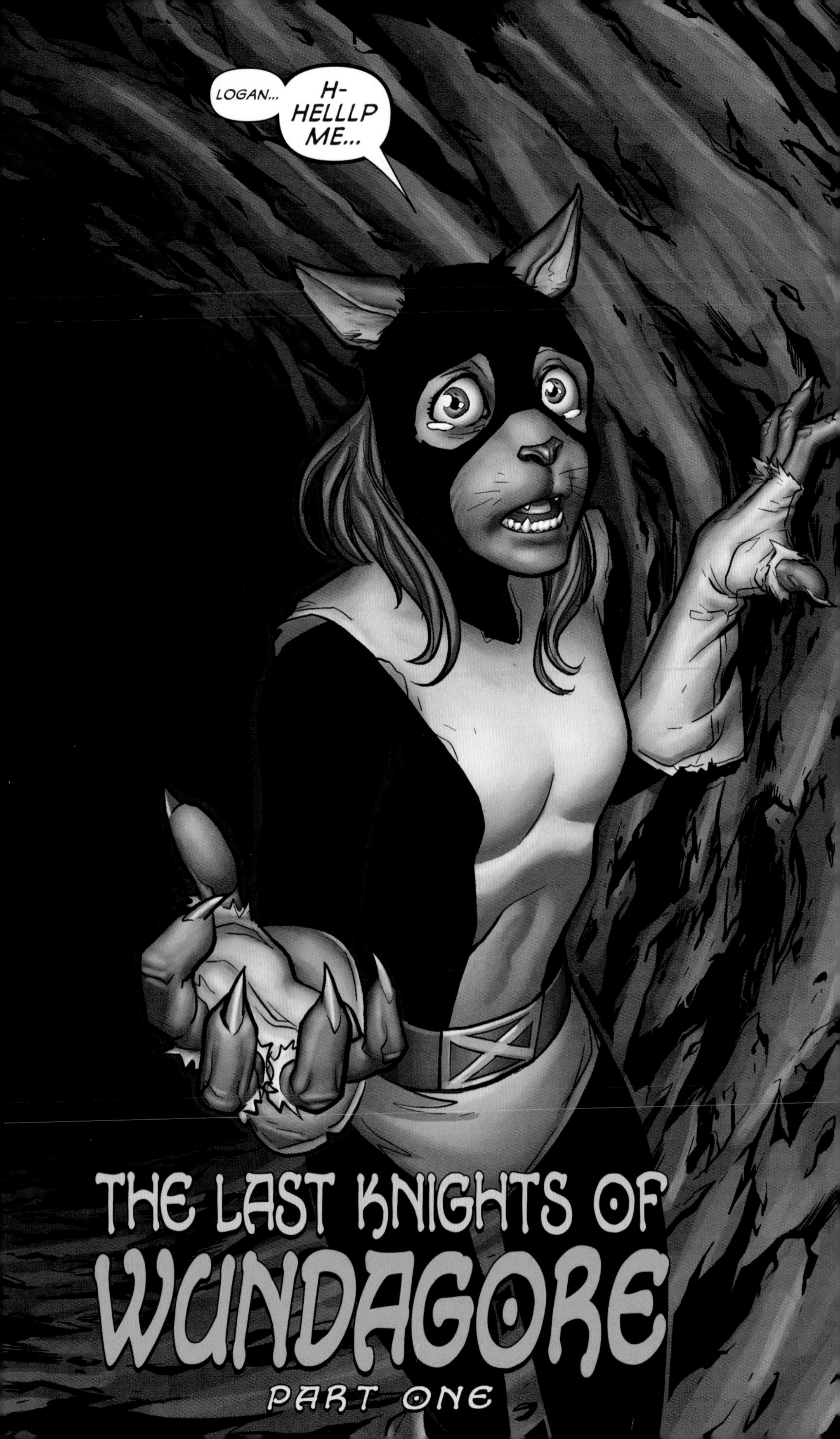
LOGAN...
H-
HELLLP
ME...
THE LAST KNIGHTS OF
WUNDAGORE
PART ONE

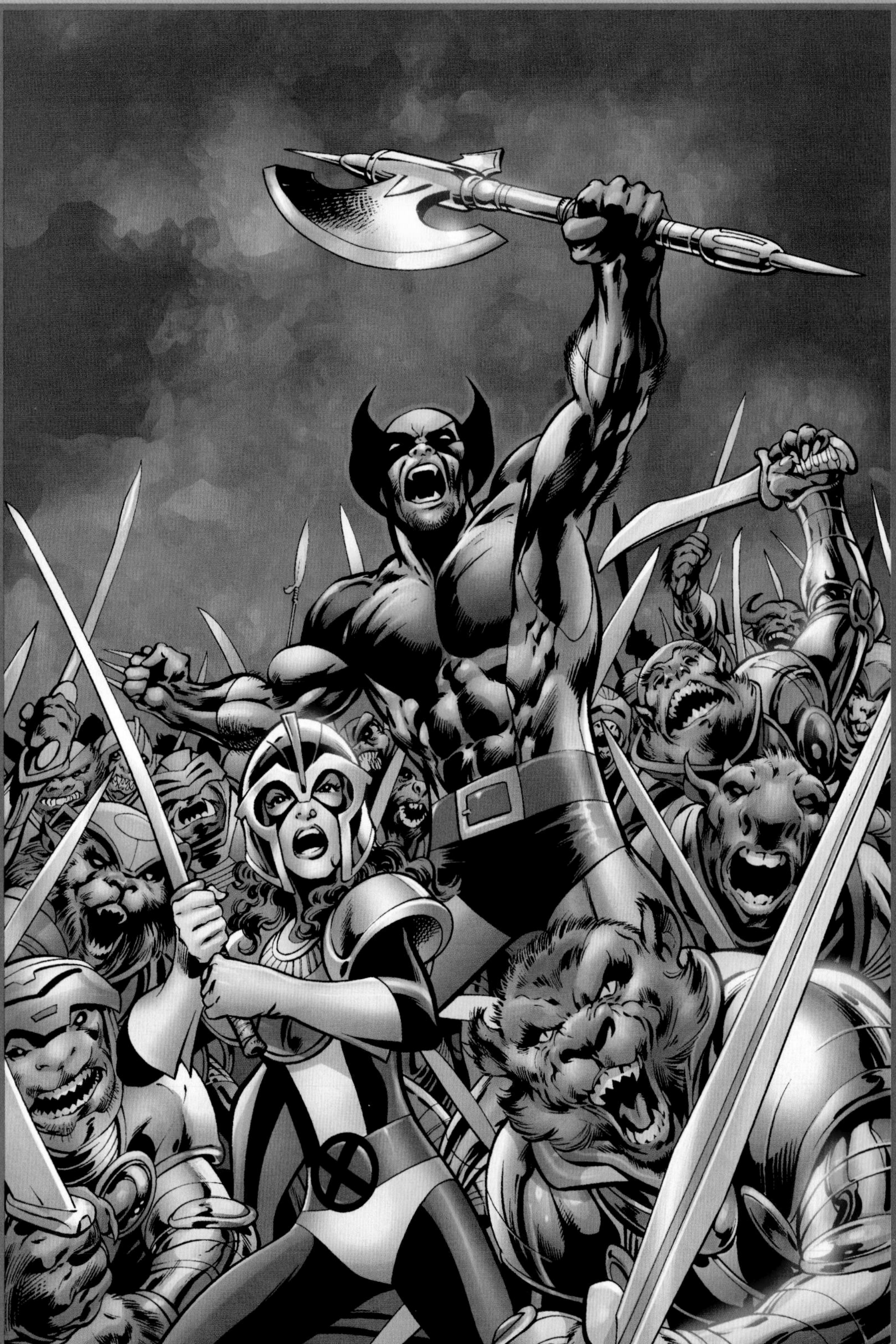

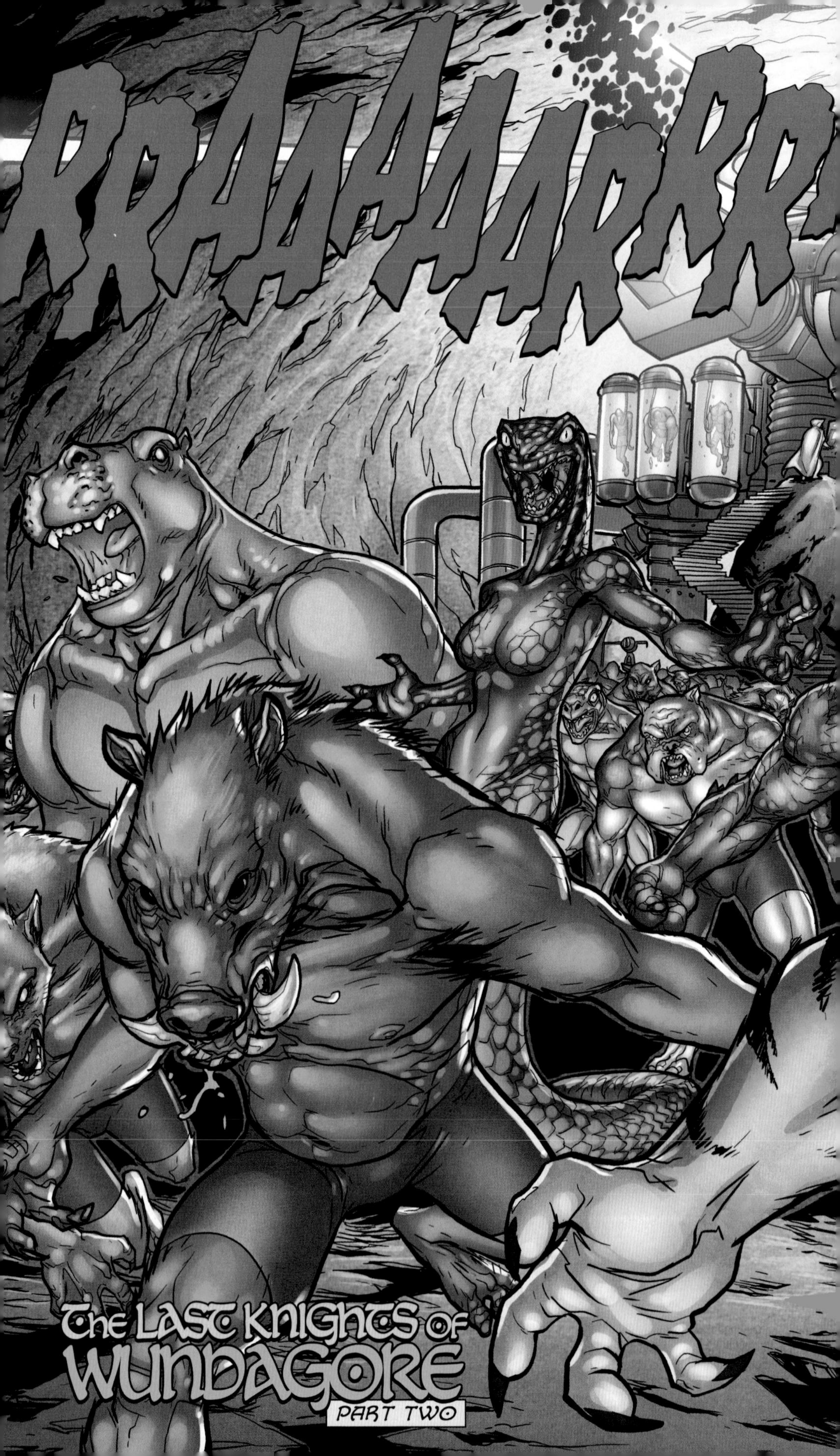
RRAAAARRR
The LAST KNIGHTS OF
WUNDAGORE
PART TWO

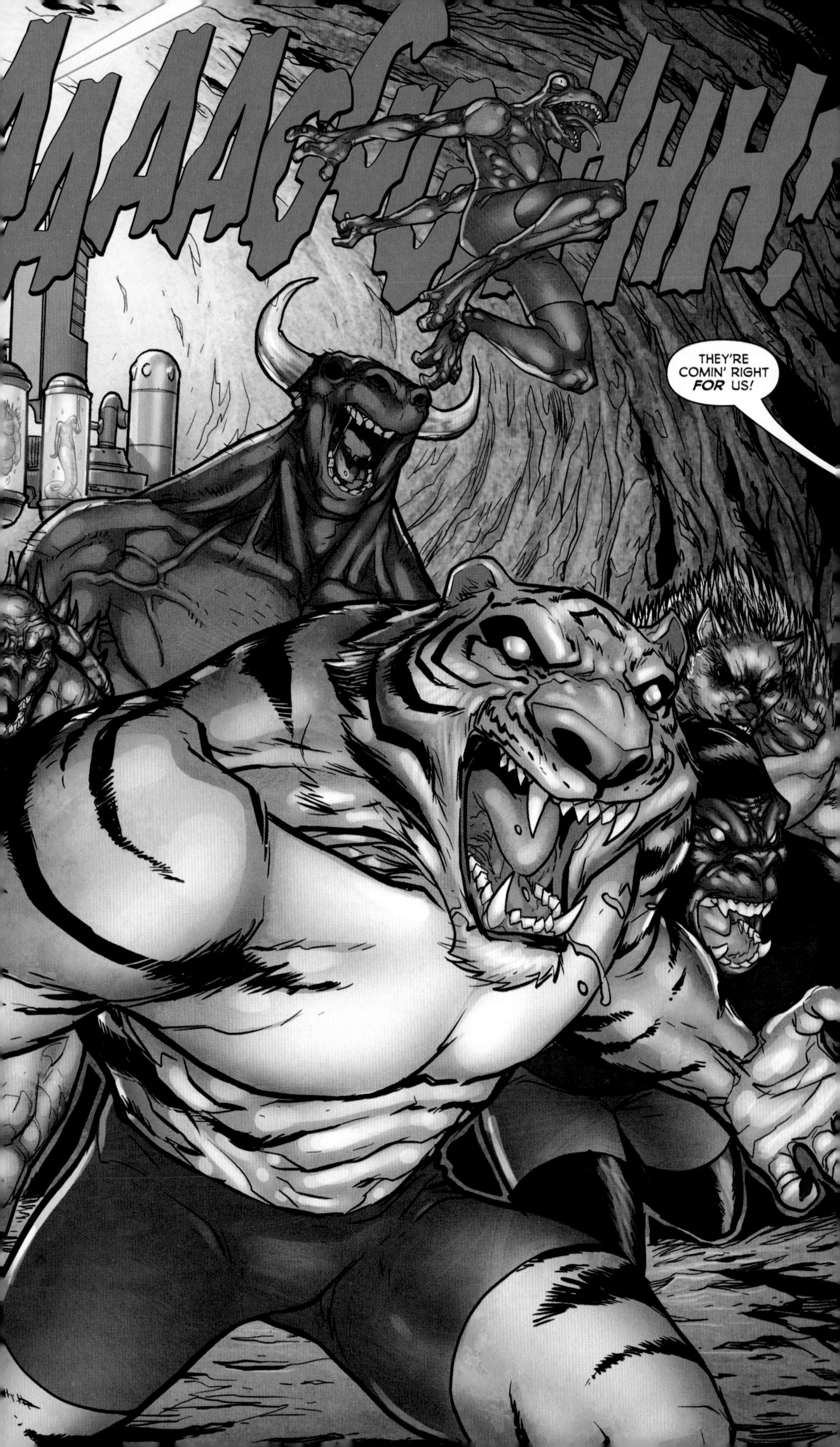
THEY'RE COMIN' RIGHT **FOR** US!

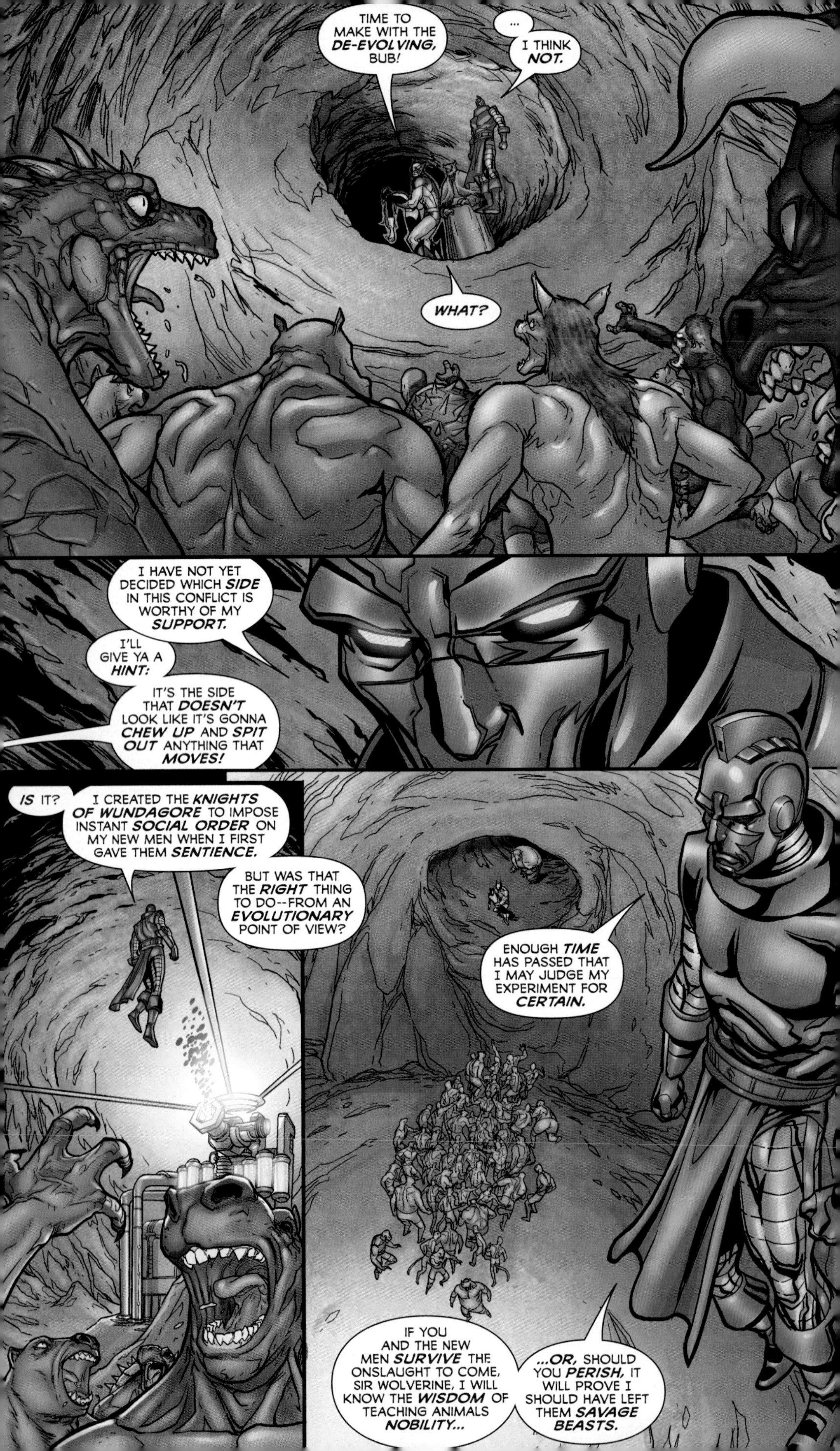
TIME TO MAKE WITH THE DE-EVOLVING, BUB!
...
I THINK NOT.
WHAT?
I HAVE NOT YET DECIDED WHICH SIDE IN THIS CONFLICT IS WORTHY OF MY SUPPORT.
I'LL GIVE YA A HINT:
IT'S THE SIDE THAT DOESN'T LOOK LIKE IT'S GONNA CHEW UP AND SPIT OUT ANYTHING THAT MOVES!
IS IT?
I CREATED THE KNIGHTS OF WUNDAGORE TO IMPOSE INSTANT SOCIAL ORDER ON MY NEW MEN WHEN I FIRST GAVE THEM SENTIENCE.
BUT WAS THAT THE RIGHT THING TO DO--FROM AN EVOLUTIONARY POINT OF VIEW?
ENOUGH TIME HAS PASSED THAT I MAY JUDGE MY EXPERIMENT FOR CERTAIN.
IF YOU AND THE NEW MEN SURVIVE THE ONSLAUGHT TO COME, SIR WOLVERINE, I WILL KNOW THE WISDOM OF TEACHING ANIMALS NOBILITY...
...OR, SHOULD YOU PERISH, IT WILL PROVE I SHOULD HAVE LEFT THEM SAVAGE BEASTS.

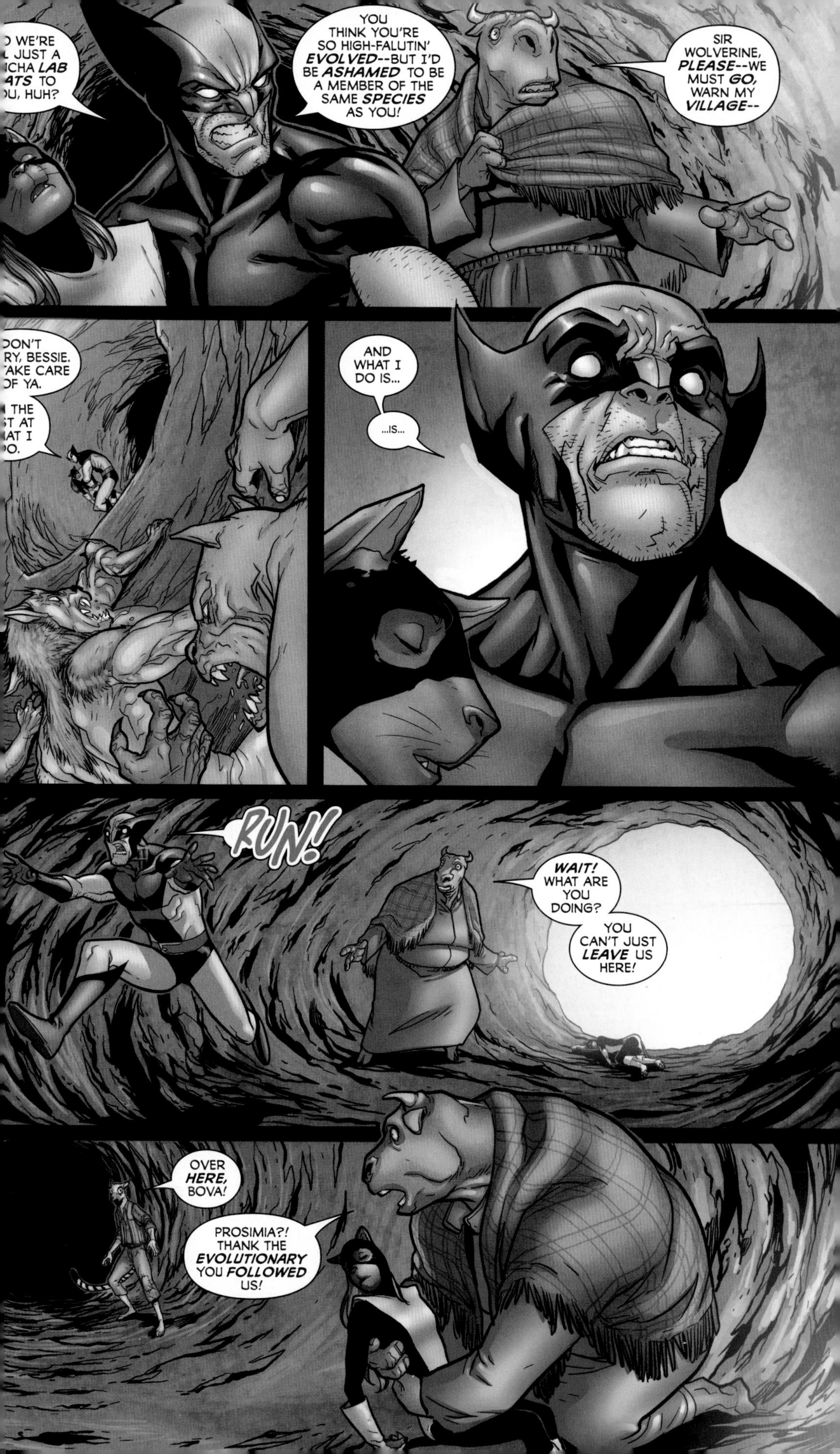

O WE'RE L JUST A ICHA LAB ATS TO U, HUH?
YOU THINK YOU'RE SO HIGH-FALUTIN' EVOLVED--BUT I'D BE ASHAMED TO BE A MEMBER OF THE SAME SPECIES AS YOU!
SIR WOLVERINE, PLEASE--WE MUST GO, WARN MY VILLAGE--
DON'T RY, BESSIE. TAKE CARE OF YA.
THE ST AT AT I O.
AND WHAT I DO IS...
...IS...
RUN!
WAIT! WHAT ARE YOU DOING?
YOU CAN'T JUST LEAVE US HERE!
OVER HERE, BOVA!
PROSIMIA?! THANK THE EVOLUTIONARY YOU FOLLOWED US!

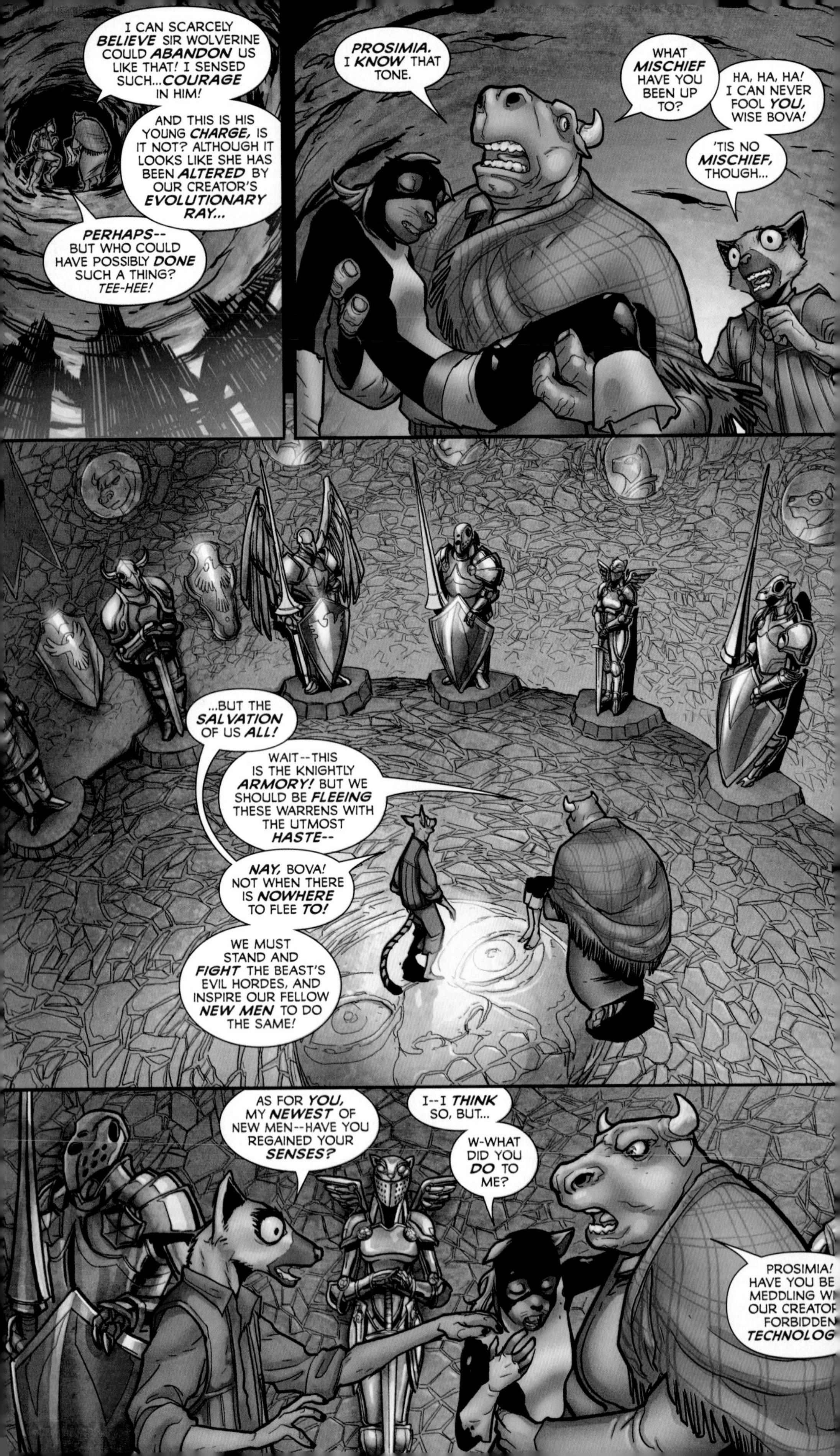
I CAN SCARCELY BELIEVE SIR WOLVERINE COULD ABANDON US LIKE THAT! I SENSED SUCH...COURAGE IN HIM!
AND THIS IS HIS YOUNG CHARGE, IS IT NOT? ALTHOUGH IT LOOKS LIKE SHE HAS BEEN ALTERED BY OUR CREATOR'S EVOLUTIONARY RAY...
PERHAPS-- BUT WHO COULD HAVE POSSIBLY DONE SUCH A THING? TEE-HEE!
PROSIMIA. I KNOW THAT TONE.
WHAT MISCHIEF HAVE YOU BEEN UP TO?
HA, HA, HA! I CAN NEVER FOOL YOU, WISE BOVA!
'TIS NO MISCHIEF, THOUGH...
...BUT THE SALVATION OF US ALL!
WAIT--THIS IS THE KNIGHTLY ARMORY! BUT WE SHOULD BE FLEEING THESE WARRENS WITH THE UTMOST HASTE--
NAY, BOVA! NOT WHEN THERE IS NOWHERE TO FLEE TO!
WE MUST STAND AND FIGHT THE BEAST'S EVIL HORDES, AND INSPIRE OUR FELLOW NEW MEN TO DO THE SAME!
AS FOR YOU, MY NEWEST OF NEW MEN--HAVE YOU REGAINED YOUR SENSES?
I--I THINK SO, BUT...
W-WHAT DID YOU DO TO ME?
PROSIMIA! HAVE YOU BE MEDDLING WI OUR CREATOF FORBIDDEN TECHNOLOG

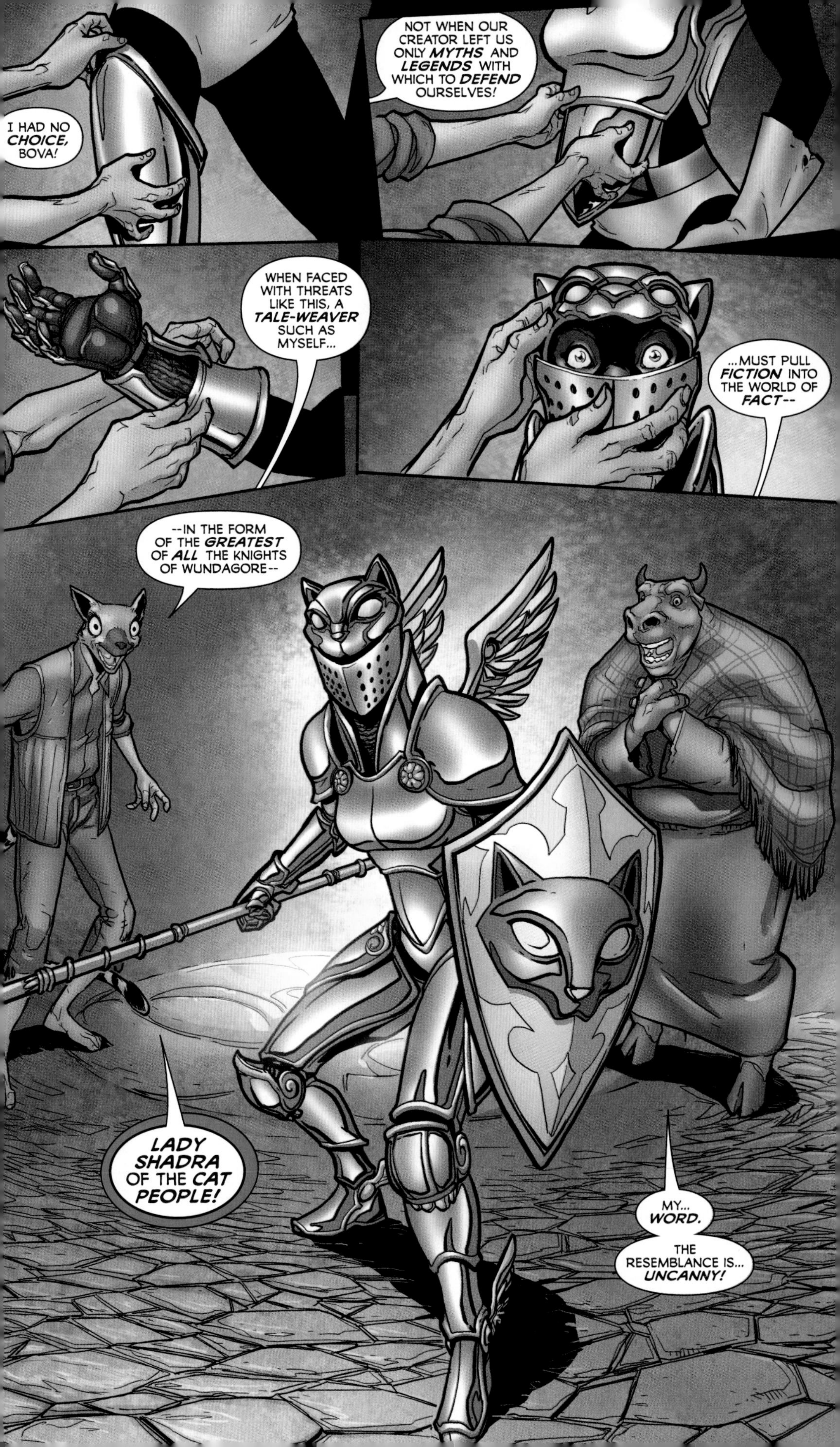
I HAD NO CHOICE, BOVA!
NOT WHEN OUR CREATOR LEFT US ONLY MYTHS AND LEGENDS WITH WHICH TO DEFEND OURSELVES!
WHEN FACED WITH THREATS LIKE THIS, A TALE-WEAVER SUCH AS MYSELF...
...MUST PULL FICTION INTO THE WORLD OF FACT--
--IN THE FORM OF THE GREATEST OF ALL THE KNIGHTS OF WUNDAGORE--
LADY SHADRA OF THE CAT PEOPLE!
MY... WORD.
THE RESEMBLANCE IS... UNCANNY!

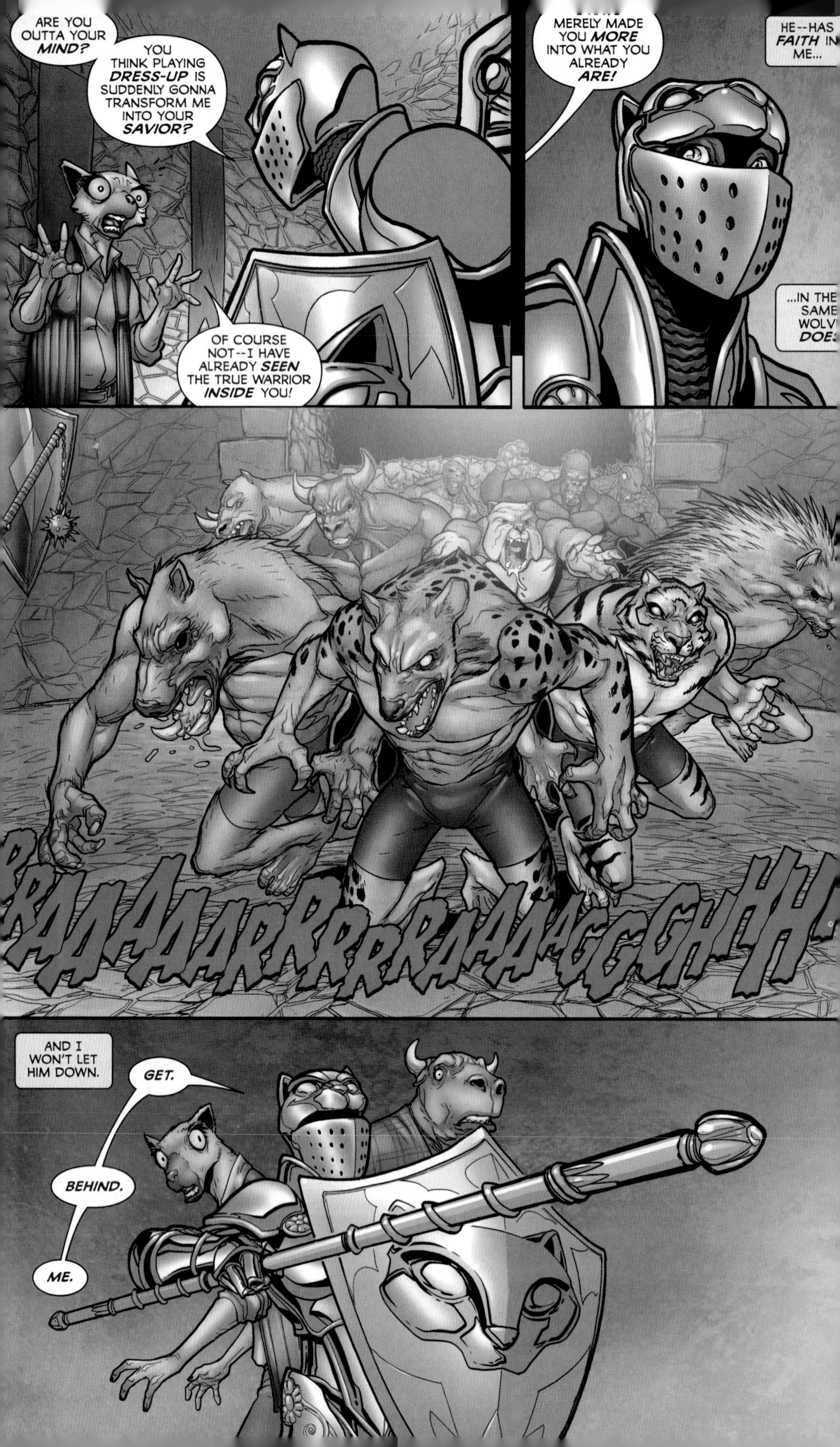
ARE YOU OUTTA YOUR MIND?
YOU THINK PLAYING DRESS-UP IS SUDDENLY GONNA TRANSFORM ME INTO YOUR SAVIOR?
OF COURSE NOT--I HAVE ALREADY SEEN THE TRUE WARRIOR INSIDE YOU!
MERELY MADE YOU MORE INTO WHAT YOU ALREADY ARE!
HE--HAS FAITH IN ME...
...IN THE SAME WOLV DOES
RAAAAAARRRRRAAAAGGGHHH
AND I WON'T LET HIM DOWN.
GET.
BEHIND.
ME.

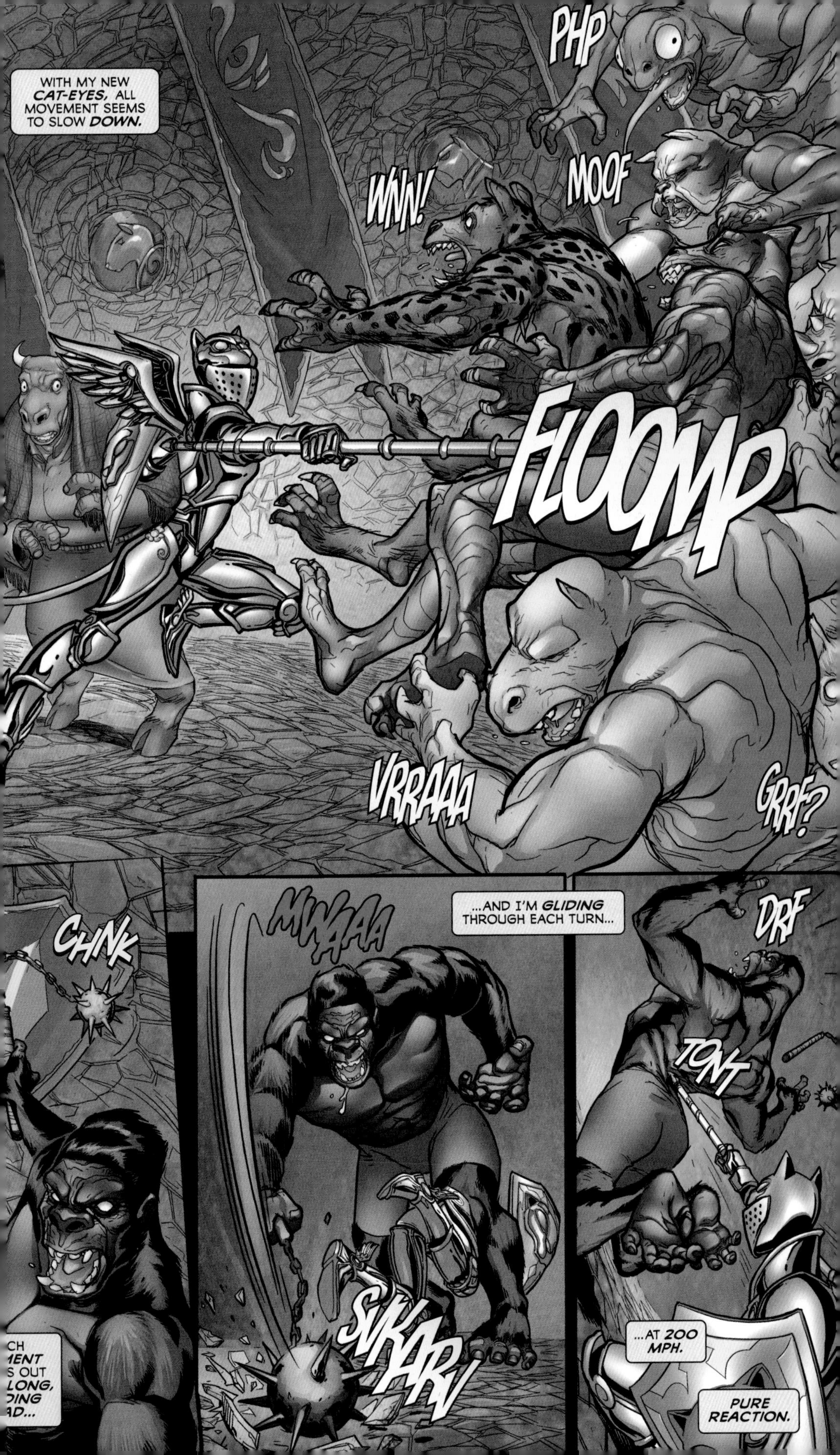
WITH MY NEW CAT-EYES, ALL MOVEMENT SEEMS TO SLOW DOWN.
PHP
WNN!
MOOF
FLOOMP
VRRAAA
GRRF?
CHINK
CH
MENT
S OUT
LONG,
DING
AD...
MWAAA
SKARV
...AND I'M GLIDING THROUGH EACH TURN...
DRF
TONT
...AT 200 MPH.
PURE REACTION.

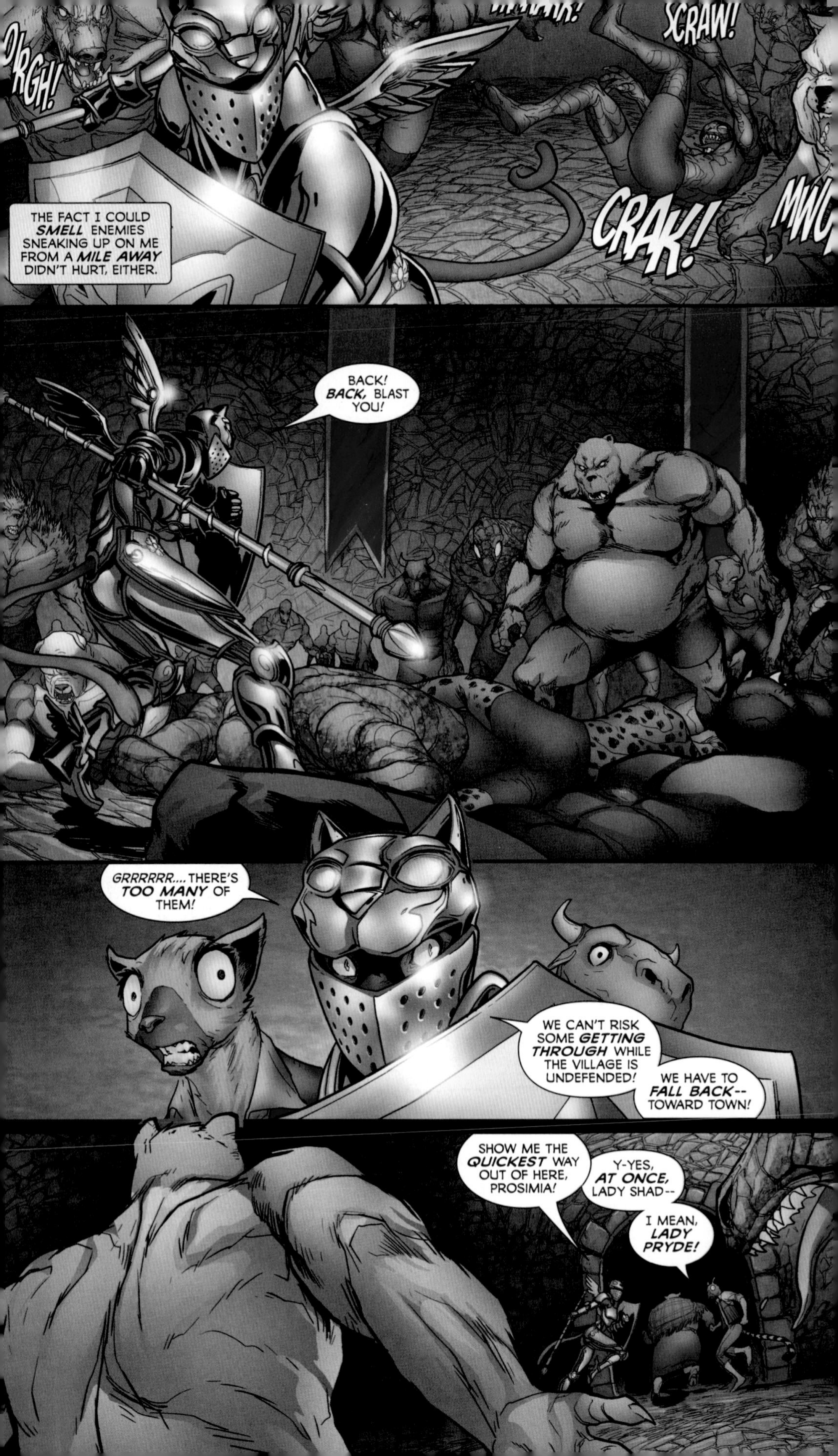
SCRAW!
THE FACT I COULD *SMELL* ENEMIES SNEAKING UP ON ME FROM A *MILE AWAY* DIDN'T HURT, EITHER.
CRAK!
BACK! *BACK,* BLAST YOU!
GRRRRRR.... THERE'S *TOO MANY* OF THEM!
WE CAN'T RISK SOME *GETTING THROUGH* WHILE THE VILLAGE IS UNDEFENDED!
WE HAVE TO *FALL BACK*-- TOWARD TOWN!
SHOW ME THE *QUICKEST* WAY OUT OF HERE, PROSIMIA!
Y-YES, *AT ONCE,* LADY SHAD--
I MEAN, *LADY PRYDE!*

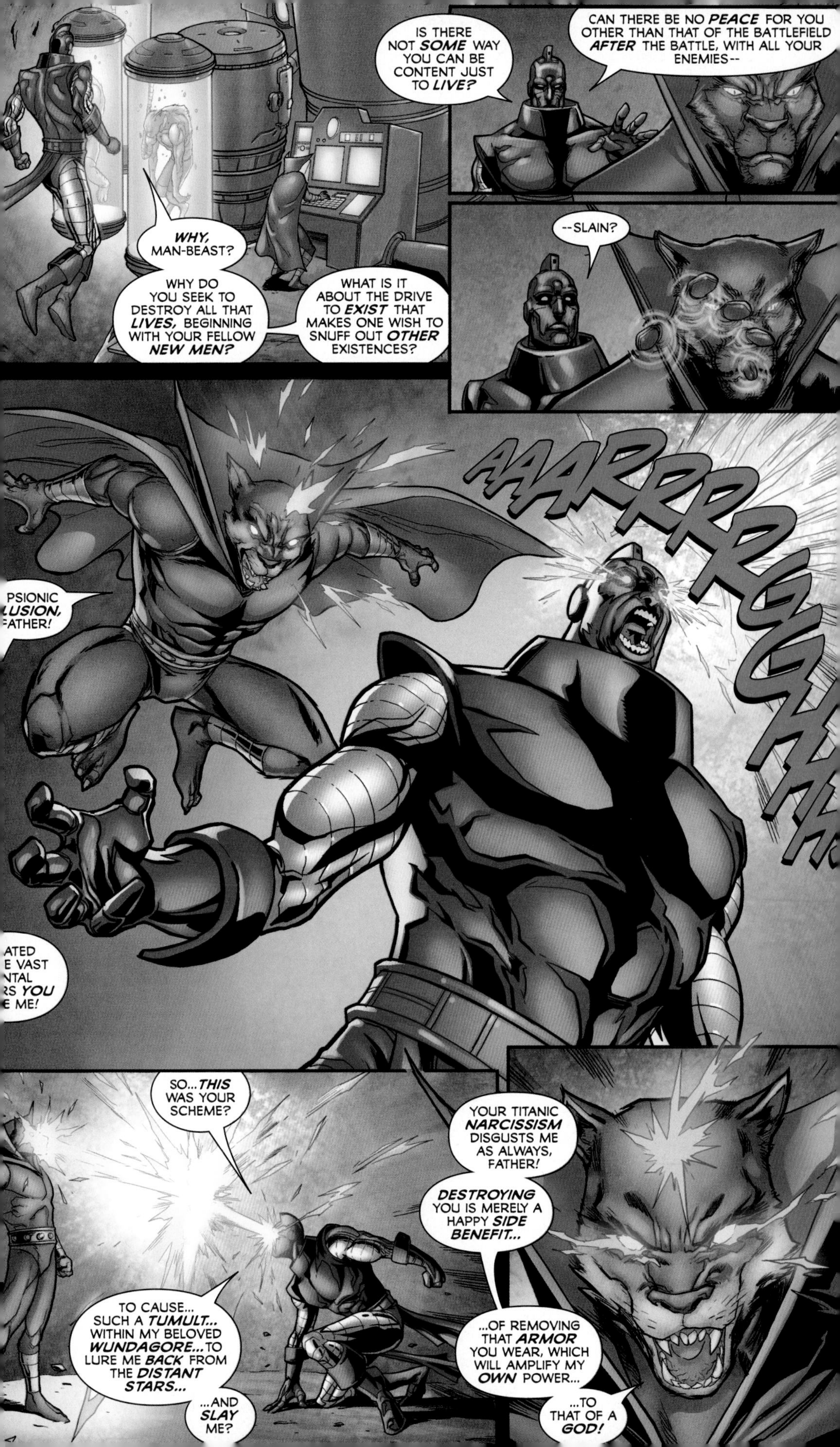
WHY, MAN-BEAST?
WHY DO YOU SEEK TO DESTROY ALL THAT LIVES, BEGINNING WITH YOUR FELLOW NEW MEN?
WHAT IS IT ABOUT THE DRIVE TO EXIST THAT MAKES ONE WISH TO SNUFF OUT OTHER EXISTENCES?
IS THERE NOT SOME WAY YOU CAN BE CONTENT JUST TO LIVE?
CAN THERE BE NO PEACE FOR YOU OTHER THAN THAT OF THE BATTLEFIELD AFTER THE BATTLE, WITH ALL YOUR ENEMIES--
--SLAIN?
AAARRRRGHHH
PSIONIC LUSION, FATHER!
ATED E VAST NTAL RS YOU E ME!
SO...THIS WAS YOUR SCHEME?
TO CAUSE... SUCH A TUMULT... WITHIN MY BELOVED WUNDAGORE...TO LURE ME BACK FROM THE DISTANT STARS...
...AND SLAY ME?
YOUR TITANIC NARCISSISM DISGUSTS ME AS ALWAYS, FATHER!
DESTROYING YOU IS MERELY A HAPPY SIDE BENEFIT...
...OF REMOVING THAT ARMOR YOU WEAR, WHICH WILL AMPLIFY MY OWN POWER...
...TO THAT OF A GOD!

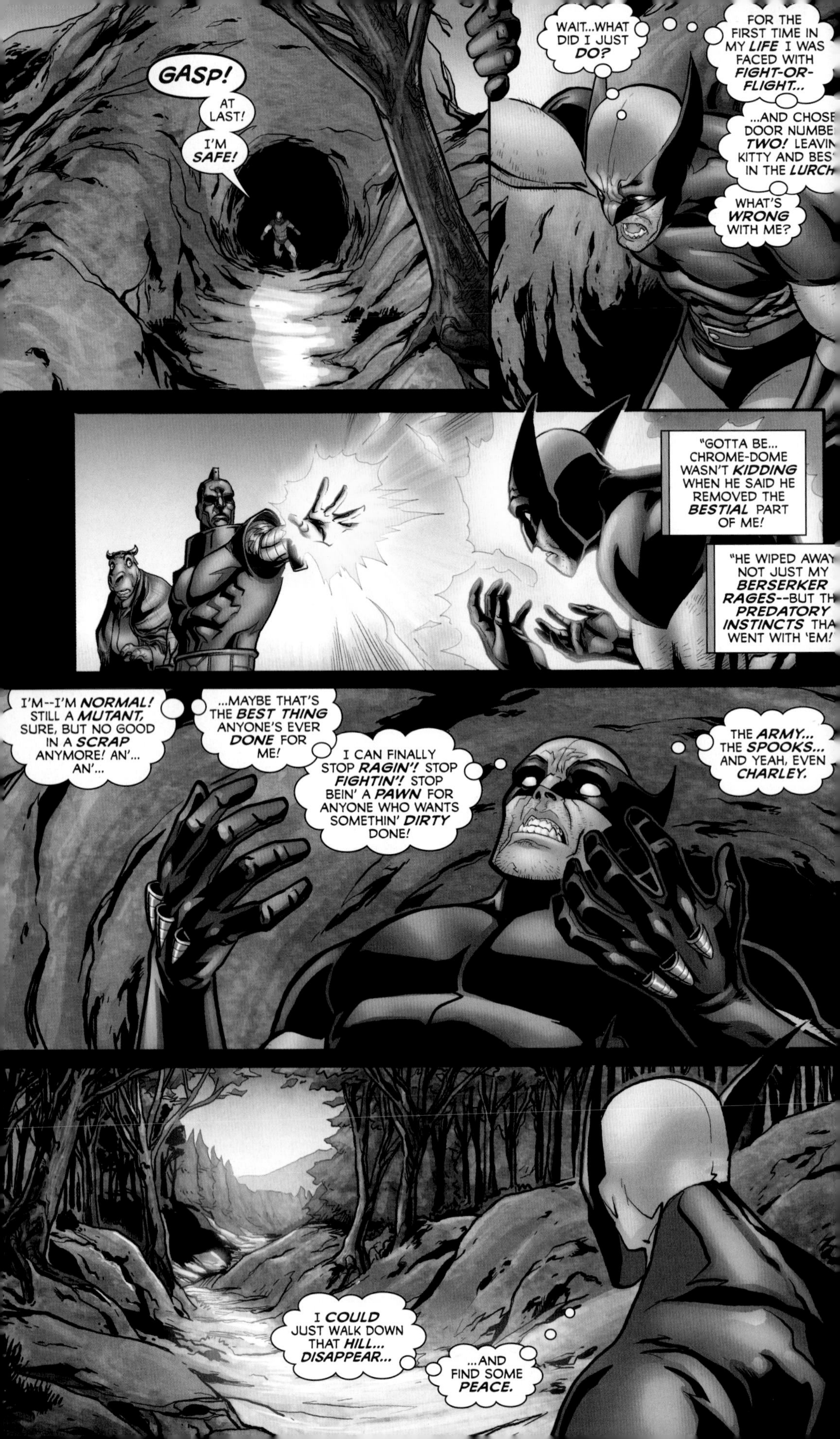
GASP!
AT LAST!
I'M SAFE!
WAIT...WHAT DID I JUST DO?
FOR THE FIRST TIME IN MY LIFE I WAS FACED WITH FIGHT-OR-FLIGHT...
...AND CHOSE DOOR NUMBE TWO! LEAVIN KITTY AND BES IN THE LURCH
WHAT'S WRONG WITH ME?
"GOTTA BE... CHROME-DOME WASN'T KIDDING WHEN HE SAID HE REMOVED THE BESTIAL PART OF ME!
"HE WIPED AWAY NOT JUST MY BERSERKER RAGES--BUT TH PREDATORY INSTINCTS THA WENT WITH 'EM!
I'M--I'M NORMAL! STILL A MUTANT, SURE, BUT NO GOOD IN A SCRAP ANYMORE! AN'... AN'...
...MAYBE THAT'S THE BEST THING ANYONE'S EVER DONE FOR ME!
I CAN FINALLY STOP RAGIN'! STOP FIGHTIN'! STOP BEIN' A PAWN FOR ANYONE WHO WANTS SOMETHIN' DIRTY DONE!
THE ARMY... THE SPOOKS... AND YEAH, EVEN CHARLEY.
I COULD JUST WALK DOWN THAT HILL... DISAPPEAR...
...AND FIND SOME PEACE.

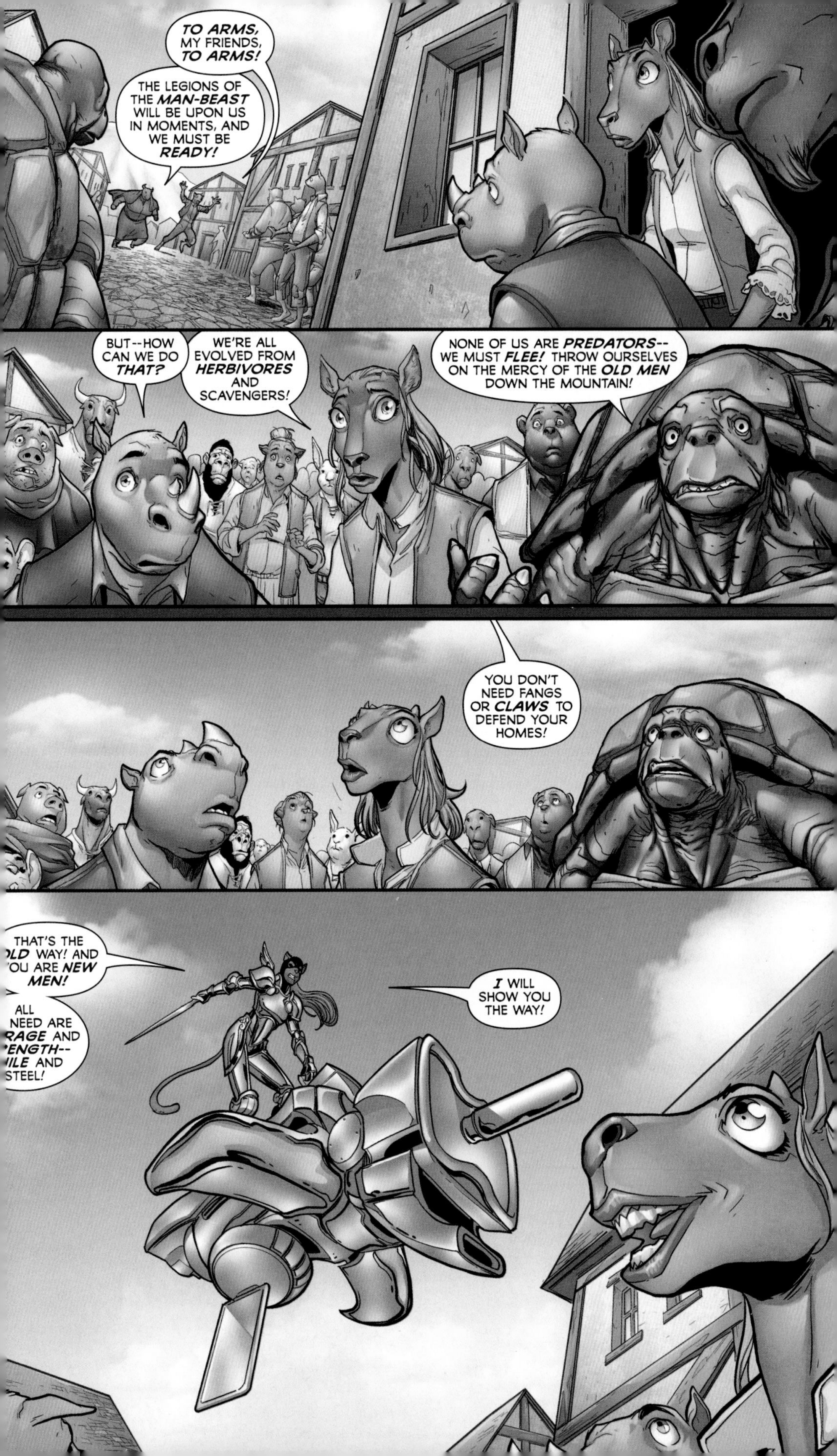
TO ARMS, MY FRIENDS, TO ARMS!
THE LEGIONS OF THE MAN-BEAST WILL BE UPON US IN MOMENTS, AND WE MUST BE READY!
BUT--HOW CAN WE DO THAT?
WE'RE ALL EVOLVED FROM HERBIVORES AND SCAVENGERS!
NONE OF US ARE PREDATORS-- WE MUST FLEE! THROW OURSELVES ON THE MERCY OF THE OLD MEN DOWN THE MOUNTAIN!
YOU DON'T NEED FANGS OR CLAWS TO DEFEND YOUR HOMES!
THAT'S THE LD WAY! AND OU ARE NEW MEN!
ALL NEED ARE RAGE AND ENGTH-- ILE AND STEEL!
I WILL SHOW YOU THE WAY!

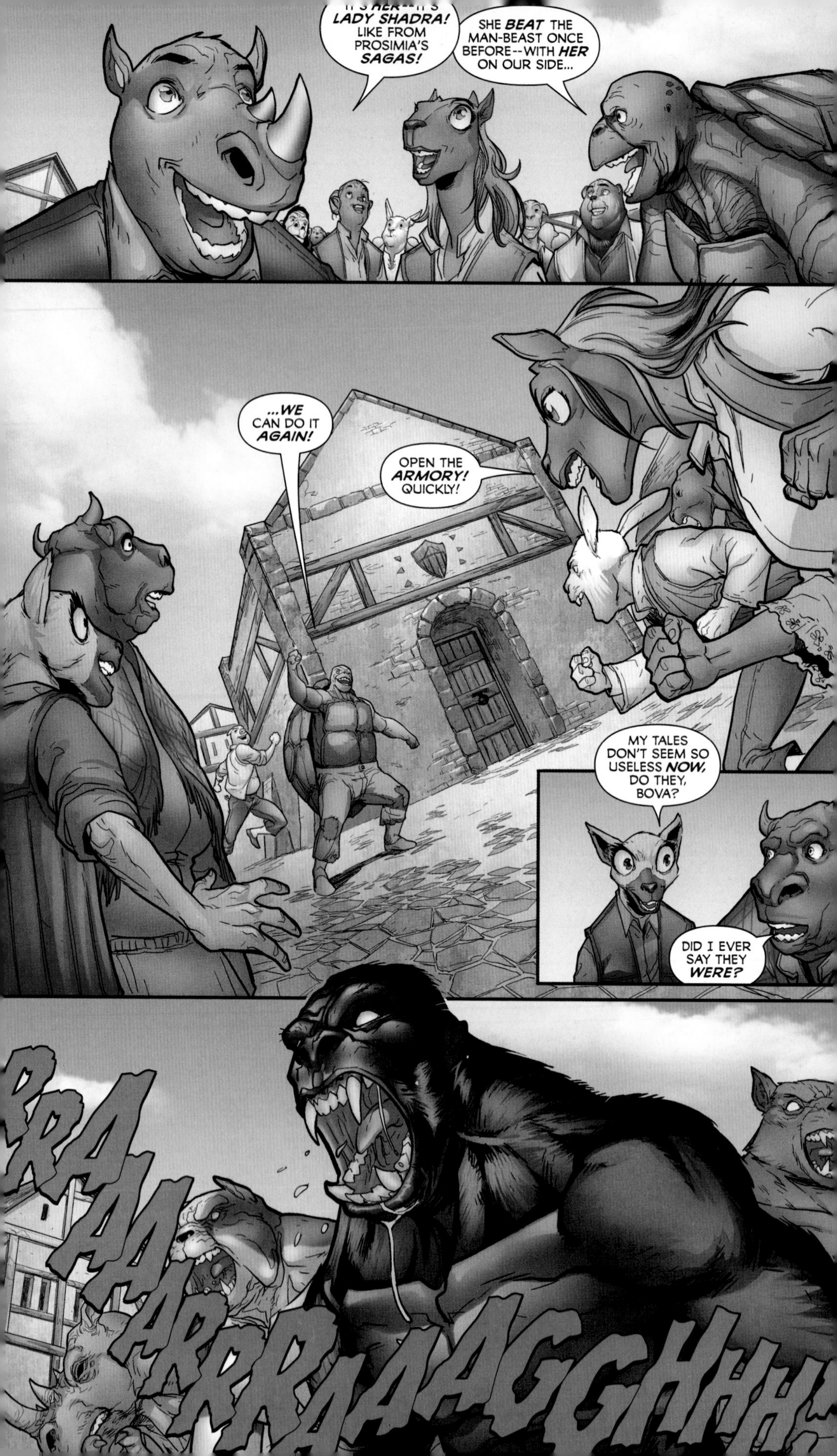
LADY SHADRA! LIKE FROM PROSIMIA'S SAGAS!
SHE BEAT THE MAN-BEAST ONCE BEFORE--WITH HER ON OUR SIDE...
...WE CAN DO IT AGAIN!
OPEN THE ARMORY! QUICKLY!
MY TALES DON'T SEEM SO USELESS NOW, DO THEY, BOVA?
DID I EVER SAY THEY WERE?
RRAAAARRRAAAGHHH

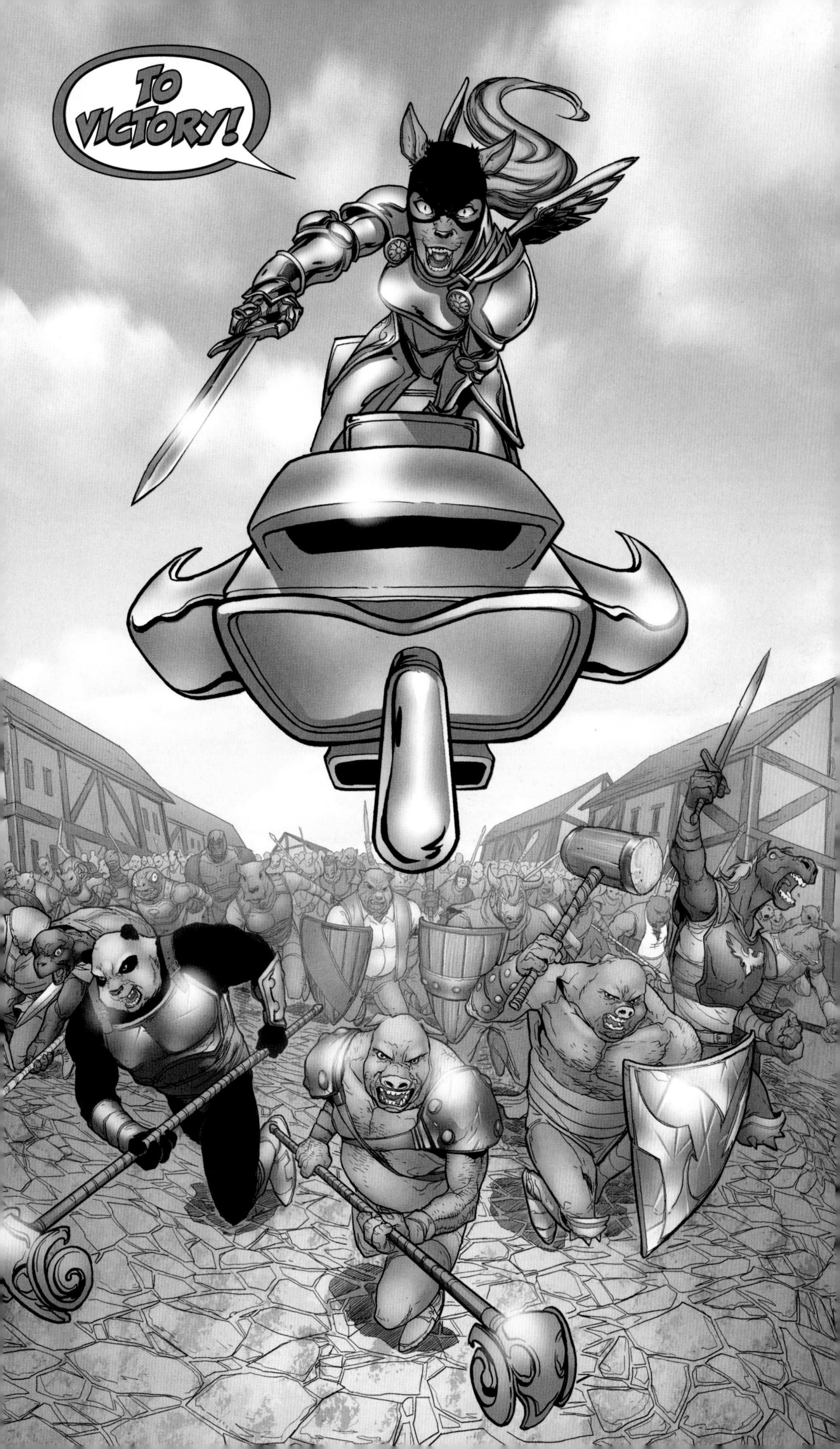
TO VICTORY!

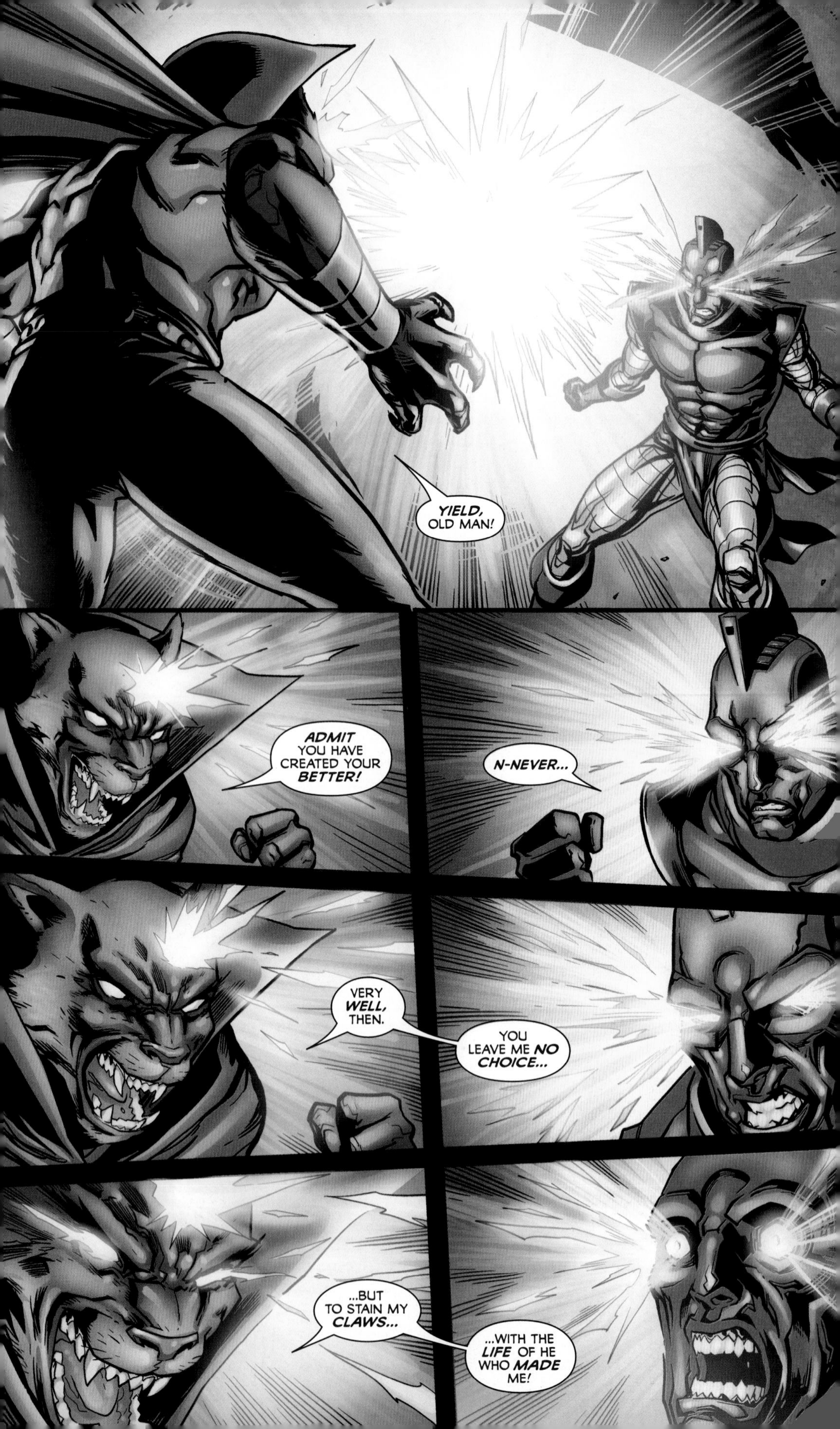
YIELD, OLD MAN!
ADMIT YOU HAVE CREATED YOUR BETTER!
N-NEVER...
VERY WELL, THEN.
YOU LEAVE ME NO CHOICE...
...BUT TO STAIN MY CLAWS...
...WITH THE LIFE OF HE WHO MADE ME!

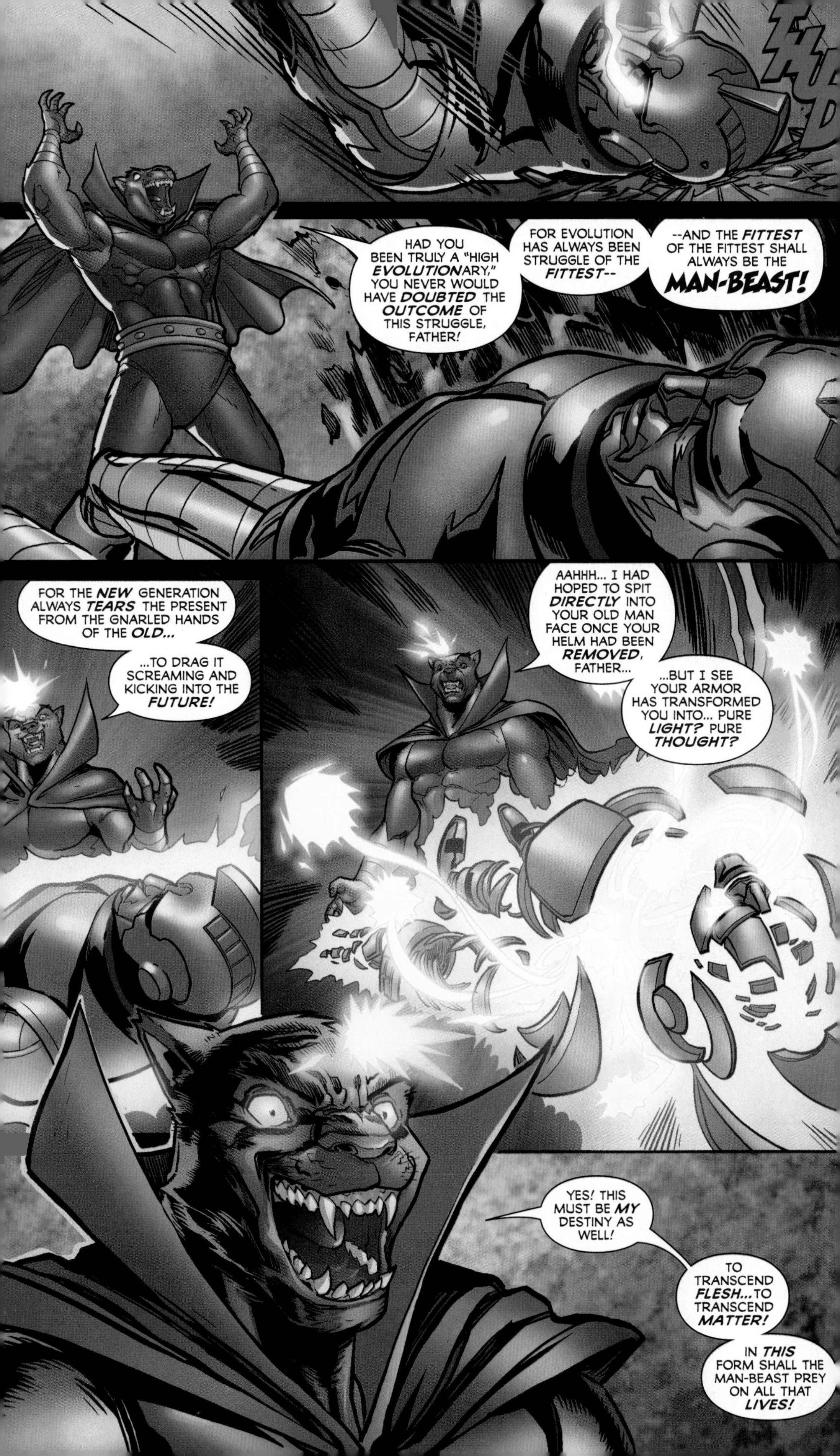
THUD
HAD YOU BEEN TRULY A "HIGH EVOLUTIONARY," YOU NEVER WOULD HAVE DOUBTED THE OUTCOME OF THIS STRUGGLE, FATHER!
FOR EVOLUTION HAS ALWAYS BEEN STRUGGLE OF THE FITTEST--
--AND THE FITTEST OF THE FITTEST SHALL ALWAYS BE THE MAN-BEAST!
FOR THE NEW GENERATION ALWAYS TEARS THE PRESENT FROM THE GNARLED HANDS OF THE OLD...
...TO DRAG IT SCREAMING AND KICKING INTO THE FUTURE!
AAHHH... I HAD HOPED TO SPIT DIRECTLY INTO YOUR OLD MAN FACE ONCE YOUR HELM HAD BEEN REMOVED, FATHER...
...BUT I SEE YOUR ARMOR HAS TRANSFORMED YOU INTO... PURE LIGHT? PURE THOUGHT?
YES! THIS MUST BE MY DESTINY AS WELL!
TO TRANSCEND FLESH...TO TRANSCEND MATTER!
IN THIS FORM SHALL THE MAN-BEAST PREY ON ALL THAT LIVES!

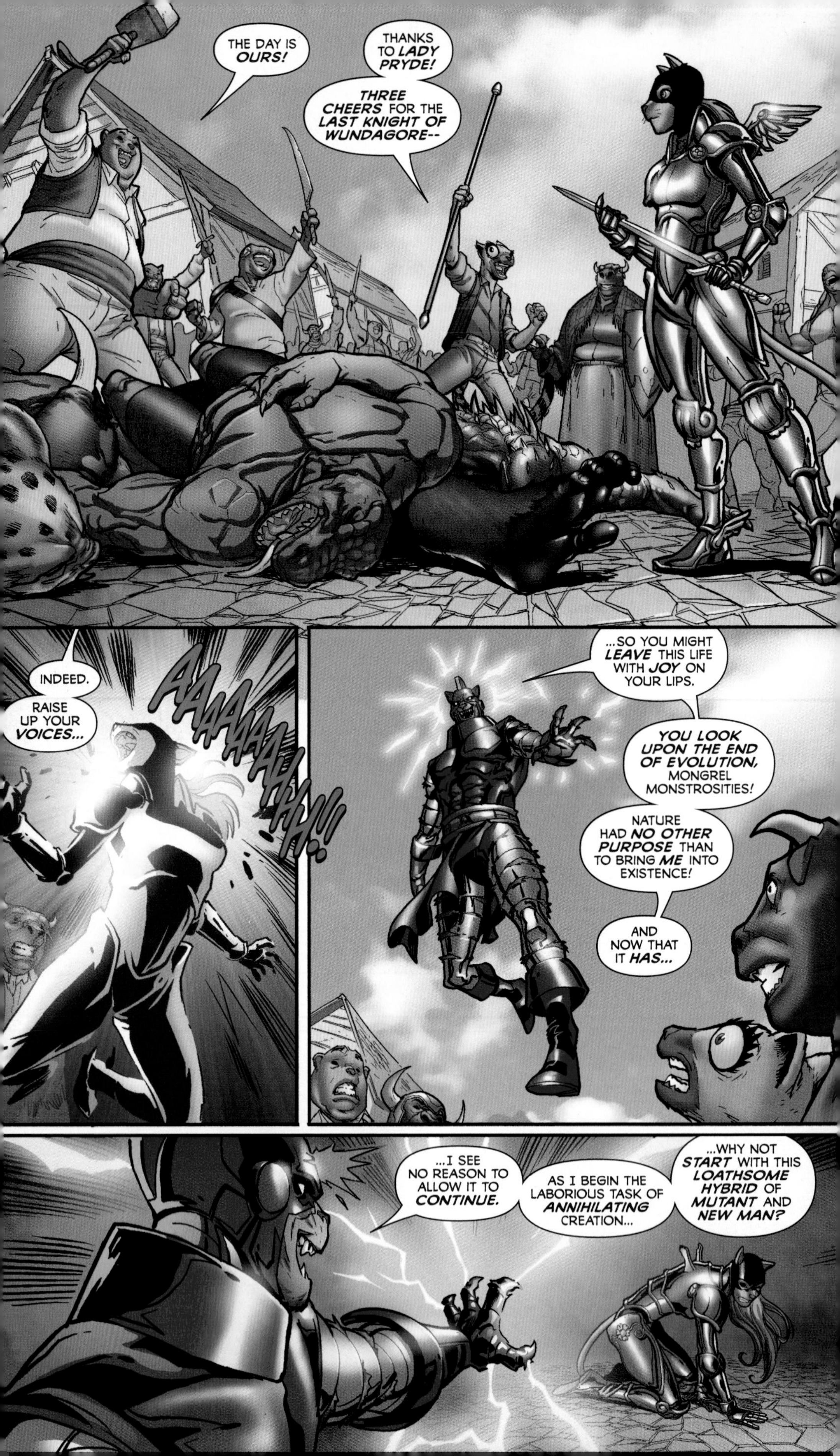
THE DAY IS OURS!
THANKS TO LADY PRYDE!
THREE CHEERS FOR THE LAST KNIGHT OF WUNDAGORE--
INDEED.
RAISE UP YOUR VOICES...
AAAAAAAAHH!!
...SO YOU MIGHT LEAVE THIS LIFE WITH JOY ON YOUR LIPS.
YOU LOOK UPON THE END OF EVOLUTION, MONGREL MONSTROSITIES!
NATURE HAD NO OTHER PURPOSE THAN TO BRING ME INTO EXISTENCE!
AND NOW THAT IT HAS...
...I SEE NO REASON TO ALLOW IT TO CONTINUE.
AS I BEGIN THE LABORIOUS TASK OF ANNIHILATING CREATION...
...WHY NOT START WITH THIS LOATHSOME HYBRID OF MUTANT AND NEW MAN?

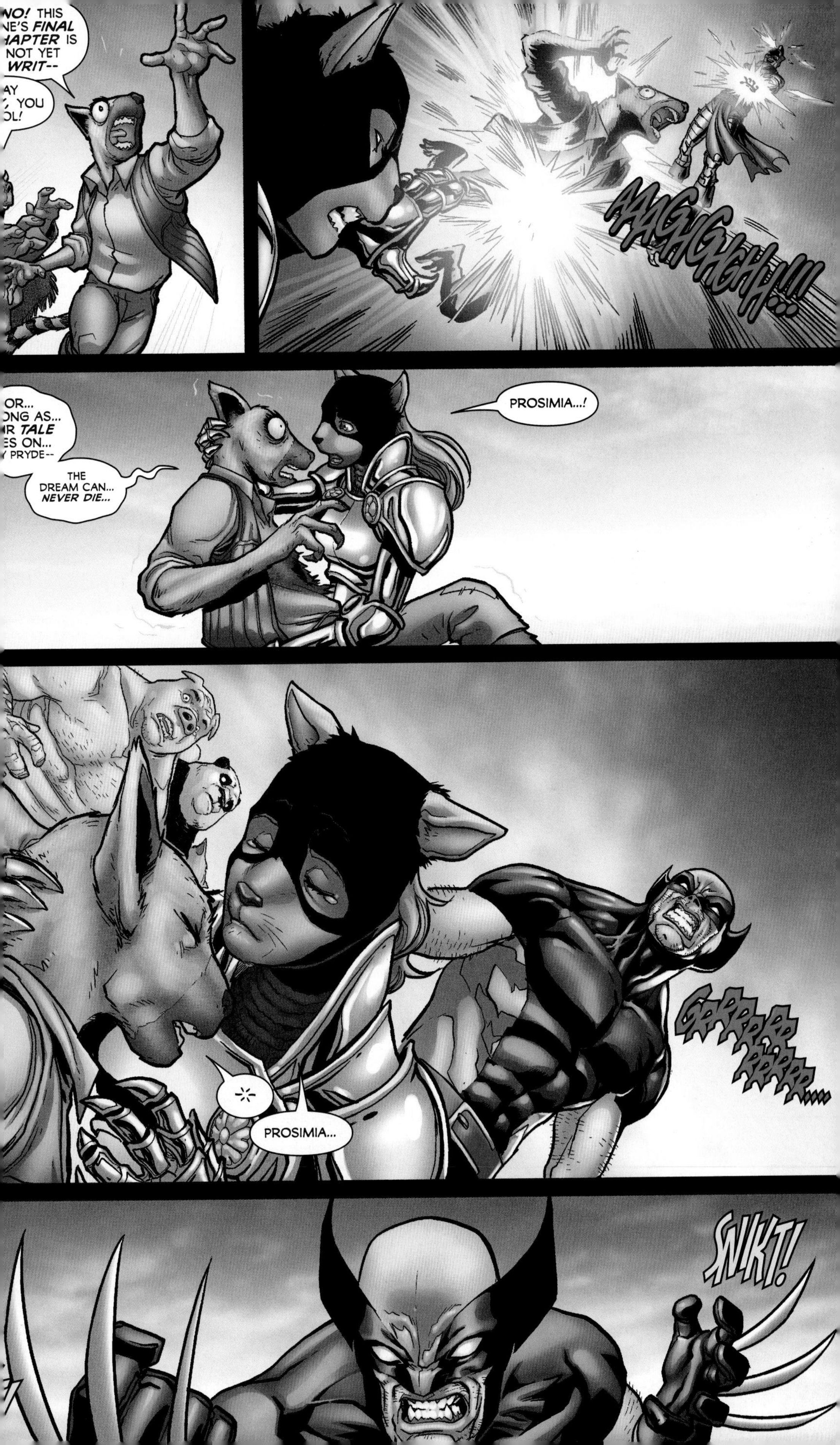
NO! THIS NE'S FINAL HAPTER IS NOT YET WRIT--
AY , YOU OL!
AAAGHGHGHH!!!
OR... ONG AS... R TALE ES ON... Y PRYDE--
THE DREAM CAN... NEVER DIE...
PROSIMIA...!
GRRRRRR RRRRR....
PROSIMIA...
SNIKT!

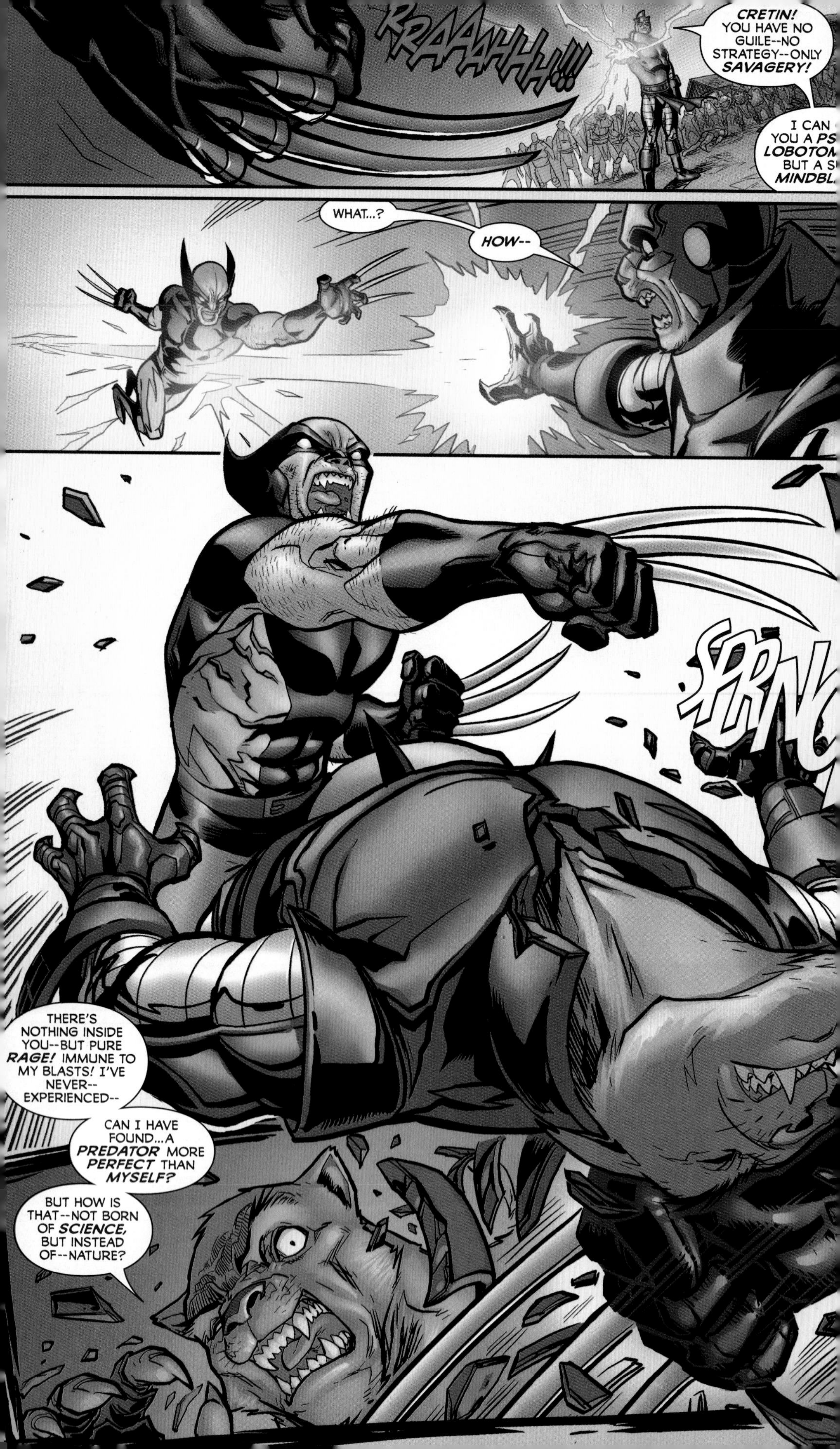

KRAAAHHH!!!
CRETIN! YOU HAVE NO GUILE--NO STRATEGY--ONLY SAVAGERY!
WHAT...?
HOW--
SPRNG
THERE'S NOTHING INSIDE YOU--BUT PURE RAGE! IMMUNE TO MY BLASTS! I'VE NEVER--EXPERIENCED--
CAN I HAVE FOUND...A PREDATOR MORE PERFECT THAN MYSELF?
BUT HOW IS THAT--NOT BORN OF SCIENCE, BUT INSTEAD OF--NATURE?

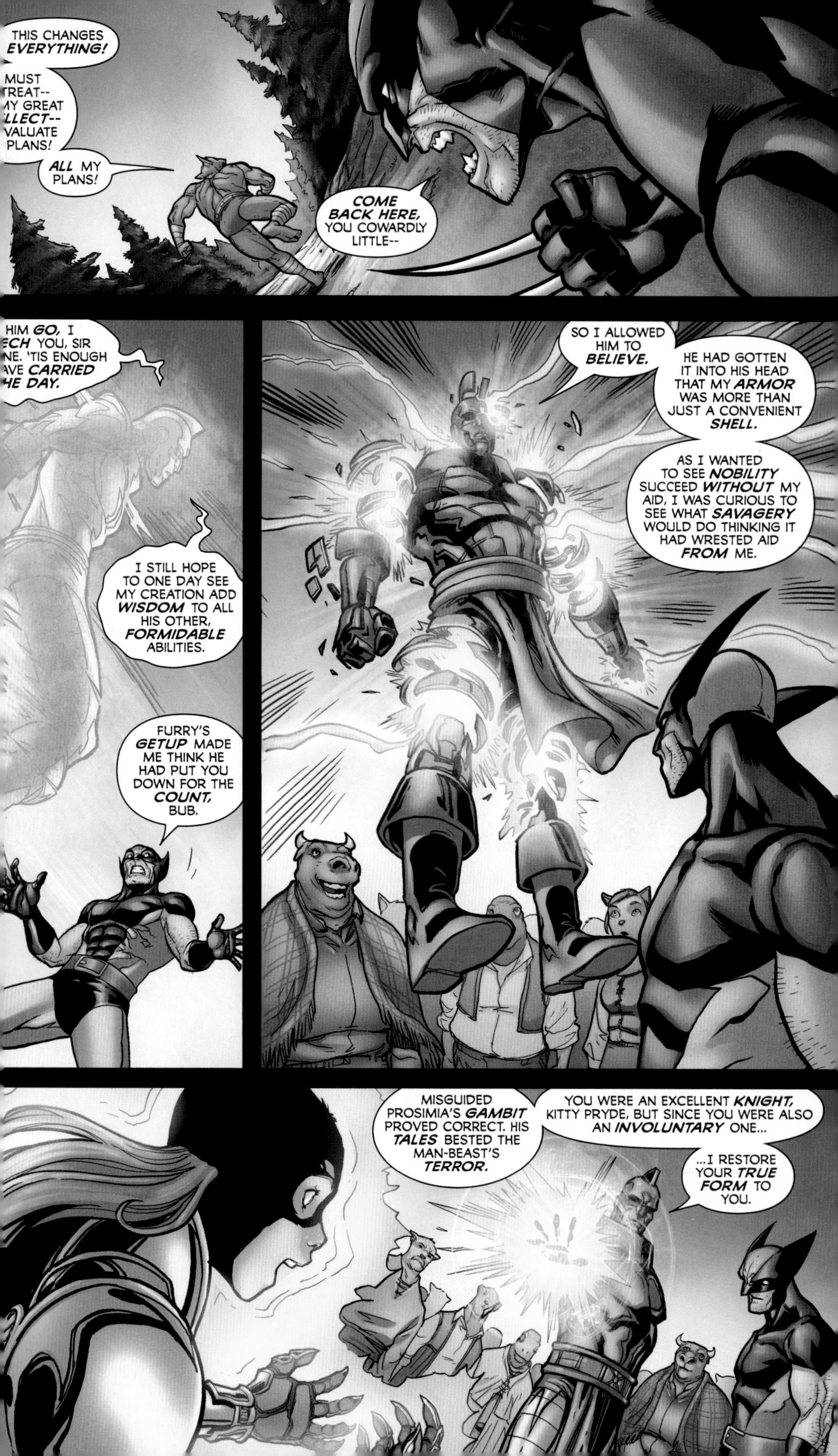
THIS CHANGES EVERYTHING!
MUST TREAT-- MY GREAT LLECT-- VALUATE PLANS!
ALL MY PLANS!
COME BACK HERE, YOU COWARDLY LITTLE--
HIM GO, I ECH YOU, SIR NE. 'TIS ENOUGH AVE CARRIED HE DAY.
I STILL HOPE TO ONE DAY SEE MY CREATION ADD WISDOM TO ALL HIS OTHER, FORMIDABLE ABILITIES.
FURRY'S GETUP MADE ME THINK HE HAD PUT YOU DOWN FOR THE COUNT, BUB.
SO I ALLOWED HIM TO BELIEVE.
HE HAD GOTTEN IT INTO HIS HEAD THAT MY ARMOR WAS MORE THAN JUST A CONVENIENT SHELL.
AS I WANTED TO SEE NOBILITY SUCCEED WITHOUT MY AID, I WAS CURIOUS TO SEE WHAT SAVAGERY WOULD DO THINKING IT HAD WRESTED AID FROM ME.
MISGUIDED PROSIMIA'S GAMBIT PROVED CORRECT. HIS TALES BESTED THE MAN-BEAST'S TERROR.
YOU WERE AN EXCELLENT KNIGHT, KITTY PRYDE, BUT SINCE YOU WERE ALSO AN INVOLUNTARY ONE...
...I RESTORE YOUR TRUE FORM TO YOU.

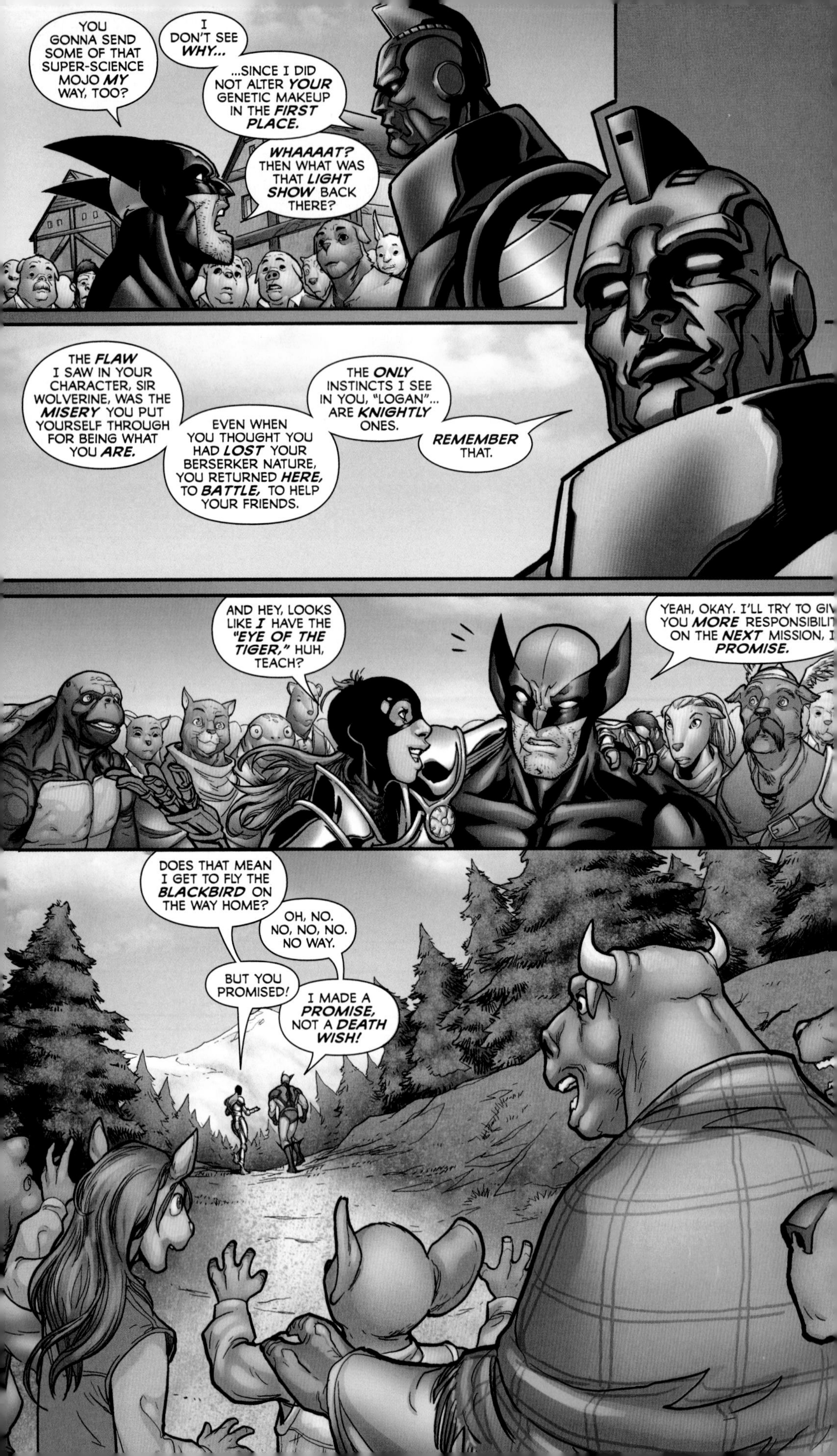
YOU GONNA SEND SOME OF THAT SUPER-SCIENCE MOJO *MY* WAY, TOO?
I DON'T SEE *WHY...*
...SINCE I DID NOT ALTER *YOUR* GENETIC MAKEUP IN THE *FIRST PLACE.*
WHAAAAT? THEN WHAT WAS THAT *LIGHT SHOW* BACK THERE?
THE *FLAW* I SAW IN YOUR CHARACTER, SIR WOLVERINE, WAS THE *MISERY* YOU PUT YOURSELF THROUGH FOR BEING WHAT YOU *ARE.*
EVEN WHEN YOU THOUGHT YOU HAD *LOST* YOUR BERSERKER NATURE, YOU RETURNED *HERE,* TO *BATTLE,* TO HELP YOUR FRIENDS.
THE *ONLY* INSTINCTS I SEE IN YOU, "LOGAN"... ARE *KNIGHTLY* ONES.
REMEMBER THAT.
AND HEY, LOOKS LIKE *I* HAVE THE *"EYE OF THE TIGER,"* HUH, TEACH?
YEAH, OKAY. I'LL TRY TO GIV YOU *MORE* RESPONSIBILIT ON THE *NEXT* MISSION, I *PROMISE.*
DOES THAT MEAN I GET TO FLY THE *BLACKBIRD* ON THE WAY HOME?
OH, NO. NO, NO, NO. NO WAY.
BUT YOU PROMISED!
I MADE A *PROMISE,* NOT A *DEATH WISH!*

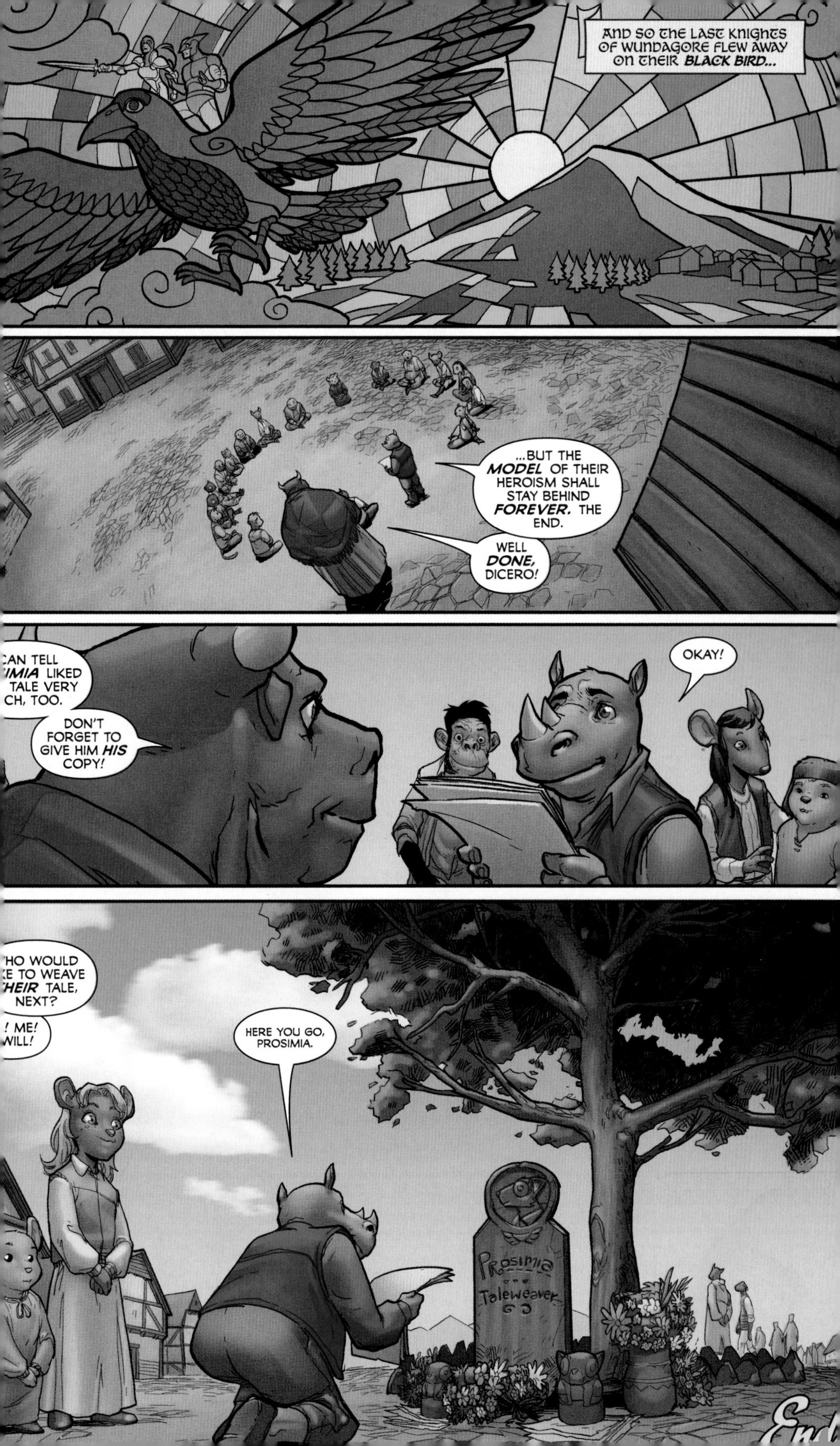
AND SO THE LAST KNIGHTS OF WUNDAGORE FLEW AWAY ON THEIR BLACK BIRD...
...BUT THE MODEL OF THEIR HEROISM SHALL STAY BEHIND FOREVER. THE END.
WELL DONE, DICERO!
CAN TELL
IMIA LIKED
TALE VERY
CH, TOO.
DON'T FORGET TO GIVE HIM HIS COPY!
OKAY!
HO WOULD
E TO WEAVE
THEIR TALE,
NEXT?
! ME!
WILL!
HERE YOU GO, PROSIMIA.
Prosimia
Taleweaver

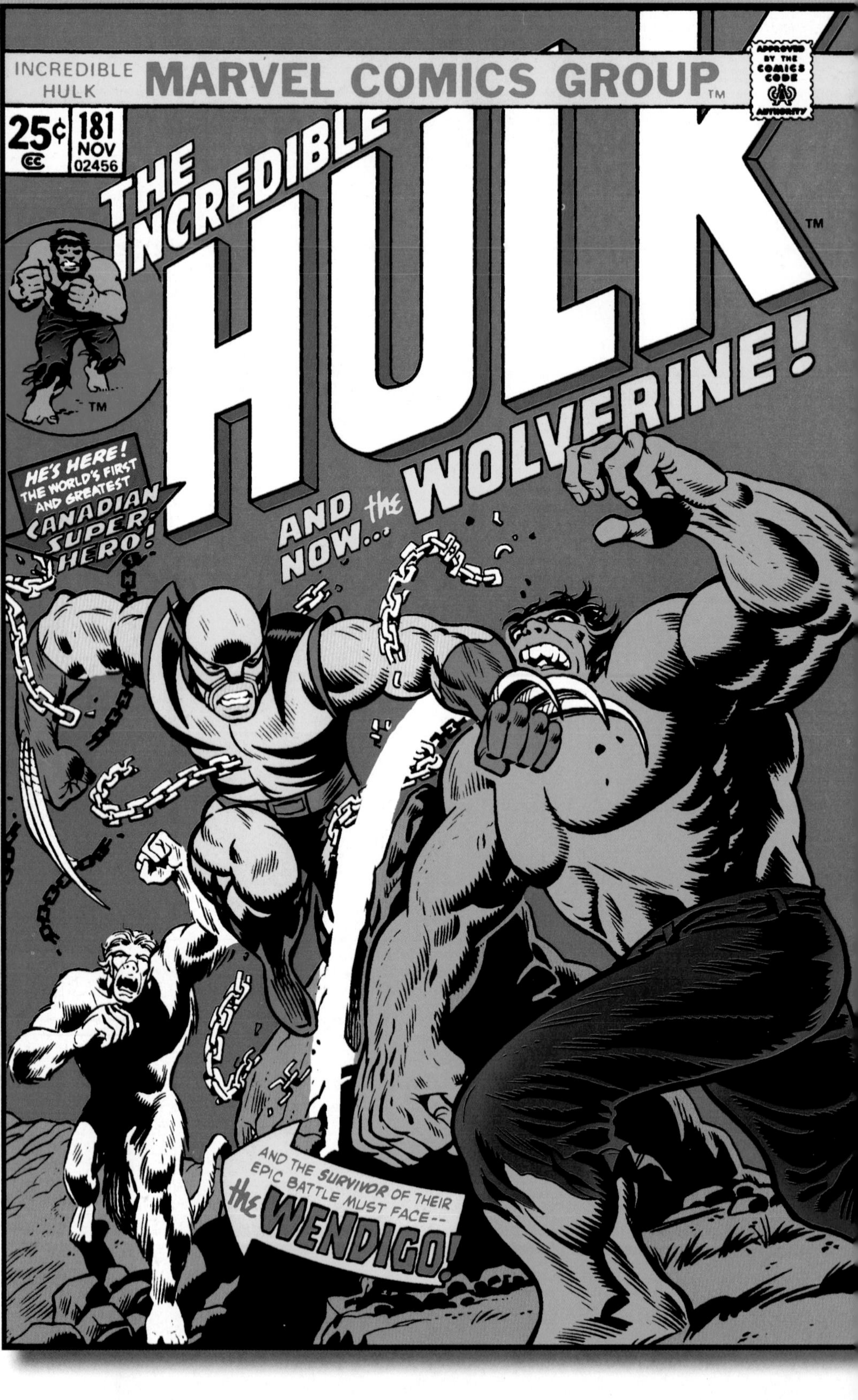
INCREDIBLE HULK
MARVEL COMICS GROUP
APPROVED BY THE COMICS CODE AUTHORITY
25¢
181 NOV
02456
THE INCREDIBLE HULK
HE'S HERE! THE WORLD'S FIRST AND GREATEST CANADIAN SUPER-HERO!
AND NOW... the WOLVERINE!
AND THE SURVIVOR OF THEIR EPIC BATTLE MUST FACE-- the WENDIGO!

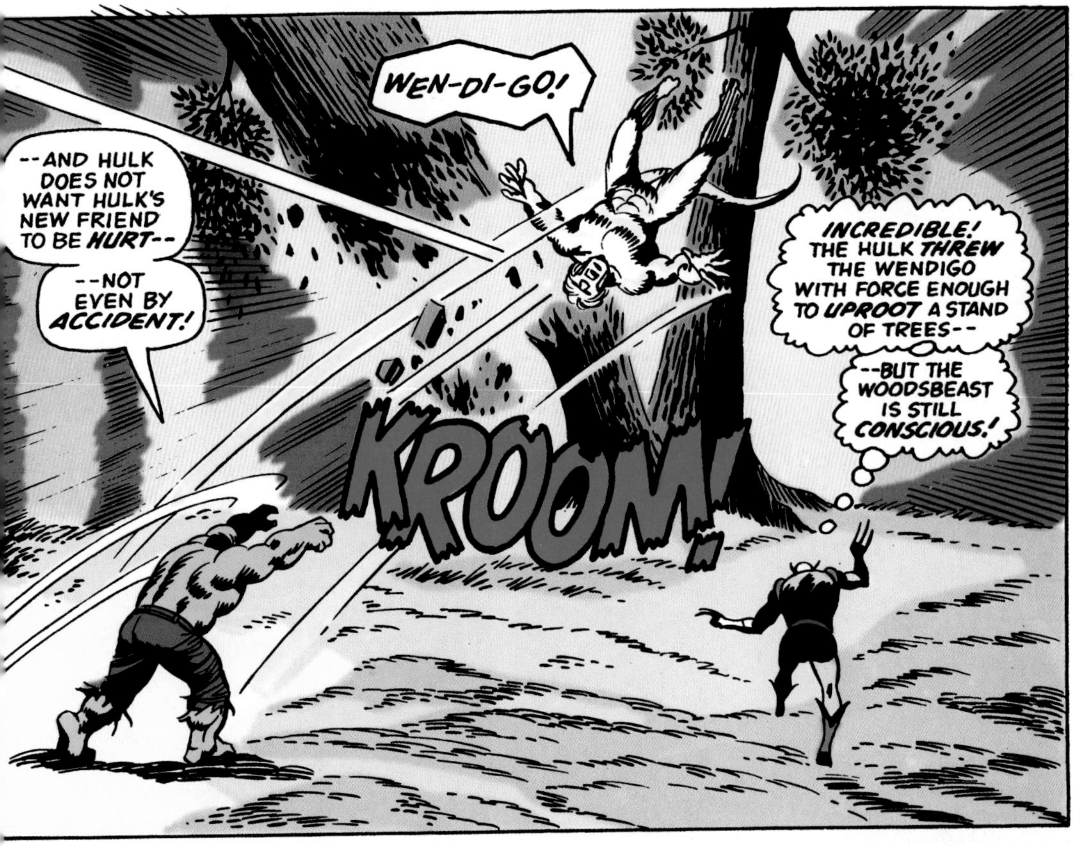
WEN-DI-GO!
--AND HULK DOES NOT WANT HULK'S NEW FRIEND TO BE HURT--
--NOT EVEN BY ACCIDENT!
INCREDIBLE! THE HULK THREW THE WENDIGO WITH FORCE ENOUGH TO UPROOT A STAND OF TREES--
--BUT THE WOODSBEAST IS STILL CONSCIOUS!
KROOM!

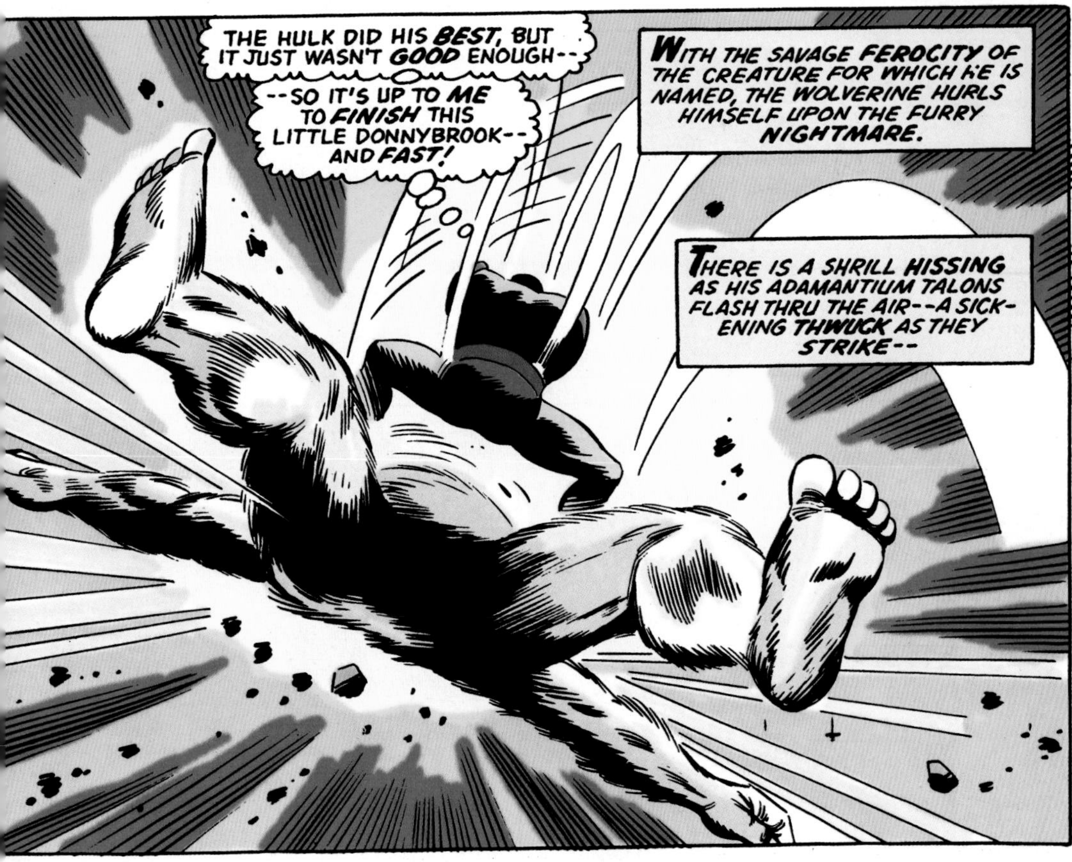
THE HULK DID HIS BEST, BUT IT JUST WASN'T GOOD ENOUGH--
--SO IT'S UP TO ME TO FINISH THIS LITTLE DONNYBROOK--AND FAST!
WITH THE SAVAGE FEROCITY OF THE CREATURE FOR WHICH HE IS NAMED, THE WOLVERINE HURLS HIMSELF UPON THE FURRY NIGHTMARE.
THERE IS A SHRILL HISSING AS HIS ADAMANTIUM TALONS FLASH THRU THE AIR--A SICKENING THWUCK AS THEY STRIKE--

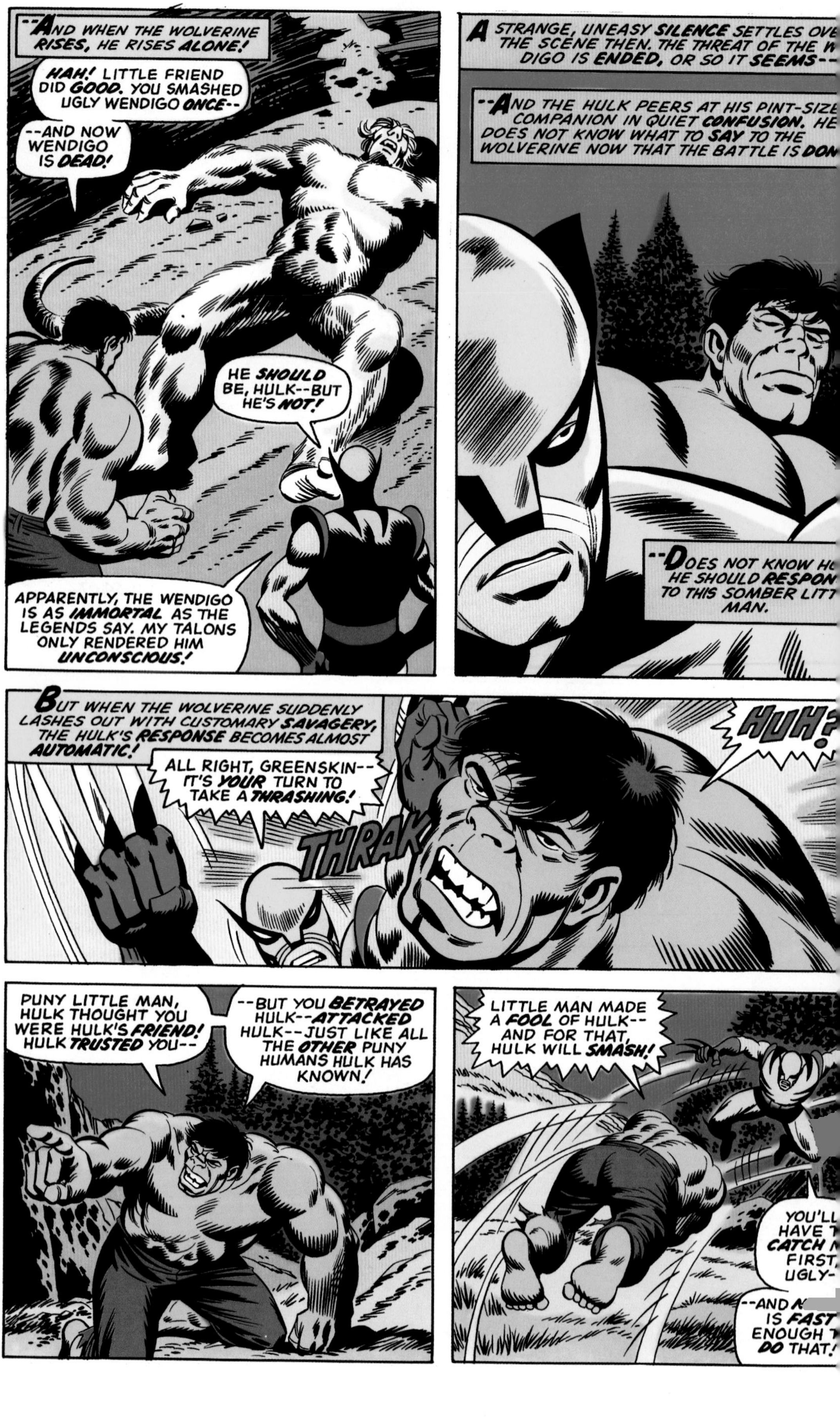
--AND WHEN THE WOLVERINE RISES, HE RISES ALONE!
HAH! LITTLE FRIEND DID GOOD. YOU SMASHED UGLY WENDIGO ONCE--
--AND NOW WENDIGO IS DEAD!
HE SHOULD BE, HULK--BUT HE'S NOT!
APPARENTLY, THE WENDIGO IS AS IMMORTAL AS THE LEGENDS SAY. MY TALONS ONLY RENDERED HIM UNCONSCIOUS!
A STRANGE, UNEASY SILENCE SETTLES OVE THE SCENE THEN. THE THREAT OF THE W DIGO IS ENDED, OR SO IT SEEMS--
--AND THE HULK PEERS AT HIS PINT-SIZE COMPANION IN QUIET CONFUSION. HE DOES NOT KNOW WHAT TO SAY TO THE WOLVERINE NOW THAT THE BATTLE IS DON
--DOES NOT KNOW H HE SHOULD RESPON TO THIS SOMBER LITT MAN.
BUT WHEN THE WOLVERINE SUDDENLY LASHES OUT WITH CUSTOMARY SAVAGERY, THE HULK'S RESPONSE BECOMES ALMOST AUTOMATIC!
ALL RIGHT, GREENSKIN-- IT'S YOUR TURN TO TAKE A THRASHING!
HUH?
THRAK
PUNY LITTLE MAN, HULK THOUGHT YOU WERE HULK'S FRIEND! HULK TRUSTED YOU--
--BUT YOU BETRAYED HULK--ATTACKED HULK--JUST LIKE ALL THE OTHER PUNY HUMANS HULK HAS KNOWN!
LITTLE MAN MADE A FOOL OF HULK-- AND FOR THAT, HULK WILL SMASH!
YOU'LL HAVE T CATCH M FIRST, UGLY-
--AND N IS FAST ENOUGH T DO THAT!

HIDDEN IN THE PRE-DAWN SHADOWS NEAR AN UNCOMFORTABLE *GEORGES BAPTISTE*, A GRIM *MARIE CARTIER*--THE GIRL WHO LURED THE HULK TO QUEBEC--WATCH THE RAGING BATTLE WITH A MIXTURE OF *HORROR* AND ANXIOUS *ANTICIPATION.*

THERE, MARIE. DO YOU SEE WHAT YOUR *MADNESS* HAS *WROUGHT?* YOUR BROTHER HAS *FALLEN*--PERHAPS MORTALLY *WOUNDED*--AND IT IS ALL *YOUR* FAULT!

NONSENSE, GEORGES--EVERY-THING GOES EVEN *BETTER* THAN EXPECTED!

THE WENDIGO CAN'T BE *HARMED*--YOU *KNOW* THAT.

THE HULK AND THE ONE CALLED *WOLVERINE* MERELY SAVED US THE TASK OF *OVERCOMING* PAUL ALL BY OURSELVES!

NOW *QUICKLY*--WHILE THEY'RE STILL *DIS-TRACTED*--HELP ME *CARRY* PAUL'S BODY INSIDE.

THE SOONER THINGS ARE *PREPARED*, THE SOONER WE'LL BE READY TO BEGIN THE *TRANSFORMA-TION!*

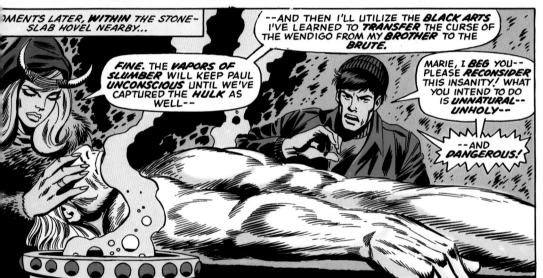

MOMENTS LATER, *WITHIN* THE STONE-SLAB HOVEL NEARBY...

FINE. THE *VAPORS OF SLUMBER* WILL KEEP PAUL *UNCONSCIOUS* UNTIL WE'VE CAPTURED THE *HULK* AS WELL--

--AND THEN I'LL UTILIZE THE *BLACK ARTS* I'VE LEARNED TO *TRANSFER* THE CURSE OF THE WENDIGO FROM MY *BROTHER* TO THE *BRUTE.*

MARIE, I *BEG* YOU-- PLEASE *RECONSIDER* THIS INSANITY! WHAT YOU INTEND TO DO IS *UNNATURAL*-- UNHOLY--

--AND *DANGEROUS!*

OUTSIDE, THE JADE-HUED JUGGERNAUT FIGHTS ON, *UNAWARE* OF THE TERRIBLE *FATE* THE MANIACALLY OBSESSED GIRL HAS PLANNED FOR HIM--

--*U*NAWARE OF THE GOLD-AND-CRIMSON *SPLENDOR* SPREAD ACROSS HIS BATTLE-FIELD BY THE SWIFTLY RISING *SUN*--

--*A* SUN ALSO RISING BEHIND A SECRET CANADIAN *MILITARY COM-PLEX* NESTLED DEEP IN THE SHELTERING HILLS NOT TOO VERY FAR *AWAY.*

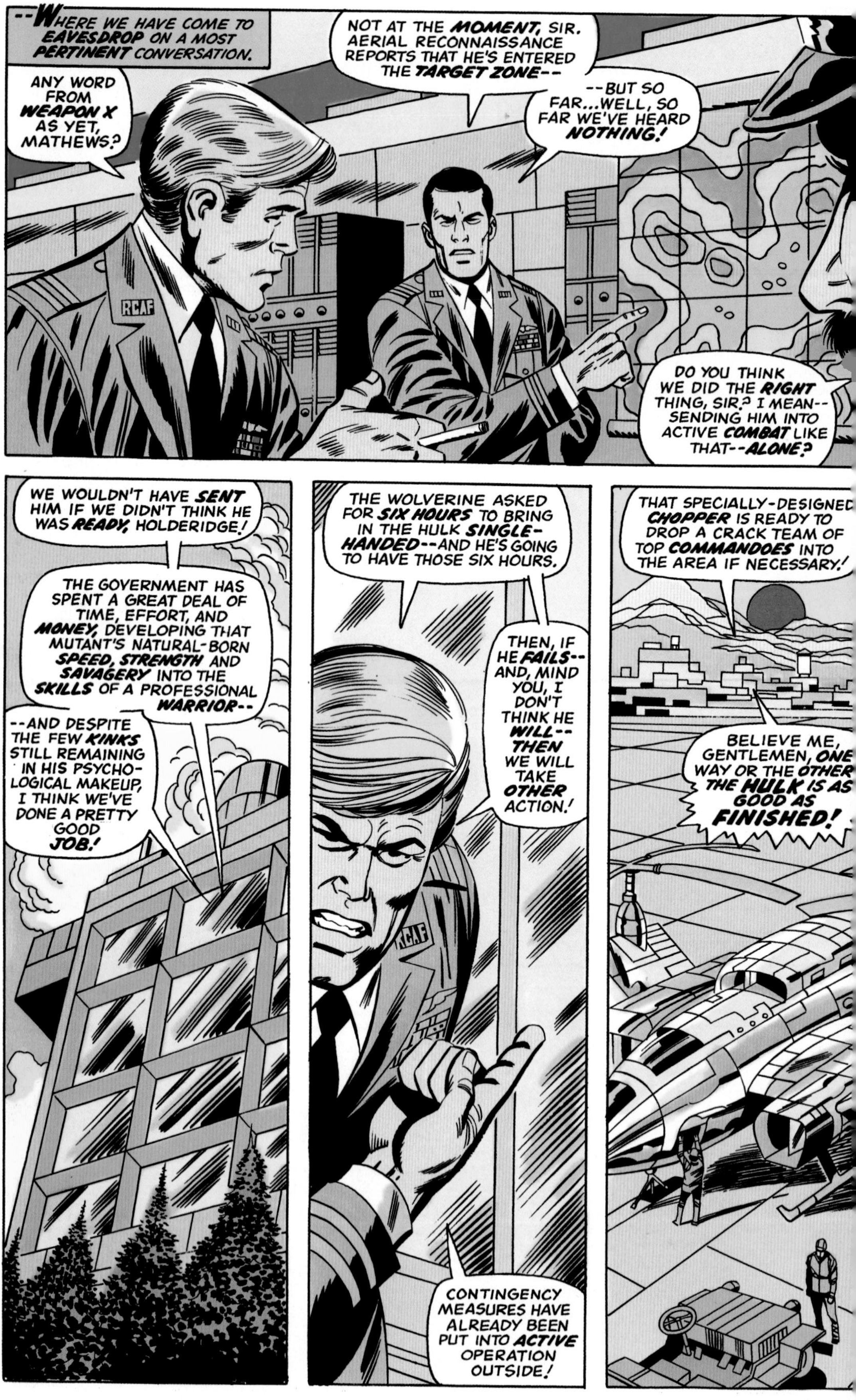
--WHERE WE HAVE COME TO EAVESDROP ON A MOST PERTINENT CONVERSATION.
ANY WORD FROM WEAPON X AS YET, MATHEWS?
NOT AT THE MOMENT, SIR. AERIAL RECONNAISSANCE REPORTS THAT HE'S ENTERED THE TARGET ZONE--
--BUT SO FAR...WELL, SO FAR WE'VE HEARD NOTHING!
DO YOU THINK WE DID THE RIGHT THING, SIR? I MEAN--SENDING HIM INTO ACTIVE COMBAT LIKE THAT--ALONE?
WE WOULDN'T HAVE SENT HIM IF WE DIDN'T THINK HE WAS READY, HOLDERIDGE!
THE GOVERNMENT HAS SPENT A GREAT DEAL OF TIME, EFFORT, AND MONEY, DEVELOPING THAT MUTANT'S NATURAL-BORN SPEED, STRENGTH AND SAVAGERY INTO THE SKILLS OF A PROFESSIONAL WARRIOR--
--AND DESPITE THE FEW KINKS STILL REMAINING IN HIS PSYCHOLOGICAL MAKEUP, I THINK WE'VE DONE A PRETTY GOOD JOB!
THE WOLVERINE ASKED FOR SIX HOURS TO BRING IN THE HULK SINGLE-HANDED--AND HE'S GOING TO HAVE THOSE SIX HOURS.
THEN, IF HE FAILS--AND, MIND YOU, I DON'T THINK HE WILL--THEN WE WILL TAKE OTHER ACTION!
CONTINGENCY MEASURES HAVE ALREADY BEEN PUT INTO ACTIVE OPERATION OUTSIDE!
THAT SPECIALLY-DESIGNED CHOPPER IS READY TO DROP A CRACK TEAM OF TOP COMMANDOES INTO THE AREA IF NECESSARY!
BELIEVE ME, GENTLEMEN, ONE WAY OR THE OTHER THE HULK IS AS GOOD AS FINISHED!

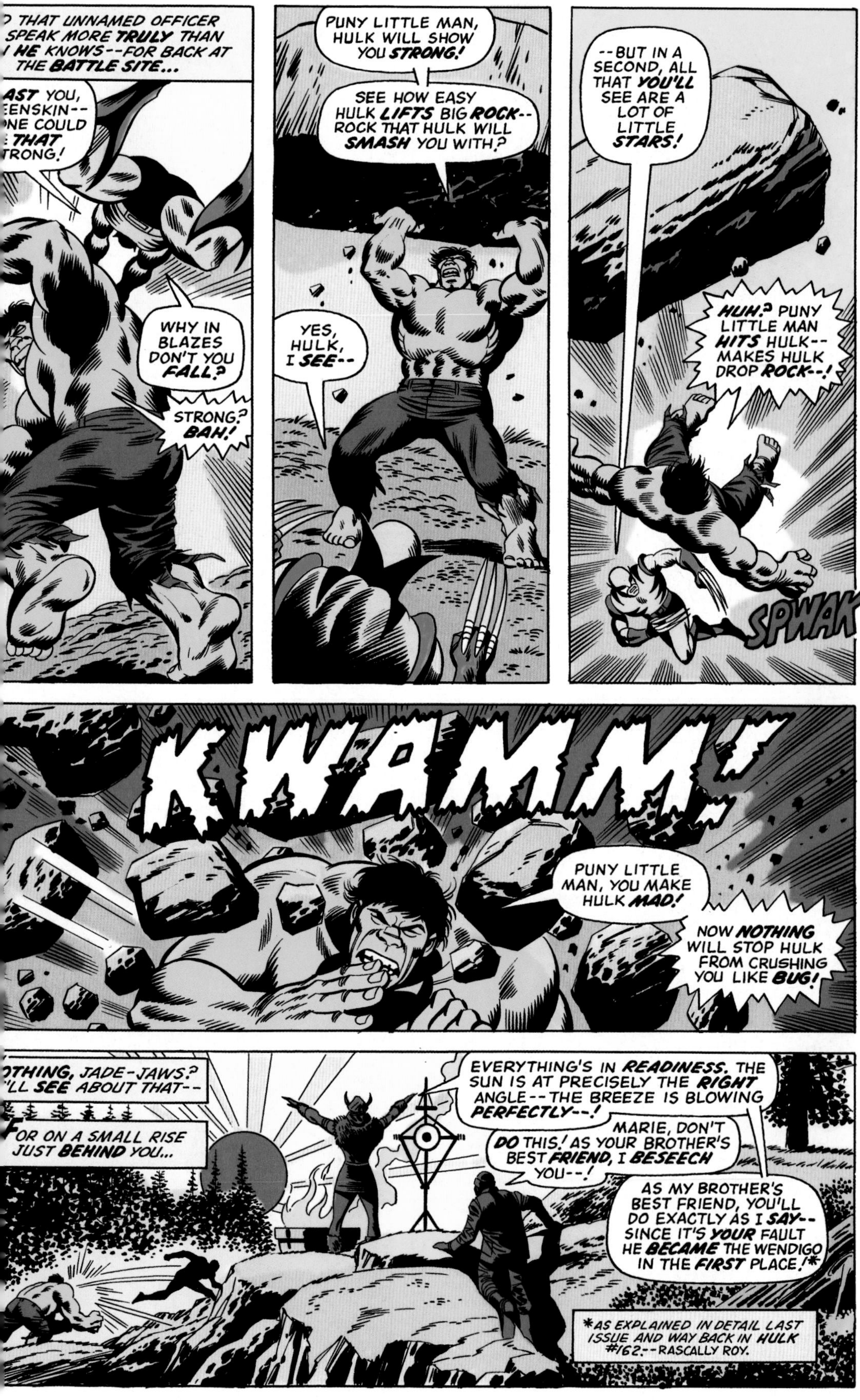

...D THAT UNNAMED OFFICER ...SPEAK MORE TRULY THAN ...HE KNOWS--FOR BACK AT THE BATTLE SITE...
...AST YOU, ...EENSKIN-- ...NE COULD ...THAT ...TRONG!
WHY IN BLAZES DON'T YOU FALL?
STRONG? BAH!
PUNY LITTLE MAN, HULK WILL SHOW YOU STRONG!
SEE HOW EASY HULK LIFTS BIG ROCK--ROCK THAT HULK WILL SMASH YOU WITH?
YES, HULK, I SEE--
--BUT IN A SECOND, ALL THAT YOU'LL SEE ARE A LOT OF LITTLE STARS!
HUH? PUNY LITTLE MAN HITS HULK--MAKES HULK DROP ROCK--!
SPWAK
KWAMM!
PUNY LITTLE MAN, YOU MAKE HULK MAD!
NOW NOTHING WILL STOP HULK FROM CRUSHING YOU LIKE BUG!
...OTHING, JADE-JAWS? ...'LL SEE ABOUT THAT--
FOR ON A SMALL RISE JUST BEHIND YOU...
EVERYTHING'S IN READINESS. THE SUN IS AT PRECISELY THE RIGHT ANGLE--THE BREEZE IS BLOWING PERFECTLY--!
MARIE, DON'T DO THIS! AS YOUR BROTHER'S BEST FRIEND, I BESEECH YOU--!
AS MY BROTHER'S BEST FRIEND, YOU'LL DO EXACTLY AS I SAY--SINCE IT'S YOUR FAULT HE BECAME THE WENDIGO IN THE FIRST PLACE!*
*AS EXPLAINED IN DETAIL LAST ISSUE AND WAY BACK IN HULK #162.--RASCALLY ROY.

NOW STAND ASIDE AS I PREPARE THE MYSTIC *SPELL OF SUBJUGATION*--

--OR *YOU* MAY BE CAUGHT IN ITS GRASP AS *WELL!*

WITH THAT, MARIE CARTIER TURNS HER FACE *SKYWARD*-- MUTTERS AN ARCANE *CHANT* BENEATH HER BREATH--

--*T*HEN POURS A DUSTY GRAY *PUMICE* FROM THE VIAL IN HER HAND.

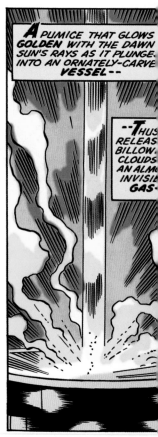

A PUMICE THAT GLOWS *GOLDEN* WITH THE DAWN SUN'S RAYS AS IT PLUNGE*S* INTO AN ORNATELY-CARVE*D VESSEL*--

--*T*HUS RELEAS*ING* BILLOW*ING* CLOUDS *OF* AN ALM*OST* INVISI*BLE GAS*--

--*A* GAS CARRIED DOWN THE RISE TO THE BATTLE- FIELD BELOW BY THE BRISK MORNING *BREEZE.*

*F*OR SEVERAL SECONDS, THE CONFLICT *CONTINUES,* UNMINDFUL OF THE ALL- PERVADING *MIST.*

*T*HEN THE TWO COMBATANTS *STAGGER*--GASP DESPERATELY FOR *BREATH*--AND *FALL!*

*A*ND IT IS A *TRIUMPHANT* ENCHANTRESS WHO COMES TO CLAIM HER *PRIZE.*

YOU *SEE,* GEORGES? I *TOLD* YOU EVERY- THING WOULD *WORK OUT* IN THE END, DIDN'T I?

UNFORTUNA*TELY,* MARIE, EV*ERY-* THING IS N*OT ENDED*--*NOT YE*T!

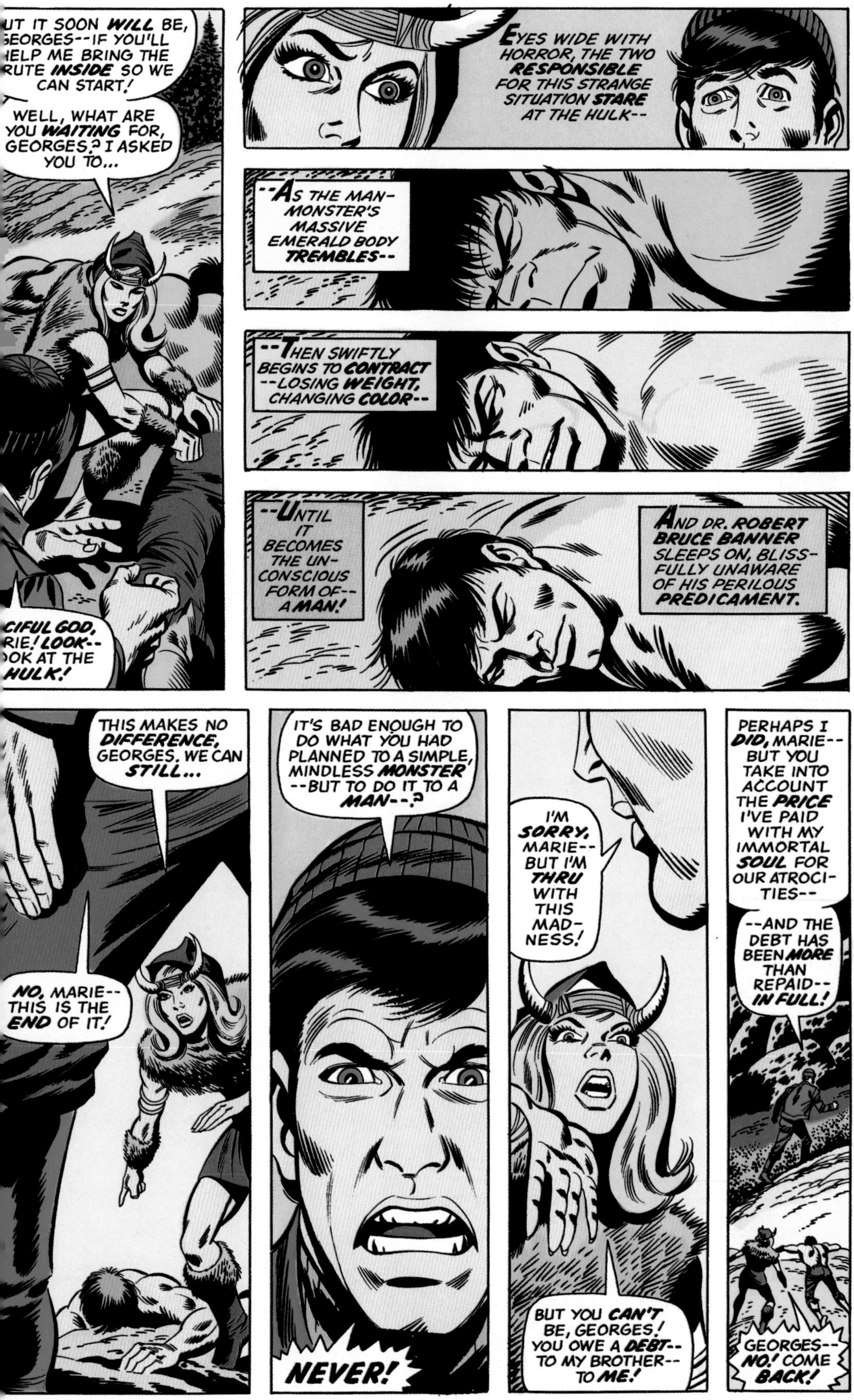
UT IT SOON WILL BE, GEORGES--IF YOU'LL HELP ME BRING THE RUTE INSIDE SO WE CAN START!
WELL, WHAT ARE YOU WAITING FOR, GEORGES? I ASKED YOU TO...
CIFUL GOD, RIE! LOOK-- OOK AT THE HULK!
EYES WIDE WITH HORROR, THE TWO RESPONSIBLE FOR THIS STRANGE SITUATION STARE AT THE HULK--
--AS THE MAN-MONSTER'S MASSIVE EMERALD BODY TREMBLES--
--THEN SWIFTLY BEGINS TO CONTRACT --LOSING WEIGHT, CHANGING COLOR--
--UNTIL IT BECOMES THE UN-CONSCIOUS FORM OF--A MAN!
AND DR. ROBERT BRUCE BANNER SLEEPS ON, BLISS-FULLY UNAWARE OF HIS PERILOUS PREDICAMENT.
THIS MAKES NO DIFFERENCE, GEORGES. WE CAN STILL...
NO, MARIE--THIS IS THE END OF IT!
IT'S BAD ENOUGH TO DO WHAT YOU HAD PLANNED TO A SIMPLE, MINDLESS MONSTER --BUT TO DO IT TO A MAN--?
NEVER!
I'M SORRY, MARIE--BUT I'M THRU WITH THIS MAD-NESS!
BUT YOU CAN'T BE, GEORGES! YOU OWE A DEBT--TO MY BROTHER--TO ME!
PERHAPS I DID, MARIE--BUT YOU TAKE INTO ACCOUNT THE PRICE I'VE PAID WITH MY IMMORTAL SOUL FOR OUR ATROCI-TIES--
--AND THE DEBT HAS BEEN MORE THAN REPAID--IN FULL!
GEORGES--NO! COME BACK!

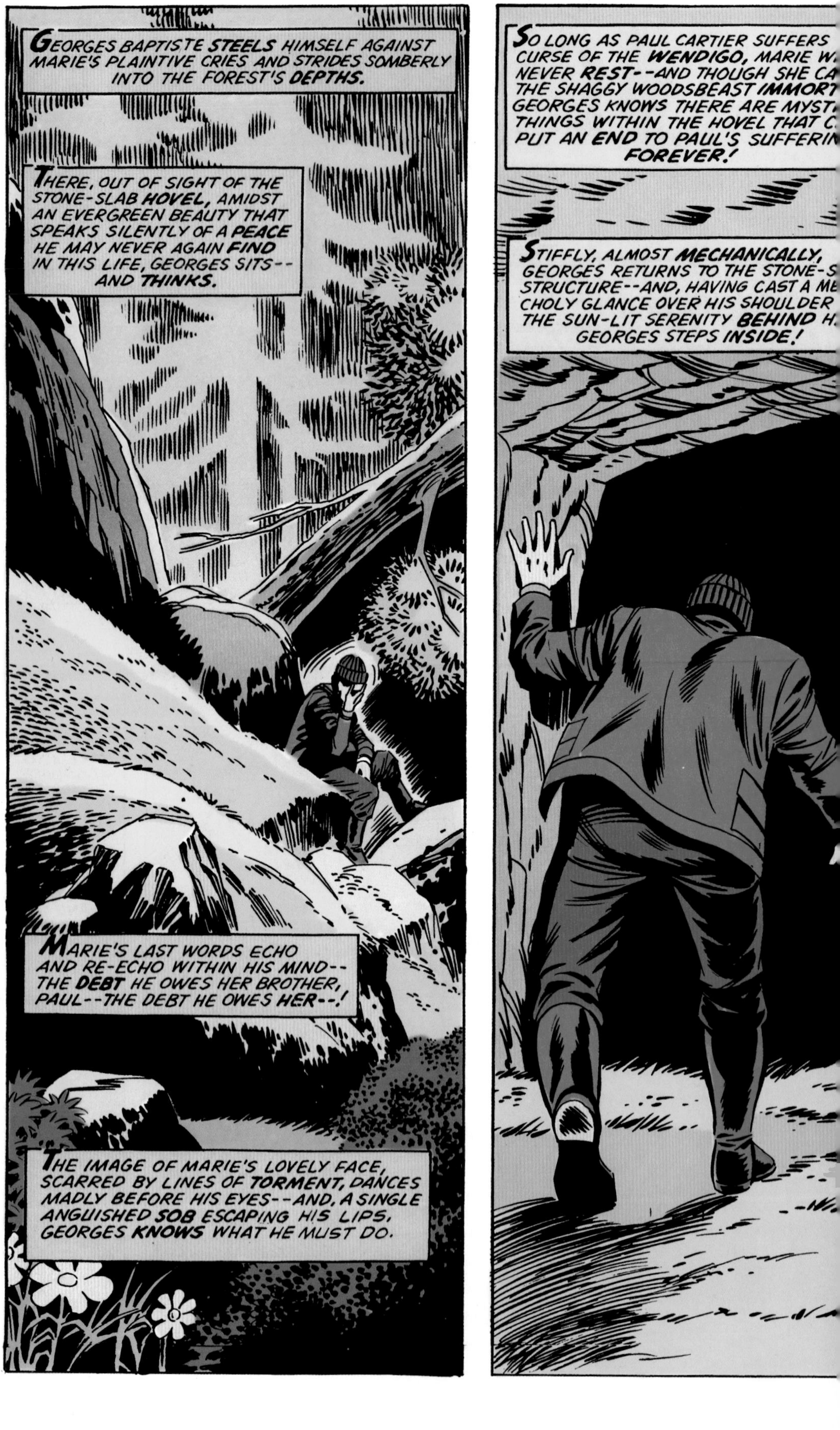
GEORGES BAPTISTE STEELS HIMSELF AGAINST MARIE'S PLAINTIVE CRIES AND STRIDES SOMBERLY INTO THE FOREST'S DEPTHS.
THERE, OUT OF SIGHT OF THE STONE-SLAB HOVEL, AMIDST AN EVERGREEN BEAUTY THAT SPEAKS SILENTLY OF A PEACE HE MAY NEVER AGAIN FIND IN THIS LIFE, GEORGES SITS-- AND THINKS.
MARIE'S LAST WORDS ECHO AND RE-ECHO WITHIN HIS MIND-- THE DEBT HE OWES HER BROTHER, PAUL--THE DEBT HE OWES HER--!
THE IMAGE OF MARIE'S LOVELY FACE, SCARRED BY LINES OF TORMENT, DANCES MADLY BEFORE HIS EYES--AND, A SINGLE ANGUISHED SOB ESCAPING HIS LIPS, GEORGES KNOWS WHAT HE MUST DO.
SO LONG AS PAUL CARTIER SUFFERS
CURSE OF THE WENDIGO, MARIE W
NEVER REST--AND THOUGH SHE CA
THE SHAGGY WOODSBEAST IMMORT
GEORGES KNOWS THERE ARE MYST
THINGS WITHIN THE HOVEL THAT C
PUT AN END TO PAUL'S SUFFERIN
FOREVER!
STIFFLY, ALMOST MECHANICALLY,
GEORGES RETURNS TO THE STONE-S
STRUCTURE--AND, HAVING CAST A ME
CHOLY GLANCE OVER HIS SHOULDER
THE SUN-LIT SERENITY BEHIND H
GEORGES STEPS INSIDE!

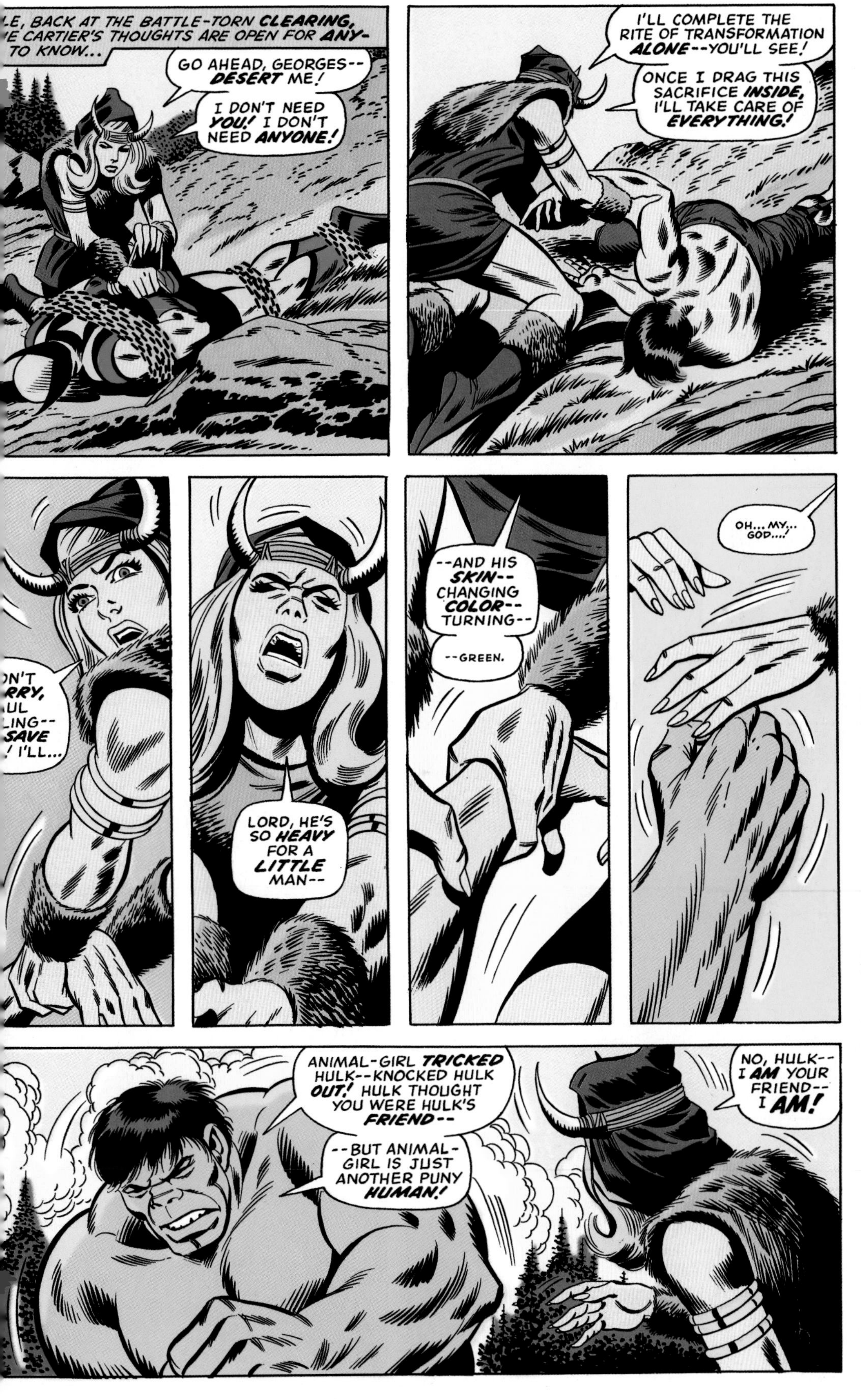

LE, BACK AT THE BATTLE-TORN CLEARING, E CARTIER'S THOUGHTS ARE OPEN FOR ANY- TO KNOW...
GO AHEAD, GEORGES-- DESERT ME!
I DON'T NEED YOU! I DON'T NEED ANYONE!
I'LL COMPLETE THE RITE OF TRANSFORMATION ALONE--YOU'LL SEE!
ONCE I DRAG THIS SACRIFICE INSIDE, I'LL TAKE CARE OF EVERYTHING!
N'T RRY, UL LING-- SAVE I'LL...
LORD, HE'S SO HEAVY FOR A LITTLE MAN--
--AND HIS SKIN-- CHANGING COLOR-- TURNING--
--GREEN.
OH... MY... GOD....!
ANIMAL-GIRL TRICKED HULK--KNOCKED HULK OUT! HULK THOUGHT YOU WERE HULK'S FRIEND--
--BUT ANIMAL-GIRL IS JUST ANOTHER PUNY HUMAN!
NO, HULK-- I AM YOUR FRIEND-- I AM!

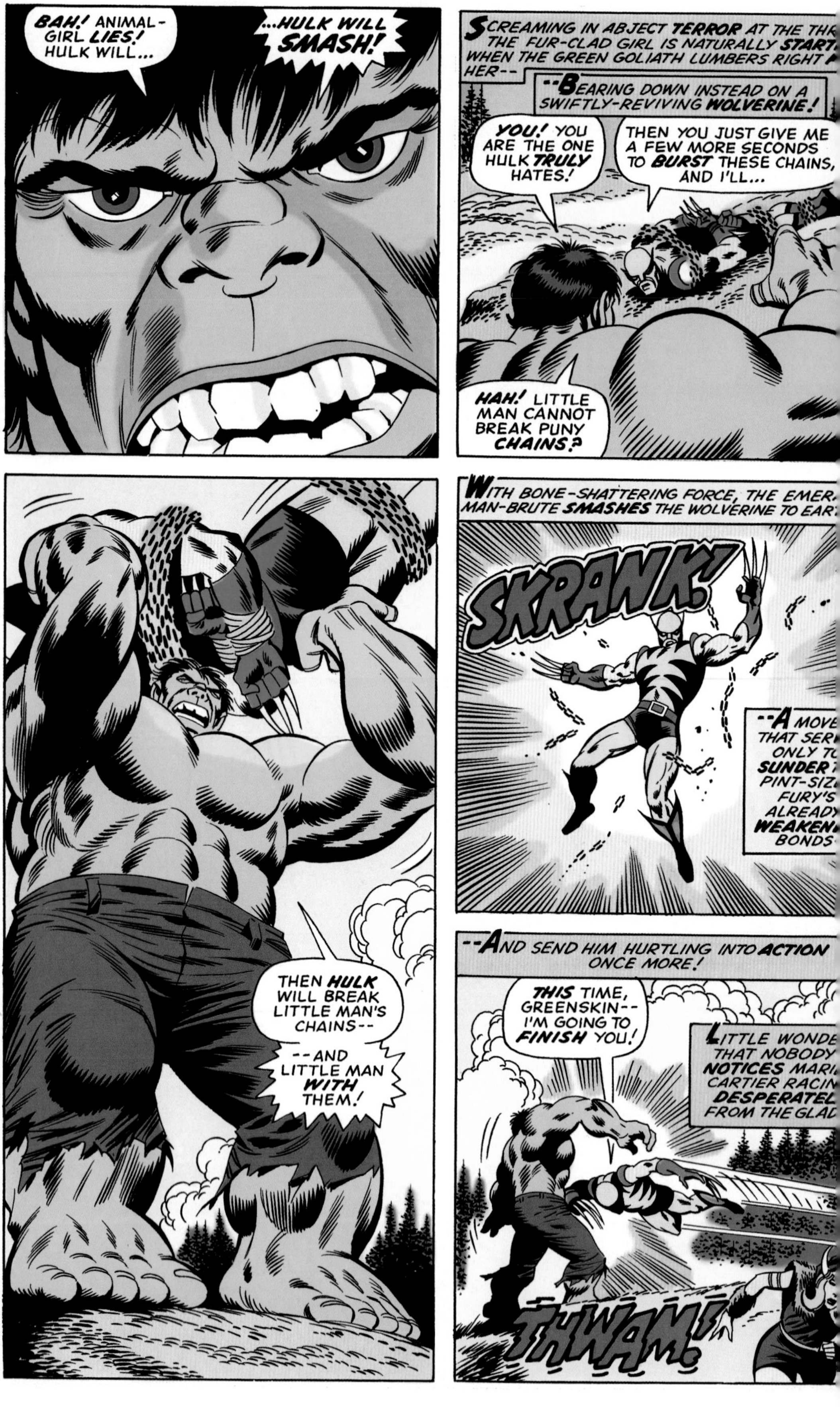

BAH! ANIMAL-GIRL LIES! HULK WILL...
...HULK WILL SMASH!
SCREAMING IN ABJECT TERROR AT THE THR THE FUR-CLAD GIRL IS NATURALLY START WHEN THE GREEN GOLIATH LUMBERS RIGHT HER--
--BEARING DOWN INSTEAD ON A SWIFTLY-REVIVING WOLVERINE!
YOU! YOU ARE THE ONE HULK TRULY HATES!
THEN YOU JUST GIVE ME A FEW MORE SECONDS TO BURST THESE CHAINS, AND I'LL...
HAH! LITTLE MAN CANNOT BREAK PUNY CHAINS?
THEN HULK WILL BREAK LITTLE MAN'S CHAINS--
--AND LITTLE MAN WITH THEM!
WITH BONE-SHATTERING FORCE, THE EMER MAN-BRUTE SMASHES THE WOLVERINE TO EAR
SKRANK!
--A MOVE THAT SER ONLY TO SUNDER PINT-SIZ FURY'S ALREADY WEAKEN BONDS
--AND SEND HIM HURTLING INTO ACTION ONCE MORE!
THIS TIME, GREENSKIN-- I'M GOING TO FINISH YOU!
LITTLE WONDE THAT NOBODY NOTICES MARI CARTIER RACIN DESPERATEL FROM THE GLAD
THWAM!

...ND BACK TO THE STONE-...AB *SHACK* WHERE HER ...ONSTROUS *BROTHER* LIES SLEEPING.

SOUNDS GREET HER ENTRANCE--

A NERVE-CHILLING WAIL--AND THE *FRENZIED RENDING* OF WHAT COULD BE *HUMAN FLESH!*

*I*N THAT INSTANT, SHE REMEMBERS *GEORGES*--AND, HER HEART *HAMMERING* IN HER CHEST, SHE MOVES CAUTIOUSLY FORWARD--

--TO FIND HER PATH *BLOCKED* BY THE THREATENING FORM OF A NEWLY-AWAKENED *WENDIGO!*

NO! OH-- NO!

MARIE'S *SCREAM* SLICES THE MORNING AIR LIKE THE STROKE OF A FINELY-HONED *RAZOR.*

EEEEEEEEE

*F*OR AN INSTANT, THE TWO COMBATANTS *CEASE* THEIR VIOLENT *BATTLE*--

WHAT IN HADES WAS THAT?

--*B*UT FOR *ONLY AN INSTANT.*

*F*OR, DESPITE ITS MANY *FLAWS*, THE GREAT GREEN GOLIATH'S *MIND* GENERALLY RUNS ON *ONE* TRACK--

--AND ONCE HAVING **BEGUN** SOMETHING, OL' GREENSKIN DOESN'T LIKE TO **STOP** UNTIL HE'S **FINISHED** IT!

GIVE THE WOLVERINE **CREDIT**: HE **SENSES** WHAT'S COMING, THEN SNAPS HIS HEAD ASIDE WITH SUCH **SPEED** THAT THE BLOW IS ONLY A **GLANCING** ONE!

BWOK!

UUNNFF!!

AND IT'S PROBABLY **THAT** PLUS HIS ASTONISHING **STAMINA** THAT SAVES HIS L...

--FOR, BY RIGHTS, EVEN A **GLANCING** BLOW FROM FISTS THAT CAN SHATTE... MOUNTAINS SHOULD BE **FATAL!**

LITTLE MAN TRIED TO **TRICK** HULK--BUT HULK WAS **SMARTER**-- HULK WAS **STRONGER**--

--AN... THA... WH... HUL... **WO...**

WHILE WITHIN THE ROCK-HEWN HOVEL, A TIMOROUS MARIE CARTIER STRIVES IN VAIN TO **COMPREHEND** THE URGENT GESTURES OF THE IVORY-PELTED **BEAST** WHO STANDS BEFORE HER--

I--I DON'T **UNDER-STAND,** PAUL. WHAT ARE YOU TRYING TO **TELL** ME?

WHAT'S **HAPPENED?**

THE WENDIG... SAYS **NOTHI...** MERELY **BOW...** ITS SHAGGY HEAD SORRO... FULLY--

--**T**HEN STABS A TALONED **FINGER** TOWARDS THE WEIRDLY-LIT **CHAMBER** BEYOND.

FEARFULLY, MARIE STEPS INTO THE ROOM--

--**A**ND IS FILLED WITH **SHOCK** AND **REVULSION** SU... AS SHE HAS NEVER BEFORE KNOWN.

OH, DE... GOD-- **COUL...** YOU...

G-GEORGES!?!

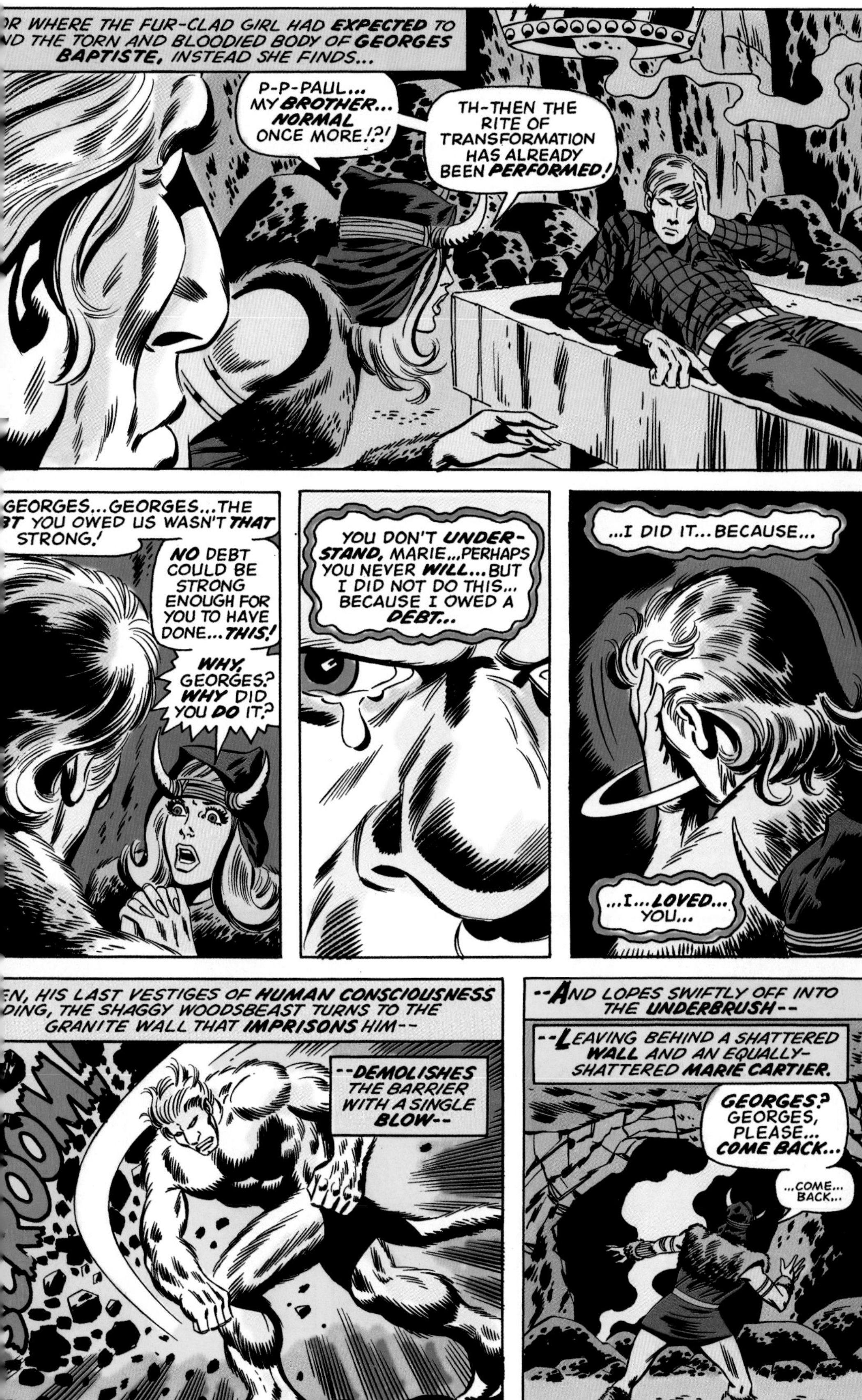

OR WHERE THE FUR-CLAD GIRL HAD EXPECTED TO ND THE TORN AND BLOODIED BODY OF GEORGES BAPTISTE, INSTEAD SHE FINDS...
P-P-PAUL... MY BROTHER... NORMAL ONCE MORE!?!
TH-THEN THE RITE OF TRANSFORMATION HAS ALREADY BEEN PERFORMED!
GEORGES...GEORGES...THE BT YOU OWED US WASN'T THAT STRONG!
NO DEBT COULD BE STRONG ENOUGH FOR YOU TO HAVE DONE...THIS!
WHY, GEORGES? WHY DID YOU DO IT?
YOU DON'T UNDER-STAND, MARIE...PERHAPS YOU NEVER WILL...BUT I DID NOT DO THIS... BECAUSE I OWED A DEBT...
...I DID IT...BECAUSE...
...I...LOVED... YOU...
EN, HIS LAST VESTIGES OF HUMAN CONSCIOUSNESS DING, THE SHAGGY WOODSBEAST TURNS TO THE GRANITE WALL THAT IMPRISONS HIM--
--DEMOLISHES THE BARRIER WITH A SINGLE BLOW--
--AND LOPES SWIFTLY OFF INTO THE UNDERBRUSH--
--LEAVING BEHIND A SHATTERED WALL AND AN EQUALLY-SHATTERED MARIE CARTIER.
GEORGES? GEORGES, PLEASE... COME BACK...
...COME... BACK...

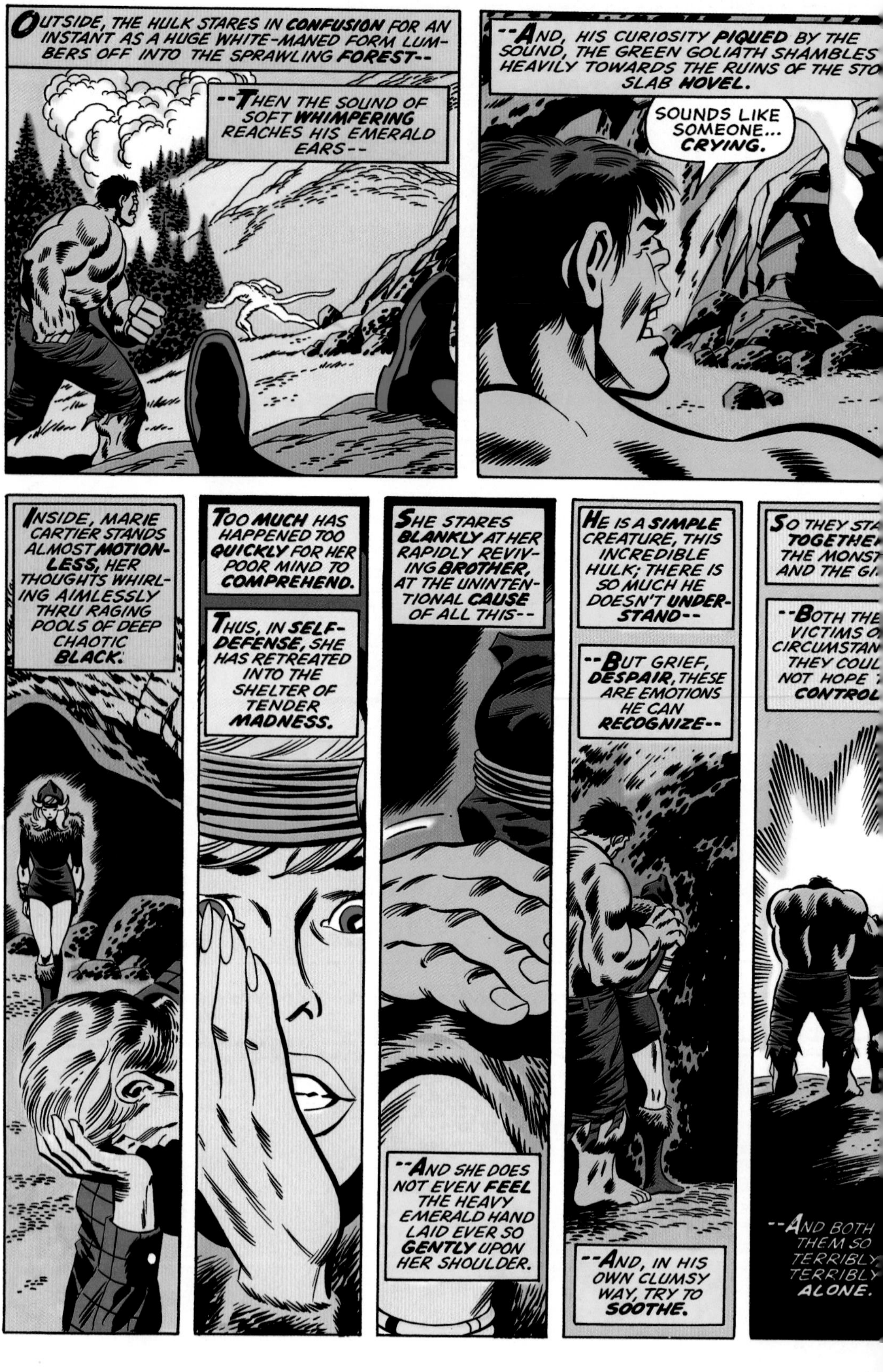
OUTSIDE, THE HULK STARES IN CONFUSION FOR AN INSTANT AS A HUGE WHITE-MANED FORM LUMBERS OFF INTO THE SPRAWLING FOREST--
--THEN THE SOUND OF SOFT WHIMPERING REACHES HIS EMERALD EARS--
--AND, HIS CURIOSITY PIQUED BY THE SOUND, THE GREEN GOLIATH SHAMBLES HEAVILY TOWARDS THE RUINS OF THE STO SLAB HOVEL.
SOUNDS LIKE SOMEONE... CRYING.
INSIDE, MARIE CARTIER STANDS ALMOST MOTIONLESS, HER THOUGHTS WHIRLING AIMLESSLY THRU RAGING POOLS OF DEEP CHAOTIC BLACK.
TOO MUCH HAS HAPPENED TOO QUICKLY FOR HER POOR MIND TO COMPREHEND.
THUS, IN SELF-DEFENSE, SHE HAS RETREATED INTO THE SHELTER OF TENDER MADNESS.
SHE STARES BLANKLY AT HER RAPIDLY REVIVING BROTHER, AT THE UNINTENTIONAL CAUSE OF ALL THIS--
--AND SHE DOES NOT EVEN FEEL THE HEAVY EMERALD HAND LAID EVER SO GENTLY UPON HER SHOULDER.
HE IS A SIMPLE CREATURE, THIS INCREDIBLE HULK; THERE IS SO MUCH HE DOESN'T UNDERSTAND--
--BUT GRIEF, DESPAIR, THESE ARE EMOTIONS HE CAN RECOGNIZE--
--AND, IN HIS OWN CLUMSY WAY, TRY TO SOOTHE.
SO THEY STA TOGETHE THE MONST AND THE GI
--BOTH THE VICTIMS O CIRCUMSTAN THEY COUL NOT HOPE T CONTROL
--AND BOTH THEM SO TERRIBLY TERRIBLY ALONE.

Character Sketches by Salva Espin

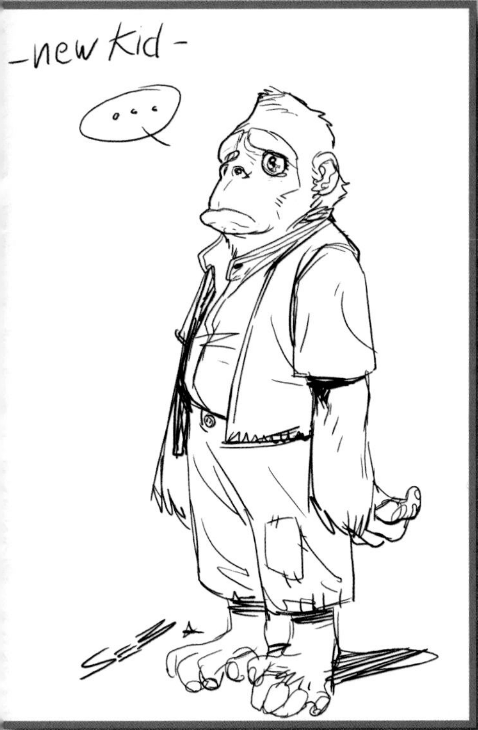
-new Kid-
...

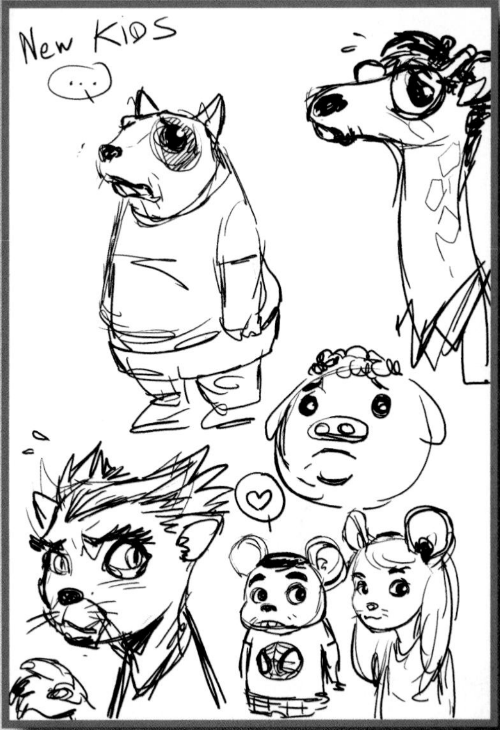
New KIDS
...

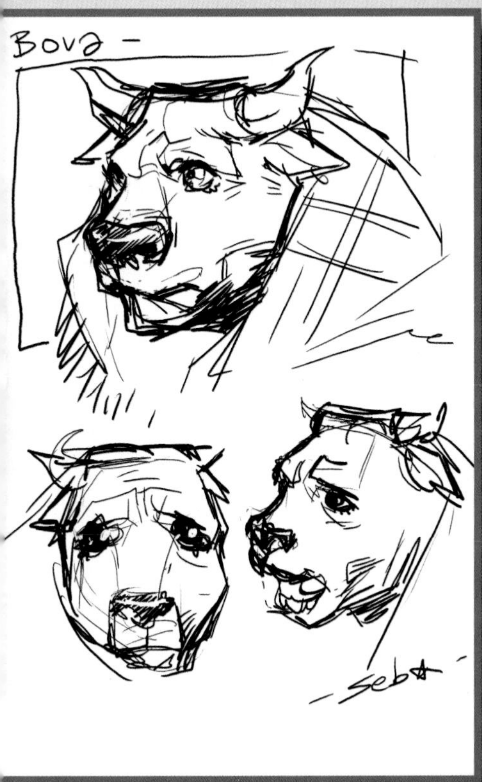
Bova -
- seb

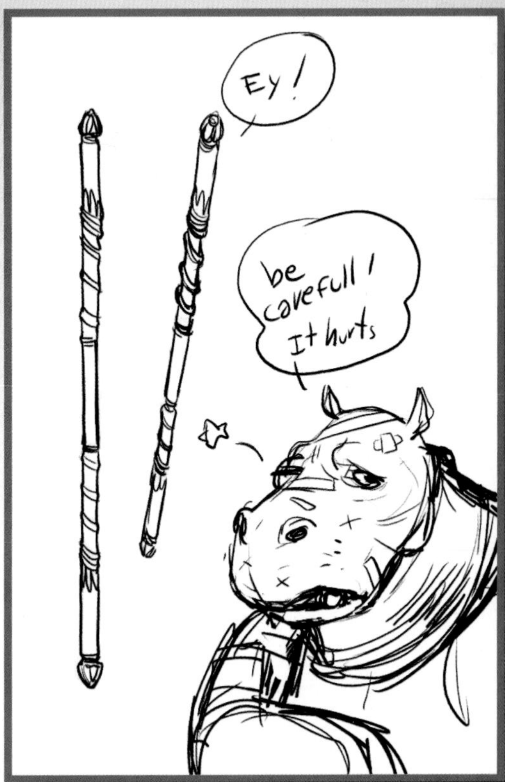
Ey!
be carefull!
It hurts

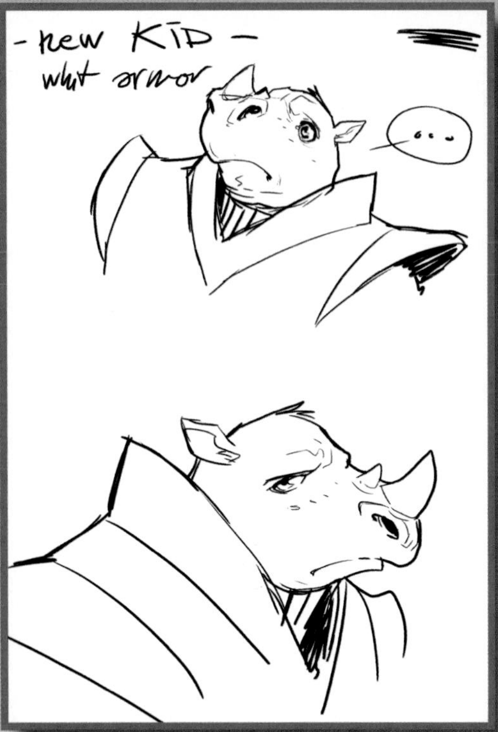
- new KID -
wht armor

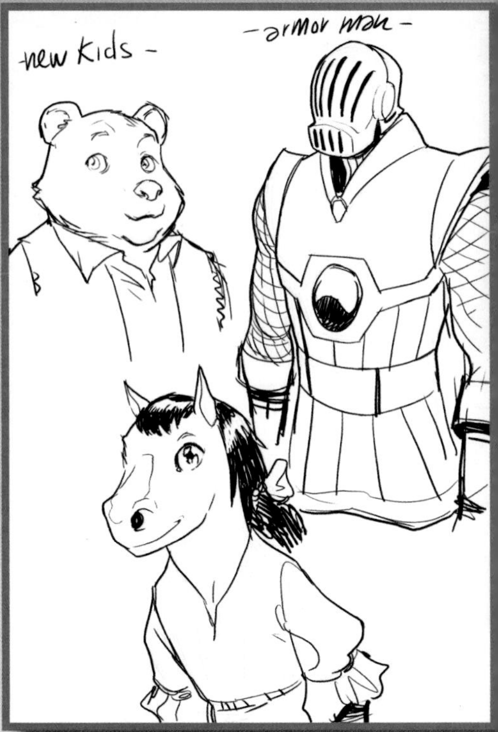
new kids -
- armor man -

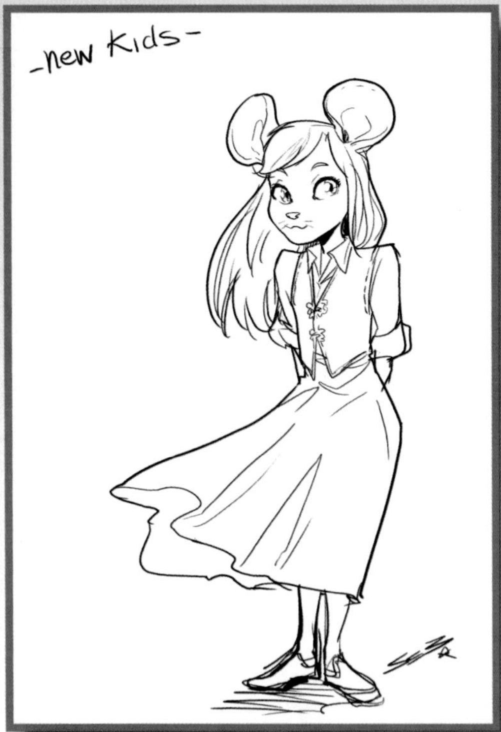
-new kids-

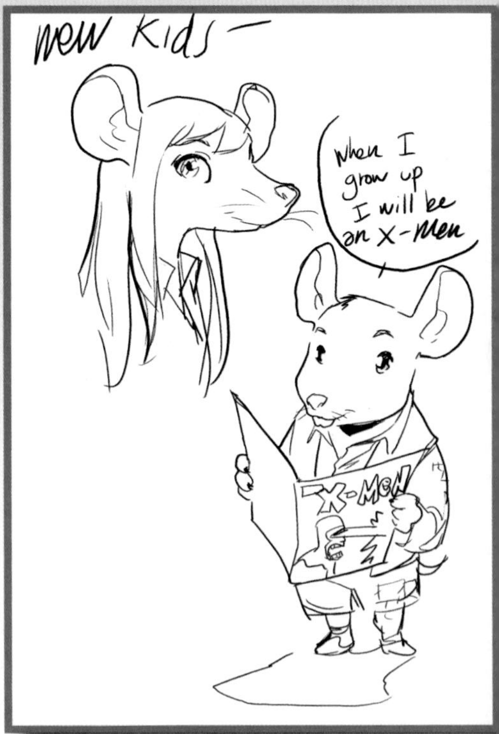
new kids —
when I grow up I will be an X-Men
X-MEN

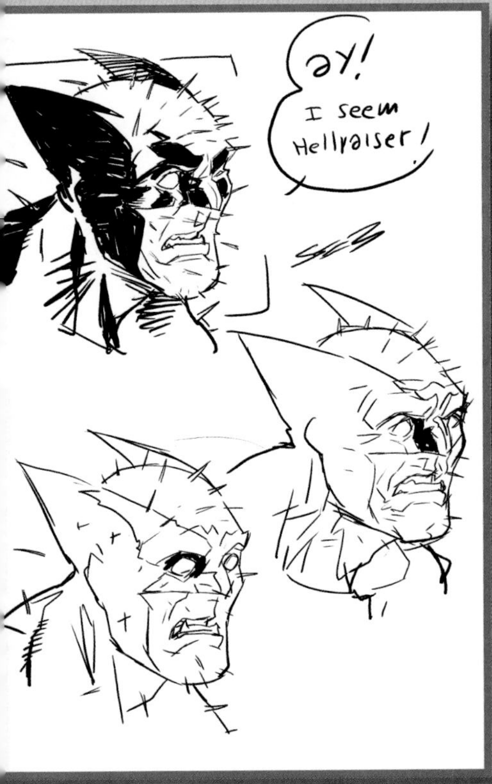
ay!
I seem Hellraiser!

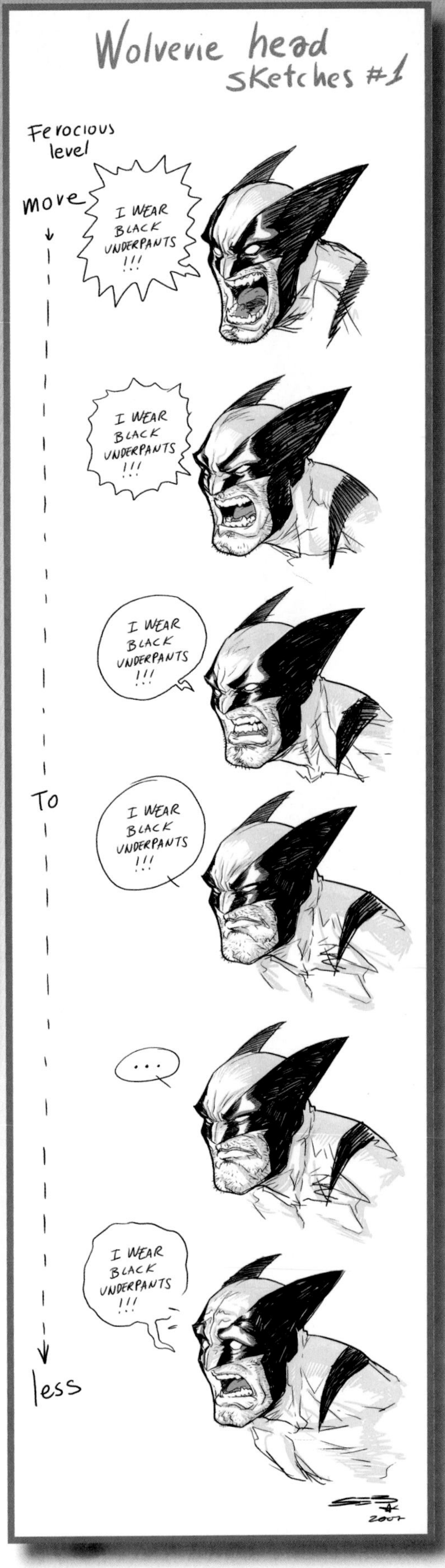
Wolverie head sketches #1
Ferocious level
more
I WEAR BLACK UNDERPANTS !!!
I WEAR BLACK UNDERPANTS !!!
I WEAR BLACK UNDERPANTS !!!
To
I WEAR BLACK UNDERPANTS !!!
...
I WEAR BLACK UNDERPANTS !!!
less

Cover Sketches

COVER SKETCHES
X-MEN 1st CLASS

- I WASN'T SURE
WHICH COSTUME YOU
WANTED ON SABERTOOTH
SO I GAVE HIM HIS
MORE RECENT ONE.
I CAN CHANGE THAT.

WOLVERINE: FIRST CLASS #2

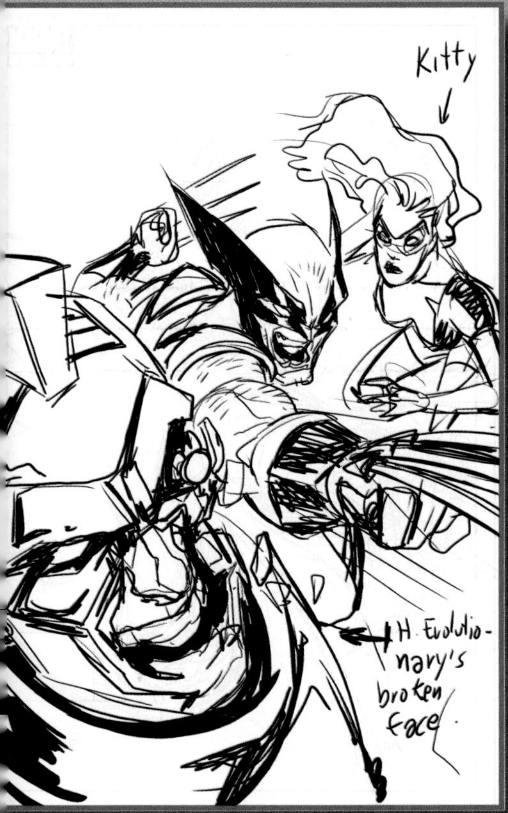

Kitty
H. Evolutionary's broken face

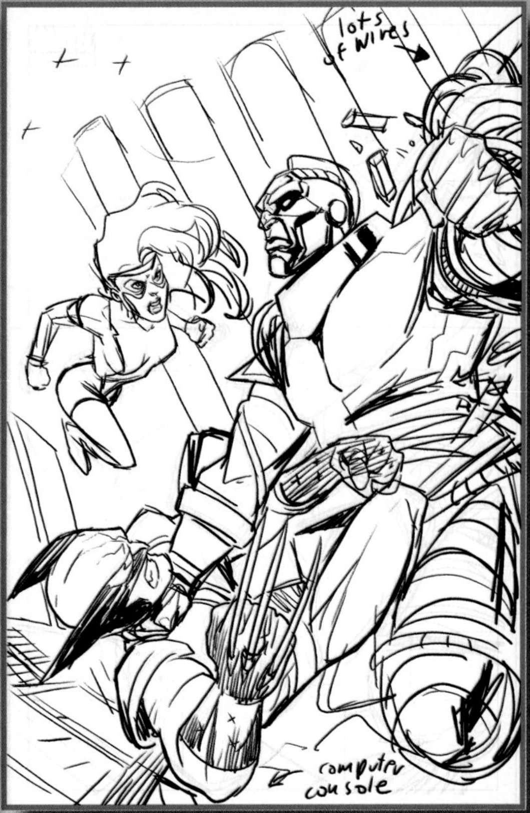

lots of wires
computer console

WOLVERINE: FIRST CLASS #3

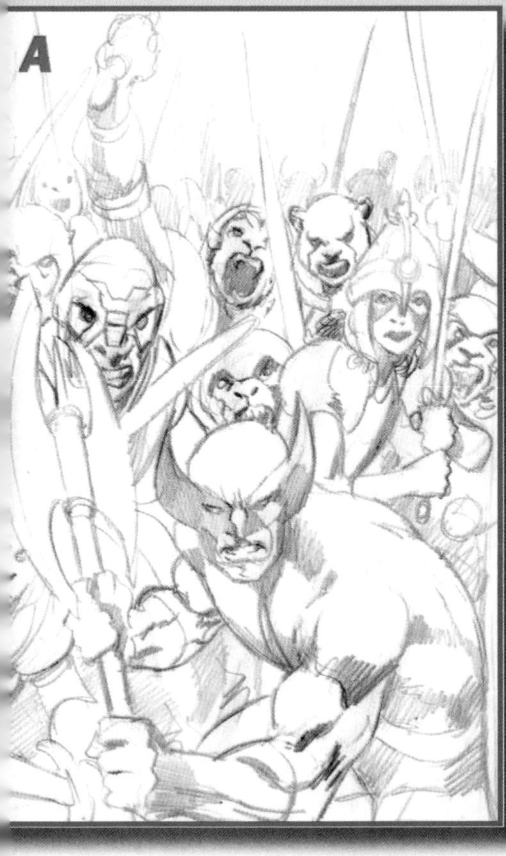

A

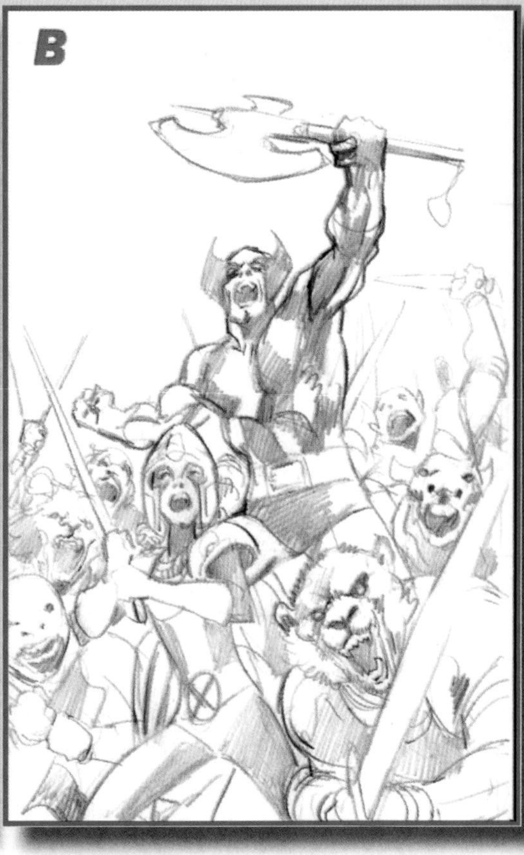

B

WOLVERINE: FIRST CLASS #4

AN'T MISS X-MEN COLLECTIONS!

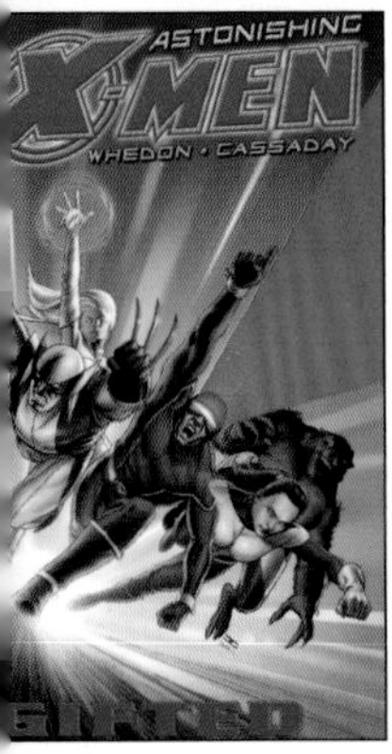
ASTONISHING
X-MEN
WHEDON • CASSADAY

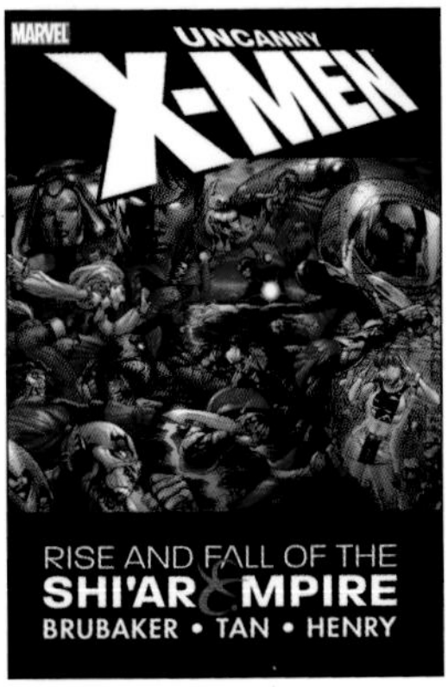
MARVEL
UNCANNY
X-MEN
RISE AND FALL OF THE
SHI'AR EMPIRE
BRUBAKER • TAN • HENRY

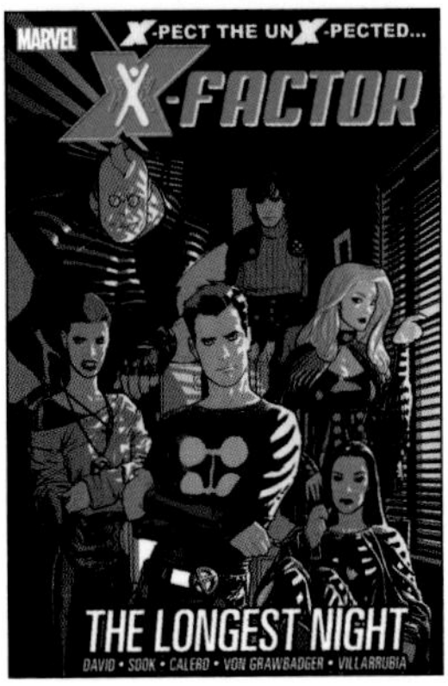
MARVEL
X-PECT THE UNX-PECTED...
X-FACTOR
THE LONGEST NIGHT
DAVID • SOOK • CALERO • VON GRAWBADGER • VILLARRUBIA

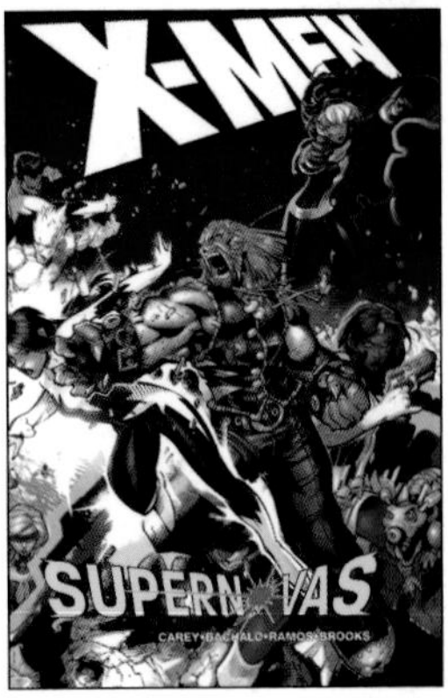
X-MEN
SUPERNOVAS
CAREY • BACHALO • RAMOS • BROOKS

ASTONISHING X-MEN

ASTONISHING X-MEN VOL. 1: GIFTED...$14.99
(ISBN: 0-7851-1531-5)
ASTONISHING X-MEN VOL. 2: DANGEROUS...$14.99
(ISBN: 0-7851-1677-X)
ASTONISHING X-MEN VOL. 3: TORN TPB...$14.99
(ISBN: 0-7851-1759-8)
ASTONISHING X-MEN VOL. 4: UNSTOPPABLE TPB...$17.99
(ISBN: 978-0-7851-2254-8)

X-MEN

X-MEN: SUPERNOVAS HC...$34.99
(ISBN: 0-7851-2514-0)
X-MEN: GOLGOTHA TPB...$12.99
(ISBN: 0-7851-1650-8)
X-MEN: BIZARRE LOVE TRIANGLE TPB...$9.99
(ISBN: 0-7851-1665-6)
X-MEN/BLACK PANTHER: WILD KINGDOM TPB...$11.99
(ISBN: 0-7851-1789-X)
DECIMATION: X-MEN - THE DAY AFTER TPB...$15.99
(0-7851-1984-1)
X-MEN: BLOOD OF APOCALYPSE TPB...$17.99
(ISBN: 0-7851-1985-X)
NEW X-MEN - ACADEMY X VOL. 1: CHOOSING SIDES TPB...$14.99
(ISBN: 0-7851-1538-2)
NEW X-MEN - ACADEMY X VOL. 2: HAUNTED TPB...$12.99
(ISBN: 0-7851-1615-X)
NEW X-MEN - ACADEMY X VOL. 3: X-POSED TPB...$14.99
(ISBN: 0-7851-1791-1)
NEW X-MEN: CHILDHOOD'S END VOL. 1 TPB...$10.99
(ISBN: 0-7851-1831-4)
NEW X-MEN: CHILDHOOD'S END VOL. 2 TPB...$10.99
(ISBN: 0-7851-2024-6)
NEW X-MEN: CHILDHOOD'S END VOL. 3 TPB...$10.99
(ISBN: 0-7851-2025-4)
NEW X-MEN: CHILDHOOD'S END VOL. 4 TPB...$10.99
(ISBN: 0-7851-2238-9)
NEW X-MEN: CHILDHOOD'S END VOL. 5 TPB...$17.99
(ISBN: 0-7851-2239-7)
NEW X-MEN: HELLIONS TPB...$9.99
(ISBN: 0-7851-1746-6)

UNCANNY X-MEN

UNCANNY X-MEN: RISE & FALL OF THE SHI'AR EMPIRE HC...$34.99
(ISBN: 0-7851-2515-9)
UNCANNY X-MEN - THE NEW AGE VOL. 1: THE END OF HISTORY TPB...$12.99
(ISBN: 0-7851-1535-8)
UNCANNY X-MEN - THE NEW AGE VOL. 2: THE CRUELEST CUT TPB...$11.99
(ISBN: 0-7851-1645-1)
UNCANNY X-MEN - THE NEW AGE VOL. 3: ON ICE TPB...$15.99
(ISBN: 0-7851-1649-4)
HOUSE OF M: UNCANNY X-MEN TPB...$13.99
(0-7851-1663-X)
UNCANNY X-MEN - THE NEW AGE VOL. 4: END OF GREYS TPB...$14.99
(ISBN: 0-7851-1664-8)
UNCANNY X-MEN - THE NEW AGE VOL. 5: FIRST FOURSAKEN TPB...$11.99
(ISBN: 0-7851-2323-7)
X-MEN: DEADLY GENESIS TPB...$19.99
(ISBN: 0-7851-1830-6)
X-MEN DARK PHOENIX SAGA TPB...$24.99
(ISBN: 0-7851-2213-3)
X-MEN: DAYS OF FUTURE PAST TPB...$19.99
(ISBN: 0-7851-1560-9)
X-MEN: MUTANT GENESIS TPB...$19.99
(ISBN: 0-7851-2212-5)

X-FACTOR

X-FACTOR VOL. 1: THE LONGEST NIGHT TPB...$14.99
(ISBN: 0-7851-1817-9)
MADROX: MULTIPLE CHOICE TPB...$13.99
(ISBN: 0-7851-1500-5)
X-FACTOR VISIONARIES: PETER DAVID VOL. 1 TPB...$15.99
(ISBN: 0-7851-1872-1)
X-FACTOR VISIONARIES: PETER DAVID VOL. 2 TPB...$15.99
(ISBN: 0-7851-2456-X)
X-FACTOR VISIONARIES: PETER DAVID VOL. 3 TPB...$15.99
(ISBN: 978-0-7851-2457-3)

X-23

X-23: INNOCENCE LOST TPB...$15.99
(ISBN: 0-7851-1502-1)
X-23: TARGET X TPB...$15.99
(ISBN: 0-7851-1971-X)

X-MEN: FIRST CLASS

X-MEN: TOMORROW'S BRIGHTEST TPB...$19.99
(ISBN: 978-0-7851-2427-6)

or a comic store near you, call 1-888-comicbook.

Return with us again to the early days of the all-new, all-different X-Men for the thril untold adventures of Wolverine and Kitty Pryde! The next generation of students arrived at Xavier's School — Colossus, Storm, Nightcrawler and the mysterious Wolver — and with them, new teaching methods. Professor X pairs up green recruit Kitty Pr with the been-everywhere, done-everything vet Logan — and neither of them is all t happy about it. Featuring Sabretooth, the High Evolutionary, the Man-Beast and more

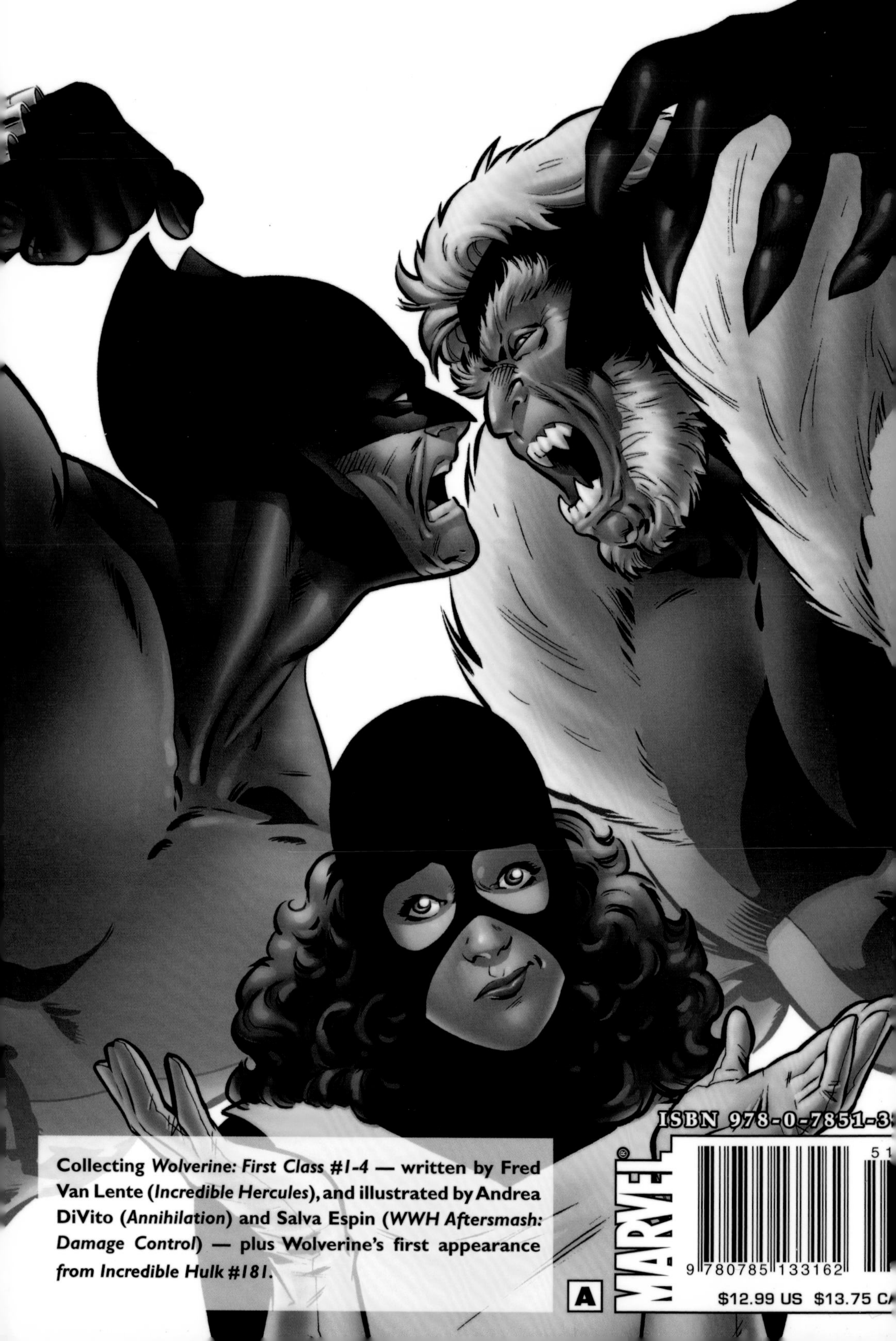

Collecting *Wolverine: First Class #1-4* — written by Fred Van Lente (*Incredible Hercules*), and illustrated by Andrea DiVito (*Annihilation*) and Salva Espin (*WWH Aftersmash: Damage Control*) — plus Wolverine's first appearance *from Incredible Hulk #181*.

ISBN 978-0-7851-3

9 780785 133162 51

A

MARVEL

$12.99 US $13.75 C